LA
shorts

LA
shorts

Edited by Steven Gilbar

Heyday Books
Berkeley, California

Library of Congress Cataloging-in-Publication Data

LA shorts / edited by Steven Gilbar.
    p. cm.
  ISBN 1-890771-29-5
  1. Los Angeles (Calif.)—Social life and customs—Fiction. 2. Short stories, American—California—Los Angeles. I. Title: L.A. shorts. II. Title: Los Angeles shorts. III. Gilbar, Steven.
  PS572.L6 L28 2000
  813'.010897494—dc21
                         00-008216

ISBN: 1-890771-29-5

Cover Art: "Van Nuys" by Peter Alexander, 1987. Courtesy James Corcoran Gallery, Los Angeles, California
Cover Design: Dave Bullen Design
Interior Design: Rebecca LeGates
Printing and Binding: Publishers Press, Salt Lake City, Utah

Orders, inquiries, and correspondence should be addressed to:
    Heyday Books
    P. O. Box 9145, Berkeley, CA 94709
    510/549-3564, Fax 510/549-1889
    heyday@heydaybooks.com
    www.heydaybooks.com

Printed in the United States of America

10 9 8 7 6 5 4 3 2 1

Contents

Introduction

Steven Gilbar

LA Story, LA Confidential, LA Law, LA Woman...movies, television, rock lyrics, all offer up images of Los Angeles. Typically they showcase the glitz, the decadent, the shallow; the city, as one critic put it, of lapsed angels. Such is the media take on LA. A more telling counterpoint to these modern myths emerges in literature, whether in the classic novels of James Cain, Raymond Chandler, or Joan Didion, or in the best-selling suspense fiction of Michael Connolly, James Ellroy, or Faye Kellerman. If in days to come historians attempt to discover how life was lived in *fin de millennium* Los Angeles they could do no better than to read the fiction set there over the last couple of decades, especially the short stories. While literary LA novels might furnish a more spacious vista of the social panorama of this city on the edge, it is the stories, as Gary Krist has written, that "peer directly into our houses." Over the past twenty years the short story has given us, he adds, "the more nuanced picture of the way we live now— the ironic rhythms of our speech, the casual heartbreak of our small domestic failures, the twisted warp and woof of our daily moral compromises." This is due, in part, to the pared down, precise nature of the form; there is simply no room for excess baggage.

If the short story is, as Lorrie Moore once described it, "a bright light shone on a character in conflict, turmoil, or simple comic confusion," then you will discover that the stories collected here illuminate the rich diversity of contemporary LA's topographical and emotional landscapes so that we can clearly see the city as both refuge and hell, a place both of fresh starts and of failed dreams. In settings that range from Watts to Malibu, from East LA to the Valley, each writer has given us a vision of LA life filtered through his or her unique sensibility vivified through a rare gift of language.

This collection is not an attempt at an official canon of the contemporary LA short story, nor is it meant as a display of current LA writing—both tasks would be impossible in a volume so slender. For one thing, many superb fiction writers in LA don't write short stories. Others do write short stories, but not set in LA—at least not in any recognizable LA. Simply put, these stories were selected to reflect the diversity of the city, its depth and breadth of experience. They portray people born in LA; people escaping from it—or trying to escape from it; people who are waking from an unreal dream of LA; and people who are putting their lives back together after disillusionment. There is sorrow, integrity, common sense, humor, irony—the gamut of experience. The writers lend their insights through the hard distilled work of the craft. All of the stories here are filled with invention and passion, and can be read and reread with pleasure. This is an unflinching literary view into the lives of people as they are played out on the ground without the distortions of film and television.

LA Shorts is both a demonstration of the power and vitality of the short story as literature and a stimulating ride through the "LA experience" in all its glory and infamy; a taste of life in what is—love it or loathe it—one of the most vital and protean new capitals of the world.

LA
shorts

Eternal Love

Karen E. Bender

AFTER LENA AND BOB WERE MARRIED in the Chapel of Eternal Love, Ella told them that new husbands and wives were not allowed to share a hotel bedroom. Married couples, she told her retarded daughter, learned to be married slowly, in separate rooms. For the first two days of the honeymoon, Ella shared her room at the El Tropicale with Lena, while her husband, Lou, slept in the other room with Bob. The four of them elbowed their way to the two-fifty, ninety-seven-item buffet table, piling their plates with fat-laced barbecued ribs; they lay, sun-doped, on a sparkling swath of concrete by a pale blue swimming pool. The sounds by the pool echoed, amplified by the water; even the children's shrieks were transformed into the caws of aroused, hysterical birds. Ella could pretend she didn't hear at first when Lena said very softly that she wanted to share a room with Bob.

Ella told Lena about sex in a quiet lounge off El Tropicale's main casino. Her thirty-year-old daughter sat patiently, twirling a pink vinyl coin purse embossed *Las Vegas: City of Luck.* "You're a wife," Ella began. Her daughter smiled. "There are certain things you can do."

"I'm called Mrs.!" squealed Lena.

A cocktail waitress holding an empty tray strode swiftly across the lounge, her nylon stockings an opalescent orange under the subdued light of the chandelier.

"First," began Ella, then stopped. "Well, how do you feel when Bob kisses you?"

"My mouth feels wet."

"Do you—like it?"

"I like it." Lena paused. "Sometimes he puts his tongue in too much. I don't like that."

A sign by the Canary Room said: EIGHT P.M. TONIGHT: HILO HATTIE AND THE HAWAIIANS. Loud tourists flowed eagerly through the lounge toward the casino, flashing slabs of sunburnt skin. "Married people—are naked in bed, Lena," Ella said.

"Naked!" Lena said with a tiny shriek.

Ella felt something very tall collapse slowly inside her. "Don't be scared," she said, trying to fit her voice around the immense gentleness that surged inside her. "It's just—skin."

"I liked it when he touched—here," Lena said, reaching up and squeezing her breast.

"Where did he do—"

"In the bathroom. At House of Pancakes." She giggled.

"No," said Ella. "You don't do that in House of Pancakes. You don't do that in any—public place. You do it in your bedroom. Nowhere else."

"In my bedroom," repeated Lena.

"After, you take a shower. You wash your hands with soap."

"It smelt like the ocean."

Ella let go of Lena's hand.

"When he put his hand in my panties. I liked that. He took his hand out and he smelt like me." She clapped her hand over her mouth and giggled, a guilty, thrilled sound.

"Lena," said Ella, "when did Bob do—"

"We came in through the back yard."

"You let him do that in my back yard?"

"I liked it."

"Soap," said Ella, a little desperately. "You use soap."

"Mother," said Lena, "what about when we're naked?"

Ella did not want to continue. Apparently Lena and Bob were doing well enough on their own.

"If he's ever not gentle with you, Lena, tell me."

"Tell what?"

Far away, Ella heard the distant clink of breakfast dishes being washed in the hotel coffee shop, the whir of a vacuum being pushed across the lobby, the gentle sounds of maids and waiters cleaning the guests' messes of the day.

"If he ever does something you don't like."

"Mother," said Lena impatiently, "does everyone married sleep naked in a bedroom? Him?" She pointed to a porter leafing through a newspaper with the headline WAR OF THE BOSOMS CONTINUES. "Him?" A man pushed a rack of pink and peach-feathered costumes toward the Lido de Paris show. "Her?" A tall showgirl, her hair in a rumpled bouffant, sipped a large glass of orange juice and blinked awake. Her feet were swollen in silver sandals, and her eyes were ringed with fatigue.

"They use soap," said Ella. She tried to think of one more crucial rule to tell her daughter, but her mind was filled with only this—in the deep green of her back yard, somewhere amid the walnut and lemon trees, Bob had plunged his hand into Lena's panties. Now everyone flowing through the lounge seemed profoundly tainted. Ella noticed the raw nubbiness of the bandleader's ruby velvet jacket, the too-proud grip a tourist had on his white-blond wife, the obsessive way a waitress counted her tips, turning all the green bills in the same direction, before she vanished into the dim, clockless casino again.

Bob had first called six months ago, an April day in 1961. Ella had picked up the phone and heard a male voice whisper, almost plead, "Lena. Lena. Lena there?"

It was a question she rarely heard. "Who may I say is calling?" Ella asked.

"Bob. Goodwill. I drive trucks—Bob—"

She knocked on Lena's door. "Lena. There's a...Bob on the phone for you."

Lena burst out of her room with a nakedly joyous expression on her face. "Tell him to wait," she exclaimed.

She was wearing a little rouge and perfume when, five minutes later, she deigned to pick up the phone. At first Ella couldn't figure out why her daughter smelt familiar. Then she knew. Lena had put on some of her Chanel; Lena smelt like her.

Lena had been working at the Van Nuys Goodwill for five years. Her job was to sit at a long table and sort socks and blouses that no one else wanted to own. Ella called Dolores, the coordinator of Goodwill's disabled employees, to check Bob out.

"Bob. Bob," muttered Dolores. "Why?"

"A Bob called Lena on the phone."

"This is so nice!" said Dolores. "We have five Bobs. Bob Winters is considerate, but a drooler. Bob Lanard I wouldn't let in my house, not if you care about your china surviving the night." She paused. "Are you sure it's not a Rob? We have a Rob who's—well—a former convict, but I think he's very nice, too."

"It was Bob. He said he drove trucks."

"Trucks," muttered Dolores. "Bob Silver."

"Tell me about him."

"A sweetie. Short, quiet, brown hair, good driver."

Ella tried to feel relieved but didn't honestly know what she felt. Bob Silver. It was just a name, but it seemed ferocious as a comet, hurtling toward her home to do some new damage.

Bob called again that night. "Is Lena there?"

"Lena who?" Ella said.

She was sorry she said it; she could actually hear the terror mount in his breath. "Lena Rose."

"Who may I say is calling?"

"Bob."

"Why?"

Now he was dying. She heard his breath, everything slow on his end as he struggled not to tell her why he was calling.

"I just want to talk to her," said Bob.

Bob was half an hour early for their first date. He pulled up in an old, candy-apple red Ford that gleamed dully in the afternoon. While Lena sprayed her hair upstairs, Ella and Lou huddled in the sheer-curtained window by the door and watched him come toward them. Bob rushed up the walkway, his hands plunged deep into his pockets, head down as though he was walking into a wind.

Lou opened the door. "Glad to meet you," he boomed.

Bob kept his hands in his pockets, not lifting them to shake with Lou. The part in his hair was crooked.

"Bob, Lena's not ready," Ella lied, touching his arm; she wanted to see how normal he felt. His shoulder was a little damp and surprisingly muscular. Quickly, she removed her hand.

Bob glided deftly past her into the den and plucked up the *TV Guide.* He flipped wildly through its pages for a moment, then stumbled across the room and clicked the channels until he found *Gunsmoke.*

Bob propped his feet on Lou's green vinyl footstool, sunk down into the couch and thoughtfully eyed the action in *Gunsmoke.* He looked about forty. His short, bristly hair was gray, but his feet, in blue sneakers, bounced on the footstool with the blunt, coarse merriment of a boy. Ella was used to Lena's stubbiness, the way she seemed to bump up unsuccessfully against adulthood. But it seemed strange in Bob, and she could not help thinking that, even though he was taller than she, he resembled an aging dwarf.

Lou sat on the couch and rubbed his palms rapidly against his knees. His face looked as though it had been sculpted hurriedly into an expression of calm—the cheeks were uneven, the smile was off. He surveyed Bob as he did any stranger—as though deciding whether he would hire him. "You like *Gunsmoke?*"

Bob clasped his hands on his lap. "I like the man in the hat," he said.

Lou began to lean into another question; Ella felt he would ask the wrong ones. "How is the job?" Ella asked.

Bob arranged his hands around an invisible steering wheel and twisted it to the right until the wheel came to an abrupt stop. "I drive," he said. "I like to drive."

"Do you like—big trucks or small ones?" Ella asked.

"I just drive big ones," he said, as though insulted.

Cowboys galloped, yelling, across a desert. Ella kept glancing at her aquamarine vase right by his elbow, pretending not to stare at him. There had to be reasons to like him. His fingernails shone. He had tied his shoes neatly. He had blue eyes. And the main point —he wanted Lena. "How long have you worked for Goodwill?" she asked.

"Awhile."

"And you live?"

"On a cot."

"Excuse me?"

"With the Ensons."

"And they are?"

"A man and a wife."

Before she could inquire more, Lena appeared. Ella had helped her match her yellow rhinestone earrings and scarf with a yellow shift, the one she'd worn when she'd gotten the Goodwill job. It seemed lucky. Bob lifted his eyes from the TV. Ella had never looked at Lena the way a man would. Dressing her was like adorning a child—for a specific, decorative purpose, but not for men. Now, creamy lavender eye shadow gleamed iridescent on her eyelids, and her hair was expansive with spray. Bob gazed at her frankly, as though he had a right to her.

Lena whisked past Ella, bumping her with her purse. "I've been talking to your guest," Ella began, "and—"

"Hi, Bob," said Lena.

Bob smiled. "Finish your socks?"

"Shut up!" squealed Lena, clapping her hand over her mouth.

"Excuse me?" asked Ella.

"Learn to park!" Lena said.

"I'm the best parker," Bob said. "I'm the number-one parker. And you know it."

Lena screeched with giggles. "Liar!" She rushed to the door with an exuberant haughtiness. Bob ran after her, as though afraid she would disappear.

"Where are you going?"

"We're going to walk down to House of Pancakes," said Lena.

"House of—it's going to be crowded," said Ella, feeling vaguely hysterical. "There'll be a long wait—"

"I'm hungry," said Bob, tugging Lena.

"Do you have enough money? Let me give you some—"

"Bob has money."

Bob gazed at Lena. His eyes were clear and intelligent with desire. He put his hand on her arm.

"Bye!" Lena said, waving tentatively.

Ella could not speak.

"Bye!" said Lena. "You—you look very pretty."

And they left.

She watched them bound across the lawn. Lena's yellow dress seemed to flutter in slow motion as she ran, as though governed by new physical laws.

Lou sprang back from the window, like a child embarrassed by what he had just seen. He pushed his hand into his glossy gray hair.

"Well," he said, "we're not losing a daughter—we're just gaining another mouth to feed."

Lou had never owned Lena the way she had. For thirty years he had tried hard not to look too closely at their daughter, instead cultivating a relentless optimism that Ella had found incomprehensible, yet also necessary. Now it made her feel alone.

"We're not gaining anything," said Ella. She grabbed her sweater and followed the two figures walking down the street.

She walked briskly, but casually, keeping a block between herself and her daughter. When Lena and Bob turned into a shopping center at the corner, Ella stopped beside a hefty Buick that was parked at one end of the lot.

They walked through the empty parking lot. It spread, like a dark lake, between House of Pancakes and a Hallmark, an ice cream parlor, a laundromat, and a pet store. It was Sunday, and all the stores were closed, but Bob and Lena stared hard at the windows as though willing them to open. Ella waited for something to go wrong. Bob went over to cars, rubbed their dusty tops, nodded like an expert, returned to Lena. She put coins into a newspaper rack, removed a paper and handed it to him; he rolled it up and tapped it against his leg.

Lena and Bob walked around the parking lot slowly, once, twice, three times. The orange flanks of House of Pancakes loomed, unreal, candied in the pale light. Customers left the restaurant and walked toward their cars with a casual confidence; Bob and Lena watched them walk. As the two of them finally went through the coffee shop's glass doors, Bob touched Lena's back, just for a moment; his hand reached for the yellow fabric, trying, gently, to hold on.

Bob began to come to the house once a week. Lena was always dressed and ready an hour beforehand; she sat absolutely still on her bed, as though the fact of his imminent arrival was so fragile she had to take care not to disturb even the air. But she always made him wait. One night, while Bob installed himself in the den and waited for Lena to join him, Ella swept in to quiz him about his life. "Where is your cot?" she asked.

"Near the garage."

"Who are the Ensons?"

"A man and a wife."

She dragged out of him the following scintillating facts: he preferred lamb chops to chicken, and peas to potatoes.

Ella ruled that Lena and Bob had to spend part of the date somewhere in the house. They sat on the patio while Ella washed the dishes, observing them through the kitchen window. Toward nine o'clock, when the sky had turned dark, Ella heard a jump and rustle and the sound of running; she looked out a window onto the shining, moon-silver lawn. Lena and Bob were not kissing or touching but just chasing each other, endlessly, like large, slow bears. Their sound was of the purest joy, a soft, hushed giggling as they followed each other through the dark yard.

Dolores told her that Bob lived with the Ensons—a couple—in Sherman Oaks, and had a brother in Chicago, Hugh, who paid them rent. Ella got Hugh's number and called him up.

When she told him that Bob was dating her daughter, there was a silence so hostile she wondered what she had actually said.

"I'm sending money," Hugh said irritably. "I'm sending money."

"I'm not asking—"

"It's not easy, lady. Do you think it's easy sending—"

"Sir," she said, "I'm not asking for money. I just want to know what he's like."

Another silence. "Well, you see what he's like."

"For the last few months. What about before?"

"What is there to know? He's forty-one. Three years older than me."

"Where has he lived?"

"The folks had him at an institution for a while. They didn't know what the hell to do with him. He's been at the Ensons' six years, since the folks died. They got him to Goodwill. He likes driving, I hear."

"What else?"

"You might want to know this. He had a vasectomy."

She pressed the phone more firmly to her ear.

"They did that early. When he was sixteen, seventeen. No little Bobs running around."

Ella did not know how to digest this fact, so she decided to move on. "Anything else? Health problems, disorders, anything?"

"No, he's just real slow."

"And you?" she asked, in spite of herself.

"Me?"

"You, what do you do?"

"I'm in insurance. Life and homes. I just got married two years ago. I've got a son now," he said, his voice suddenly soft and eager to please.

"How nice," she said coolly.

"I hope he and your daughter get along real well," he said, his voice high-pitched with false sincerity. "I'll call back to see how he is—" He hung up. She never heard from him again.

———

One night, as Ella put on her sweater, preparing for her usual reconnaissance mission to House of Pancakes, she felt Lou's hands on her shoulders. He turned her around.

"I have to go," she said.

"Have dinner with me."

"Dinner?" she asked. "But they're—"

"They're just going to House of Pancakes." He looked away from her. "Who else is going to marry her?" he asked.

He was wearing an undershirt, and his shoulders were thinner now, at sixty-two, almost girlish. She followed him to the kitchen. Lena had recently discovered her own perfume, a chirpy lavender scent from Sav-On, and it floated through the hall. In the kitchen the shiny appliances hummed.

Lou paced around while Ella heated chicken with mushrooms. "What do you think they're doing?" she asked him.

"Eating," he said.

"They'll forget to pay," she said.

"Then they'll get arrested," he said. He folded his arms. They were caramel-colored, dusted with silver hair. His gaze stopped on her, held her. "Let's fool around," he said, a soft huskiness in his voice.

She stopped; she wished she could feel interested. "If you want to," she said, a little hopefully, "then come over here."

She turned away from him and, gently, he wound her long hair into his hands. His after-shave smelt drugstore-blue and sharp. His breath was a hot current against her neck. His hands slid down her bare arms and gently cupped her breasts, and Ella tried to let herself go against him, but she couldn't.

Lou stopped, sensing her resistance. "She's fine," he said.

Delicately Ella disentangled herself from him.

"I need you too," Lou said. He lightly slapped her hip, as though she were a cow, and she heard him walk away from her.

———

Lena and Bob marched into the kitchen one evening, their fingers wound together tightly, as though they had been assigned to each other as buddies on a school trip. Lena held up their hands. A plastic yellow ring encircled her index finger.

"I'm married!" said Lena.

Bob swiped a bruised pear off the table and took a big, juicy bite.

"You're what?" Ella asked.

"He gave me a ring!"

"You're engaged," said Ella.

"I'm going to have a husband!" screeched Lena. She pulled Bob to her side, like a purse.

Ella slowly laid her dishtowel on the sink. She touched Lena's taut hand, the yellow ring; it was the type that fell, encased in a plastic bubble, out of a gumball machine. Bob's breath was loud and puppyish, and his bristly hair seemed a harder silver than before. Lena giggled. She said to Bob, "Say what I said to—"

"Do I have to?"

"Yes."

Bob slowly got to his knees in front of Ella. He rubbed his hands on the sides of his gray pants and looked at the floor.

"I forget," he said to Lena.

"You know," said Lena. She whispered loudly, "I want to—"

"I want to propose a marriage," Bob said, addressing Ella's knee.

"Lena," Ella said, "honey, he's supposed to kneel in front of you, not me."

"But he's asking you."

Ella looked down at the rosy, bald circle on Bob's scalp. He looked like a gardener sprawled across a patch of lawn, pressing seeds into a plot of dirt. He was inevitable, and perhaps because of that, she felt an unexpected rush of love for him.

"Lou," Ella called carefully. "Lou."

"I'm married!" Lena shrieked as her father came into the room, and then she rushed into his arms. It was something she rarely did; Lou was unsure how to hold her, and his arms curved awkwardly around her. He stepped away and looked at her, blinking.

"Married," Lou said.

"Stand up," Ella said. Bob rocked back onto his feet and stood slowly, grabbing Lena's hip for balance. He was standing up, one of them now.

"We have to have a toast," said Lou.

Ella lifted a pitcher of cranberry juice from the refrigerator and filled the glasses. Lou arranged Lena's and Bob's arms into the gesture of a toast. Lena and Bob clutched their glasses fiercely, as though expecting them to rise to the ceiling, pulling them, legs kicking, off the floor.

"L'chayim," Lou said.

It was Lou's idea that they get married in Las Vegas. They had a nine P.M. appointment at the Chapel of Eternal Love, at the other end of South Fifth, but Bob played the slots too long and almost made them late. Lena played right beside him, a little wobbly in her heels, her veil plopped on top of her machine.

The four of them walked down the Strip to the Chapel of Eternal Love, past the Stardust and the Thunderbird and the Riviera. The streets glowed with the hotels' gaudy pink and orange and white light. Lena wore a polyester puff-sleeved ivory dress, which they had purchased off a mannequin in the window of Treasureland, a discount emporium. The mannequin rose grimly out of a litter of golden ashtrays and inflatable palm trees. Lena had stopped by the window, pointed to the mannequin and said with great assurance, "Her."

Ella held Lena's hand in hers; with the other, she touched Lou's arm. "They do know we're coming?"

"Yes."

"What about flowers? Do they provide them?"

"Relax." He did not look at her. "It's going to be beautiful."

She wanted to ask him if love was truly good, if marriage made you safe, if the right man or woman would make anyone happy. She wanted to ask Lou if she had, in fact, given birth to Lena—if her daughter truly lived outside her body.

Outside the chapel, Ella took Lena to the far corner of the parking lot, drew Red Plum lipstick across her trembling lips.

"Ready?"

Lena nodded.

"Scared?"

Lena shrugged.

Ella took her hand. She wanted to tell her something. Marriage, she thought, was not simply choosing your mate, but the person you wanted to be for the rest of your life. There were other wives Ella could have been. Ella's marriage had shaped her, firmly and precisely, but she could not see the marks of her own evolution; she could not see how the love she gave and took made her what she was.

And here was her daughter with one suitor, one choice.

"Do you understand what this means, Lena?"

"It means that Bob and I will be together and we will be happy."

Ella adjusted Lena's veil with trembling fingers. "Where's your bobby pin?" she asked. "Don't let this fall off. Don't keep touching it."

Lena swatted her hand away. "I want to get married now."

The justice of the peace looked worn down by all the eternal love he'd seen that day. His assistant, wearing a red-sequined dress and a sparkly name tag that said WITNESS, took the wedding fee of twenty dollars from Ella, then flung open the door to a large refrigerator. Rows of cold bouquets were lined up like a silent, aloof audience inside. She shivered. "What color roses, hon? Red, pink, white or silver?"

"I would like silver, please," Lena said.

Lena stood beside Bob, their elbows touching. She tugged her wedding dress straight and nodded obediently at the justice. Her hand gripped the refrigerated spray of silver roses, which were the color of a dull nickel. Her face had the alertness of true happiness.

Ella, the maid of honor, stood beside Lena; Lou removed his navy fedora and held it as he stood beside Bob.

"By the power invested in me by the state of Nevada, I pronounce you man and wife," said the justice. He coughed. He suddenly seemed uncomfortable, as though just realizing he was intruding upon a family gathering.

Lena moved first. She raised her hand to Bob's face with a great tenderness, her fingers spread as though to capture as much of him as she could. Ella stared at Lena's fingers, which looked eerie and remote as a sea animal, and she did not know where Lena had learned to touch someone like that.

The witness hauled over a large, blue-sequined sack of free gifts for the newlyweds. "Something to start off your new home," she said. It was brimming with boxes of detergent, spatulas, colanders. The justice thrust his arm inside and brought out a box of Tide.

"Yuck," Lena said.

"This is your free gift," the assistant said.

"I don't want that one," Lena said, pouting.

"You don't want it?" asked the justice.

"Let them pick," Ella said.

The justice glared at Ella and checked his watch. "Lady, I'd like to stay here all night, but—"

"Let them pick," Ella hissed. She would not let them walk back into the streets of Las Vegas with a bad gift. Lena and Bob plunged their hands into the sack together. They began to bring out another box of Tide, pale detergent flowing out through a crack in the top. Ella pushed in front of Bob and Lena and slapped the box back into the bag. She grabbed hold of a spatula and pushed it into Lena's trembling hand.

"Congratulations," Ella said.

Out by the pool, the Las Vegas sun hammered down on their faces. Ella watched her daughter spread herself on a bright plastic chaise. Lena's eyes were masked by her horn-rimmed sunglasses, and her nipples were visibly erect under her lemon-yellow bathing suit. She lay on the chaise in an aloof silence, as though she were spinning quiet, magnificent thoughts.

"Do you want some lotion?" Ella asked.

Lena did not answer. She stood up regally and walked over to the pool. Standing a little unsteadily on its edge, she looked down at Bob in the water. Bob yanked her leg, and Lena crashed in.

Ella was not the only one who watched while Lena and Bob tumbled and splashed, cheerful, muffled bellows rising from their mouths. Their slick arms smacked the surface and swooped under the water, and their faces butted and kissed, but it was not exactly clear what they were doing to each other, and the crowd around the pool was riveted. Ella felt the backs of her knees tense. She got ready to stand up.

But after a minute Lena swung herself casually out of the pool. She glittered like an unearthly creature, with water shining on her arms, her hair. Lena came right to her chaise and sat beside her.

"I would like to share a room with Bob," Lena said.

That night the four of them stood in El Tropicale's dim hallway. Bob's arm circled Lena's shoulder with a brave attempt at propriety.

"Honey, may I have your key," Ella said.

Lena handed her mother the key. Lou was silent. Bob's fingers fluttered on Lena's shoulder, and Ella tasted fear, metallic, in her throat.

"Lena," Ella started, as her daughter took Bob's hand, "Lena, knock if you need anything." Lena whisked into her room and closed the door.

Lou had assumed a posture of odd, formal politeness. "Do we want to go sit at the piano bar?" he asked.

"I don't feel like it."

"Do we want to play the slots?"

"No," she said, opening the door to their own room next door.

They went inside, twitchy as a couple meeting each other illicitly for the first time. With a sharp, definite motion, Lou shrugged off his wine-colored jacket. His white shirt stuck to his shoulders in the heat.

"Have you noticed the footwear they sell here?" he asked.

"Footwear?"

He tossed his jacket over a chair. "People are on vacation, they lose their shopping sense." He took a deep, sharp breath. "Pink loafers. They take them home and they realize, where the hell am I going to wear pink loafers?"

"They're going to have to live with us," said Ella.

"They probably don't want to."

"She can't cook or clean," said Ella.

"I don't think he'd notice."

She thought she heard the TV's muffled garble start in the other room. "I hear them," she said.

The two of them froze, listening. "No," he said. "You don't hear them."

She put her hands on the wall dividing their room from Lena's. It was strangely cool. She heard only a faint, staticky wave of audience laughter.

"Look!" said Lou. He knocked on the wall sharply, twice. "Hello!" he called. Breathless, they awaited an answer; there was none. "See?" he said. "They can't hear us." He turned abruptly and walked away from the wall. "Come away from there," he said.

She wanted, vaguely, to accuse him of something; she wanted to see pain on Lou's face, a sorrow she could recognize.

"Leave her alone," he said, not sounding entirely convinced. He sank wearily into the sofa and rubbed his hands vigorously over his face. "Let's have a drink."

She couldn't. Instead, Ella pulled the ice tray out of the refrigerator and, in a gesture that felt both normal and alien, shook out cubes of ice and dropped them into a glass. She sat on the bed and crunched the ice cubes slowly and deliberately, trying to listen only to the hard clink they made as they fell back into the glass.

At about one A.M. there was a sharp knocking. Ella opened the door to Lena, who was shivering in her nightgown. Bob was right behind her, naked, holding a white towel across his waist with only middling success.

"What?" Ella demanded. "What's wrong?"

"I'm bleeding, Mother. There's blood—"

Ella yanked Lena into the room. Bob toddled in behind her, wearing the frozen, frightened smile of a child unsure what he was expected to do. Lou stood up. "What's—" he began, and she saw his face melt to alarm.

"I've got her," Ella announced. She pulled Lena into the bathroom. "Sit," she said. Ella wound a long ribbon of toilet paper around her hand. "Show me where."

Lena sat on the toilet and daintily flipped up her nightgown. Ella saw a smear of blood on Lena's large beige panties; she reached up, grapped the elastic and pulled the panties down to the floor. Ella dabbed Lena's vagina with the toilet paper; it came back pale red.

Ella knelt and peered critically between her daughter's legs. She had no idea what she was looking for; there was just a little blood. She held a towel under warm water and gently dabbed Lena's pubic hair.

"Am I okay, Mother?"

Ella didn't speak.

"Am I okay?"

"I don't know." Ella let Lena wonder a moment. "Answer me. Was he nice to you?"

"I think so."

"Does it still hurt?"

"I started bleeding."

"Do you feel better now?"

Lena touched her vagina tenderly, then stood up.

Ella knelt before her daughter and reached for her hands. "You've had"—Ella spoke slowly—"intercourse now, Lena."

Lena slapped Ella's hands away, impatient. "I have to go see my husband."

Bob was waiting in a chair, the towel arranged, like a large white napkin, across his lap. Lou was sitting in a chair on the other side of the room. They each had the alert demeanor of someone trying very hard not to speak.

"I stopped bleeding," Lena said proudly to Bob.

Bob folded the towel around his waist and jumped up; he hurried out of the room. Lena bounded after him, and Ella followed into the hallway. "The TV's still on," he called to Lena.

"Leave it on," said Lena.

As Lena began to follow him into their room, Ella saw Lena's nightgown sticking, indecent, over her hips; she reached forward to tug it down. But Lena pushed grandly past her mother. The pink door shut, and Ella was left standing in the corridor alone.

Back in the room, Lou looked at her. "Is she all right?"

Ella nodded.

He gingerly lifted Lena's beige lace panties off the floor. "She left these," he said.

She remembered when she had bought these panties for Lena—on sale at Henshey's, two for one. Lou folded them gently, barely touching the edges, then handed them to Ella. She was moved by the way he folded them. She went to the bathroom and threw them out.

She opened the refrigerator and took out a perfect, tiny bottle of Dewar's. She unscrewed the cap, swallowed half the bottle and handed it to her husband.

There was only one thing she could think to do.

She went to Lou and kissed him.

They kissed in the strange, clean room, surrounded by lampshades and bedspreads and dressers that were not their own.

Ella let her husband kiss her neck, her breasts, her knees, hard enough to erase Lena. Ella had not expected to feel abandoned. She had not expected that Lena's closing the door would make her turn to Lou. The kindest thing he could do was make her forget. And as Lou had been, since Lena's birth, second place to her daughter, Ella sensed, in the muscular trembling of his fingers, how much he wanted to make her forget. She felt the nakedness of their lips in the deep, cooling dark.

Long after Lou had fallen asleep, she sat awake beside him. Then she went to the window and looked down at the street. It was the street Lena had walked down to her wedding, and it burnt with the hotel's twenty-four-hour lights. She watched the lit messages—BINGO and POKER and WIN!—that flashed a brilliant display of pink and orange and yellow into the empty street. Ella believed, suddenly, absolutely, that Lena was also looking out her window. She saw her daughter leaning naked on the ledge, her hair streaming over her bare shoulders, gazing at the bright casino lights and their strange, insistent attempts to illuminate the sky.

Stupid Girl

Louis Berney

NO ONE EVER DIES AT DISNEYLAND, at least that's what she'd heard, so even though it was obvious the old dude's heart was history—when the ride ended he was sagging in his safety harness like he weighed a thousand pounds, his eyes rolled back to the milky whites—paramedics loaded his body onto a stretcher, clipped an oxygen mask to his face, and whisked him safely off park property. Where, she supposed, Disney authorities would finally release his soul and allow the emergency room attendant at Anaheim Memorial to check him out.

Snow White, who'd been strapped in with the dead man, clawed her way out of the bobsled, ripping one of her pleated, mutton-leg sleeves in the process. She stumbled to the nearest trash can. Even on the best of days? The swoops and dips of the Matterhorn always made her feel like pitching. And today was most definitely *not* the best of days. The old dude they'd paired her with for an in-action publicity shot was some high-roller insurance tycoon from Houston. Potbelly, pink piggy eyes, cigar smoke, and Old Spice. When she first gave him her hand to shake, he held it a little longer, got it a little moister, than was really necessary.

No *way*, she'd thought, am I getting on that bobsled with you.

But then she'd felt sad, like somebody had jabbed her heart with a fork. Here she was, only nineteen years old, and always she looked at life as something about to sneak up on her and pounce. Maybe this old dude was a nice old man, a dad and granddad who gave the kids dollar bills and root beer barrels whenever they stopped by. Maybe?

Smiling at the insurance tycoon smiling back at her, Snow White (Suzanne Elizabeth Bailey when she was off the clock) had made up her mind, as she did periodically, to screw past experience and try thinking the best of people. To be less jaded in the hope that the world, somehow—she tried not to think too much about this logic—might therefore turn out nicer.

That, and she really really needed the extra money she'd get for the job, you betcha.

Hunched over a trash can trimmed with glitter-paint fairy dust, Suzanne wondered now if it was possible for a girl to die of chronic dumb judgment. Right before he kicked, right after the bobsled shot into the last fast curve, the insurance tycoon had hooked a fat pimply arm around her shoulder and—smack!—grabbed a handful of boob.

She'd seen too many people dead or dying (her dad, her first stepmother, a grandmother, a boyfriend sheared from his Yamaha by the kingpin of a jackknifed semi) to feel anything but sympathy for the man; she wasn't pissed off, only tired. And glad to be off the Matterhorn, somewhere she could puke in peace.

When she finished doing that, she felt better, though not by much. She had three hours left on her shift, and nights in August were almost as hot as the days; her scalp smoldered inside the black, bow-topped wig.

Her own hair was dirty blonde. Brown eyes, a gap between her two front teeth. Very embarrassing, those claw-hammer teeth of hers, but when she scored the TV series they'd been part of her so-called charm; the producers had even written a clause into her contract. After that, well—the fact of the matter was that stepfathers, and the boyfriends of ex-wives of former stepfathers, didn't invest hundreds of orthodonto-dollars in little girls to whom they were barely connected.

With the back of her hand she swiped at the black mascara sweating spider legs down her cheeks. Worse than the heat or the heaves was the thought that they'd never use 8 x 10s of a corpse. They'd probably still pay her, she considered, but then again what if they didn't?

She kicked the side of the trash can. That money, whenever it finally came, she'd already promised to her stepsister, who'd been waiting two months for her June rent. The stepsister, really just the ex-wife of one of Suzanne's half brothers, wouldn't believe what had happened on the Matterhorn. She'd conclude that Suzanne had snorted away the cash, even though Suzanne had been moderately clean for almost a year and absolutely so since the Fourth of July, since the day after the Fourth of July. A fight would erupt, Tita would call her an ungrateful coke-head tramp—this from a woman who considered crystal meth one of the four basic food groups—and then Suzanne would end up sleeping in her friend Robert's van, if she was lucky.

The thought of all that was too much to bear on an emptied stomach. She glanced around. At the foot of the Matterhorn, security was busy trying to hustle everyone along to Mr. Toad's Wild Ride. Her own lead, a guy in charge of shadowing her through the park, in case she dehydrated and collapsed in costume and traumatized some moron kid who'd think Snow White was dead, was searching for her in exactly the wrong direction.

She dodged a pair of eight-year-old autograph piranhas and slipped into the Skyway to Tomorrowland, a timber and cake-frosting facade that was supposed to look like a Swiss chalet. Taped yodeling. The greeter, a skinny blonde kid in lederhosen, passed her through, and a heartbeat later she was in one of the buckets that coasted on cables, forty feet above the asphalt surface of the park.

It was cooler up there, and quieter. No shrieking kids, no hydraulic spitting of the rides, no dink-dink-tinkle of "It's a small world, after all," piped through speakers hidden in the bushes. From inside her bodice, from the elastic edge of her jog-bra, she plucked a match and a joint. She slouched in her seat so that, from the ground, the only thing you could see above the wall of the gondola was her polka-dot bow. Not that she gave a shit if she got fired. But if she was caught getting baked on the Skyway, the jarheads from security might search her locker and find the rest of the Chocolate Tide she had stashed there. And that would mean another three months of court-ordered treatment, another ninety-day twelve-step recovery drill.

"God grant me the serenity to blah blah blah."

Please. But she was golden up here, as long as she slouched. No worries. *Hakuna* fucking *matata*.

She lit the joint and blew out the match with a smudge of gray breath. She took a good, deep rip, pulled the smoke up and over her heart like a goose-down quilt, pulled and pulled until her brain was tucked in as well.

Every time was like the first sweet time. She'd been nine. Her TV dad, now a born-again bass player for a Christian rock group, had turned her on to bong hits between takes of an episode about cheating. Should little Cathy (that was the character Suzanne had played, little Cathy raised in the station house by a band of kooky firemen), should she copy her best friend's test answers? She had, of course, and they'd been nabbed by the teacher, of course, and there'd been some important lessons, of course, to be learned right after the commercial break.

The lessons? Little Cathy learned the importance of personal integrity, etc.; little Suzanne learned that weed was good and good weed turned your lips to liquid rubber. They'd had to tape the last scene three times, because she'd sounded like she was speaking Chinese.

Suzanne closed her eyes, smiled her first sincere one of the day, and enjoyed the slosh of blood in her veins as the gondola rocked along above the canals of Storybook Land.

The show hadn't set the world on fire, but for two seasons and a half, at least, she'd had a manager, a theatrical agent, a commercial agent, a tutor, an acting coach. She had a woman who was in charge, as far as she could tell, of nothing else but slathering her up with sunscreen every time she even thought about going outside.

After the show was cancelled, when she was eleven, Steven Spielberg didn't exactly come knocking. So she did the school thing for a few years, then worked a delightful array of bad jobs and worse jobs—Baskin-Robbins, JCPenney's, a cocktail place on Hollywood. About a year ago she landed the part-time Disney gig, where the money wasn't much, but steady.

"I beg your pardon!" someone shouted, loud. "Pardon me!"

She sighed. Was that too much to ask, she wondered, four minutes of peace without some asshole father, down below, throwing a hissy fit because Minnie Mouse hadn't signed his kid's book yet?

"I BEG YOUR PARDON!"

Something stung her on the arm and she swatted at it. Another something, hard and small, pinged off the metal wall of the gondola; she heard it fall to the floor.

Startled, she sat up, leaned forward, patted the floor with the palms of her hands. After a minute she found it, pinched it, sniffed it: a chocolate-covered raisin.

A chocolate-covered raisin?

She peeked over the lip of her gondola. In the gondola directly behind her stood a big black man.

Really black and *really* big. Three hundred and fifty pounds if he was an ounce, butt as broad as a love seat. He wore a short-sleeved dress shirt, striped tie, and glasses with dark plastic frames.

"PARDON ME!" he roared. He stamped his foot and whipped another Raisinet at her. Another one. "Snow White does not smoke!" he roared. "PLEASE EXTINGUISH THAT AT ONCE!"

Oh, she thought, my fucking God. She flicked her roach away and bonked her head on the plastic seat when she ducked back behind the wall of the gondola. She sat there for a minute, stunned, wondering what in the *fuck* her Chocolate Tide had been dusted with. Because she was tripping, wasn't she? What other explanation could there possibly be?

Very cautiously she took another peek at the gondola behind her, but it was still there, *he* was still there. He'd stopped roaring and stomping and winging Raisinets, but he kept glaring at her. There was another guy in the gondola, a white guy about half his size. She could hear the crackle of cussing as he tried to yank the monster dude back down to his seat.

Her own bucket swung into the wheelhouse. Suzanne hitched her skirt over her knees, crouched next to the hatch, tried to think, to *think*. If the big black guy called security on her, she was fucked. That stupid weed: she swore to herself she'd never do another drug for as long as she lived. And what if he decided not to bother with security at all and came tearing after her himself? He could probably twist her head off like you'd twist the cap off a bottle. She thought she was going to have a heart attack.

"Welcome to Tomorrowland," the attendant said. When he popped her door open, she jumped to the ground and didn't look back. The cast member locker room was behind Aladdin's Oasis, so she blew across the Central Plaza and made for Adventureland. She started to relax, a little, when she hit the bridge, but then she was blindsided by a Dopey, who must have spotted her from the Castle Forecourt. He grabbed her around the waist and tried to waltz her back to a group of giggling Japanese tourists.

"Fucker," she hissed. She shoved him away and he went reeling backward. His big, molded-plastic dwarf head hit the bridge railing like a bomb, with a colossal hollow boom that scattered the birds from the trees. Everyone turned to see what had happened, and in that instant she shimmied through the crowd, over the bridge, shimmied safe and sound through the bamboo portcullis hung with bunches of plastic bananas.

He'd had this game, her dad, that he liked to play with her when he was drunk or stoned or whatever. Which, in other words, was most of the time. He'd come home and open the front door and pretend she was invisible.

"Suzanne, girl, where are you?" he'd cry. "I can't see you!"

"Daddy!" she'd holler. "Right here!" She'd pound her fists against his legs.

"Suzanne!"

"Daddy!"

He'd trip over her, stumble, knock her gently down to the shag with him, tickle her until she could barely breathe, until her laughter was just weak, wet, happy squeaks.

"Suzanne! Where are you darlin'?"

Well, when he wasn't drunk or stoned, lifting her over his head like a surfboard and tickling her down to the grass and threatening to surf her heinie all the way to Australia, then she really was invisible to him. Sobriety, she would have to conclude, was as a general concept highly overrated.

She always seemed to think about her dad late at night, when it was time to go home. She'd been only five years old when he died, and yet her memories of him were sharper than yesterday's. Particles of dust churning in a shaft of July light. The texture and taste of American cheese slices, the crinkle of the cellophane wrapper. American cheese was his favorite snack, and sometimes he'd flip squares to her like fish to a seal.

Marvin punched her card—1:03 A.M.—and motioned her through the gate with a flick of his *Sports Illustrated*. She slid her time card up under the sun visor. It was 1:03 A.M. and her day from hell was officially over.

She turned off the AC, which was worthless anyway. Her hand, she noticed, was trembling, and no wonder. One dead man on the Matterhorn; one giant psycho; forty dollars worth of perfectly good Chocolate Tide flushed down the toilet. A cool, fishy breeze had managed to work its way inland, and there wasn't much smog; what smog there was even seemed kind of romantic, made the stars down along the horizon look fuzzy and soft.

Not another car in sight, either direction, but the light stayed red. She wasn't in any particular hurry, come to think of it. Right turn, left turn, straight? The apartment in West Hollywood was out of the question, of course, because of the wicked stepsister and the rent money Suzanne didn't have; Robert's van was a possibility, if it hadn't been impounded since she last talked to him, but it was a *van* for God's sake, decorated with yellow tennis balls he'd cut in half and glued to the walls. The thought of a night alone in there (Robert worked the dog shift till dawn) was just too lonely, too depressing, for words.

That song by Garbage was on the radio again, "Stupid Girl," her own personal anthem. The light changed and Suzanne eased off the clutch, whispered a short prayer of the please-God-please variety. The engine fluttered for a second, but her Rabbit rolled out of the employee lot and onto the street without conking again.

"Thank you, God," she murmured, just in case. You never know, right?

She turned…left. Why not? Ahead of her were the guest lots, empty now, three motels, every window dark and curtain drawn, the Pick-N-Pay, another motel, and an abandoned Church of the Holy Pentecost. On the wall of the church there was a faded picture of a child riding an escalator up to heaven, up out of a tangle of pale yellow flames. Suzanne wondered if there was a down escalator too, if there was a food court in heaven, a Nordstrom's, and (drowsy, floating in that weird in-between, that trippy frappe of asleep and awake and Garbage on the radio) she almost didn't see the car with its hood up and engine smoking; she almost didn't see the man who stepped out to flag her down.

Reflex, she tapped the brakes, gave the wheel a jerk. That was a mistake, she realized, even before she'd done it. Her little Rabbit was pretty single-minded when it came to following instructions; you could turn, or stop, but not really both at the same time. The car stalled, blew a big sweet breath of gasoline at her, and rolled into the parking lot of the Holy Pentecost.

Fuck, Suzanne mused. Fuck. Fuck. She cranked the ignition, just for the fun of it. Nothing.

The guy tapped on her window. She glanced up at him—he was unshaven, about forty years old, with blue bloodshot eyes and a stringy ponytail. Perfect: just the sort of drifter you'd want to encounter late at night, in an abandoned Orange County parking lot. She tried the ignition again.

"Hey," he said through the glass, "could you give us a lift to a gas station?"

Us? she wondered, just as (Did she need this shit? Did she really need this shit?) rumbling up into the puddle of yellow streetlight came the big black maniac from the Skyway.

"Charlie," he said, "you didn't let me finish explaining my theory about Critter Country." He saw her. "Snow White!"

Suzanne gave up on the *fucking* ignition and reached for her purse. She found the can, pushed open her door, stepped out of the car. The drifter backed off a few steps.

"Leave me alone!" Suzanne screamed. She shook the can hard so that they could hear the rattle of the aerosol bead. "Leave me alone! I've got Mace! Why do you keep bothering me?"

"Wait!" the drifter said. "Shit!"

"Don't move!"

"Shit! I won't!"

"Don't move! *Both* of you!"

"Take it easy!" the drifter yelled. "Christ Almighty!"

"I swear to God I'm going to mace you both if you don't leave me the *fuck* alone!"

"What the fuck is your problem?" He edged away, palms up.

"What the fuck is my *problem?* What the fuck is *my* problem?"

"I know *you!*" the big maniac said suddenly, excited. He rumbled closer.

"Shit, Walter!" the drifter said. He dropped to one knee on the broken asphalt and covered his face with his hands.

"Leave me *alone!*" Suzanne screamed. She stared up, up, up the slope of the big guy. It was impossible, how huge he was. "Get the fuck *back!*"

He studied her face intently, one long, surprisingly slender finger pressed against the bridge of his glasses. He lifted his chin and lowered it very slowly.

"Come on down and meet some friends of mine," he began to sing—to *sing*—in a frail little wisp of a voice that couldn't possibly come out of a monster bod like that, "meet some friends of mine, down at engine house, engine house number nine."

The drifter friend had hunched down into himself, his hands still wrapped around his face. "Walter, goddammit," he warned softly. "Get *back.*"

Suzanne couldn't help but snort. "You *remember* that?"

"You lived with your dad who was a fireman," the big guy said, "and a dalmatian named Lazy."

"Nobody remembers that," Suzanne said. "It was only on two seasons and a half."

"Sunday nights on the Disney Channel. The plotting was somewhat derivative, but the acting was superb. You reminded me of a young Hayley Mills. Suzanne Bailey."

Somewhere, not far away, a dog barked, paused to hack something up, then started barking again; across the street, razor wire coiled down off the dead Best Western sign like a strand of Christmas tree tinsel.

"Listen," Suzanne said, "if you guys are star-stalkers? I'm guessing you could do better. I know a girl who played a girl in *Forrest Gump*, if you want her number. One of the minor hippies. My career is currently on hiatus."

"Don't lose heart," the big guy said. "Look at Walt Disney, for example. *Pinocchio*, when it was first released, was a financial disaster. My name is Walter. This is my friend Charlie. I'm sorry we acted so impetuously on the Skyway, but you shouldn't smoke cigarettes when you're in costume. You really shouldn't smoke at all, you know."

"Could you put that down, please?" the drifter said, peeking through his fingers. "I have some really bad tear-gas memories."

Suzanne shrugged, snorted again. "Just Aqua Net." She flashed them her best spokesmodel smile, dazzling and insincere, swept spokesmodel fingers across the can's label, then pitched it up onto the roof of the Church of the Holy Pentecost. "And it's empty," she said. "Story of my life."

The white drifter guy slowly unfolded from his crouch, groaned, and stretched out flat on his back.

"It must be very exciting," the black guy said, "to be a cast member at Disneyland. "Would you like to know what I think is the only negative aspect of Disneyland?"

"The stupid shows?" said his friend. He had his arms flung out and looked as if he'd been dropped there from a helicopter. "The right-wing patriotism and corporate butt-licking? The colorful audio-animatronic Third World peasants?"

"The only negative aspect," he continued cheerfully, "is that eventually you have to *leave*. Not so at Walt Disney World in Florida. When you go home for the night, you can take the monorail to the Polynesian Resort and wake up in the morning to a stunning view of the castle." He straightened his glasses. "Suzanne," he said, "what would you consider the ten most indelible moments in Disney animated history?"

"Jesus Christ," the drifter muttered.

"Indelible?"

"Memorable," the big guy said. He bounced on his toes and Suzanne wouldn't have been surprised if he'd soared off suddenly like a helium-filled cartoon parade balloon.

"No offense?" she said. "But are you like some sort of fanatical Disney freak?"

"The proper appellation," the drifter said, in what she had to admit was a pretty dead-on imitation of his friend, "is Disney enthusiast."

"Of course one must include the final scenes of both *Snow White* and *Pinocchio*," the big guy went on, "but I'd argue the final sequence of *Cinderella* is just as rich with possibilities."

She shrugged. "Never seen it," she said, and you'd have thought from the horrified look on his face that she'd suggested he go in for a rectal swab. "I liked *The Lion King.*"

"*The Lion King?*" He chuckled.

The drifter guy sat up, rubbed his thumb along his bottom lip, contemplated the torn toe of his Chuck Taylor high-top. He wore rings on all the fingers of his right hand, even the thumb. "What show did you say you were in?" he asked.

"*Engine House Number Nine*," the black guy said. "Oh, she was superb, Charlie. Suzanne had the sort of elusive Disney star quality one doesn't see much of anymore. A young Hayley Mills."

"You know," he said, rubbing his bottom lip, hooking a lank of hair behind his ear, "I might have an idea. I might have just stumbled across the opportunity of a lifetime."

Suzanne leaned back against her Rabbit. She took off her Dodgers cap and raked fingers through her hair. For a moment she pretended there was someone, out there, who was tracking her progress across the wide, white face of a clock, in a cheerful kitchen, someone who was sipping coffee and watching a *Cheers* rerun and expecting her home at such and such a time, on the dot, and would be worried if she was a minute late.

"What?" she asked, before she could stop herself.

"Picture this," Charlie said. He set his coffee cup down on the counter and gazed up at the ceiling, at the fluorescent tubes lisping and fluttering there. He was telling her how famous and rich it was going to make her, his opportunity of a lifetime, how she'd get soap operas and sitcoms and all the parts Alicia Silverstone turned down, how she'd have a condo in Malibu with room for as many dogs as she wanted.

They were at the International House of Pancakes, a couple of miles from the park and across the street from the gas station where she'd driven them. Two A.M. They'd offered to buy her breakfast, and she'd agreed. Why not? She hadn't had anything to eat since her shift break at four, and then only a bagel with hummus. She knew she shouldn't trust the two of them, but she had to keep reminding herself. Not once had either one of them brushed against her boob or tried to slide an arm around her shoulders. She hadn't caught them, not once, looking at her with the subtle, acquisitive, half-lidded lizard stare she was used to. They might be dangerous—she wasn't *that* naïve—but at least, she reasoned, they would be dangerous in original ways.

Charlie made a fist and pressed it against his ear. She realized the rings on his fingers weren't rings at all, but tattoos. A black-ink circle of vines and tiny thorns tooled around each finger, just beneath the second knuckle.

"Hello?" he said, fist still pressed to his ear.

"What?" she asked.

He shushed her. "I've got a call. Hello? This is Pepsi. Who was that blonde girl I saw on the tube last night? Suzanne Bailey? Get her in here. We want her for our Super Bowl spot."

"Please," she told him. "National commercials are impossible. There are a million girls for the smallest part."

"You're not a million girls," he said. "It's all about exposure. Once they see you, they'll have to have you."

She finished her eggs and noticed that Walter, perched on a stool that had disappeared beneath him, was leafing very slowly, very seriously, through a coffee-table book on the art of *Pinocchio*. He was humming softly to himself, a tune she recognized after a second—"Hi-diddle-de-dee, an actor's life for me." She propped her elbows on the counter, lit a cigarette, and smoked through a faint smile. For a minute it seemed the most normal thing in the world, to be sitting here at the International House of Pancakes, two o'clock in the morning, with a long-haired drifter and a giant black Disney enthusiast, considering a proposal for your own abduction. She tapped ash into her coffee saucer and turned to Charlie.

"And what makes you think you're the best possible applicants for this position?" she asked. "Do you have references? What would you say are your three greatest strengths as a kidnapper?"

He stared at her very intently. His eyes were blue, with shifting shadows inside, like light at the bottom of a swimming pool. She wanted to ask him about the significance of the thorn tattoos, but figured it was none of her business. "Just keep an open mind," he said. "It's very simple. It's so simple that absolutely nothing can even possibly go wrong. We fake a kidnapping, we send a ransom note, we collect the money."

"The money?" she laughed. "From who? I hate to rain on your parade, but there's no one in the continental United States who would pay to get me back. There's no one in the continental United States, actually, who'd even notice I'd been kidnapped, which let me tell you is a really pleasant thought to consider." The roof of her mouth itched and she wished she had some snow, some good old snow, just a taste.

"Disney will," he said. He had a narrow angular shape to his face, like a wedge, and a way of leaning a little bit forward all the time, as if he was always in the middle of squeezing through a tight place. "They don't give a shit about you *now*, I know. But once the word gets out that Snow White has been *kidnapped*—do you know what kind of media coverage that will get? What's Disney going to do then, when every evening over Tom Brokaw's shoulder there's a blue box with your picture: Day 17—the Snow White Crisis. They'll pay a million dollars. Two million. That's ashtray change for a company like that. And you'll be famous. Suzanne Bailey. Ten minutes after it's all over you'll be curled up on a sofa across from Barbara Walters, telling the tale of how you survived your terrifying ordeal."

"In Florida, you see, Walt learned anticipated urban development," Walter said. He reached across Charlie and touched her wrist. "He bought up forty square miles of virgin orange grove. At Walt Disney World in Florida, you can avoid the real world altogether."

Charlie snorted, but Suzanne had to admit that she wasn't particularly pro-reality herself. There was something to be said for clean streets and plenty of toilet paper and no cockroaches sifting through the Grape-Nuts and no neighbors above who, seriously, once dragged a goat up the stairs for some sort of Santeria thing. Once in a while, riding in the Electrical Parade, she'd stare so hard at some girl's smiling face that she'd fall into it; she'd daydream herself down into a life that seemed so happy (she wasn't dumb enough to think it actually was) she'd stop pelting the crowd with posies.

"Forget it," she told Charlie. "You've got to be kidding. Do I look that stupid and pathetic that I'd go for something like that? Tell me, OK, because if I do? I might as well kill myself right now."

"We'll be the ones who rescue you," he said. "Picture this. An old abandoned warehouse. A couple of guys driving along and a flat tire, or a belt goes flapping, and then through the flap of the fan belt they hear a muffled cry for help."

"Forget it," she said.

"We'll make the place look like the Manson family's been living there. Empty water jugs, cookie wrappers, duct tape with your blonde hairs stuck to it. Our two heroes creep inside and there she is, Suzanne Bailey. The nation rejoices."

"You're whacked," she said. She watched the line-cook scrape grease off the grill with a plastic spatula. "No way. Don't you think they're going to know it's a scam?"

"How?" he demanded. Those spooky blue eyes—it was a good thing, she supposed, her head wasn't made of flammable materials. "Who's going to call Snow White a liar, after her ordeal, this sweet weepy-eyed Disney Channel blonde girl? It's foolproof."

"No," she said. "Forget it."

No.

No.

And then, finally:

"OK."

She sighed a smoky sigh that could have been the last long sigh on earth, winding out to the outer eternal reaches of the universe. OK.

"Hey, Suzanne," Charlie said, "I know it's a crazy thing I'm asking you to do, but—"

"I've done crazier," she said with a shrug, which shut him up, a miracle. "Believe it or not."

Believe it or not. The fact of that matter made her want to giggle and cry at the same time, so she just lit another cigarette and watched the shreds of tobacco redden, crumble.

"*The Lion King,*" Walter said, out of the blue, "is certainly a *secondary* classic. But one would be hard pressed to rank it in the same group as *Cinderella.*"

She lay with her head tilted back, so that when she opened her eyes she stared up at the torn cloth ceiling and the tuft of stripped copper wires where the overhead light should have been. She'd always meant to get it fixed. Charlie was driving, just his fingertips on the wheel because the plastic was so hot; Walter was in the backseat, humming "Whistle While You Work," and flipping through the pages of his *Pinocchio* book. Every time he shifted on his monster haunches she thought they'd had a blow-out.

She'd been dozing. The sun had finally rolled over the horizon, like an egg off a table, but it was still hot. A hundred and twenty degrees, Charlie said, and he was probably exaggerating only a little. She thought her nostrils were going to melt every time she tried to inhale.

"I hate the fucking desert," she said. The heat made the macadam squiggle. "Hate it, hate it, hate it."

Charlie concentrated on the road ahead, didn't answer. He was convinced the desert was the place to go. He'd already figured out a place to hole up—the abandoned silver mines high in the hills above the Colorado River, just across the border into Arizona. He'd been there years ago, though she wasn't exactly clear why. It was critical they get off the beaten track, he said, and those old, high-desert silver mines were as far off the beaten track as you could get.

"It'll be like hiding on the moon," he'd said. "The whole world could be looking for you, the whole world could be holding hands and looking for you, and they'd never find you out here."

She counted the cigar-stub stumps of organ-pipe cactus, watched the telephone lines, barbed with desert birds, go spinning past. Charlie was prepared—she'd give him that much. He had details worked out that she wouldn't have thought of in a million years. The photos, for example; he was going to take pictures of her to go with the ransom note, once they got to the hideout. He was high if he really thought the scam was foolproof, but there was a chance they could pull it off. Stranger shit had happened. When the police questioned her afterwards? She'd be the fucking ice queen; she wouldn't give a fucking inch. "Three Asian men...bound and gagged...frightened for her life." Et cetera. She'd stick to her story and they could hammer at her morning and night, for all the good it would do them.

She reached over and touched one of Charlie's tattoos, traced the curve of thorns with the tip of her finger. "Are they religious?" she asked him.

He glanced at her, blinked. "What?"

"Are they supposed to be religious?" She was thinking of the crucifix her grandmother had hung on the wall above her bed the summer Suzanne had stayed there, the foot-long Jesus carved from dark, oily wood, the crown of thorns. He was one buff Jesus, she remembered, all knotted muscles and tendons and just the skimpiest scrap of loin cloth, which she'd actually peeked under once.

Charlie thought about the question. "Yeah," he said finally.

"Hey," she said. "How did you and Mr. Disney back there end up together?"

Charlie was staring hard at the road again, looking for the turn-off. "Shit," he said. "Don't ask."

Greasewood spurs, a few clumps of prickly pear, dry shallow washes scored east to west across the desert floor. Along the highway shoulder there were occasional smears of blood, pin-feathers, single scattered reptile scales that caught the light and blinked like sequins.

Maybe it was the dusk, the soft toasted orange of it, or maybe it was the half a lude Charlie had scored for her back at a gas station in Twenty-Nine Palms, to show his good faith, but for the moment she felt rosy as hell; she was so hopeful her heart felt pinched, like a green olive squeezed until out comes shooting an exclamation point pimento. This was the absolute last time, she promised herself, she'd do something this nutty.

They were off the state highway now and onto a dirt road that branched out from it. After a few minutes Charlie turned off and angled across the desert floor, toward the mesas, stumps listing like guttered candles in the mess of their own wax.

"I thought we were going to cross the river first," she said.

He checked the gas gauge, gave it a thump with his knuckle. She turned to watch their dust, drifting off toward the empty road, and noticed that Walter, in the backseat, was weeping. Very quietly, with just the slightest pucker of his lips, the slightest shiver to his shoulders. There was a spot of wet shine on each dark cheek.

Charlie glanced into the rearview mirror. "Shut up," he told Walter softly. "Shut up, goddammit."

Suzanne turned back around, stretched out her legs and kicked her feet up onto the dashboard. "What's wrong with *him?*" she asked Charlie.

He flipped on the headlights, gave her a wink.

"Almost there," he said.

Temporary Light

Kate Braverman

IT IS EARLY IN DECEMBER. Suzanne Cooper drives down Wilshire Boulevard through Beverly Hills and the city is not as she knew it. Overnight, wide red ribbons have been entwined around street lamps, there is simulated snow and frost in shop windows, and legions of slaughtered pines are everywhere decorated and displayed. It is as if the earth had suddenly divested itself of the ordinary and revealed its pagan interior. Or perhaps the world had without warning gone mad, she decides, garish red and green and silver like a bleeding forest under moonlight. This is a landscape of dangerous wounds and corrupted vegetation.

At a traffic light she finds herself staring at a Santa Claus with a sleigh of reindeer strung on wires across the intersection. Everywhere, strands of light bulbs rise into the air. Even the sky seems delirious and experimental. It is the winter of the wild surprise. The old regime does not apply. Have a drink, the voice in her head says.

It is Suzanne Cooper's second sober Christmas. She has learned to recognize the voice of her illness, the demonic chorus it employs and the genius motivating its attempts to destroy her. The voice could be articulate, brilliant, and seductive. It is the disaster that never sleeps.

I have a killer disease that wants me dead, she remembers. I have a daily reprieve based on the maintenance of my spiritual life. She repeats the slogans she has memorized in Alcoholics Anonymous, the banalities designed to provide a rudimentary form of counterattack against the onslaught of her alcoholism. It is like a chess game played by two computers to a series of perpetual stalemates. She is always black and on the defensive. Her sickness is aggressive and white, the color of vodka, gin, and wine.

At the next stop sign, she glances into a shop window dense with a red-and-green geometric motif. Mirrors amplify the distortion. Mannequin elves offer demented smiles. They look as if they have taken enormous doses of mescaline.

You're pathetic, the voice says, with your tiny arsenal, your squalid weaponry. And it won't be enough, not nearly. Consider the thin air beneath you. You have no net. You will fall and shatter and your blood run. One small glass of eggnog with a drop of brandy. No one will know.

Suzanne Cooper turns her car into the monumental parking structure beneath the Beverly Center. This year she is shopping early. Last Christmas she was in the hospital. This year will be different. This year she will see her children. Stephanie and Mark will spend Christmas Eve and Christmas Day with her. This has become her imperative, the irrefutable meaning of her present life. Her actions derive from the fact of Christmas. It has become the spine of her world, the anatomy she accepts as necessary.

In a boutique on the sixth level of the mall, yard-square aluminum representations of snowflakes sway above her head. She wonders if each one is in fact different and unique from the others. "Jingle Bells" plays relentlessly, asserting itself from unseen speakers. The voice in her head substitutes the word "martini" for jingle bells. "Mar-ti-ni, mar-ti-ni, mar-ti-ni to-day," the voice intones tirelessly as she lifts scarves and sweaters and cannot focus her eyes. She is conscious of the sharp-edged metallic snowflakes just above her. She is holding clothing between her fingers, bolts of fabric, some square, others vertical. She feels confused, suddenly hot, as if she has been struck with a virulent flu. Then she walks out of the store.

On a higher level of the mall, Suzanne finds herself standing in a shop excessive with Christmas manifestations. Six tall trees straddle stacks of wrapped and ribboned gifts. A colossal wreath is suspended from the ceiling. The walls glow with strings of gold lights. This is not Christmas as Suzanne Cooper remembers it.

Last year she did not even send Christmas cards. She was only one month sober. She could barely walk the hospital corridors. It seemed that there had been rain and carolers had come, schoolchildren wearing bells. She had closed the door.

It occurs to her that the other Christmasses of her life are partial memories, images in a blackout, something like a village glimpsed in a blizzard. There are the meals she burned, the gifts she forgot to wrap or send. The line in the post office was offensive and boring, she thought as she drank from a bottle stashed in her car. She would return later, when the line was smaller, but of course she didn't, drove to Malibu instead and crashed the car. She is thinking of the Malibu sheriff's station and the ambulance on the Pacific Coast Highway as she stands beneath a gigantic wreath suspended from the ceiling. Then, somehow, she buys her first gifts of the season.

Even as the packages are being wrapped, the dark blue velvet dress with a white lace collar for Stephanie and a red-and-green sweater with a border of reindeer for Mark, a discreet implication of Christmas adorning the area near the shoulders, Suzanne feels dissatisfied. The wrapping paper is red embossed with green trees and the red seems to glare challengingly. She is conscious of the voices in her head complaining, mimicking her children. "Oh, another dress," the condemning voice of Stephanie says, allowing herself the restrained disappointment of understatement. In the silence, Stephanie would not have to say, how dull, how could you? It's riding pants I long for.

"There are reindeer on here," the representation of Mark accuses, using the inflections of mock astonishment. "Mother, I can't wear reindeer," the approximation of Mark tells her, his voice soft like his father, the phrasing that of a lecture.

In their eyes she is something like a slow child to be tutored. She realizes they do not expect much from her, she of the ruined dinners and automobiles and hospitals. She of the diminished capacities. And she recognizes that their estimation is similar to her mother's. Somehow she has managed to replicate that which she most loathes.

And somewhere, always near, her mother Candace, her tone sharp and offended, says, "Put that down, dear. You can't afford it. They won't appreciate it. They never do. How could they, with that breeding? I told you, put that back." It occurs to Suzanne that she is trembling. She reaches out her hands for the packages, the red that glares dangerously, and walks out of the extravagantly wreathed store. For a moment, she experiences a sense of triumph.

She has at last purchased something. Suzanne feels as if she has finally drawn blood in the consumer hunting season. She enters a stationery store. A wordless version of "Jingle Bells" descends from the wall and ceiling speakers like an invisible flock of tiny, menacing birds. "Mar-ti-ni, mar-tin-i, mar-tin-i to-day." Then she begins to study the boxes of Christmas cards. She considers her potential selections methodically, working her way first vertically and then horizontally across the rows.

Suzanne Cooper weighs the resonances of the cards, not merely the issue of style and content, typeface and graphics, but the more elusive fundamental essence. There are subtleties. She rules out snow scenes in any guise. This is California and it would be, after all, contrived. Santa Claus in any form is too childish and cute. The elves are unspeakable. Birds of peace are a possibility. And flowers and bells and cards from nonprofit agencies. There is also the matter of recycled paper. She stacks her first round of potential selections in a pile near the counter. The stack rises beside the cash register.

Suzanne Cooper considers the implications of "Merry Christmas" versus "Joy," and the distinctions implicit in "Season's Greetings" and "Happy Holidays." The voice in her head objects to all of her selections. Too religious, it chides her. Too flamboyant, it comments, voice stern. Suzanne feels inadequate. She experiences a sudden sense of rage that takes her breath away.

Of course, "Merry Christmas" is too specific. What if one doesn't celebrate Christmas? What if one isn't merry, has just gone through a divorce, a suicide, or drug overdose in the family? Or a malignant biopsy, a touch of cancer perhaps? What if one is an alcoholic and has been removed from her family and then banished to a small apartment in Santa Monica? Was there a card appropriate to her circumstances?

She finds herself holding a box offering "Joy" in pastels. The motif is simultaneously intimidating and seductive, avant-garde in a terrifying way. It could mean anything, this "Joy," even things she could not articulate or control. Finally, Suzanne decides to buy three boxes of "Season's Greetings." These permutations seem manageable. Still, she feels little confidence as she departs from the store.

On the top level of the mall, in a kind of enclosure past the movie theaters that remind her of a Greyhound bus station in a depressed city, Suzanne Cooper drinks a café au lait and wishes that she could smoke again. If she had a cigarette, she could make more accurate assessments in her shopping, she would be calmer and more assured. Her brain and hand-eye coordination would be vastly improved. She watches someone smoking near her and it occurs to her that if she smoked, she would look glamorous and capable. Store clerks would not dare defraud her. Smoke a cigarette, just one, the voice in her head says. It's Christmas. You can have one.

Suzanne turns her attention to the Christmas cards she has just selected. She views the cards as if they were the distillation of her personality, the highest tangible achievement of her sensibility. She notices that the card approximates a kind of typewriter script and duplicates the phrase "Season's Greetings" relentlessly, as if struck by a mental illness or a form of repetitive nervous disorder. She feels repelled and somehow betrayed. There is a lack of authenticity about the card that profoundly saddens her. She recognizes that she would not wish to receive such a card.

She walks to a Mrs. Field's Cookies bordering the eating enclosure and purchases four large white chocolate with macadamia nut cookies. She eats two of them, quickly, and immediately feels better. This year she will manage the ritual of Christmas, with all its garish atrocities and bizarre paraphernalia. These pathetic rituals are our cumulative definition, she thinks, concurrently agitated and resigned.

This year she will decorate a Christmas tree and hang a wreath of noble fir on her front door. She will bake cookies shaped like Christmas trees. She will cover them with green sugar that resembles bits of glass. She has practiced the recipe already. She has told Stephanie about their striking stained-glass appearance. Stephanie, with polite silence accentuating her lack of enthusiasm, has reluctantly agreed to participate. They will wear matching white aprons Suzanne has purchased just for this activity. She has imbued the baking activity with spiritual qualities that require special garments like vestments. They will bake cookies together and this action will resonate and subtly bond them. She will duplicate the winter landscape with a version of her own, green and white, like a form of voodoo, or the manifestation of a powerful concurrency.

Suzanne realizes that the stained-glass cookie project has attained an almost mystical significance for her. She wants her entire life filled with tangible manifestations of the calming and predictable. Her personal evolution has been characterized by what she now views as fierce years of barbarism. Her own private ice ages, so to speak, her centuries of retrograde behavior and perception. Now she is committed to the larger traditional demarcations. Events such as Christmas have been clarified and redeemed. She no longer views them as acts of indifferent hypocrisy but rather as collective cultural statements of faith.

She eats another white chocolate and macadamia nut cookie and reviews this knowledge of personal evolution with herself. It occurs to her that she might be preparing for an oral exam in a subject in which she is not comfortable and has merely memorized themes. She glares at the Christmas cards with their leaden assertion of greetings and the words seem to leave the page, to somehow retreat and pale.

"I don't drink anymore," she told Candace. It was the previous summer. She had taken her mother out for lunch. It was July. They sat in the Polo Lounge at the Beverly Hills Hotel. The air seemed somehow yellow and pink, tropical but tamed and elegant. She had taken Candace out of the institution on a half-day pass.

"But you can have one glass of wine with your mother. Of course you can," Candace chided her. Her mother was dressed entirely in pink, a pink Chanel suit and hat and silk scarf. Even the diamonds on her brooch and rings seemed pink in the filtered and restrained midafternoon light. Such a sweet lady, a passing stranger might think. Candace ordered a scotch on the rocks. She drank it quickly and signaled with a diamond-tiered hand for another.

"Have a drink with your mother," Candace ordered. Her voice was fueled with rage. Her face was flushed. Even her eyes looked pink. Her eyes were the pink of certain predatory birds, or perhaps more distinctly reptilian like chameleons. Have a drink with your mother, you must, the voice within her announced.

"You're contemptible," Candace decided, drinking with exaggerated relish and ordering another. She wore pink lipstick. Even the scotch in her glass looked pink.

"What kind of celebration is this?" Candace demanded. "You always disappoint me. No"—she paused, then faced her daughter—"you betray me. That is a constant."

Candace pushed her chair away from the table. She stood up, unsteady. She pointed a finger encased with diamonds at her. Her voice was loud now. "You always lie to me," Candace shouted. She was still holding her scotch glass. She studied the glass in her hand as if she was uncertain what the object was. Then she threw it in Suzanne's face.

Suzanne had been startled by the liquor, how cool it was, how familiar the scent. She closed her eyes then, the better to breathe it in.

Later, she had telephoned her former husband. She told Jake that she had been forced to call the hospital. Candace had been taken from the Polo Lounge in an ambulance.

"Naturally," Jake had said distantly, as if adjusting something while they spoke, a shoelace, perhaps, or the television, the newspaper, the skirt of a new woman, or jogging shoes. "She's mentally ill."

"I didn't drink," Suzanne had told her former husband.

"Why would you?" Jake had answered, surprised, as if the thought had never occurred to him. "You don't drink anymore."

He made it sound as if she had a minor infection and had received the appropriate antibiotic and now it was over, done with, part of her ancient history, less than a footnote. It was remote to him because she was no longer important. He had filed for divorce while she was still in the hospital. The outcome of her hospitalization did not matter to him. She could drink herself to death or remain abstinent, in either event he was finished with her. He had kept the house in Beverly Hills and the children remained with him. She had gone from the hospital to a one-bedroom apartment in Santa Monica. She had been banished. It had never occurred to her that this might happen. It had been, literally, unthinkable.

Suzanne Cooper drives from the Beverly Center shopping mall west toward the ocean. The landscape is manicured and swept clean, a perpetual warm winter of bougainvillea and poinsettia on sunny hillsides above the loitering Pacific. On impulse, she parks her car on the bluffs above Santa Monica Bay. It occurs to her, suddenly, that there are certain moments and angles that are almost bearable. There are white sailboats on the bay. The water seems anemic and dazed. Waves break slowly and without malice. The Pacific is simply a fact for her, a blue beyond judgment, taken for granted. A sense of definition asserts itself at the periphery of her awareness. She realizes that nuances and the blue increments will come later, if at all.

She finds it necessary to reiterate the central facts of her existence, that she is thirty-seven years old, the divorced wife of Jake, the mother of Stephanie and Mark. She is a sober member of Alcoholics Anonymous. She doesn't drink anymore, ever. This year her children will spend Christmas Eve and Christmas Day with her. She will not fall asleep with a lit cigarette burning in an ashtray or pass out in the garden with her nightgown on. She no longer smokes and she no longer has a garden. She is reliable now. Even Jake's attorney has finally agreed to accept, provisionally, this concept. Yes, she is becoming the sort of woman who puts the appropriate change into parking meters and mails her Christmas cards on time. She is becoming the sort of woman one could exile to an apartment in Santa Monica knowing that she would accept it with quiet dignity. She is the sort of woman one could banish with little expense.

Suzanne Cooper walks along the Santa Monica cliffs feeling oddly hollow, as if her bones are merely a grid, a suggestion for an armature not yet developed. She walks into a gift shop bizarre with decorations, its shelves flaunting color and pyramids of oddities she can barely decipher. She holds a plastic ashtray with a picture of the Santa Monica Bay, overly representational, the water is never that shade of ineffable blue anymore. *"Feliz Navidad"* is written in an offensive red script across the exaggerated too-green shoreline. Her hand feels soiled.

You need a drink, her voice reminds her. It is a patient voice. No one will know, it tells her. They don't care anyway. Drunk or sober, they have no use for you. One Bloody Mary. It won't kill you. 'Tis the season. 'Tis the season to be jolly. And you won't be surprising anyone. They expect it. They expect you to slip. They'll forgive you. You can always go back to AA after the holidays, in January, when the world turns dull and normal.

As she walks to her car, the light sea breeze brushes her body and she feels insubstantial, as if she might blow away. Then she drives to her noon AA meeting. She raises her hand and is called on to share. She wants to tell them how she has been exiled to an apartment in Santa Monica but she does not. Instead, she talks about her difficulty selecting the absolutely perfect Christmas card. Everyone laughs sympathetically. The women nod their heads with recognition. But she does not tell them that Stephanie and Mark will be spending Christmas with her. She imagines her children climbing the stairs to her apartment with their sleeping bags, their eyes expertly adjusting to her limited perimeters. Stephanie and Mark exchanging glances that say, Look at her minuscule domain. She is even less than we thought.

Suzanne Cooper spends her alloted three minutes making a humorous anecdote of her inability to choose a Christmas card that will solve all of her problems. She does not mention the fact that Stephanie and Mark will be spending Christmas with her under duress. They have both telephoned, separately, asking to be released from this obligation. Jake is going skiing in Aspen with his current girlfriend, the redhead with the free concert tickets. The one who took them to David Bowie and U2. Jake had suddenly become a skier. He had discovered rock and roll. He can take airplanes now, his fear of plane crashes has disappeared. It is as if her miniaturization has somehow enlarged him. This is what Suzanne is actually thinking while she talks about Christmas shopping. When she finishes, she glances at the women she has successfully deceived. Quite unexpectedly, she realizes that she detests them all.

That night the wind becomes agitated and cold. There is a storm and then, almost immediately, another. It rains for the next two weeks. The night wind seems increasingly personal and specific. She prepares her apartment for the arrival of her children who do not want to be there. She has never before managed the literal details of Christmas by herself. She ties a Christmas tree to the roof of her car and drives with branches splayed across the windshield. She drags the tree up the stairs to her apartment as it rains. She decorates it with new ornaments. The hand-sewn sequined snowflakes her grandmother made remain with Jake and the children. Her tree seems pathetic in comparison, deformed like a kind of dwarf, something small enough for her to carry, and adorned with the standard and ordinary. She tries to erase her sense of humiliation about the tree as she hangs a wreath on her front door. She stockpiles cookie-baking ingredients.

It rains the night of her children's Christmas pageant. It has been decided that she will pick them up after their performance. Jake's attorney has relented and she will be allowed to be with her children in an automobile for the first time in years. Then she will take them to her tiny dominion, which they will translate into something squalid. They will be excessively polite with her. Their eyes will be angry and bored.

She is imagining her children's eyes as she parks her car in the school parking lot. She is struck by the force of the wind as she walks. The sudden cutting press of it seems more than a function of literal climate. It seems to be a revelation of some brutal interior.

She finds a seat in the school auditorium. A seat for one. There is a moment of darkness and then the lights come on, soft and pink and radiant, as if there had been a kind of clarification. The pageant unfolds gracefully. The program is titled *Fiesta de las Luces*. Children rush across the darkened stage holding flashlights. They are comets. They are comets in the void or perhaps they are meant to represent random pulses of inspiration. Suzanne considers this, breathlessly. A child with a white robe speaks into a microphone, explaining that it is not only Christmas and Hanukkah, but a rare conjunction of planets and calendars makes this also the Hindu celebration of Ramadan and the African festival of Kwanza.

Suzanne Cooper is stunned by the implications of this universal recognition of light. Children appear and sing a Christmas carol in Spanish and then a chant in an African dialect. An older boy appears and recites passages from Genesis and the Upanishads. Suzanne is struck by the thought that somewhere, candles are being put into boats and they are gliding across unpronounceable rivers. Stephanie appears and stands in a circle with five other girls, singing a lullaby about stars in winter. The stage fills with children wearing African masks and others dancing like dervishes.

It occurs to her that this is her first Christmas pageant. Last year she was in the hospital. Before that, each year by this time she was drunk. Now she is sober and the spectacle seems to be winding down. There is a song in what seems to be Chinese. Later, she recognizes the music as Bach. Children part the shadows with flashlights, simulating comets and inspiration, desire and intelligence. The simplicity of this resonates through her with an intensity for which she is absolutely unprepared.

She recognizes that this essential drama is being enacted, in slight variation, throughout the world. White-gowned children sing of the light in remote nations and languages. It is more than a holy day, one holy day or another, but a recognition of the evolution of life. From the fundamental darkness, there is a random juxtaposition of energy, of thought and light. On this night and this night only, Buddha, Christ, Muhammad, and Moses inform the winter waters with a brilliance that glows. Suzanne Cooper finds herself weeping.

When she meets her children after the performance, Mark with his saxophone case, Stephanie still in a white robe, they seem distant and restrained. She notices that they are not carrying their sleeping bags.

"We've decided to go skiing," Mark informs her, barely looking at her.

"That is, if you agree, Mother," Stephanie adds. Her eyes say, Deny me this and I will hate you forever.

Suzanne recognizes that she needs a cigarette. They will go to Aspen and she will go to a 7-Eleven and buy a package of Marlboros. She sees her former husband on the far side of the almost deserted auditorium. Stephanie and Mark are joining their father. They call good-bye to her over their retreating shoulders and this sentiment, at least, sounds authentic. Then she is alone in the auditorium. She walks to the parking lot in the rain, buys a package of cigarettes at a liquor store, and drives to her apartment.

She lies awake smoking and listening to the rain. She has had insomnia since she stopped drinking. She is used to this forced examination of the night while the voice within her demands that she drink. The voice which is male and yet speaks with the cadence of her incarcerated mother, she suddenly realizes.

In the morning Suzanne gets down on her knees and prays to the God she does not believe in to keep her sober one more day. She has been instructed to do this by her sponsor, a woman with eight years of sobriety who has rebuilt her life one painful molecule at a time. Her sponsor did not believe in God in the beginning, either. Suzanne Cooper begins each morning of her sobriety in this fashion, feeling fraudulent and somehow debased. Now it occurs to her that the voice of destruction within her is silent when she prays. She has never noticed this cause-and-effect relationship before.

Something feels as if it is awakening, inside, where she has lived with her secret glaciers, the fields of ice which surround her, which encase her, which keep her protected and inaccessible. The ice which seems pink when the sun chances to touch it. On impulse, she telephones her mother in the hospital. She describes Stephanie in her ankle-length white robe singing about stars in an African dialect. There is something transcendent that she wishes to transmit to her mother. She expects nothing in return, not shared recognition, certainly, not even polite indifference.

"I would have wanted to see this," Candace says from the hospital. Suzanne does not reply. She is looking out her living-room window, into the window of an apartment identical to her own. She can see a Christmas tree and Christmas cards opened across the mantel.

Suddenly Suzanne finds herself offering to pick up her mother. She is telling her mother that she can have a Christmas pass. Suzanne had not planned to see her mother. Candace is too disruptive. It is simply too much pain.

"I'll be good," Candace says, and softer, after a pause, "I promise."

"You won't throw a drink in my face?" Suzanne asks, lighting a cigarette. The package is almost finished. She recognizes that she has started to smoke again.

"I would never do such a thing," Candace replies, voice hurt. "I know you don't drink anymore."

"But I'm smoking," Suzanne reveals.

"You'll stop again, I'm certain," Candace assures her. "You don't drink. That's the important thing."

"The children aren't coming," Suzanne says. She reports the fact of it, simply.

"They will appreciate you when they are older," Candace tells her. "You will see. They will surprise you."

Later, Suzanne Cooper will drive to the hospital, pick up her mother, and carry her suitcase into her apartment near the ocean. Candace will behave appropriately or she will not. They will, perhaps, wear matching white aprons and bake cookies in the form of green stained-glass Christmas trees or they will not. Perhaps they will sit on a bluff above the slow lingering white sails of boats on the Santa Monica Bay, sipping hot chocolate and recalling anecdotes from her childhood. Perhaps Stephanie and Mark will telephone from a ski lodge, suddenly missing her. They might say that Jake and his girlfriend keep the door of their room locked and it doesn't seem like Christmas, really, in that distant lodge, without her.

Of course she will always be disappointed by the traditional demarcations. She accepts this dispassionately. The voices she has internalized will always degrade her efforts and pronounce her inadequate and flawed in all circumstances. They will evaluate the stimuli and tell her she is not loved enough.

But it is this particular morning, following the *Fiesta de las Luces* that occupies her attention. She is hanging up the telephone, staring out the window and taking the morning into her. She is smoking a cigarette in the living room of her apartment in Santa Monica. The storms have stopped. The morning is brilliant with the kind of purified light often seen in high altitudes, a light which implies the revelatory, absolution and forgiveness. It is the light of Christmas and Hanukkah, Ramadan and Kwanza. It is the light of candles on mantels and candles in boats on rivers and moored in harbors in the ports of all the world. It is the light of a billion schoolchildren wearing white robes and white gowns rushing across auditoriums to announce the birth of a myriad of deities. It is the light of children everywhere holding flashlights as they sing into the darkness, and beyond that darkness are great ridges of white mountains covered with white snow and punctuated by uncountable pines, all the massacred trees of Christmas somehow risen and returned. And further, there are green rivers lit by the white of flames in boats. There are ports where rivers empty their caravans of temporary light. And somewhere, in the place above that men perpetually pray to, comets startle the void and inexplicable juxtapositions inspire the darkness into forms of birth.

Suzanne Cooper is smoking a cigarette, racks of cookies are cooling. Her kitchen curtains are wide open. Sunlight is pouring into the room, brushing against the white apron she is wearing. And she is startled by the thought that she is somehow a candle in the window and she is lit, at this moment, from within.

Where We Are Now

Ethan Canin

WHEN I MET JODI, she was an English major at Simmons College, in Boston, and for a while after that she tried to be a stage actress. Then she tried writing a play, and when that didn't work out she thought about opening a bookstore. We've been married eleven years now, and these days she checks out books at the public library. I don't mean she reads them; I mean she works at the circulation desk.

We've been arguing lately about where we live. Our apartment is in a building with no grass or bushes, only a social room, with plastic chairs and a carpet made of Astroturf. Not many people want to throw a party on Astroturf, Jodi says. She points out other things, too: the elevator stops a foot below the floors, so you have to step up to get out; the cold water comes out rusty in the mornings; three weeks ago a man was robbed in the hallway by a kid with a bread knife. The next Sunday night Jodi rolled over in bed, turned on the light, and said, "Charlie, let's look at houses."

It was one in the morning. From the fourth floor, through the night haze, I could see part of West Hollywood, a sliver of the observatory, lights from the mansions in the canyon.

"There," I said, pointing through the window. "Houses."

"No, let's look at houses to buy."

I covered my eyes with my arm. "Lovebird," I said, "where will we find a house we can afford?"

"We can start this weekend," she said.

That night after dinner she read aloud from the real estate section. "Santa Monica," she read. "Two bedrooms, yard, half-mile to beach."

"How much?"

She looked closer at the paper. "We can look other places."

She read to herself for a while. Then she said that prices seemed lower in some areas near the Los Angeles airport.

"How much?"

"A two-bedroom for $160,000."

I glanced at her.

"Just because we look doesn't mean we have to buy it," she said.

"There's a real estate agent involved."

"She won't mind."

"It's not honest," I said.

She closed the paper and went to the window. I watched a muscle in her neck move from side to side. "You know what it's like?" she said, looking into the street.

"I just don't want to waste the woman's time," I answered.

"It's like being married to a priest."

I knew why she said that. I'm nothing like a priest. I'm a physical education teacher in the Hollywood schools and an assistant coach—basketball and baseball. The other night I'd had a couple of other coaches over to the house. We aren't all that much alike—I'll read a biography on the weekend, listen to classical music maybe a third of the time—but I still like to have them over. We were sitting in the living room, drinking beer and talking about the future. One of the coaches has a two-year-old son at home. He didn't have a lot of money, he said, so he thought it was important to teach his kid morality. I wasn't sure he was serious, but when he finished I told a story anyway about an incident that had happened a few weeks before at school. I'd found out that a kid in a gym class I was teaching, a quiet boy and a decent student, had stolen a hat from a men's store. So I made him return it and write a letter of apology to the owner. When I told the part about how the man was so impressed with the letter that he offered the boy a job, Jodi remarked that I was lucky it hadn't turned out the other way.

"What do you mean?" I asked.

"He could have called the police," she said. "He could have thanked you for bringing the boy in and then called the police."

"I just don't think so."

"Why not? The boy could have ended up in jail."

"I just don't think so," I said. "I think most people will respond to honesty. I think that's where people like us have to lead the way."

It's an important point, I said, and took a drink of beer to take the edge off what I was saying. Too much money makes you lose sight of things, I told them. I stopped talking then, but I could have said more. All you have to do is look around: in Beverly Hills there's a restaurant where a piece of veal costs thirty dollars. I don't mind being an assistant coach at a high school, even though you hear now about the fellow who earns a hundred thousand dollars with the fitness truck that comes right to people's homes. The truck has Nautilus, and a sound system you wouldn't expect. He keeps the stars in shape that way—Kirk Douglas, the movie executives. The man with the truck doesn't live in Hollywood. He probably lives out at the beach, in Santa Monica or Malibu.

But Hollywood's fine if people don't compare it with the ideas they have. Once in a while, at a party, someone from out of town will ask me whether any children of movie stars are in my classes. Sometimes Jodi says the answer is yes but that it would violate confidentiality to reveal their names. Other times I explain that movie stars don't live in Hollywood these days, that most of them don't even work here, that

Hollywood is just car washes and food joints, and that the theater with the stars' footprints out front isn't much of a theater
anymore. The kids race hot rods by it on Thursday nights.

Hollywood is all right, though, I say. It's got sun and
wide streets and is close to everything.

But Jodi wants to look anyway.

Next Sunday I drive, and Jodi gives directions from the map.
The house is in El Segundo. While I'm parking I hear a loud
noise, and a 747 flies right over our heads. I watch it come
down over the freeway.

"Didn't one of them land on the road once?" I ask.

"I don't remember it," Jodi says. She looks at the map.
"The house should be on this block."

"I think it was in Dallas. I think it came right down on
top of a car."

I think about that for a minute. It shakes me up to see a
huge plane so low. I think of the people inside the one that
landed on the road—descending, watching the flaps and the
ailerons, the houses and automobiles coming into view.

"The ad says there are nice trees in back," says Jodi.

She leads us to the house. It's two stories, yellow stucco
walls, with a cement yard and a low wire fence along the
sidewalk. The roof is tar paper. Down the front under the
drainpipes are two long green stains.

"Don't worry," she says. "Just because we look doesn't
mean anything." She knocks on the door and slips her arm
into mine. "Maybe you can see the ocean from the bedroom
windows."

She knocks again. Then she pushes the door a little, and
we walk into the living room. There are quick footsteps, and
a woman comes out of the hallway. "Good afternoon," she
Says. "Would you sign in, please?"

She points to a vinyl-covered book on the coffee table,
and Jodi crosses the room and writes something in it. Then

the agent hands me a sheet of paper with small type on it and a badly copied picture. I've never shopped for a house before. I see two columns of abbreviations, some numbers. It's hard to tell what the picture is of, but then I recognize the long stains under the drainpipes. I fold the sheet and put it into my pants pocket. Then I sit down on the couch and look around. The walls are light yellow, and one of them is covered with a mirror that has gold marbling in it. On the floor is a cream-colored shag rug, with a matted area near the front door where a couch or maybe a trunk once stood. Above the mantel is a painting of a blue whale.

"Do the appliances and plumbing work?" Jodi asks.

"Everything works," says the agent.

Jodi turns the ceiling light on and off. She opens and closes the door to a closet in the corner, and I glimpse a tricycle and a bag full of empty bottles. I wonder what the family does on a Sunday afternoon when buyers look at their house.

"The rooms have a nice feel," the agent says. "You know what I mean?"

"I'm not sure I do," I say.

"It's hard to explain," she says, "but you'll see."

"We understand," says Jodi.

In the marbled mirror I watch Jodi's reflection. Three windows look onto the front yard, and she unlatches and lifts each one.

"I like a careful buyer," says the agent.

"You can never be too thorough," Jodi answers. Then she adds, "We're just looking."

The agent smiles, drumming her fingers against her wrist. I know she's trying to develop a strategy. In college I learned about strategies. I worked for a while selling magazines over the phone: talk to the man if you think they want it; talk to the woman if you think they don't. I was thinking of playing ball then, semi-pro, and the magazine work was evenings. I was twenty-three years old. I thought I was just doing work until I was discovered.

"Why don't you two look around," I say now to the agent. "I'll stay here."

"Perfect," she says.

She leads Jodi into the next room. I hear a door open and shut, and then they begin talking about the floors, the walls, the ceiling. We aren't going to buy the house, and I don't like being here. When I hear the two of them walk out through the back door into the yard, I get up from the couch and go over to look at the painting above the mantel. It's an underwater view, looking below the whale as it swims toward the surface. Above, the sunny sky is broken by ripples. On the mantel is a little pile of plaster powder, and as I stand there, I realize that the painting has just recently been hung. I go back to the couch. Once on a trip up the coast I saw a whale that the tide had trapped in a lagoon. It was north of Los Angeles, along the coastal highway, in a cove sheltered by two piers of man-moved boulders. Cars were parked along the shoulder. People were setting up their cameras while the whale moved around in the lagoon, stirring up the bottom. I don't like to think about trapped animals, though, so instead I sit down and try to plan what to do tomorrow at practice. The season hasn't started yet, and we're still working on base-running—the double steal, leading from the inside of the bag. Baseball isn't a thing you think about, though; baseball *comes*. I'm an assistant coach and maybe could have been a minor league pitcher, but when I think of it I realize I know only seven or eight things about the whole game. We learn so slowly, I think.

I get up and go over to the painting again. I glance behind me. I put my head next to the wall, lift the frame a little bit, and when I look I see that behind it the plaster is stained brown from an interior leak. I take a deep breath and then put the frame back. From outside in the yard I hear the women speaking about basement storage space, and rather than listen I cross the room and enter a hallway. It smells of grease. On the wall, at waist level, are children's hand marks that go all the way to the far end. I walk down there and enter the kitchen. In it are a Formica table and four plastic chairs, everything made large by the low ceiling. I see a door in the corner, and when I cross the room and open it I'm surprised to find a stairway with brooms and mops hung above the banister. The incline is steep, and when I go up I find myself in the rear of an upstairs closet. Below me Jodi and the agent are still talking. I push through the clothes hanging in front of me and open the door.

I'm in the master bedroom now. A king-size bed stands in front of me, but something's funny about it, and when I look closer I think that it might be two single beds pushed together. It's covered by a spread. I stop for a moment to think. I don't think I'm doing anything wrong. We came here to see the house, and when people show their homes they take out everything of value so that they won't have to worry. I go to the window. Framing it is a new-looking lace curtain, pinched up in a tieback. I look out at a crab apple tree and some telephone wires and try to calculate where the ocean might be. The shadows point west, but the coastline is irregular in this area and juts in different directions. The view of the crab apple is pretty, spotted with shade and light—but then I see that in the corner behind the curtain the glass is splintered and has been taped. I lift the curtain and look at the pane. The crack spreads like a spider web. Then I walk back to the bed. I flatten my hands and slip them into the crevice between the two mattresses, and when I extend my arms the two halves come apart. I push the beds back together and sit down. Then I look into the corner, and my heart skips because I see that against the far wall, half-hidden by the open door, is an old woman in a chair.

"Excuse me," I say.

"That's all right," she says. She folds her hands. "The window cracked ten years ago."

"My wife and I are looking at the house."

"I know."

I walk to the window. "A nice view," I say, pretending to look at something in the yard. The woman doesn't say anything. I can hear water running in the pipes, some children outside. Tiny, pale apples hang among the leaves of the tree.

"You know," I say, "we're not really looking at the house to buy it."

I walk back to the bed. The skin on the woman's arms is mottled and hangs in folds. "We can't afford to buy it," I say. "I don't make enough money to buy a house and—I don't know why, but my wife wants to look at them anyway. She wants people to think we have enough money to buy a house."

The woman looks at me.

"It's crazy," I say, "but what are you going to do in that kind of situation?"

She clears her throat. "My son-in-law," she begins, "wants to sell the house so he can throw the money away." Her voice is slow, and I think she has no saliva in her mouth. "He has a friend who goes to South America and swallows everything, then comes back through customs with a plastic bag in his bowel."

She stops. I look at her. "He's selling the house to invest the money in drugs?"

"I'm glad you don't want to buy," she says.

I might have had a small career in baseball, but I've learned in the past eleven years to talk about other things. I was twenty-three the last pitch I threw. The season was over and Jodi was in the stands in a wool coat. I was about to get a college degree in physical education. I knew how to splint a broken bone and how to cut the grass on a golf green, and then I decided that to turn your life around you had to start from the inside. I had a coach in college who said he wasn't trying to teach us to be pro ballplayers; he was trying to teach us to be decent people.

When we got married, I told Jodi that no matter what happened, no matter where things went, she could always trust me. We'd been seeing each other for a year, and in that time I'd been reading books. Not baseball books. Biographies: Martin Luther King, Gandhi. To play baseball right you have to forget that you're a person; you're muscles, bone, the need for sleep and food. So when you stop, you're saved by someone else's ideas. This isn't true just for baseball players. It's true for anyone who's failed at what he loves.

A friend got me the coaching job in California, and as soon as we were married we came west. Jodi still wanted to be an actress. We rented a room in a house with six other people, and she took classes in dance in the mornings and speech in the afternoons. Los Angeles is full of actors. Sometimes at parties we counted them. After a couple of years she started writing a play, and until we moved into where we are now we used to read pieces of it out loud to our six housemates.

By then I was already a little friendly with the people at school, but when I was out of the house, even after two years in Los Angeles, I was alone. People were worried about their own lives. In college I'd spent almost all my time with another ballplayer, Mitchell Lighty, and I wasn't used to new people. A couple of years after we graduated, Mitchell left to play pro ball in Panama City, and he came out to Los Angeles on his way there. The night before his plane left, he and I went downtown to a bar on the top floor of a big hotel. We sat by a window, and after a few drinks we went out onto the balcony. The air was cool. Plants grew along the edge, ivy was woven into the railing, and birds perched among the leaves. I was amazed to see the birds resting there thirty stories up on the side of the building. When I brushed the plants the birds took off into the air, and when I leaned over to watch them, I became dizzy with the distance to the sidewalk and with the small, rectangular shapes of the cars. The birds sailed in wide circles over the street and came back to the balcony. Then Mitchell put his drink on a chair, took both my hands, and stepped up onto the railing. He stood there on the metal crossbar, his wrists locked in my hands, leaning into the air.

"For God's sake," I whispered. He leaned farther out, pulling me toward the railing. A waiter appeared at the sliding door next to us. "Take it easy," I said. "Come on down." Mitchell let go of one of my hands, kicked up one leg, and swung out over the street. His black wingtip shoe swiveled on the railing. The birds had scattered, and now they were circling, chattering angrily as he rocked. I was holding on with my pitching arm. My legs were pressed against the iron bars, and just when I began to feel the lead, just when the muscles began to shake, Mitchell jumped back onto the balcony. The waiter came through the sliding door and grabbed him, but in the years after that—the years after Mitchell got married and decided to stay in Panama City—I thought of that incident as the important moment of my life.

I don't know why. I've struck out nine men in a row and pitched to half a dozen hitters who are in the majors now, but when I think back over my life, about what I've done, not much more than that stands out.

As we lie in bed that night, Jodi reads aloud from the real estate listings. She uses abbreviations: BR, AC, D/D. As she goes down the page—San Marino, Santa Ana, Santa Monica—I nod occasionally or make a comment.

When I wake up later, early in the morning, the newspaper is still next to her on the bed. I can see its pale edge in the moonlight. Sometimes I wake up like this, maybe from some sound in the night, and when I do, I like to lie with my eyes closed and feel the difference between the bed and the night air. I like to take stock of things. These are the moments when I'm most in love with my wife. She's next to me, and her face when she sleeps is untroubled. Women say now that they don't want to be protected, but when I watch her slow breathing, her parted lips, I think what a delicate thing a life is. I lean over and touch her mouth.

When I was in school I saw different girls, but since I've been married to Jodi I've been faithful. Except for once, a few years ago, I've almost never thought about someone else. I have a friend at school, Ed Ryan, a history teacher, who told me about the time he had an affair, and about how his marriage broke up right afterward. It wasn't a happy thing to see. She was a cocktail waitress at a bar a few blocks from school, he said. Ed told me the whole long story, about how he and the waitress had fallen in love so suddenly that he had no choice about leaving his wife. After the marriage was over, though, Ed gained fifteen or twenty pounds. One night, coming home from school, he hit a tree and wrecked his car. A few days later he came in early to work and found that all the windows in his classroom had been broken. At first I believed him when he said he thought his wife had done it, but that afternoon we were talking and I realized what had really happened.

We were in a lunch place. "You know," Ed said, "sometimes you think you know a person." He was looking into his glass. "You can sleep next to a woman, you can know the way she smiles when she's turned on, you can see in her hands when she wants to talk about something. Then you wake up one day and some signal's been exchanged—and you don't know what it is, but you think for the first time, *Maybe I don't know her.* Just something. You never know what the signal is." I looked at him then and realized that there was no cocktail waitress and that Ed had broken the windows.

I turn in bed now and look at Jodi. Then I slide the newspaper off the blanket. We know each other, I think. The time I came close to adultery was a few years ago, with a secretary at school, a temporary who worked afternoons. She was a dark girl, didn't say much, and she wore turquoise bracelets on both wrists. She kept finding reasons to come into my office, which I share with the two other coaches. It's three desks, a window, a chalkboard. One night I was there late, after everyone else had gone, and she came by to do something. It was already dark. We talked for a while, and then she took off one of her bracelets to show me. She said she wanted me to see how beautiful it was, how the turquoise changed color in dim light. She put it into my hand, and then I knew for sure what was going on. I looked at it for a long time, listening to the little sounds in the building, before I looked up.

"Charlie?" Jodi says now in the dark.

"Yes?"

"Would you do whatever I asked you to do?"

"What do you mean?"

"I mean, would you do anything in the world that I asked you to do?"

"That depends," I say.

"On what?"

"On what you asked. If you asked me to rob someone, then maybe I wouldn't."

I hear her roll over, and I know she's looking at me. "But don't you think I would have a good reason to ask you if I did?"

"Probably."

"And wouldn't you do it just because I asked?"

She turns away again and I try to think of an answer. We've already argued once today, while she was making dinner, but I don't want to lie to her. That's what we argued about earlier. She asked me what I thought of the house we looked at, and I told her the truth, that a house just wasn't important to me.

"Then what is important to you?"

I was putting the forks and knives on the table. "Leveling with other people is important to me," I answered. "And you're important to me." Then I said, "And whales."

"What?"

"Whales are important to me."

That was when it started. We didn't say much after that, so it wasn't an argument exactly. I don't know why I mentioned the whales. They're great animals, the biggest things on earth, but they're not important to me.

"What if it was something not so bad," she says now, "but still something you didn't want to do?"

"What?"

The moonlight is shining in her hair. "What if I asked you to do something that ordinarily you wouldn't do yourself—would you do it if I asked?"

"And it wasn't something so bad?"

"Right."

"Yes," I say." Then I would do it."

"What I want you to do," she says on Wednesday, "is look at another house." We're eating dinner. "But I want them to take us seriously," she says. "I want to act as if we're really thinking of buying it, right on the verge. You know—maybe we will, maybe we won't."

I take a sip of water, look out the window. "That's ridiculous," I say. "Nobody walks in off the street and decides in an afternoon whether to buy a house."

"Maybe we've been looking at it from a distance for a long time," she says, "assessing things." She isn't eating her dinner. I cooked it, chicken, and it's steaming on her plate. "Maybe we've been waiting for the market to change."

"Why is it so important to you?"

"It just is. And you said you'd do it if it was important to me. Didn't you say that?"

"I had a conversation with the old woman in the yellow house."

"What?"

"When we looked at the other house," I say, "I went off by myself for a while. I talked with the old woman who was sitting upstairs."

"What did you say?"

"Do you remember her?"

"Yes."

"She told me that the owner was selling the house so he could use the money to smuggle drugs."

"So?"

"So," I say, "you have to be careful."

This Sunday Jodi drives. The day is bright and blue, with a breeze from the ocean, and along Santa Monica Boulevard the palm fronds are rustling. I'm in my suit. If Jodi talks to the agent about offers, I've decided I'll stay to the back, nod or shrug at questions. She parks the car on a side street and we walk around the corner and go into the lobby of one of the hotels. We sit down in cloth chairs near the entrance. A bellman carries over an ashtray on a stand and sets it between us; Jodi hands him a bill from her purse. I look at her. The bellman is the age of my father. He moves away fast, and I lean forward to get my shoulder loose in my suit. I'm not sure if the lobby chairs are only for guests, and I'm ready to get up if someone asks. Then a woman comes in and Jodi stands and introduces herself. "Charlie Gordon," I say when the woman puts out her hand. She's in a gray pinstriped skirt and a jacket with a white flower in the lapel. After she says something to Jodi, she leads us outside to the parking circle, where a car is brought around by the valet, a French car, and Jodi and I get in back. The seats are leather.

"Is the weather always this nice?" Jodi asks. We pull out onto Wilshire Boulevard.

"Almost always," the woman says. "That's another thing I love about Los Angeles—the weather. Los Angeles has the most perfect weather on earth."

We drive out toward the ocean, and as the woman moves in and out of the lines of traffic, I look around the car. It's well kept, maybe leased. No gum wrappers or old coffee cups under the seat.

"Then you're looking for a second home?" the woman says.

"My husband's business makes it necessary for us to have a home in Los Angeles."

I look at Jodi. She's sitting back in the seat, her hand resting on the armrest.

"Most of the year, of course, we'll be in Dallas."

The street is curved and long with a grass island in the middle and eucalyptus along its length, and each time the car banks, I feel the nerves firing in my gut. I look at Jodi. I look at her forehead. I look at the way her hair falls on her neck, at her breasts, and I realize, the car shifting under us, that I don't trust her.

We turn and head up a hill. The street twists, and we go in and out of the shade from a bridge of elms. I can't see anything behind the hedges.

"The neighborhood is lovely," the woman says. "We have a twenty-four-hour security patrol, and the bushes hide everything from the street. We don't have sidewalks."

"No sidewalks?" I say.

"That discourages sightseeing," says Jodi.

We turn into a driveway. It heads down between two hedges to the far end where a gravel half circle has been cut around the trunk of a low, spreading fig tree. We stop, the agent opens Jodi's door, and we get out and stand there, looking at the house. It's a mansion.

The walls are white. There are clay tiles on the roof, sloped eaves, hanging vines. A narrow window runs straight up from the ground. Through it I can see a staircase and a chandelier. In college once, at the end of the season, the team had a party at a mansion like this one. It had windows everywhere, panes of glass as tall as flagpoles. The fellow who owned it had played ball for a while when he was young, and then gotten out and made big money. He was in something like hair care or combs then, and at the door each of us got a leather travel kit with our name embossed and some of his products inside. At the buffet table the oranges were cut so that the peels came off like the leather on a split baseball. He showed us through the house and then brought us into the yard. He told us that after all these years the game was still inside him. We stood on the lawn. It was landscaped with shrubs and willows, but he said he had bought the place because the yard was big enough for a four-hun-dred-foot straightaway center field.

Now the agent leads us up the porch stairs. She rings the bell and then opens the door; inside, the light is everywhere. It streams from the windows, shines on the wood, falls in slants from every height. There are oriental carpets on the floor, plants, a piano. The agent opens her portfolio and hands us each a beige piece of paper. It's textured like a wedding invitation, and at the top, above the figures, is an ink drawing of the house. The boughs of the fig tree frame the paper. I look down at it in my hand, the way I used to look down at a baseball.

The agent motions us into the living room. From there she leads us back through a glass-walled study, wisteria and bougainvillaea hanging from the ceiling, down a hallway into the kitchen. Through the windows spread the grounds of the estate. Now is the time, I think to myself, when I should explain everything.

"I think I'll go out back," Jodi says. "You two can look around in here."

"Certainly," the agent says.

After she leaves, I pretend to look through the kitchen. I open cabinets, run the water. The tap has a charcoal filter. The agent says things about the plumbing and the founda-tion; I nod and then walk back into the study. She follows me.

"I know you'll find the terms agreeable," she says.

"The terms."

"And one can't surpass the house, as one can see."

"You could fit a diamond in the yard."

She smiles a little bit.

"A baseball diamond," I say. I lean forward and examine the paned windows carefully. They are newly washed, clear as air. Among them hang the vines of bougainvillaea. "But some people look at houses for other reasons."

"Of course."

"I know of a fellow who's selling his house to buy drugs in South America."

She looks down, touches the flower in her jacket.

"People don't care about an honest living anymore," I say. She smiles and looks up at me. "They don't," she says. "You're absolutely right. One sees that everywhere now. What line of work are you in, Mr. Gordon?"

I lean against the glassed wall. Outside, violet petals are spinning down beneath the jacarandas. "We're not really from Dallas," I say.

"Oh?"

Through the window I see Jodi come out onto the lawn around the corner of the house. The grass is beautiful. It's green and long like an outfield. Jodi steps up into the middle of it and raises her hands above her head, arches her back like a dancer. She was in a play the first time I ever saw her, stretching like that, onstage in a college auditorium. I was in the audience, wearing a baseball shirt. At intermission I went home and changed my clothes so that I could introduce myself. That was twelve years ago.

"No," I say to the agent. "We're not really from Dallas. We moved outside of Dallas a while back. We live in Highland Park now."

She nods.

"I'm an investor," I say.

Free Your Mind and Your Ass Will Follow

Michelle T. Clinton

IT WAS THE TIME that made them get their hair all wild. Nappy is what Debra's momma called it. "Nappy, nasty, and downright niggerish, like some boo just crawled out of the bush," she fussed.

"But we proud, Mrs. Garnette," Sandra said. "God made us this way. We proud and happy to be nappy-headed."

"Them naps done soaked into your brains and kinked up your sense till you ain't got none left. How a nigger gone be proud of being a nigger?" Debra's momma kept fussing while Debra just snorted and grabbed Sandra by the forearm, and pulled her into the bathroom where all the hair care bottles, the Afro grease and Afro combs sat shining under the water-stained mirror.

"So what," Debra cursed, "fuck her," as she sprayed and picked out Sandra's hair. The tiny bathroom filled with the sour mist of the Afro Sheen. "We got something to do tonight, girl. Man and them want us to go riding. Plus they gonna pick up some juice, just like last time. You got to look pretty. You got any money?"

"Fifty cents."

"Okay. I got seventy-five. Let's only tell them we got a quarter apiece. I seen a picture in Life magazine of this white girl, must have been Jewish, 'cause her hair was rough just like a nigguh's 'cept she had braids on the side. Here. Hand me the comb." Debra plaited two braids right above Sandra's ears that framed her brown face. "Girl, you so cute," she said, and shoved the red, black, and green comb in the back pocket of her jeans.

Their jeans were Levi's, shrunk bootie tight, cuffed at the bottom and topped by a solid color T-shirt. No bras: Their breasts bobbed when they left Debra's momma's house, nipples alert with all the juice and arrogance of adolescence. The beads around their necks were psychedelic rainbows, just the perfect touch, Debra figured, to telegraph to the wide and open world that they were ready.

Man and them were older and had a car. A nineteen-fifty-something Chevy that broke down once a week but could get to Venice Beach and back on one dollar worth of gas. Man and them meant some fast riding boys, but safe, 'cause Man was Debra's older brother, and Sandra was too young anyway and read too many books. Smart girls, Debra and Sandra, kind of cute, but way too smart-mouth for women, so didn't nobody mess with them. The Chevy got loaded down: Man, then Debra, then big Rufus, Man's ace boon coon, in the front seat, with Sandra and Stevie in the back.

"Debra," Man said, "you got Sandra looking like some kinda hippie white girl." All the boys busted up like it was a joke they'd been holding in. Sandra let out her breath and blinked.

"You so ignorant," Debra said, "you wouldn't know fine if it jumped up and slapped your ass in the face."

"We so ignorant," Rufus said, "we want to take you riding with us. You all got any money?"

"All we got is fifty cents between us. And we don't have to give you that. Better hope some fine white boy with a bunch of money don't see hippie-looking Sandra and snatch her ass up."

"What you got, Sandra, a quarter? I know you got more than that. Don't lie to me, girl. You want to have fun, you want to go to the beach, you got to pay," Rufus said.

"All I got is twenty-five cents. Here. Take it."

"Here's my quarter," Debra said. "You cheap-ass, broke-down nigguhs, always trying to take some woman's money." Man collected quarters from everybody and headed out to the Primo Discount Gas station, right next door to King's Liquor and Fine Beverages' blinking neon sign. Rufus, who had almost had a mustache, had to try and buy, but came back stomping to the car, pissed and frustrated that he couldn't pass for grown. Then four more liquor-store stops, four more ID requests that Rufus didn't have, until a half-buzzed, half-nodded wino offered to help.

"I could get that brew for you," he said, his eyes bloodshot.

"Don't want brew. We looking for that wine connection, Spanada, need three bottles."

The wino took the money and got four. He was already drinking, the bottles turned up inside the paper bag, when he walked out the store. He handed over three bottles.

"Aw man," Rufus said, "why you wanna do some kids like that?"

"You wanna play, you got to pay," the wino laughed.

"Fuck that drunk-ass, scabby motherfucker," Debra started up. "If you all was men, you'd take his money."

"Nigguh ain't got no money. Why you think he's drinking?" Man said. "Rufus, just get your ass in the car and let's ride. We got the juice, don't we? Let's just ride."

The clunky car made it up the ramp and whizzed into the lights of the Santa Monica Freeway. Man and Rufus and them always kept the window down in summer so the quick LA night air hit your face and made you feel like everything in speed. The white and red ribbonlike streaks of color could almost wrap you like wire and cut your happiness if you were too slow or thought too much. But Sandra couldn't help thinking, even riding the lucky ride to the beach with safe boys and her best friend: Nothing but fun was coming at her, she knew it and her mind kicked in anyway. The rhythm of the lights bouncing into her eyes made her wonder what was in everybody's head. I'll never know what's in anybody's head but mine, she figured, and that made her feel safe, that made her feel calm.

"I said free your mind," blasted out the radio, "and your ass will follow. The kingdom of heaven is within," said the music of the machine that carried them.

"Love me some funk," said Rufus, as he leaned over Debra and cranked up the radio. "Love me some hard-hitting, funkadelic music."

"Yeah, we ride," said Man, claiming the dark side of the night as his own. "Yeah, we drinking and we riding tonight."

The alleys of Venice are known to be sexy to men and dangerous to women, so teenagers are drawn like ants. Around the garbage cans and many arrogant cats, everybody thinks something is about to happen, something that you'll love, or something that will seriously mess with your mind. The wildest of the jealous gods is gonna go off on somebody with bad or excellent luck. Somebody, maybe you, maybe your running buddy, is about to pay or be paid, you could end up laughing so hard your stomach would cramp, or you might bust out crying, running back toward the car, or catch a brick in the lip and give up a front tooth: The alleys excited and warned them. But like most places everywhere, mostly nothing happens, mostly people wander and wait, mostly the alleys are still.

The front of Man's car bounced over the curb to the Clubhouse Court, an alley just three blocks off the beach, and began a steady creep up the alleys in prayer for the luck of an empty parking space. Man twisted the tops off the green wine bottles in the brown paper bag and handed one bottle to Debra. "This here is for you all," he said. "Best try and chug it. Drink it fast as you can without throwing up, gives you the best head rush." Debra turned the bottle up, gagged, wiped her mouth and passed the bag to Sandra. Sucking on the bottle like that, her neck all the way back, Sandra could feel a perfect loneliness, stronger than the lights on the freeways, thicker than the danger in the alleys, and even with the horrible liquor sourness in her nose, she was strong and got down three gulps. This is it, she thought. This is drinking now like a grown-up. This is what they do and I'm doing it now, she thought, because it was her first time and she didn't know shit and she always did what Debra told her anyway. She knew they was gonna get drunk and fucked up. Debra told her she did it last weekend and how she could be a wino. She could understand they trip. Because wine juice in the vein and head is a pure wish for fun and peace and no worry can make you mad. Which sounded pretty good to Sandra. So, with her head back, her nose fizzing with Spanada, she couldn't tell one reason not to gulp and drink. But how to tell if you were drunk and how much, were you really drunk? When does it get completely easy, she wondered when she hit the bottle a fourth and fifth time and then stopped counting.

"Yo, man, let's cruise," Man declared, and all four doors of the car opened at once; all five of them hit the pavement and turned in the direction of the waves. A big inhale of salt sucked in by open mouths made the whole gang light-headed and happy. That plus the booze.

The group split off into the boy bunch and the girl couple. The girl couple walked half a dozen paces behind the boys and in general made more noise, mostly laughing. They knew they wasn't nothing but fools; they liked to be loud fools, prowling for the trouble in fun, ready for the fun in trouble. Pretty scary for the fragile tourist white folks, but with laughing girls in back, that was the easiest way to make anybody willing to take a second glance comfortable.

But it wasn't hardly anybody on the boardwalk, no tourists at all, just a few of the local white folks, people of strange and mysterious culture. Beach people. Hippies. White people of peculiar color combinations: pink and orange, yellow and purple. Their hair dripped and hung shaggy. Their eyes all smokey and red, the hippie women obviously without bras, and everybody, even at night, bare-footed. Just a few couples, a few small groups were out walking under the boardwalk lights, the rose color vibrated above them all. Like the same jealous god sent down a spot-light that seemed no relation to the beach at all, no relation to the reason all of them were there. The lack of shadow and electric buzz made them all look and feel cold, to themselves and to each other. But the light did not affect the girls at first. Debra eyeballed everybody. Sandra was busy with her Spanada grin, trying out her theory on telepathic communi-cation with people of the same nature. She had on her tight jeans, true she wasn't barefooted, but she had braids in her natural and bells tied to her orange and purple beads.

"Can a nigguh be a hippie?" she asked.

"Hell yeah, look at you." Debra laughed.

"Debra, we dressed exactly the same way."

"Yeah, but I'm passing." Debra laughed more. "I'm vis-iting these white folks' planet. I would never act the same kinda fool as these fools act. 'Cept when I'm with you." She hit Sandra on the butt and took off running toward the water.

"Okay, so now I gotta run," Sandra thought, and walked to the nearest bench just past where the sand started and undid her shoelaces and carried her shoes. By then Debra was halfway to the ocean, and Man and Rufus was nowhere seemed like, the boardwalk totally empty. She wouldn't run in no cold sand, the cold bit into her toes and reminded her that the lights were hard, just like the lights that hit her eyes in the car, and maybe the whole night was poisoned and it wasn't even scary.

"Help. Help!" Sandra heard and she didn't even flinch.

"Help, please I desperately need your help," and it wasn't nobody but Debra, in a white lady voice, still wanting to be

chased. "Please come to my rescue. I need help immediately."
Sandra grinned and started an easy run toward the ocean.
She could see Debra balanced on the rocks, waving her
hands above her head, begging and yelling for attention.

"I have come," Sandra shouted, soon as she got close. "I
am the lifeguard, the prince ready to do battle with the
waves. Ready to protect you from the evil fish men!"

"Fish men!" Debra barked. "Fish men, girlfriend, I wish
some fish men would try and come after me." She was bust-
ing up.

"Are you okay?" someone said behind her, and Sandra
jerked around and faced him. A man, a white man hippie in
thin beard and T-shirt said, "Is your friend cool? I came to
see if anything was happening, anything weird."

"Nothing weird," Debra said. "Nothing weird happening here."

The white man exhaled. "She was yelling for help."
Behind him Sandra saw other people, more than a dozen,
coming toward them in a steady pace, their heads bent a little against the wind.

"We was just playing," Sandra said. "Wasn't nobody for
real hurt."

The white man exhaled again and turned to the other
people and yelled, "Everything is cool. Nothing weird is
happening."

The people slowed down and stopped. They swayed a
minute and looked at them.

"Then why the fuck did she cry for help?" a pissed-off
somebody white said.

"Because they are kids," the man with the beard
answered. "And they stink like they've been drinking."

"Hell, I was drinking too." The pissed-off one got closer
and pushed his face toward Debra. "Listen, kid," he said.
"It's not cool to stress out your community support, you
dig?"

"We're not from here," Sandra said. "We was just playing. We didn't think nobody was listening." And by then

most of the people had turned and begun to walk back to the lights of the boardwalk.

"Hell, I was drinking too," he said again, and turned away from them, and pushed his feet into the sand.

Then Sandra felt cold. She could see Debra sucking the corner of her bottom lip the way she did when she was tripping. Behind her the ocean was too big, too loud, and the air cut at her checks with soft slaps.

"I know where it's some swings," she told Debra. "And forget him anyway. What he know about nothing, white man who live at the beach." Their feet moved through the cold sand in one rhythm, Debra's shadow a few inches in front of Sandra, Sandra's eyes lowered like her friend's, their eyes stuck in the sand.

"I don't wanna go to no swings," Debra said.

"Tell me what he know, drunk sucker. He should have kept on drinking. Why he gotta come bother us?"

"They was good to come. They was good people." Debra's voice was depressed and scared Sandra.

"I don't like this wino mess," she told Debra. "Wine don't keep you from getting mad. And it tastes so nasty. Let's just find us them swings."

"The swings probably be broke anyway." Then Debra was silent. They were both quiet, and the wine and the cold and the human silence came down on them, and pushed them into the sand. "I feel so bad," Debra said. "I feel so bad."

Sandra loved the way Debra could loud talk and curse, the way her angry mother's fussing could never mess up her head. Teachers couldn't make her cry. Boys could not trip her out unless she liked them. When she was hurt she knew how to talk, she was quick and evil. All the bad-mouthing, all those pretty curse words were in public, outside the bathroom, in Man's car. But in front of mirrors, at beaches, times happened with Debra when sadness was a fist in your throat and you couldn't do nothing but feel it.

They were too big to ask for a push, so they got on the swings, in identical shadows, and they started to pump with their knees. Only way to get high fast. The sky looked blacker and blacker. There wasn't hardly no stars so nobody started dreaming: Debra hung her head back and kept her eyes open. Sandra closed her eyes when she was going backward. "Free your mind," Debra whispered, her eyes wide, coming up and then down on the swing. "And your ass will follow. The kingdom of heaven is within," she whispered into the wicked lights of the beach. "Free your mind," she said louder and pushed her feet out over the edge of the black sky.

"And your ass will follow," said Sandra, lifting her head, her eyes greedy for the emptiness on the beach. "The kingdom of heaven is within."

"Free your mind," loud, together, they chanted, and sent out the words with heat and arrogance, slamming them into the spoiled night, like the threat of a whipping about to crack into your body and make you bleed. Like some punishment that only makes you meaner, like they found the secret of some sacred law and it was a lie, like all lies, like everything.

"And your ass will follow." Sandra stood up on her swing. "The kingdom of heaven is within." They swore it like an oath, like they believed they could always hold back, hold in from the world and the sneaky ways it hurts you. Underneath their voices the comfort adolescents find in movement was faster and higher and cold.

"Yo, Sister Love," and it was big Man, his hands in his pockets, his shoulders hunched, the color in his skin as regular as any brother could be. "You all ready?"

"Check it out, man." Rufus showed his friendly teeth. "These women is tore down. Look like that Spanada done done its work."

"Jump!" Man yelled. "Can you all jump?"

Sandra swooped straight out from her swing and came down on her palms, her knees, with the palm trees and rose lights spinning with the dizzy sickness in her stomach.

"Bop on that," Debra said, and dug her heels down into the sand. "You all help me stop this thing."

The five of them regrouped, again in formation, like the points of a dark star, a whole unit, a perfect distance apart. They bent their heads against the sharp nightwind and headed back to the car, their faces and feelings finally ready for the foreignness to close behind them. The bumper on Man's heavy car pushed through the alleys of Venice and broke out into the wide city intersections. With the streetlights and other cars, the city expanded its indifference and they were small again, practically sober. Their luck stayed halfway good and Man made all the lights. Her head against the glass of the backseat window, Sandra closed her eyes and gave herself to the car that slid back down onto the Santa Monica Freeway, into the ribbon of white and red lights that would take them back to their mother's home.

Night Sky

Bernard Cooper

As Kay shouted instructions in the background, I angled the telescope down the mountain toward the home of her ex-husband, but no matter how carefully I focused the lens or adjusted the tripod, I couldn't make out much more than a tile roof surrounded by trees. Each time I blinked, my eyelashes splayed against the glass.

"It's the wall to the left of the front door," she yelled. "Just below his driveway. See any damage?"

What little I could see of Warren's house looked fine to me, no gaping hole or trace of rubble. When I turned around and shrugged at Kay, she shrugged, too. She stood above me on the patio, lit by the blaze of an orange afternoon, her bathrobe flapping. The fierce wind blew her hair to one side, where it whipped from her head like a wind sock. The patio was as far as she could stray from the house before her electronic ankle bracelet set off an alarm at the Bel Air Police Department. Whenever this happened, a concerned officer phoned within a minute and interrogated whoever answered in order to verify Kay's whereabouts. Even if she answered the phone herself, which was usually the case, they had a way of quizzing her to make sure the voice didn't belong to some kind of Kay impersonator.

According to Kay, the main problem with house arrest was the fact that her swimming pool, embedded in a flagstone terrace several steps below the patio, was now off-limits. She loved nothing more than drifting on an inflatable raft and dangling her hands in the tepid water, a kind of mindless hydrotherapy that helped her forget a vindictive divorce. Now that she couldn't bob across it, the water flaunted its soothing blue. The only thing that made exile from her own swimming pool tolerable was Kay's fear that the ankle bracelet would electrocute her once she dove in, even though Our Lady of Corrections, as she called her probation officer, assured her the device was waterproof. Still, Kay swore she dangled one leg outside the tub when she took a bath, largely, it seemed to me, to add yet another inconvenience to an already long list—all, she claimed, because Warren had the gall to report her.

The telescope stood on a small promontory just beyond the pool, a vantage point from which, on a day as windy as this, the city beneath us stretched in unexpected directions, the world more vivid and unfamiliar than it had been for several smoggy months. Skyscrapers jutted from downtown on one end of the horizon, and Century City on the other. A silver ribbon of sea glittered in the distance. I worked a crimp from my lower back and promised Kay I'd spy again later.

"Investigate," she said.

I climbed back toward the patio. "You'd be a lot better off if you learned to control your temper."

She shot me the look of stunned betrayal she usually reserved for Warren. "Don't tell me *you* don't believe me either?" Kay settled onto a chaise lounge, tapped a cigarette from the pack, and tried unsuccessfully to light it against the wind. Only when I bent to cup the flame did she realize the steps had left me out of breath. She patted the chaise.

"I believe you," I said, squeezing beside her, "but I also believe some accidents happen on purpose."

"It was a strange car, Sam, a make I've never driven before."

"Every car has an emergency brake. To keep the thing from rolling downhill."

"I put it in park!" She flicked an ash into the wind. "I'm almost certain."

When my laughter turned into hacking, I had to sit upright. Each cough felt like pumice in my lungs. Lights exploded when I closed my eyes. Kay stubbed out her cigarette and pounded me between the shoulder blades, firm like I liked it, until the coughing stopped.

"Alright," she conceded. "Maybe it was subconscious..."

"*Un*conscious."

"Don't correct me when I'm venting!" She cinched her robe, then tied the belt in a big angry bow. "Maybe it was *un*conscious. But I don't care about that bastard enough to back a rental car into his living room. Besides, I wouldn't have had to rent the car in the first place if he hadn't completely cleaned me out." She threw an arm behind her head, pointing in the general direction of her huge French Regency house, now vacant except for a box spring and mattress, a television set propped on a stack of phone books, and a checkered picnic blanket where the dining room table used to seat fourteen. I lay back beside her, and we listened to shuddering palm fronds and the distant clatter of what must have been a trash bin overturning. If you let yourself, it was easy to imagine the Santa Ana turning doorknobs and peeling paint. After a while, Kay raised a lotion-polished leg—I used to love to run my cheek along those legs—and gazed at the contraption strapped to her ankle. "It's really no different than a ball and chain," she said, pointing her toes and flexing her foot to emphasize the shapely calf.

"Or one of those tracking devices they attach to wild animals."

Kay turned to face me, touched my arm and smiled. In the ten years I'd known her, I'd never been able to second-guess what little remark would make her grateful.

When I awoke, I saw that Kay still lay beside me, nursing a tumbler of scotch. The sun was dousing itself inch by inch in the Pacific, the dying light reflected in her Ray Bans. She gazed toward the sunset in steely contemplation, like someone prepared for the next grim surprise. When I first met Kay she'd been a student, the kind of young woman who pronounced "chaise lounge" with a sarcastic French accent and didn't care about the difference between cheap whiskey and single malt scotch. But all of that had changed when she married Warren. "Sam," she'd told me shortly after they met, holding my hand to buffer the blow, "Warren can give me the things I need most." I knew it was true. A successful lawyer, Warren offered Kay the constancy I couldn't, not to mention a six-figure salary and a mansion in Bel Air. And, if Warren was even half as horny as Kay implied, the guy could provide her with sex on tap. In short, Warren was a man with plenty of extras, and no one deserved them more than my wife.

Kay and I had been married—a quick civil ceremony after breakfast at Denny's—while attending graduate school at Cal Tech. Our Pasadena apartment, furnished with orange crates and cinder-block shelves, held the sum of our possessions, mostly books for classes on calculus, astrophysics, and a seminar devoted to the hypothesis that black holes swallowed their own light. Kay was a brilliant student, vocal in class, asking the professors challenging questions. I felt proud of Kay, safe in her presence, as though her rigorous powers of reason could protect me from harm.

Soon enough, though, Kay's scholastic daring showed its dark side. She turned in long argumentative essays for exams she could have aced. She offered a group of physics majors the unsolicited opinion that their model of cold fusion, with its Styrofoam balls and plastic tubing, looked like a kid's project for a science fair. She filed her nails during peer reviews. All this happened in the second year of our marriage, and I couldn't help but see myself as the cause. Kay's brazenness existed in direct proportion to my secrecy. The more I suppressed my desire for men, the more keenly Kay seemed to sense its strength. Even if this conviction—that the changes in her behavior hinged on my inner life—arose from youthful egotism, her alertness to my moods was real, and precisely the trait that made leaving her so difficult.

Then along came Warren Scofield for a graduate lecture on scientific patents. Kay returned from his lecture all hopped up about the ethical and legal ramifications of a bio-engineered bacteria that was supposed to eat oil spills, though no one was certain what else it might feast on when thrown in the ocean. She paced back and forth and recounted the lecture point by point, calling Warren by his first name once too often. I knew right then they would sleep together, and this freed me to flirt with the handsome guy in financial aid who filed my paperwork. After the split, Kay and I were amazed at how quickly we shifted into friendship—though we still can't talk about those old infidelities without a fight—as if divorce had been the prelude to a far more doable union.

That night on her patio, moments from our marriage reached me like starlight, their origins a long way off. I lay there as Kay sipped liquor, wind ruffling the collar of her robe. She chewed an ice cube, huffing at thoughts, I supposed, of Warren. While I'd slept, she'd covered me with a blanket, and now the idea of trying to untangle myself was exhausting. Those were the days before protease, when I thought the virus was going to destroy me sooner rather than later, and sleep was the only antidote to my fearful, finite point of view: last visit with Kay; last windy night; last glance through a telescope—the litany would begin the instant I opened my eyes. When Kay felt me stirring she reached over and, without shifting her gaze from the view, yanked at the blanket, setting me free. I yawned and stretched, clenched the feeling back into my fingers. While I waited for wakefulness to take hold, the avenues below us ignited with lights. Underneath a darkening sky, the city looked sad and dazzling, like a picture postcard someone never sent.

And then I saw, or thought I saw, a surge of light. An electrical charge was sucked from the air, leaving an indescribable void as every refrigerator, power tool, garage door opener, and chandelier in the neighborhood went dead. Houses all around us were suddenly extinguished. A new moon, still low in the east, cast a faint glow.

"Say it's not me," said Kay. She grabbed my hand—we both winced at a shock of static—and peered into her dark yard. Lit from within only seconds ago, the swimming pool had disappeared. Wind stripped the leaves from trees, the air alive with grit and friction. Below us, the only lights left in the city belonged to traffic that had no doubt come to a halt at dim intersections. In the vicinity of West Hollywood, a hospital with its own generator twinkled like a sequin on a bolt of black fabric.

Kay's shadowy figure rose from the chaise, ice cubes clinking. "I'm making a break," she said, gulping the dregs of her scotch.

"What?"

"I'm returning to the scene of the crime. Bet the damage isn't half as bad as he claimed in the police report."

"You're not going to Warren's."

"Why not?"

"You're under house arrest, remember?"

"Oh, honey. You're too good for your own...good."

"What'll I tell Our Lady?"

Kay raised her leg and dangled her ankle. "I'm sure this thing won't work during a blackout."

"It runs on batteries, Kay. And the phones work during a power outage."

She stepped into a pair of sandals. "What I'm saying is, the precinct will be swamped with calls, and no one's going to go chasing after a first offender. Or nouveau offender, as they say in these parts." Before I could stop her, she dashed inside the house. I followed the scent of Bain de Soleil. It was a good thing Warren had taken all the furniture because the place was pitch dark, and I would have caused a fortune in damage or broken my neck. In her white robe, Kay made a spectral exit out the front door. "Stay here, Sam," she called over her shoulder. "I'll be back in no time."

The phone began to ring. "See, Kay," I shouted, but she kept on padding down the street.

I didn't relish the idea of having to talk to Kay's probation officer; in previous conversations, she'd been far too canny to fall for a lie. Still, I ran to get it because I hate the ring of an unanswered phone—a sound close to hopeless. I plucked the phone off the living room floor. "Hi," I panted. "Kay's indisposed…"

"This is an important message from the brokerage firm of Hansen and Wong. Are you one of the thousands of Americans who's put off preparing for retirement?" I would have hung up—the message, after all, was prerecorded—but I needed a moment to catch my breath. "Whether you're looking for the security of low-risk bonds or the adventure of high-growth stocks, it's never too late to invest in the future." The male voice was without inflection, like a robot's admonishment. It gave the night a futuristic tinge. I stood in the empty living room, with its panoramic view of the missing city, and wondered why I'd studied science.

It was foolish to try and catch up with Kay. Even if my lungs could get me downhill, there was uphill to contend with. But anything was better than being alone in Kay's empty house, waiting for the phone to echo through its rooms.

I set off from the front porch with an unusual burst of energy, but soon found that the best way to make progress was to take small, methodical steps. It was one thing for me to walk haltingly at my supermarket in West Hollywood, where the shoppers had seen so many failing bodies that no one gawked at the sight of lesions, Hickman catheters, or gaunt young men shuffling down the aisles. But a lone man lurching down Copa de Oro was another matter, especially since there aren't any sidewalks in Bel Air and the residents tend to panic at the sight of foot traffic. Several houses had motion detectors bolted to their fences and stone walls; anyone so much as sneezing within a thirty-foot radius would set off a floodlight worthy of San Quentin. But now, of course, none of them worked, the gloom a kind of protective cloak. Without electricity, perhaps the rules of etiquette relaxed. Even Kay wandering about the neighborhood in her bathrobe might strike the ordinarily wary onlooker as a neighbor's endearing response to the crisis. *Under cover of darkness,* I said to myself, forging ahead.

Each house I passed—at least the ones I could see behind high walls and extravagant foliage—was another brand of fantasy: rustic Tudor, low-slung ranch, boxy modern. Here and there, windows flickered with the beams of flashlights or the mild, floating coronas of candles. In one house I heard the cries of children, lost it seemed in a labyrinth of rooms. I passed enormous monogrammed gates, a birdbath shaped like a giant champagne glass, and a formerly Negroid lawn jockey who hoisted a plaster lantern, his face repainted to look Caucasian. Under a tunnel, of jacarandas, I tramped through a blizzard of lavender petals, the hot wind ballooning inside my shirt.

Once I'd been a jogger. Sure of my body. I used to lift my lover off his feet and make him yelp like a gleeful child, and even later, when he grew too weak to walk on his own, I carried him to and from the bed. Now every exertion, every gesture, no matter how brief or easy or routine, exacted a price.

When I turned the corner onto Belagio, I spotted Kay sitting on a manicured lawn across the street from Warren's. The night was sweltering, but she hugged her knees as though she were cold. I buckled beside her and tried to speak, a wheeze at the crest of every breath.

"You sound awful," she said. "I told you not to follow me."

"He's not worth it, Kay. He wants some demure little flower for a wife."

"A woman who knows when to set her emergency brake."

"Exactly. Besides, you'll get a huge chunk of money when you sell the house."

Kay sighed. "And live the life to which I've grown accustomed." She rubbed her skin where the ankle bracelet chafed.

"I hate to say it, Kay, but I wouldn't mind having problems like yours."

"I know," she said, turning to face me. Even in the dark, I could see her moist, red-rimmed eyes. "Why do you think I go on and on about Warren when you're around? I hate hearing myself, but I'm afraid if I stop, there's only one topic. Your health, I mean. Your T-cells dropping. It scares me to death. And there's nothing I can do." Dogs around us began to bark at some disruption only they could hear.

Save me, I wanted to say. Ever since my diagnosis I'd said it silently, again and again, to no one in particular. I heard the words in my head like a pulse, blurted them to strangers in dreams. And there I was, fighting the urge to say it to Kay, a plea so unequivocal and blunt, resisting it took the rest of my strength.

I lay back on the grass and, gazing overhead, saw a swath of night sky. Stars congested the deep regions of space, a spectacle I'd missed while watching my steps on the leaf-strewn roads. "Kay," I said, tugging her down. Hard-pressed to take her eyes off Warren's house, she lowered her head slowly, long hair coiling beneath her like rope. Kay ran her hands through the brittle grass and her robe fell open, revealing the yellow bikini underneath. I pointed at the sky. "It's like floating on a raft."

"It is," she whispered. Some people might have searched for constellations—ram, hunter, charioteer—but Kay bristled when earthly forms were imposed on the cosmos, which we'd dubbed in school The Big Abstraction. The two of us squinted at a quadrant of sky where Kay had once located the misty hint of a nebula through her telescope. Its cosmic debris and clouds of dust sailed outward at fantastic speeds, though the nebula would look, from this vast a distance, completely still for the next billion years. In a few minutes, the power around us would sputter back to life, and we'd sit up and see, through a hole Kay had made in the house across the street, Warren peering toward us, just as a patrol car screeched around the curve. But for now we lay back on a stranger's lawn, pointing to what we guessed were red dwarfs, stars formed long before the earth, their matter decaying so slowly it defies all measure of time.

The Rocky Hills of Trancas

William Harrison

SETTING

WE LIVED FAR OUT IN MALIBU on the wrong side of the highway. In those scraggly, rocky, desert hills above Trancas—which is really just a crossroads with a seedy supermarket, a gas station, and a bar and grill that constantly changes ownership and names—there are a number of shabby, low-rent houses and tiny ranches. Many of the places feature eccentric gates: the residents' names fashioned out of horseshoes, an arch of used tires painted in reds and yellows, mailboxes adorned with the bleached skulls of animals, seashells in tacky patterns on the gateposts. Our gate was composed of two stone columns: desert rocks stuck together with too much mortar so they resembled fountains of lava that had exploded upward and dried in place above the surrounding dust. Our forlorn house had the same look: a melted mass created out of my father's labors. When he wasn't writing another unwanted screenplay, he did rock work. Either behind the typewriter or behind his wheelbarrow, he trapped us inside the crafts and dreams he never mastered. He was also a womanizer who often left home, calling to say that he was staying in the city for script conferences or making other lame excuses. The world was filled with gullible women and girls for him to charm, and the lies he told them became part of the arid spaces in my early teenage years.

Not a mile from that monstrosity we called home, just across the Pacific Coast Highway, was Broad Beach: rows of seaside mansions and exquisite beach houses where the movie stars and famous producers lived. One could cross the parking lot at the Trancas Market where all the migrant workers gathered in hopes of getting day jobs, wait at the traffic light there at the far end of Zuma Beach, then enter the infectious dream that makes our coast so seductive. Go along the main road and you pass Dustin Hoffman's place, then, further on, Spielberg's. Go down a lane toward the lower beach and there's Mel Gibson's. I could never fault my father for being so susceptible to the movie business at this close proximity to success. Broad Beach was newer and even more potent than the old Malibu Colony behind its closed gates; there was gold dust in the air, the heavy pollen of talent and money, and it was always real enough if just beyond one's own capacity to breathe it into the lungs.

BACKSTORY

One day when I was barely thirteen years old I came home early from school to find my father in bed with another woman. I stood in the doorway, watching their copulation and the strange prop they shared, the old Hasselblad camera that had once belonged to my grandfather. A curious and irrational thing happened inside me as I stood there watching: I assumed, suddenly and without the least doubt, that my mother—not just my father carrying on before my eyes—was having an affair, too. My mother in those days was an assistant to the dean at the nearby university, a hardworking woman who provided the family's means of support, and she was always in the company of the dean, a tall man with gray skin and silver hair, and so my adolescent assumption had its basis in odd pieces of evidence. The two of them often went away to academic conferences or my mother frequently went back to the university in the evenings for seminars or cultural activities at the dean's side. He was the distinguished father figure in some of my odd fantasies, the successful Dean Havens who somehow enhanced my mother, Jenna, with his attentions.

Standing there in the doorway, then, watching my father hold the camera at arm's length, snapping off photos as he thrust himself into this anonymous young woman, I assumed that my parents—both of them—were into free love and open marriage.

These intuitions ultimately proved wrong. Dean Havens was a gentleman of the old school: a family man, a community leader, straight-arrow all the way, if somewhat lazy. My mother did most of his work—and hated his laziness, I learned, while taking pride in her work for the university and for our family. I knew, finally, without having to ask her, that there was nothing remotely intimate between them.

My father eventually caught sight of me in the doorway.

"Roper," he called to me. "Hey, fella, would you mind going out on the patio? I'll be with you in a minute."

I waited on the unfinished patio—the eternal project with bags of cement mix lying around—and kept my eyes on a Ford Mustang, red, parked at the top of our driveway. At last my father came outside, fully dressed, and began an elaborate and hollow explanation about taking photographs, art pictures, a hobby of his until that time unknown to me. He talked loudly and too long, punctuating his words with short bursts of embarrassed laughter.

"Nudity, you see, well, it's controversial. Some people don't understand the difference between, well, art and smut. Your mother, for instance, probably wouldn't understand."

"I won't tell," I promised, and as he talked on, relieved, I watched the young woman hurrying out the back door and getting into her car. She wore leotards and rolled double socks: the standard uniform of girls who worked out at the gyms in those days.

STORYLINE

I met Mirelle, the love of my sixteenth year, at Malibu High School. We both lived in absurd houses up in the hills—more about that in a moment—and among our wealthy and wildly spoiled classmates we would've been outsiders except that she was beautiful and, although I never played on the team because of my part-time job, I was probably the best tennis player in school.

I learned to play on the school's courts. Few others wanted to be seen on them. Surrounded by a cheap chain-link fence that curled at the bottom so balls constantly went through, made of grainy concrete scarred with hideous cracks, they were regarded as an eyesore. After all, half the kids at school had tennis courts at home: the newest hard surfaces, well-kept clay courts, even one grass layout—neatly trimmed by a battery of gardeners—up the winding road at Las Flores Canyon. My time off was usually spent at these private tennis courts—Mirelle, eventually, on the sidelines sipping cola and cheering me—and because I rarely lost a set, and because a few of the snootier players hoped to beat me, I kept getting invitations.

Mirelle's beauty intimidated everyone. Tall and thin with hardly any breasts, she had a look of icy cool and had already made money as a model when we first became acquainted. I owned an old junker, a battered Chevy Nova that cost less than three hundred dollars. I drove it to school and to my various assignments for Creative Caterers. Mirelle didn't have a car, so suffered the indignities of the school bus. Occasionally, since she lived up a canyon road not far from our house, she allowed me to drop her at her gate after school—never allowing me to venture up her driveway. Then one day she saw our rockpile. She stopped off with me to borrow a library book I had checked out. When she saw my house she broke into laughter. Embarrassment flooded over me.

"No, you don't understand," she assured me, and after we located the book she allowed me to drive beyond her gate for the first time.

She had a rock house, too, studded with seashells, chunks of crude ceramic, pieces of colored bottles, and metallic strips: a terrible stucco heap decorated with the shiny artifacts of bad taste.

"Your dad should meet Stella," she said of her mother, smiling at me with those perfect teeth and touching my hand as I steered us into the carport. A big Persian cat jumped on the hood of the car. Cats everywhere: perched in windows, strolling the slate roof, lounging around a dry fountain and pool adorned with glinting ceramic and shards of glass.

Stella, her mother, who wasn't home, had been a soap opera actress, but now, according to Mirelle, she drank too much and stayed on call for a battery of ex-husbands. She was also a mystic and the world's worst potter, Mirelle said, whose bowls and ashtrays could be lifted only by musclemen.

"Stella says that she helps me through life by serving as a bad example," Mirelle added, sighing.

We sat in the kitchen with mixing bowls and plates heavy on the shelves around us, drinking orange juice. In some miraculous way we talked about our parents' sex lives—about which we had very few actual facts—then about our own and those of our classmates.

"I'm a virgin and mean to stay that way," Mirelle announced.

"In spite of all my efforts, I'm a virgin too," I admitted, and thankfully she laughed.

"Every girl I know does it," she confided.

"What about Karen Highsmith?"

"You don't know about her?"

"No, what about her? She doesn't go steady with anybody."

"That's because she bangs anybody who asks."

"Karen? You're kidding."

"If you want her, just ask. She likes the direct approach. And I guess you'll ask if you're all that interested."

"It's not Karen I'm interested in, not at all," I said, giving her a look that made my meaning clear.

Mirelle studied me over the rim of her glass. In an enormous mixing bowl above us on a shelf, a cat lay curled in sleep.

"I guess we both have promiscuous parents," she finally began, thoughtfully. "We love them, I guess, but we don't want to be like them. You know, we could possibly go together. I mean, you're perfect for me because you get invited everywhere to play tennis."

"You get invitations, too."

"No, I don't, that's the point. The boys seem to be afraid of me and the girls know I'm poor and can't keep up with them. I mean, guess where Anna and Susie went for their summer break? The Himalayas. To see the Dalai Lama or something. Ginger Dickinson says she only skis in Switzerland these days. Half of them have new convertibles. Look at their clothes, then look at mine. When they heard I had a modeling job, they considered me a working girl. And except for the tennis it's probably the same for you. I mean, you work for the catering service. They see you at their parents' parties wearing a white jacket and serving the hors d'oeuvres, don't they?"

"Sometimes I even have to wear white gloves," I admitted. "But let's get back to you and me."

"We're perfect, but no sex," Mirelle said, putting the deal straight. "I like you, I mean, but this is for the social situation. Because our parents have these god-awful houses. And because I'm miserable, but I'm twice as pretty as Becky or Ginger or any of them."

"You're ten times more beautiful," I added. "So what about kissing?"

She smirked and placed her empty glass on the rough kitchen table. "Just kissing?" she asked, again thoughtfully.

"I believe we should kiss each other all the time," I suggested, trying to sound rational about it. "In front of everbody. At tennis matches. In the hallway at school. You know, to keep up appearances."

She considered this argument. Then she moved over and sat on my lap, sighing and saying, "All right. Let's see how it goes."

The kiss she gave me, open mouthed, slow, wet, deep, filled with the subtleties of arousal, ignited all my hopes.

She liked it, too. "Goodness," she said afterward, and she got up and walked to the window where she stroked a fat little Siamese who sunned himself there. "Goodness, you have strong arms."

Strong arms. It was a compliment I've remembered all my life.

She came back to me, shoved her kitchen chair against mine, sat facing me, pulled closer, placed her long legs over mine, and kissed me again. In pleasure and in misery we practiced kissing that whole afternoon. Afterward, everywhere, just as I had suggested, we were considered ardent lovers, kissing on the mouth, the neck, the cheek, constantly, in a conspiracy against those around us and in the turmoil of our own early confusions.

Close Up

Unlike my father, Tally, who never went on walks, my mother and I enjoyed strolling along the beaches. At low tide we sometimes walked from Broad Beach up toward the Ventura County line, passing all those elegant houses and the raw cliffs filled with wildlife. We saw a bobcat, once, and often ran across rattlesnakes, the small dark ones that hunted for rodents and rabbits beneath the gorse and windblown trees. Out at sea windsurfers turned their bright sails into the breeze, making sharp cuts at the edges of our thoughts. Overhead, gulls called to one another and rode the wind. Surfers in their black wet suits waited for the waves, adream, like a special species of ocean creatures.

During those walks I often wanted to talk about my father, about the demanding dean, about Mirelle, or all the restlessness inside me, but somehow didn't.

In a rocky cove one day, sheltered from a fierce afternoon breeze, we ate apples and slices of cheese as my mother's silken scarf billowed softly in the air. She had a soft look, a serenity, and used her scarves to dress up a modest wardrobe bought on sale far from the fashionable shops. At Christmas or on her birthdays I usually gave her a new scarf, something expensive bought out of my wages—a Fendi or a Picasso—and I always promised myself that I'd someday buy her a new car, a new house, or a new life.

We talked about my Grandfather Roper that day in the cove. "I know he was a cowboy and an atheist and I've heard all the stories about how tough he was," I said. "But can you remember anything else? Something about him you've never told me?"

She bit into her apple, looking at the ocean horizon where, far offshore, an oil tanker passed. I was my grandfather's namesake, and she knew I loved the old anecdotes.

"He once told me that he just loved revenge," she said slowly, grinning and remembering.

"Getting even, you mean?"

"Exactly. Payback. He was even a little cruel about it. He said it was one of life's wicked pleasures. He beat up that deputy sheriff, the one who stole the antique saddle."

"You told me that story. You said grandfather almost had to go to jail himself."

"When he thought he was in the right, he was terrible. He sometimes overdid it with my brother and me. But you're not like that. You're gentler. More like your father, I believe."

I didn't want to hear that and she sensed it.

"Let's finish the walk," I suggested.

"Throw your apple core up on the cliffs for the little animals," she reminded me, and we set out again.

Not only did I consider my mother wrong about how I was like my father, but the mystery of her marriage to Tally always nagged me. How could she love this philanderer? This typewriter bum? It was far beyond me. Angry in this uncertainty, I threw my apple core high onto the cliff as we walked on.

PANNING LEFT

Back when my father temporarily had an agent—not a good one, of course—he went to a script conference with a producer who was guiding the career of young Tom Cruise. It was the most important meeting of my father's writing career.

He spent the morning dressing himself, getting the casual outdoor look: sneakers, black jeans, a crisp white shirt, and the old black leather jacket with the little dangling chain. He noted for us later that the actor's producer, the assistant, and the recording secretary all wore essentially the same costume: jeans and fancy new shirts. They drank Diet Pepsi and spoke his name in a litany of friendliness: Tally Jones, yes, Tally old pal, Tal, Tally this and that. They were doing a boxing movie, he told us, and already had the storyline. He sat in that studio office, he said, turning his Diet Pepsi in his fingers, excited, trying not to say the wrong things. Too much, he told us: sitting at a real studio, sound stages just beyond the window, talking to real producers about a possibly real movie for which he would really get paid.

The story was about a crude southern boy who had been in prison and his new black manager. It was about racial prejudice and how the two become friends. In the last act, the young boxer, Tom Cruise, wins the title.

"You have the storyline already," my father says he told them. "So what can I do for you?"

The crucial moment of the meeting had arrived. All script meetings are actually auditions, and the writer is supposed to have a good idea or two if he expects to land a writing assignment.

The second act is the problem, the assistant pointed out. You know, the part where Tom and his manager—Morgan Freeman, say—become pals. Characterization. All that.

At this point, Tally told us that he had an inspiration. The black manager, see, reads Miss Manners, he said to them. The manager believes in courtesy the way some people believe in the Bible. So he carries around this big book of etiquette by Miss Manners and reads passages to Tom Cruise. While he's teaching Tom to box, he reported telling them, he also teaches him table etiquette and how to talk to women. And Tom discovers that courtesy works. Tom even learns to quote Miss Manners himself, using some of her arch diction, in a reverse bit when Morgan Freeman loses his cool.

The producer, assistant, and recording secretary laughed, my father told us, and slapped him on the back. Wonderful stuff, they said. Softens the movie with humor. Terrific. As the last handshakes began, my father said he knew he had the assignment.

On the freeway driving back out to Trancas, my father said he felt clever and successful. It was a day clear of smog in Los Angeles, he said, and some distant Filipino volcano provided a vivid sunset, as if God had used the right filter.

We heard the details of this meeting for a week. He took me aside—we went into the bathroom where he sat on the edge of the tub—to tell me that his dreams could come true, they really could, and that everything would be different. He loved both my mother and me, he said, and he would give us everything he had failed to provide in the past. He meant it, I knew, as all apology for that time I caught him in bed with that strange woman—and for all his shortcomings.

A week later the second-rate agent phoned. The producer had decided to go with another writer, a former black boxer who wanted to try his first script. Later my father learned that the producer had asked a dozen or so writers to stop around, writers looking for work, picking their brains in a flurry of first names and Diet Pepsi, so they could provide the novice screenwriter with material.

I felt sorry for Tally. The world out there was cruel to him even when he was allowed to briefly touch it. And I suppose, even now, if they ever make a movie about a boxer and his black manager with Tom Cruise, Morgan Freeman, or the next incarnations of movie stars, whenever such a movie goes into production, at whatever studio in this decade or the next, Miss Manners might be part of the story. Sadly, my father did give them something nice, a little thought to be ground up, along with some of his supply of hope, in the machinery of the business.

RACKING FOCUS

We were at the Spencer house in the Colony playing on their clay court. Mirelle flashed her smile, sipped lemonade, and hung around with us talking about colleges. Craig was going up to Stanford, while Charlie was waiting on Harvard but would probably end up at Berkeley.

Charlie and I had just started a game of singles when Mr. Spencer came out. Craig's father had an unruly mop of dyed hair, hunched shoulders, and a pipe in his mouth. He concentrated on Mirelle and soon asked her to go into the house with him to look at his paintings. Mr. Spencer's seascapes featuring young women in diaphanous lingerie strolling among the sand dunes were in some of the galleries up in Santa Barbara, but in my opinion they were silly, amateurish works. Besides, Mr. Spencer remained one of the few men in Malibu living off alimony payments from a famous wife, a singer, and we all knew that both Mr. Spencer and his son Craig were braggarts and fools in spite of their clay court.

"Be right back!" Mirelle sang out, waving, and as I watched her stroll away with Mr. Spencer I had this odd, sinking feeling.

I liked playing with Charlie Beringer well enough, but that afternoon I made quick work of him: passing shots, a lob here, a dropshot there, my whole repertoire. He became a bit surly, but I couldn't give him points as I usually did. I beat him in two love sets, so we could get indoors.

We found Mirelle and Mr. Spencer seated at opposite ends of a big leather couch in his studio. I went over and sat between them, pretending to admire his most recent surf-and-dune epic perched on an easel before us. The house, by the way, had a pulse in it: with each wave breaking on the nearby beach, the windows shook and the floors gave us a definite tremor. Mr. Spencer said it was soothing. Anyway, Charlie and Craig turned on a TV set in another room and Mr. Spencer wanted to know if I appreciated art.

Guarding against a sarcasm, I gave him a humble no.

"I'd think you'd be turned on by the arts," he replied. "Isn't your father a writer?"

"My father's a failed writer," I corrected him, and that ended the discussion. Mr. Spencer probably fretted that I might have artistic standards, and he was a painter who certainly didn't want to be drawn into a discussion of those.

After small talk, a last lemonade, and a moment in front of the oversize TV screen with Craig and Charlie, we said our good-byes. Suddenly, Mr. Spencer, acting wildly formal, grabbed Mirelle's hand and kissed it, and for a crazy moment I thought Craig might do it, too.

As I was driving us back home in my rattling Chevy, Mirelle told me that I had been rude to Mr. Spencer.

"He's a nerd," I said. "Who can like that guy?"

"Also, you were jealous," she accused me, and she seemed proud of herself for making me feel that way.

"I'd be stupid if I wasn't," I told her. "You're gorgeous and you drive us all crazy."

She liked that, so pulled her legs up and encircled her knees with her arms. Smug and beautiful, her future assured, she closed her eyes against the oncoming western sun. My own future in comparison was far less certain. Others spoke of college and what lay ahead, but all my hopes were vague, poorly defined, even though I sensed that I would soon be expelled from Eden and should worry about it all.

JUMP CUT

A family dinner up in Oxnard at Sal's.

My parents called one another by their names that night, Jenna this and Tally that, stiffly, so I suspected they were making up after an argument and taking me along in order to remember why they were still married.

We talked about Tally's screenplays—which at this time must have numbered about thirty—and they tried to draw me into the discussion.

"Which one do you like best?" my mother wanted to know.

"I haven't even read them all."

"Of those you've read, which one?"

"Maybe the science fiction epic."

"Really? You like that one?" my father asked, biting into his taco. "I thought you told me it was over the top. Too weird, you said, remember?"

Sal's served my mother's favorite Mexican food. It was a big noisy place with checkered tablecloths, families, enchiladas, and beer, and if we went out to dinner it was the place my mother felt we could afford. Of course the whole question of family money remained a mystery to me: How could

Tally afford, at times, to disappear for a couple of days? Did Grandfather Roper leave us anything? We were poor, that was always made clear, and my own money, hard-earned, went for Mirelle's pleasure and mine—we usually dated in packs—and even when we drove over Kanan Road and went to the movies in Agoura we often ended up eating at places like Fettucine's because the others were oblivious to what things cost.

My father that night insisted on analyzing the sci-fi script while I tried to concentrate on my steak asada.

"The wizard shouldn't be the main character," I finally told him. "Otherwise, the whole thing's a good idea. Original."

"So who should be the main character?" Tally asked with sarcasm, his taco stopped in front of his mouth.

"Not the wizard because he's too old. A young audience won't identify with him. Maybe a new character, a kid, like his apprentice."

"Listen to him," Tally said to my mother. "The script doctor."

That ended the conversation. They had little to say to each other after that, and we drove home in silence.

Later that evening Tally asked to borrow twenty dollars.

"You didn't pay me back last time," I reminded him.

"Yes I did," he argued. "And, look, I'm driving Ellis Kerry's car up to Ventura tomorrow. I don't even have gas money. He's paying me for the favor and I'll pay you back right away."

"Ellis Kerry, the producer?"

"We've known each other for years. He almost bought a script from me once."

"And you do what for him now? Errands?"

"Roper, c'mon, don't make me ask twice. I'll pay you back with interest. Promise."

QUICK TAKE

The next day while my father was supposed to be driving up
to Ventura I laid out of school to work a big catering job at a
new house on Broad Beach. The staff had to arrive early to
set up tables, get the food into the ovens, stock the bars, and
receive assignments. Once again, I wore the white jacket and
was ordered to circulate among the two hundred guests
serving champagne and picking up empty glasses.

Built on the side of the cliff, the house had six floors and
two elevators. From the main road, like all the other houses
along that stretch, one saw only the garage doors and a modest entrance, but above the garage, tucked behind a row of
barred windows, a battery of security guards monitored
everyone who approached. Beyond the entrance and garage,
the house became a jewel of spacious salons, open decks facing out to sea, white stucco passageways, game rooms, and
vaulting glass windows. A crystal waterfall trickled down a
series of artfully arranged boulders in the middle of the
house, opening up into hidden pools, alcoves, hot tubs, and
a sense of flowing splendor.

The businessman who owned it, I was told, referred to it
as his little seaside cottage.

At one of those hidden pools, discreetly tucked away in
a nook beside the waterfall, I found my father holding hands
with a striking woman who wore a string bikini. Both their
bodies were sculpted and perfect. Tally's tanned physique, I
wanted to tell her, came from hefting big rocks into our oversize wheelbarrow and from basking in the hot sun of our
ugly patio and garden.

But I said nothing, even when she called after me asking
for a glass of champagne.

She might have been the wife of the owner or Ellis
Kerry's secretary or a porno star, but I didn't want to know.
It might have been an innocent interlude, but I saw Tally's
face and knew it wasn't.

He caught up with me at the elevator, beginning another weak explanation, stammering, but I didn't let him get started.

"Now that you're back from Ventura you owe me twenty bucks," I told him. My face must have twisted with disgust because he turned away and padded barefoot back toward his little cove.

WIDE ANGLE

It's a dreamcoast, sure, but the false optimism and elusive hope that resided in my father's deepest core, that gets into so many others out here, becomes a poison. The climate is warm and sunny; everyone hears success stories, gets glimpses of celebrities, and it's a palm-tree world, a halter-top world, where phrases like *Malibu* or *development deal* roll off the tongue, but one lives on a personal fault line where everything is shaky and terrifying.

As I began to sense this, I wondered why Tally didn't.

One evening I accompanied my mother to a university picnic up in the canyon near the Hindu temple. A soft evening in an arbor of eucalyptus: tables covered with white linen and adorned with hurricane lamps, strolling musicians with guitars and flutes. I danced with my mother, our feet shuffling over the bare earth, and found that she seemed very small in my arms. Afterward we talked for a while with Dean Havens and his wife, then sat on the ground with our backs against one of the trees. I thought of saying that I'd like to get away early so I could drop by and see Mirelle, but then I realized I couldn't hurry off.

"You okay? You seem sad," I said to her, and since I was sixteen years old it was hardly precocious of me, yet it was that rare first moment when one asks about a parent's feelings.

"Oh, I was thinking about your father," she mused, reaching over to touch my arm and reassure me. "He'll never be a writer, I sometimes think, because so much of his life is, well, physical. Like his rock walls. He doesn't read much. He doesn't have—oh, I don't know, a very strong inner life."

"He doesn't have any talent," I said, then wished I hadn't.

"Maybe not," she said, sighing, and accepting that. "But where does talent come from? How does it develop? Poor Tally. He wants to be in the mainstream so much, yet he needs to live a secret life, doesn't he?"

For me, everything about my father had become too painfully important to be discussed further. In silence, then, we sat looking up through the dark branches of the trees at the greater canopy of stars. My mother gave my arm a gentle squeeze.

"You're worried about college and money and what will happen to you, aren't you?"

"Sure," I answered, "I guess so."

"Things will become very clear. You'll see. You know what I've been thinking recently? This is odd. Don't laugh. I've been thinking that you'll do something very big. You know, famous."

"C'mon," I said, giving her a nudge. "Not me. That's scary talk, anyway." In our house, I thought, we've had too many big dreams, and my mother, my steady and practical mother, should know that.

An evening breeze rustled the leaves above us.

The musicians played "Red Sails in the Sunset."

PLOT POINT

Mirelle and her mother, Stella, came to our house for bean soup. Stella wore a tight-fitting black sheath dress, black boots, and about ten pounds of assorted jewelry that dived into her cleavage. Her hair was teased into a lopsided bird's nest. Purple lipstick. She brought a gallon of cheap red wine, two Tarot decks, a crossword puzzle in the event she got bored, her cell phone, and a Doberman pup named Coco who didn't get along with the cats, very docile because she had given it Valium. She flirted shamelessly with Tally, clomping around in her boots like a flamenco dancer while he stirred the soup at the kitchen range. Then she swept away the magazines on the coffee table and sat down cross-legged on the floor to read fortunes. Through all this, Mirelle gave us her famous smirk and rolled her eyes.

"Oh, my, dahling!" Stella cried out with each card she turned up, wildly pretentious and aware of it. Our fortunes, thankfully, were all bright and happy, although one of my cards she called "troublesome" and said we just wouldn't think about it.

My mother, slightly tipsy after two glasses of wine, put on a Dixieland CD while we ate supper. At the table Tally became the centerpiece of the evening, telling stories and doing impressions. He did a great Jack Nicholson: the nasal voice, yet back in the throat in the bass range, reciting those famous lines from the restaurant scene in *Five Easy Pieces* when the character was trying to order a chicken salad sandwich that wasn't on the menu.

Stella stood up at the table and gave him an ovation. Her dress by this time had slipped off one pudgy shoulder and a white bra strap had appeared.

After that Tally did the Godfather with pieces of French bread in his cheeks. As the women nodded and laughed, I watched his effect on them. His shirt was open to his waist, exposing the hair on his chest and his hard flat stomach. When he gave them his crooked smile it provoked all of them to smile in return. I couldn't have won their attention if I had set the room on fire; I was a boy just getting my bearings and he was a man of fearsome charm, worldly, oddly confident, in command, and it occurred to me—how old was he that night? maybe forty-three?—that he should have been an actor, not a writer, and that he possessed a special physical grace that I had never fully understood.

He drank off a glass of wine, did Cary Grant, and then, in an amazing transition, did both Bogie and Claude Rains in their famous exchange from *Casablanca*—dialogue that Mirelle liked yet didn't quite understand because she admitted never having seen the movie.

With everyone under his spell, he quit. Perfect timing.

"I'm going to make us a dessert," he announced, and went back to the kitchen.

My mother and Stella retreated to the sofa together, clasped hands, and fell into an earnest conversation like old friends. Mirelle gave her attentions to the dopey dog. I decided to help finish off the wine, so poured myself a glass and quickly drank it down.

With the evening performances ended, the five of us wandered through the house and outdoors for idle conversations. Tally made brownies. Overpowered by that single glass of wine, I stood at the bathroom mirror taking stock of my unremarkable features. A definite new pimple. Too much. When I emerged, I found Tally and Mirelle in the kitchen playing a game of slap: his palms turned down and extended, hers turned up underneath as she attempted to quickly turn her hands over and slap his. She scored on him every time and they both laughed at every twitch, feint, and success.

"Hey, you're too good," he told her, and she bit her lower lip with pride, grinning.

Alarm swept over me.

Their touching, however slight and quick and violent, was worse for me than anything that had happened with Mr. Spencer. They both looked over at me occasionally, smiling, both of them natural and having fun, yet I felt put in my place. I was a losing competitor, I knew, and I added up my assets against Tally's. I can beat him at tennis, I assured myself, and I get paid when I work. On all other counts, clearly, he had me: he was bigger, stronger, more handsome, and most surprisingly of all, more alive.

Later we ate the brownies and drank strong coffee.

At the end of the evening we stood outdoors and pointed out the constellations to one another; Stella knew them all because she was also an astrology freak, a Scorpio, and because our hills, she reminded us, sheltered the glare of lights from Santa Monica, giving us a superb view of the universe.

She and my mother hugged goodnight. Mirelle embraced everyone, too, giving Tally, I thought, a bit more enthusiasm than necessary.

"Your dad's cool," she whispered when she hugged me, then she left me without a kiss.

They almost forgot the puppy.

WILDTRACKING

The following Saturday I agreed to roll out cookie dough with the bakers for extra pay at the catering service. At noon, though, we had the job done, so I drove home to find my mother sewing. She was no better at stitching than she was at cooking, so we made conversation while she stuck needles in her fingers and swore under her breath. I asked where Tally was.

"Gone off on a hike," she said, shrugging her shoulders and shaking her head because this was definitely something new for my father. "Took the old Hasselblad with him," she added. "I guess he's going to photograph the cactus and maybe take up a new art."

My alarm went off again. I hurried to the car and drove up to Mirelle's place.

On my way I invented several excuses about why I was dropping in unannounced, then decided I didn't need any. I wondered if Stella was home, if I'd catch anybody doing naked photos, if I was going insane. Then, forgetting caution, I pressed the accelerator. In less than a minute I roared up Mirelle's driveway and skidded to a stop in a cloud of white dust. I hurried inside, running, seeing nothing except all the cats, finding no one, then with long strides I went down a hallway toward the back bedrooms.

Mirelle sat on her bed, fully dressed, eyes wide. Yet for a moment we didn't speak and I suddenly knew that all my worst fears were true. Glancing out the window, I saw Tally hurrying over the hill, making his escape, and without thinking I went after him.

He was in full flight and I couldn't catch him. Not knowing what I'd say if I did, I stood at the crest of an arroyo and hurled rocks after him. They fell around him in little white puffs of dry dust until he was finally out of range.

Back inside the house I found Mirelle still on the bed, sobbing.

"Goddammit," I said, and walked out.

SLOW FADE

That was the last time I saw my father.

I drove all around, cooling off, trying to find the right words to say to him, yet they were all wrong. Under the circumstances and because I was still so young and generally inarticulate, the phrases were all moralistic, even righteous, and I knew that just wasn't the right pitch and tone for this latitude. I drove up the PCH as far as the county line, then crossed over toward Thousand Oaks, then looped back and cruised along Broad Beach. All the celebrity houses glared at me. I had only kissed Mirelle, I kept telling myself, and I certainly didn't own her. And Tally's such a bastard. So grow up. Get used to it and get over it. And don't say anything to mother.

By the time I reached our house, though, Tally, had thrown a few clothes in the back of mother's car and without saying anything, embarrassed beyond recovery, slinking away like a dog, had left us. He left his pile of scripts on the shelf and the oversize wheelbarrow filled with stones. A week later he phoned and told Jenna that he was living in an apartment in Pasadena, giving her a phone number and arranging to send back the car.

These days he lives in San Bernadino, a million miles away. He's with a young stewardess, my mother told me, and doing what for a living nobody knows.

During my last year at Malibu High School, I fell in with the son of Ellis Kerry, the producer, and he started taking me to screenings at the studios. When we weren't playing tennis over at his place in Corral Canyon we hung out at the movie houses on Third Street in Santa Monica. Bosco was a quiet kid, serious, and thoughtful about money—for instance, he tried to stay within my budget when we did things together—and he helped me with dates after Mirelle. We took a few girls out, mostly for burgers but sometimes to the screenings—which they went crazy for—and Bosco did a strange thing: although he drove a new Nissan, he bought an old junker like mine, a beat-up Escort, and said he felt better in it. When I told him he was crazy he reminded me that he still had the Nissan, too.

From Bosco I learned about the student film competition, so entered in the screenwriting category. I dug out Tally's old sci-fi script, the one with the Wizard who was the Leonardo da Vinci of the twenty-third century, and I added the new character, the kid who was his apprentice, and a half dozen new scenes. I scanned the whole manuscript into Bosco's computer, then worked at his house, spending a month on it, and incorporating all his suggestions. After revising it again, I sent it to the student competition—which included college students, even grad students, so I knew I'd never win.

After that I considered claiming Tally's abandoned office as my own, but it didn't feel right.

I did steal his scripts, all of them. Turnabout was fair play, I decided, and, besides, that career of his—such a long indulgence—was over.

For a few weeks my mother drank too much, then, abruptly and rationally, she stopped. I never saw her cry.

That summer she went to Italy with Dean Havens, his wife, and a group of faculty members.

The wheelbarrow filled with stones was never touched.

Stella married again, and Mirelle, the model, signed some sort of contract.

TRAILER

The screenplay, *Lords and Masters,* won the competition, making me the youngest writer ever to win.

After that Bosco and I began trying to get jobs in the story departments of various studios. If this happens, I tell him, I'm going to buy my mother a new car and tie a beautiful new silk scarf on its antenna.

She sold the Trancas property—left to her by Grandfather Roper, I learned—then bought a new condo down near the old pier. The investors who bought the old place tore down the house, bulldozed away the unfinished patio, the wheelbarrow, the columns at the gate, and finally auctioned off the barren land.

When I won the competition my picture was in two or three newspapers, but I suppose Tally didn't know that because he never phoned.

The Palace of Marriage

Karen Karbo

No SOVIET EMIGRATES for any real reason. Okay, Solzhenitsyn, Sharansky. But they are movie stars of emigration. No usual émigré has their problems. Usual émigré leaves because one night he starts talking. He is drinking and he is sad. He is in bad news with his boss, let's say, or some friend has disappeared forever into psychiatric hospital. No American can understand such sadness. This man is a bathtub drain with bathwater swirling down it all at same time.

For my wife, Bella Bellinka, and me it was one February midnight. Heat and light vanished from our apartment without warning. Such cold is impossible to remember. In Los Angeles we do nothing but perspire and squint; heat and sunlight are ever present here, careless, competent, extravagant, like Americans.

But that February night we huddled in bed wearing every clothes we could get on. We boiled potatoes for our pockets and socks. I had a cold; tears of ice formed at end of my dripping nose. We drank and drank.

We talked until our throats hurt about what we wanted. A lot, it was, for people who had next to nothing. It started with heat, then bloomed into things fantastic. Bella wanted clothes, shoes, stockings, mascara, manicures, bedroom slippers, highball glasses, mail-order catalogues, marzipan, super-absorbency Tampax, *Vogue*, a subscription to *Vogue*, a job at *Vogue*, things of which I had never even heard.

I wanted a garden of cactus and a baby. First American Bogoga. Ernest Bogoga. William Bogoga. F. Scott Bogoga.

Bellinka humored me. My wishes were few and simple. Harmless dreams. But we were so stirred up. We got going. Our breath turned hot and thawed two small patches on window above our bed. I mashed a few potatoes still in my back pocket. Now I realize this sudden passion was sparked by thoughts of possibilities, not love.

One thing leads to another. Is most cruel fact on earth. *A* is one thing, *B* is other thing. *Leads to* is part no one can see or name. No one can say, "I am now living *leads to.*" *Leads to* is how whole world winds up at *B*, biggest sins and mistakes.

Suddenly I am making application for visas. I am sitting in offices, waiting for signatures. I even say I am Jew to emigrate. Jews then they were letting out. Can you imagine, saying you are Jew to get out of persecution? But there I am. I have become Bogogowicz.

Then we are on airplane, sixteen hours in Vienna, ten in New York, finally soft, hot laundromat air of Los Angeles, palm trees as tall as skyscrapers, going, going, going, ending way up in mustardy haze in tiny, disappointing cluster of half-dead fronds. Cars like stars, splattering galaxy of black asphalt streets. Fantastic.

Every morning our neighbor does things naked on her terrace. Yoga, toenail polishing, needlepoint. Today is leg shaving.

Our apartments mirror each other across narrow driveway. Both are second floor. She supposes her pots of bushy ferns, avocado plants, and camellias hide her. But no. She is betrayed; I am one who is hidden. From bedroom window I watch. I watch her pink plastic shaver sail up her shin, over her knee, and beyond.

At 6:30 A.M. every day I hear her sliding door open, close. Out of bed I stumble, fumbling, putting on my glasses. At night I leave our bedroom curtain open.

Early morning is only reasonable time in Los Angeles in September. After around nine o'clock wind comes. Wind is hot, dry, as though someone put entire city in clothes dryer. People get bloody noses. Houses in Hollywood Hills burst into flames for no apparent reason. Every day smells like campfire. At night, faces and car windshields are coated with thin layers of soot.

Our neighbor lifts her head, sniffs. Air is already brown-orange with smoke from fires burning all night. But now is pleasant. She enjoys herself. She squirts on shaving cream, whistles Chopin. She is our first American neighbor: happy, cultured, clean, her nipples dark and flat as the disks underneath our living room chairs. They are for prevention of dents on wall-to-wall carpet, these disks. My Bella Bellinka loves them. They always seem to be on sale somewhere, and she buys more than we will ever need. Same with air fresheners. All my clothes smell now like pine trees. I have not seen one pine tree since we left Soviet Union.

My wife, my sweet Bella Bellinka, is asleep. Only her back rising up and down says she is breathing and still alive. She sleeps flat on her face. This is to keep her hairstyle from mussing.

When we became émigrés, Bellinka's hair became art. Every Thursday afternoon now she returns home from a person named Roger, her head balancing a high, bright, curled, crisp tower of hair. It comes before me, her husband, and makes her wary on performing wifely duty. She is afraid I will damage her curls, despite my promises.

Real reason is not her hair, of course. I see her eyes glimmer at night while watching couples in love wrestle on television. Simple fact is I am ugly and I am old. Not age old, but life old. I am fifty-four, Soviet, bald, and nearly blind. All I want in life are cactuses for my terrace, and a son.

I stand ogling my neighbor long after my interest goes. My leg gets a cramp. I love my Bella Bellinka. I ogle only to make Bella jealous a little. I believe things might improve between us if, first thing she opens her light-gray eyes, she is faced with my interest in another woman.

Instead Bellinka is irritated. "Yuz, shame on you! People call police for this here!" She whips curtains closed, swats my arm. Her low stern voice recalls when she used to reprimand a dog we had in Moscow. This old dog was incontinent and loved our only rug.

"She is there in plain sight!" I say. "I am still a man. Don't dish me over the coals. Please Bella Bellinka, I beg of you!"

"Oh, Yuz." She goes into bathroom.

Outside, palm trees lining our street are shaken awake by burst of wind. It starts already. It is said this wind, known as Santa Ana, makes people crazy. The fronds creak and groan in unison. I have never heard a tidal wave, but this is what I imagine it sounds like.

Bella Semyonovna and I argue violently about silly things. Where to buy ice cubes trays. What is cable TV and do we need it. Which bus goes where. How to keep our apartment cooler. We avoid arguing about things upon which we truly disagree. We are afraid. Now we are in America, there is no reason for our marriage.

In Soviet Union we married for reasons of housing. Bella I met only once. She was cousin of fellow worker at laboratory, willing to do anything for permanent residency permit in Moscow. She was too talkative, overweight, provincial. As a man mostly from Moscow, my advantage was clear. Somehow I was taller than her then.

She always carried around a *Vogue* magazine she got on black market. It got rained on, snowed on so often it disintegrated. Bella wept, as though she had lost her eyesight. I found her odd, but beautiful. And I was forty-eight years old, never in love, with a twelve-by-nine-foot apartment in central Moscow I inherited from my grandfather.

When we met on steps of Palace of Marriage for ceremony, Bella didn't recognize me. She passed right by and tapped on shoulder of a much taller, much younger man. Corrected, she blushed, strangled her bouquet in embarrassment. I perspired, over-forgave her. She asked how big was apartment again. Thirteen by ten feet, I said, increasing the measurements. I invented a large kitchen, in case seeing me in cruel gray daylight changed her mind.

Accounting entered our young relationship there and then. Yuz forgives; Bella is forgiven. Yuz has Moscow apartment; Bella has nothing. Bella wants to emigrate; Yuz loses good job in applying for visas. Yuz wants a child; Bella falls asleep instantly. Bella is forty. I know what is happening. She is waiting to shift blame from herself to biology.

Yuz loves Bella; Bella tolerates Yuz, remembering all she owes him.

Every person who tries to emigrate loses his job, first thing. I worked in special research laboratory as operator of machine that washed and sterilized laboratory instruments, petri dishes. This was special lab in dull green building, huge and unmarked, on Kropotkin Street. It was place for researching in-vitro fertilization.

My petri dishes grew humans. Or tried to. They were old dishes, warped a little. They appeared to seal properly, but actually allowed all kinds of things to grow inside. Humans never got so far. There had never been a baby from that place yet. Either egg and sperm never got along, or women who came for implantation had so many abortions that no embryo could get foothold. Crude jokes went around.

Once, at end of my shift, near my last days there, when all instruments and dishes were clean, slick and steaming, I found incubator where special petri dishes were kept. Light shining on them was yellow warm. Culture medium was scab color, dishes looked innocent, empty. But I knew, I knew. Here were racks and racks of potential Soviet citizens. Dumb cells being coaxed along for eventual implantation, birth, then what? Thirty years washing laboratory instruments for lucky ones.

I went home right away. Bella was packing her china, her most beloved thing. She thought she could take it with her, even though I tried to persuade her we would never be able to get it out.

I said, "If we ever get to America we must have child." Bellinka, so anxious to emigrate, so afraid it would not happen if she made trouble, promised me yes. She says now she only said she'd think about it.

But that cold dull day is scar on memory. The rusty red disks glowing under their artificial sun, the humble worried face of my wife, her nod. A cracked teacup in her hand. A baby, yes. Frank Bogoga. Don Bogoga. Brooke Bogoga.

I cook breakfast while Bella prepares to go to work. She is TA, teaching assistant of beginning Russian at university. I do not know what this is, but I know she brings home paycheck and takes classes in Advanced Russian Syntax. Neither of us have ever heard of syntax before this job. It sounds like something to do with space.

I drop icy-hard waffles in toaster. Eggo, they are called. Syrup in babushka-shaped bottle. Instant Tang. I also open package of Sno Balls, chocolate cake with pink coconut-flavored foam outside. It seems to me all American food looks like it could be sold in toy stores.

I said this once to Claire Davis, secretary at Department of Slavic Languages, where Bella teaches. Her laugh was like bullets, Ha! Ha! Ha! She is making fun, or what? No, she said I was a stitch.

What it is, a stitch? Why is food funny? I never know if America is serious or joking.

Outside our kitchen window is something I will never understand. A billboard higher and bigger than any I ever see. Is several blocks away, looming over all smaller buildings between us. On it is redheaded girl in sunglasses standing, one hip jutted out. She has tight, fierce green pants, breasts the size of hot-air balloons floating up under black T-shirt. This is all, except TEENA spelled in big glittery plates that reflect sunlight. In middle of night I come into kitchen for water, and she is there. Lights from bottom of billboard shine on her all twenty-four hours. Through our thin curtains her legs look like two green smokestacks colliding. Who she is? Does she advertise a movie, beer, car telephones?

Bella scuttles in, sandals in hand. "What does Teena advertise?" I ask.

On television, my regular morning program is interrupted to tell what areas of Los Angeles are in danger of brush fires. People are told to water down their roofs. This is like watering down drinks? So much is confusing. Waffles are burnt around edges, still frozen in center. Morning program resumes. A dog psychologist is being interviewed. He says the dog has really got to want to change.

Bella laughs. "Teena is fantastic."

"What it is for, Teena? She actress?" I make a butter sandwich of my Eggos. I like my Tang straight from jar with no water added.

"Who knows. Not so much butter, Yuz. Bad for heart."

"How can she be fantastic if you do not know what she is? Is wasteful, all that paint. She is fantastic and no one knows what she is for? Is ridiculous."

"No," says Bella. "You are ridiculous. She is pretty, that's all. Please just to go with it, okay?"

"Go with it? What is that? With what am I supposed to go? You copy Americans like a big talking Russian bird."

"You are hopeless," she says. "I am not big." She pushes her waffle aside, begins applying her makeup. She does this at breakfast table so to have benefit of natural daylight. All her ladies' fashion magazines say makeup is best applied this way, in this light, and so she does. She is slave of those magazines.

I stare at her. To her I am like a television channel changed. She is not angry, or even flustered. She sips coffee from one of her china cups. She dragged them through after all. They are cheap, homely white. When she opened carton, second day we arrived, all handles were broken off. Broken and stolen, for they were nowhere.

Bella Bellinka is like these cups. An empty one. Broken but still able to float. Floating upon America. She is tiny and fragile, the ocean immense, but she soars in the sunshine, up one tall wave, down another, never sinking. She goes with it. I know this expression. Never would I use it. We are not so American as she likes to imagine.

"Perhaps emigration was not right," I say. "Is so difficult in Los Angeles. So difficult for Yuz."

"Yuzushka, please. You have job. We both do. Soon we will have car. Is heat making you upset? I will make you more Eggos. But no butter! Promise Bella." She hurries around kitchen. She pours me more coffee, even though I have some.

My job is as photocopier. Los Angeles motto is no place you can walk to is worth working at, but is not true. Captain Copy is eleven blocks from our apartment. Is air-conditioned, decorated with pink fishing nets hung up, painted starfish with glitter. Free coffee on all day.

Today, as I walk, a red sun sits on my bald head. The sky is thick and yellow. I have my hat, but I will not wear it in public. Is a white sailor hat, with *Yooz Andreyevich* sewn in blue thread. Except owner, everyone at Captain Copy must wear these hats. The first one they gave me said *Use*. I made them do over. New one said Yooz, a clown name, even worse.

Bogogas have dignity, I insisted. My name is Yuz. My heart slugged against my chest. They refused to try again. I forced them to add *Andreyevich*. They called me a stupid old pinko. What is that, a fish? Wind rolls an empty garbage can down middle of street against traffic. Cars swerve to miss it, but no one gets out to turn it right. My lips, they are so chapped.

I have one friend in Los Angeles. Pak, a square, wavy-haired Korean. He works at Captain Copy seven years. He has had three hats, all of them misspelled *Pack*. Most of our business is screenplays for movies. Fast rich people in shorts come in, jiggle their legs, their keys, while waiting.

When no one is there, we photocopy body parts. We read screenplays. Pak is teaching himself English this way. "*Cut to*—Lunch" he says when he goes out at noon. "*Cut to*—The Next Day," he says every morning.

We tell each other everything, but as with Americans, I don't understand all. Pak has problems with his car, he stole it or had it stolen. There is some tube situation also. Either inside his wife or the television set.

Today boss is on vacation in Mexico, someplace that starts with X. I sit by coffeemaker and eat spoonfuls of coffee whitener. I have somehow gotten on subject of cactus. Pak photocopies without putting down lid. Every few seconds a white flash bleaches his sallow face. I think he may go blind. I tell him. He nods and grins.

"I want garden, Pak. Is only matter of going, putting down two eighty-nine, taking my bunny ears, my baby toes or aloe, and starting, right? But what if I spend every moneys on powder puffs and silk pincushions, only to discover I want organ pipes and prickly pears? Too much choice. My wife says is typical Soviet fear."

"CAMERA ZOOMS IN ON YUZ," says Pak. "He is a burned-out shell of a man, but has quite a way with the ladies. Think young Burt Reynolds."

I make Pak sit down. I think perhaps hot Los Angeles wind dries his brain up.

Evening comes. Wind stays. Bella Semyonovna and I ride bus to Department of Slavic Languages for special get-together party. Invitation says we are gathering to welcome all new faculty and students. It takes forty-five minutes to go twelve miles from our apartment to university. Smells of urine, melting plastic bus seats. Bella complains her thighs are sticking. She has a new dress, new silver high-heel shoes.

We pass bank sign saying 6:30, temperature 101. A man at front of bus steals wallet from blind woman's purse. Her eye dog licks his shoe. People are desperate. Sky is blotted with sulfurous smoke. Fires wink in the hills. Like Russian steppes, Los Angeles sometimes seems emptied of weather. All clouds, rains, frosts, and fogs are scooped out, leaving only this monotonous wind. I say this to Bella. She shrugs: Is better than freezing rain. She is reading one of her magazines. "Make Your Lovemaking Aerobically Efficient!" A picture shows two tan people in bed wearing sweatbands and stopwatches.

"Huh," I say. "Why you reading that?"

She shuts magazine, pretends she hasn't heard.

Slavic Department is small and crowded. I drink four or five vodkas just so I can speak. I am shy. There are mostly professors, a few students. They huddle in circles that keep breaking apart and reforming, the way low-level life-forms reproduce. They sweat, swab their suntan faces with their hands.

Bella has propped me by food table, so she can mingle. I eat hard-boiled eggs, their yolks suffocated in black caviar. One after another I eat.

These people mean much to Bella. Her dimples work overtime. I hear her across room, through chinks in party noise, giggling and calling people Cookie. She never says Cookie at home.

Claire Davis, secretary to Slavic Department, arrives. She says she stopped for ice. She is tall. Her face is like loud music. Freckles, moles, wild eyebrows, green-gold-brown eyes, all going at once. She is not Slavic. She says when she took this job she thought Slavic was inventor of artificial heart. She only works here because she wants to write. She is illiterate, then, or what? She wants to write Russian?

She reaches over and pinches my side. "How's it going, Yuz?"

"Good, good," I mumble, my mouth full of egg.

She throws herself down in a folding chair. She wears shorts. I am drunk. Her knees stare up at me. Two doorknobs wrapped in silk, sprouting tender blond hair. "Yuz, now that is a cool tie. It looks like Las Vegas."

I look down. My tie is deep green, tiny saguaro cactus stitched on, stems bent like arms. I found it one day in Dumpster behind our apartment.

"I call it my cac-tie," I say.

"Ha! Ha! Ha!" Her bullet laugh. She loves this. She pulls over a tall, thin boy. His bony jaw chewing looks like machinery. He wears a T-shirt that says TOO MEAN TO MARRY. "Pencil Neck," she says to him, "check this out. It's his cac-tie."

"Boooooooo!" says Pencil Neck, but he laughs too.

People are interested. They stop by food table for crackers, more vodka, and stay to admire. They love that I found it among garbage. Jim Spaniel, assistant professor of Soviet Society and Culture, says he admires my audacity. I say I thought audacity was some medical procedure. I am going in for an audacity. People laugh. Claire refills my glass. You are *something*, she says.

Dr. Vera Omulchenko, department chairman, says, "Yuz, Bella never told us you were such a wit." She has arrived late, giving car trouble as reason. However, I notice she comes with Sergei Lublinsky, famous émigré writer. Lipstick is smeared around her lips, her eyes a little sleepy. Those lovers are around the age of Bella and me, I think.

"That tie is"—Sergei Lublinsky wags his finger at it, thinking—"camp."

"Camp? Only camp I know is where my father lived almost his whole life."

"Your father was in a concentration camp?" Claire's smile drops. She leans closer.

"Magnitogorsk. Labor camp. Fourteen years he lives on soup of rotten cabbage and garbage parts of animals. In deepest winter his shoes were scraps of rubber tied to his feet with wire. And what for? Stealing food ration card from dead neighbor's body."

"You guys," says Claire. "I can't imagine. I have a trauma if I can't get a new outfit." She looks at me, waiting.

I go on. Vodka is caring; it numbs you before reopening all those deep old wounds. I speak to Claire's knees.

"My father was a thermostat. This is real. Commissar had greenhouse. Is built of cypress, greenhouse. These days all are plastic, but in Soviet Union in 1937 they are cypress. Each morning my father gets up to fire boiler for heating, takes care of opening and closing of ventilation. Imagine, at labor camp, tiny greenhouse of birds-of-paradise, hibiscus, camellias. No prisoner was to know of greenhouse. Those who found out disappeared.

"Once, there is no electricity. Greenhouse goes dark, cold, snow blows inside vents, things freeze. But succulents grow, even there, even then. They huddle near ground, keep all nourishment inside. Surviving is what they do.

"My father was a cactus himself. White hair out like so, fierce expression and tough skin, tough short barrel man. Like me, you know, only better eyesight and not so bald. He manages to get his clothes patched with newspapers so he can read up on latest propaganda. He even gets friend on women's side of camp. He never sees her face but finds loose board at back of compound near latrines. He can reach through, feel her slim ankles, her breasts...." I have never talked so much to an American in my life. Waves of memories crash through my head.

"Hi, Cookies." Is Bella. She pats back of her hair. I realize no woman in this room has hair like hers. It looks like a dessert. "Has Yuz been folding your ear?"

Claire laughs. "Bending our ears. No, this stuff's great. I mean, awful. Incredible."

Bella looks at her a little icy. "Time to go," she says to me.

"A few minutes more," I say. "They like my tie."

"Yes? We purchase at downtown Bullock's department store. My friend Cricket, she is salesgirl of sportswear, instructed us. Is chic, you know."

Claire raises an eyebrow at Jim Spaniel. He has taken some notes on my story, on a tiny pad of paper with a tiny pencil. They begin to laugh. Is low, chugging laugh of people who are tired and hot. I join in. Laughter feeds laughter. We cannot stop.

Bella folds her arms, grows furious. "Yuz Andreyevich, you are laughing at me?"

"We are," I say.

I go home alone.

Claire gives me ride. Wide black streets are empty. The night smells charred. Another bank sign. Time 11:45, temperature still 101. I ask how can it be? Sign must be broken. Claire says she heard it was going to get hotter. She drifts from lane to lane. Driving by Braille, she calls it. Braille part is when she bumps over reflective lane markers. Tonight she's had six vodkas and a peach. She says she's on a diet.

When we cross Wilshire Boulevard she says, "Just think, if you took this street all the way to the end you'd hit the ocean, then Japan, then Russia."

"My thinking is not so big," I say. "That is Bella's way of thinking. She loves looking out of airplane windows."

"Oh, yeah," says Claire. "You worked in a laboratory or something."

I told her how it was. How we failed at in-vitro. "Just like you put first man on moon," I say.

"*Us?* You mean Americans? Now you're us too."

"Is impossible," I say. I smile anyway.

Claire's car is air-conditioned. I lean my head against window. I have never driven alone in a car with an American. A fire truck speeds past, lights whirling but no siren. She tells me about woman she read about who was denied artificial insemination because she wanted a baby on her own. She hated men but loved babies. Claire says this woman used turkey baster. She got some guy who was willing, then impregnates herself. And it worked. Could I believe it?

"Sure," I say. "They have dog psychologists here." I roll down my window. Claire is too young, too foreign. Breathing, even in her air-conditioning, is like inhaling gauze.

We stop in front of my apartment building. I get out. "*Spasiba,* Claire. You are good girl. Say, I mean to ask. Who is this Teena?" I point to billboard. Giantess Teena leers down at us from nighttime sky. Her lips are pink and full. Merciless.

Claire doesn't even need to look. "Nobody. That's her thing."

"She is an actress, singer?"

"She's on billboards. It's a gimmick. You know what a gimmick is? She doesn't do anything. She's a personality."

"She is famous? For doing nothing?"

"Sort of. Yeah, I guess."

I know what is turkey baster. I know because Bella Bellinka went to garage sale down our street and bought an entire drawer of kitchen instruments for fifty cents. We have this drawer sitting on our kitchen counter. At bottom of it, under bottle openers, corkscrews, spatulas, and many other mysterious things, is decal of person named Barney Rubble. Bellinka and I planned to use turkey baster for our first Thanksgiving. But I will use it now. Robert Bogoga. Madonna Bogoga. Sly Bogoga. Garage sale was being given by a woman who was going to prison.

I fill turkey baster while leaning against kitchen counter.

I am drunk, sure, but what is that? I was forty-eight when I met Bella, and am a drinker since age thirteen. I am saying I have performed this very thing while drunk for many cold decades. I still have on my tie. My mind provides its old slide show. With one hand I push open kitchen curtain. Teena Teeninka, American saint of nobody and nothing, spurs me on.

The lights of Los Angeles reflect off its smoky, smoggy ceiling, giving our bedroom a murky glow. Bella is asleep on her back, her arms and legs tossed away from her. Heat has driven her to this. Curtains and windows are open. I sit on bed edge. The bulb of turkey baster is greasy. Our neighbor is having a party. Music, a fan whirring. Someone yells *Addis Ababa!* A few people applaud. Clark Kent Bogoga. James Bond Bogoga. I know I cannot stop. To stop is to think. Outside, wind has died, but still shrieks around inside my head.

I move Bella's leg.

Suddenly her eyes click open. "Yuz?"

I throw myself on her. She doesn't yell. She growls Russian curses. She smells of toothpaste, vodka, cheese. She grabs my ears. Her nightgown slides up. "How many eyes does an earthworm have?" says someone across the way.

My hands land on her hairdo. She pulls on my ears, kicks at my thighs.

"You filthy Cossack!" she screams. She hates me. She says I am stupid old man. I rub her curls flat. This is what I've wanted, I know it now, yes! They are stiff. They crackle at my touch.

Finally, I stop. I stand. My turkey baster and future prog-
eny have rolled behind bed, to join their fate with lint and
lost shoes.

"I am sorry," I say. Sweat blinds me. My shins ache.

"You are disgusting drunken stupid man," she says. She
rubs her neck. "Claire is not impressed with you; she feels
sorry for you. She listens to your stupid stories from pity."

"Bellinka, I am sorry."

"You are joke to them, those Americans."

"We both are," I say.

She is so stunned to hear this she nods. "Yes, but at least
I know this! I have my feelers open. I am no stupid."

"Is so hot," I say.

And quiet, suddenly. Like many people holding their
breath. I look out bedroom window. Our neighbor, standing
on her terrace, among her jasmine and dwarf orange trees,
watches. She is with a man and another couple. They hold
wine goblets, bob their heads around to see. Behind them, in
living room, colorful board game is laid out on coffee table.
I try to imagine my wife with these tall, brown fun people; a
thick, simple cactus lost among lilies.

"What you are looking at!" Bella moves behind me,
crosses her arms over her chest.

One of the men asks us if everything is all right.

"They're Russian," my neighbor says.

"Oh. I didn't know."

"What, that explains it?" Bellinka says to him. "As
though we are only people to do crazy things?"

"Los Angeles is to blame," I say.

From habit Bella pats her hair, even though it stands up
like weeds.

I close the curtains.

My Father's Chinese Wives

Sandra Tsing Loh

MY FATHER DOESN'T WANT TO ALARM US. But then again, it would not be fair to hide anything either. The fact is, at seventy, he is going to try and get married again. This time to a Chinese wife. He thinks this would be more suitable than to someone American, given his advanced age.

He has written his family in Shanghai, and is awaiting response. He is hoping to be married within six months.

Let us unpeel this news one layer at a time.

Question: At this point, is my father even what one would consider marriageable?

At age seventy, my father—a retired Chinese aerospace engineer—is starting to look more and more like somebody's gardener. His feet shuffle along the patio in their broken sandals. He stoops to pull out one or two stray weeds, coughing phlegmatically. He wears a hideous old V-neck tennis sweater. Later, he sits in a rattan chair and eats leathery green vegetables in brown sauce, his old eyes slitted wearily.

He is the sort of person one would refer to as "Old Dragon Whiskers." And not just because it is a picturesque Oriental way of speaking.

"I am old now," he started saying, about ten years after my mother had died of cancer. "I'm just your crazy old Chinese father." He would rock backwards in his chair and sigh. "I am an old, old man…"

At times he almost seems to be over-acting this lizardly old part. He milks it. After all, he still does the same vigorous exercise regime—forty-five minutes of pull-ups, something that looks like the twist and much bellowing—he did ten years ago. This always performed on the most public beaches possible, in his favorite Speedo—one he found in a dumpster.

"Crazy old Chinese father" is, in truth, a code word, a rationalization for the fact that my father has always had a problem…spending money. Why buy a briefcase to carry to work, when an empty Frosted Flakes Cereal box will do? Papers slip down neatly inside, and pens can be clipped conveniently on either side.

Why buy Bounty Paper Towels when, at work, he can just walk down the hall to the washroom, open the dispenser, and lift out a stack? They're free—he can bring home as many as we want!

If you've worn the same sweater for so many years that the elbows wear out, turn it around! Get another decade out of it! Which is why to this day, my father wears only crew neck, not V-neck sweaters…

Why drive the car to work when you can take the so-convenient RTD bus? More time to read interesting scientific papers…and here they are, in my empty Frosted Flakes Box!

"Terrific!" is my older sister Kaitlin's response when I phone her with the news. Bear in mind that Kaitlin has not seen my father since the mid-'80s, preferring to nurse her bad memories of him independently, via a therapist. She allows herself a laugh, laying aside her customary dull hostility for a moment of more jocular hostility. "So who does he think would want to marry *him?*"

"Someone Chinese," I answer.

"Oh good!" she exclaims. "That narrows down the field...to what? Half a billion? Nah, as always, he's doing this to punish us."

"Think about it," Kaitlin continues with her usual chilling logic. "He marries a German woman the first time around. It's a disaster. You and I represent that. Because he's passive aggressive and he's cheap. But no, to him, it's that rebellious Aryan strain that's the problem.

"You take an Asian immigrant just off the boat, on the other hand. This is a person who has just fled a Communist government and a horrible life working in a bicycle factory for ten cents a month and no public sanitation and repeated floggings every hour on the hour. After that, living with our father might seem like just another bizarre interlude. It could happen."

Kaitlin scores some compelling points, but nonetheless...

I'm bothered for a different reason...

Perhaps it is because in describing the potential new wife, he has used only that one adjective: *Chinese.* He has not said: "I'm looking for a smart wife," or even "a fat wife," he has picked "Chinese." It is meant to stand for so much.

Asian. Asian women. Asian *ladies.*

I think back to a college writing workshop I once attended. (No credit and perhaps that was appropriate.) It was long before my current "administrative assistant" job at Swanson Films. (Makers of the ten-minute instructional video "Laughterobics! Featuring Meredith Baxter Birney," among other fine titles.)

Anyway, the workshop contained thirteen hysterical women—and one Fred. Fred was a wealthy Caucasian sixty-something urologist; he was always serene and beautifully dressed and insistent upon holding the door open for me "because you're such a lovely lady." I always wore jeans and a USC sweatshirt, sometimes even sweatpants, so at first I did not know what he meant.

We women, on the other hand, were a wildly mixed group—writing anything from wintery Ann Beattie-esque snippets to sci-fi romance/porn novels ("She would be King Zenothar's concubine, whether she liked it or not"). We attacked each other's writing accordingly. People were bursting into tears every week, then making up by emotionally sharing stories about mutual eating disorders.

But there was one moment where all thirteen women were of like minds. It was that moment when Fred would enter the classroom, laden with xeroxes, blushing shyly as a new bride. We would all look at each other as if to say, "Oh my God, Fred has brought in work *again.*"

As though springing from a murky bottomless well, each week new chapters would appear from this semi-epistolary novel Fred was penning about an elderly doctor named Fred who goes on sabbatical for a year to Japan and there finds love with a twenty-three-year-old Japanese medical student named Aku who smells of cherry blossoms.

There were many awkward scenes in which Fred and Aku were exploring each other's bodies as they lay—as far as I could gather—upon the bare floor, only a *tatami* mat for comfort. (Fred would always italicize the Japanese words, as if to separate and somehow protect them from other, lesser words.) But it was all beautifully pure and unlike the urban squalor we find in America—the rock music, the drugs, the uncouth teenagers.

Anyway, I recall the one line that I have never since been able to blot from my mind. I cannot think of it without a bit of a shiver. Nor the way he read it, in that hoarse, tremulous voice…

"I put my hand in hers, and her little fingers opened like the petals of a moist flower."

———————

It is a month later and, as in a dream, I sit at the worn formica family dining table with my father, photos and letters spread before us.

Since my father has written to Shanghai, the mail has come pouring in. I have to face the fact that my father is, well, hot. "You see?" he says. "Seven women have written! Ha!" He beams, his gold molar glinting. He is drinking steaming green tea from a beaker, which he handles with a Beauty and the Beast potholder.

Remarkably, my father doesn't make the least effort to mask his delight, no matter how inappropriate. He is old now. *He can do whatever the hell he wants,* is how I now understand it. With a sigh, I turn to the photos. In spite of myself, I am wowed!

Tzau Pa, Ling Ling, Sui Pai, Chong Zhou... "28, administrative assistant," "47, owner of a seamstress business." "39, freelance beautician." The words jump off the pages, both in English and Chinese translations. These women are dynamos, achievers, with black curly hair, in turtlenecks, jauntily riding bicycles, seated squarely on cannons before military museums, standing proudly with three grown daughters.

One thing unites them: they're all ready to leap off the mainland at the drop of a hat.

And don't think their careers and hobbies are going to keep them from being terrific wives. Quite the opposite. Several already have excellent experience, including one who's been married twice already. The seamstress has sent him two shorts and several pairs of socks; there is much talk of seven-course meals and ironing and terrific expertise in gardening.

Super-achievement is a major theme that applies to all. And the biggest star of all is my father. He clears his throat and gleefully reads from a letter by one Liu Tzun:

> Dr. Chow, your family has told me of your great
> scientific genius and of your many awards. I respect

academic scholarship very highly, and would be honored to meet you on your next visit.

"You see?" my father chuckles. "They have a lot of respect for me in China. When I go there, they treat me like President Bush! Free meals, free drinks...I don't pay for anything!"

"He had his chance. He got married once, for twenty-five years. He was a terrible husband and a worse father."

Kaitlin is weighing in. All jokes are off. Her fury blazes away, further aggravated by the fact that she is going through a divorce and hates her $50,000 a year job. Her monthly Nordstrom bills are astronomical. MCI is positively crackling.

"He's a single man," I say. "Mum's been gone for twelve years now—"

"And now he gets a second try—just like that?" Kaitlin exclaims. "Clean slate? Start right over? Buy a wife? It makes me sick. He is totally unqualified to sustain a marriage. A family structure of any kind collapses around him. Do you even remember one happy Christmas?"

Twinkling lights and tinsel suddenly swirl before me and looking deeper, through green foliage, I see my mother looking beautiful and crisp in lipstick and pearls, her wavy auburn hair done... except for the fact that she is hysterical, and my father, his face a mask of disgust so extreme it is almost parodic, is holding his overpriced new V-neck tennis sweater from Saks out in front of him like it is a dead animal—

"I try to block it out," is what I say.

"Well I was six years older than you so I can't." Kaitlin's pain is raw. "Why does he deserve to be happy...now? He made Mama miserable in her lifetime—he was so cheap! I think she was almost glad to go as soon as she did! A $70 dress, leaving the heater on overnight, too much spent on a nice steak dinner—he could never let anything go! He could never just let it go! He just could... not... let...things...go!"

Meanwhile...

On its own gentle time clock, unsullied by the raging doubts of his two daughters...

My father's project bursts into flower.

And forty-seven-year-old Liu—the writer of the magic letter—is the lucky winner! Within three months, she is flown to Los Angeles. She and my father are married a week later.

I do not get to meet her right away, but my father fills me in on the stats. And I have to confess, I'm a little surprised at how modern she is, how urban. Liu is a divorceé with, well, with ambitions in the entertainment business. Although she speaks no English, she seems to be an expert on American culture. The fact that Los Angeles is near Hollywood has not escaped her. This is made clear to me one Sunday evening, three weeks later, via telephone.

"I know you have friends in the entertainment business," my father declares. He has never fully grasped the fact that I am a typist and that Swanson Films' clients include such Oscar contenders as Kraft Foods and Motorola.

"Aside from having knitted me a new sweater and playing the piano," my father continues, "you should know that Liu is an excellent singer—" Turning away from the phone, he and his new wife exchange a series of staccato reports in Mandarin, which mean nothing to me.

"I'm sure that Liu is quite accomplished," I reply, "it's just that—"

"Oh... she's terr-ific!" my father exclaims, shocked that I may be calling Liu's musical talent into question. "You want to hear her sing? Here, here, I will put her on the phone right now..."

Creeping into my father's voice is a tremulous note that is sickeningly familiar. How many times had I heard it during my childhood as I was being pushed towards the piano, kicking and screaming? How many times—

But that was twenty years ago. I gulp terror back down. I live in my own apartment now, full of director's chairs, potted fici and Matisse posters. I will be fine. My father has moved on to a totally new pushee…

Who picks up the phone, sighs—then bursts out triumphantly:

"Nee-ee hoo-oo mau, tieh-hen see bau-hau jioo…!"

I have left you and taken the Toyota, Dr. Chow—
so there!

Five weeks later, Liu just packs up her suitcase, makes some sandwiches, and takes off in the family Toyota. She leaves her note on the same formica table at which she'd first won his heart.

My father is in shock. Then again, he is philosophical.

"Liu—she had a lot of problems. She said she had no one to talk to. There were no other Chinese people in Tarzana. She wanted me to give her gifts. She was bored. You know I don't like to go out at night. But I tell her, 'Go! See your friends in Chinatown.' But Liu does not want to take the bus. She wants to drive! But you know me, your cheap father. I don't want to pay her insurance. That Liu—she was a very bad driver—"

"Ha!" is Kaitlin's only comment.

Summer turns to fall in Southern California, causing the palm trees to sway a bit. The divorce is soon final, Liu's settlement including $10,000, the microwave and the Toyota.

Never one to dwell, my father has picked a new bride: Zhou Ping, thirty-seven, home-maker from Qang-Zhou province. I groan.

"But no... Zhou Ping is very good," my father insists. He has had several phone conversations with her. "And she comes very highly recommended, not, I have to say, like Liu. Liu was bad, that one. Zhou Ping is sensible and hardworking. She has had a tough life. Boy! She worked in a coal mine in Manchuria until she was twenty-five. The winters there were very, very bitter! She had to make her own shoes and clothing. Then she worked on a farming collective, where she raised cattle and grew many different kinds of crops—by herself!"

"I'm sure she's going to fit in really well in Los Angeles," I say.

Zhou Ping is indeed a different sort. The news, to my astonishment, comes from Kaitlin. "I received..." her voice trails off, the very words seeming to elude her. "A *birthday card.* From Papa... and *Zhou Ping.*"

My sister continues in a kind of trance of matter-of-factness, as if describing some curious archaeological artifact. "Let's see, on the front is a picture with flowers on it. It's from Hallmark. Inside is gold lettering, cursive, that says, 'Happy Birthday!' At the bottom, in red pen, it says...'Love, Zhou Ping and *your Dad.*'"

"Your 'Dad'?"

"I think Zhou Ping put him up to this. The envelope is not addressed in his handwriting. Nonetheless..." Kaitlin thinks it over, concurs with herself. "Yes. Yes. I believe this is the first birthday card I've ever received from him in my life. The first. It's totally bizarre."

A week later, Kaitlin receives birthday gifts in the mail: a sweater hand-knit by Zhou Ping, and a box of "mooncakes." She is flipping out. "Oh no," she worries, "Now I really have to call and thank her. I mean, the poor woman probably has no friends in America. Who knows what he's having her do? We may be her only link to society!"

Kaitlin finally does call, managing to catch Zhou Ping when my father is on the beach doing his exercises (which he always does at eleven and at three). Although Zhou Ping's English is very broken, she somehow convinces Kaitlin to fly down for a visit.

It will be Kaitlin's first trip home since our mother's passing. And my first meeting of either of my step-mothers.

I pull up the familiar driveway in my Geo. Neither Kaitlin nor I say anything. We peer out the windows.

The yard doesn't look too bad. There are new sprinklers, and a kind of irrigation system made by a network of ingenuously placed rain gutters. Soil has been turned, and thoughtfully. Cypresses have been trimmed. Enormous bundles of weeds flank the driveway, as if for some momentous occasion.

We ring the doorbell. Neither of us has had keys to the house in years.

The door opens. A short, somewhat plump Chinese woman, in round glasses and a perfect bowl haircut, beams at us. She is wearing a bright yellow "I hate housework!" apron that my mother was once given as a gag gift—and I think never wore.

"Kat-lin! Jen-na!" she exclaims in what seems like authentic joy, embracing us. She is laughing and almost crying with emotion.

In spite of myself, giggles begin to well up from inside me as if from a spring. I can't help it: I feel warm and euphoric. Authentic joy is contagious. Who cares who this woman is: no one has been this happy to see me in ages.

"Wel-come home," Zhou Ping says, with careful empha-sis. She turns to Kaitlin, a shadow falling over her face. "I am glad you finally come home to see your Daddy," she says in a low, sorrowful voice. She looks over her shoulder. "He old now."

Then, as if exhausted by that effort, Zhou Ping collapses into giggles. I sneak a glance over at Kaitlin, whose expres-sion seems to be straining somewhere between joy and nau-sea. Pleasantries lunge out of my mouth: "It's nice to finally meet you!" "How do you like America?" "I've heard so much about your cooking!"

My father materializes behind a potted plant. He is wearing a new sweater and oddly formal dress pants. His gaze hovers somewhere near the floor.

"Hul-lo," he declares, attempting a smile. "Long time no see!" he exclaims, not making eye contact, but in Kaitlin's general direction.

"Yes!" Kaitlin exclaims back, defiant, a kind of winged Amazon in perfect beige Anne Klein II leisurewear. "It cer-tainly is!"

My father stands stiffly.

Kaitlin blazes.

"It's good to see you!" he finally concludes, as though this were something he learned in English class.

Feeling, perhaps, that we should all leave well enough alone, the Chow family, such as we are, moves on through the house. It is ablaze with color—the sort of eye-popping combinations one associates with Thai restaurants and Hindu shrines. There are big purple couches, peach rugs, a shiny brass trellis and creeping charlies everywhere.

All this redecorating came at no great expense, though. "See this rug? my father says proudly, while Zhou Ping gig-gles. "She found it in a dumpster. They were going to throw it away!" "Throw it away!" she exclaims. "See? It very nice."

Over their heads, Kaitlin silently mouths one word to me: "Help."

Beyond, the formica dining room table is set. Oddly. There are little rice bowls, chopsticks, and a sheet of plain white paper at each place setting. It is good to know some definite event has been planned. Kaitlin, my father and I are so unaccustomed to being in a room together that any kind of definite agenda—aka: "We'll eat dinner, and then we'll leave"—is comforting.

My father goes off to put some music on his new CD player. "That bad Liu made me buy it!" he explains. "But it's nice." Zhou Ping bustles into the kitchen. "Dinner ready—in five minute!" she declares.

Kaitlin waits a beat, then pulls me aside into the bathroom and slams the door.

"This is so weird!" she hisses.

We have not stood together in this bathroom for some fifteen years. It seems different. I notice that the wallpaper is faded, the towels are new—but no, it's something else. On one wall is my mother's framed reproduction of the brown Da Vinci etching called "Praying Hands" which she had always kept in her sewing room. Right next to it, in shocking juxtaposition, is a green, red, blue, and yellow "Bank of Canton" calendar from which a zaftig Asian female chortles.

"I can't go through with this!" Kaitlin continues in stage whisper. "It's too weird! There are so many memories here, and not good ones!"

And like debris from a hurricane, the words tumble out:

"I go by the kitchen and all I can see is me standing before the oven clock at age five with tears in my eyes. He is yelling: 'What time is it? The little hand is most of the way to four and the big hand is on the eight! It was 3:18 twenty-two minutes ago—so what time is it now? What's eighteen plus twenty-two? Come on—you can do it in your head! Come on! Come on!'

"I go by the dining room and I see him hurling my Nancy Drew books across the floor. They slam against the wall and I huddle against Mum, screaming. 'Why do you waste your time on this when your algebra homework isn't finished? You… good for nothing! You're nothing, nothing—you'll never amount to anything!'

"I go by the bedroom—"

"Please—" I have this sickening feeling like I'm going to cry, that I'm just going to lose it. I want to just sit down in the middle of the floor and roll myself into a ball. But I can't. Kaitlin's rage is like something uncontainable, a dreadful natural force, and I am the gatekeeper. I feel if I open the door, it will rush out and destroy the house and everyone in it. "Please," is what I end up whispering. "Please. Let's just eat. We'll be done in a hour. Then we can go home. I promise. You won't have to do this again for another ten years—or maybe ever."

At dinner, endless plates of food twirl their way out of the kitchen, Zhou Ping practically dancing underneath. Spinach, teriyaki-ish chicken, shrimp, some kind of egg thing with peas, dumplings packed with little pillows of pork.

And amazingly, there is no want of conversational material. Photos from Shanghai are being pulled out of envelopes and passed around, of her family, his family...

I do recognize three or four Chinese relatives—a cousin, an aunt, a grand-uncle? Their names are impossible for me to remember. We had met them in China during our last trip as a family. I was fifteen; it was right before our mother started to get sick.

Shanghai is a distant, confused memory for me, of ringing bicycle bells and laundry lines hanging from buildings. What I do remember is how curious my father's family had seemed about Kaitlin and me, his odd American experiment, oohing over our height and touching our auburn hair. There were many smiles but no intelligible conversation, at least to our ears. We probably won't see any of these people again before we die.

Zhou Ping, though, is determined to push through, to forge a bridge between us. She plunges ahead with her bad English, my father almost absent-mindedly correcting her.

Their lives are abuzz with activity. Zhou Ping is taking piano lessons at the community college. My father is learning Italian and French off the Learning Channel—he sets his alarm for four in the morning. "So early!" Zhou Ping hoots. They listen to Karl Haas' "Listening to Good Music" on the classical station at ten. "Mot-sart—he very nice!" They have joined the Bahais, a local quasi-religious group. "I must cook food all the time!" My father suddenly puts his spoon down. He is chewing slowly, a frown growing.

"This meat..." he shakes his head, "is very greasy."

He turns to Zhou Ping and the lines at both sides of his mouth deepen. His eyes cloud. He says something to her in Chinese, with a certain sharp cadence that makes my spine stiffen...

Zhou Ping's face goes blank for a moment. Her eyes grow big. My stomach turns to ice.

How will she respond? By throwing her napkin down, bursting into tears, running from the room? Will she knock the table over, plates sliding after each other, sauces spilling, crockery breaking? Will we hear the car engine turn over as she drives off into the night, to leave us frightened and panicked?

It is none of these things.

Zhou Ping's head tilts back, her eyes crinkle...

And laughter pours out of her, peal after peal after peal. It is a big laugh, an enormous laugh, the laugh of a woman who has birthed calves and hoed crops and seen harsh winters decimate countrysides. Pointing to our father, Zhou Ping turns to us with large glittering eyes and says words which sound incredible to our ears:

"Your Papa—he so funny!"

My jaw drops. No one has ever laughed out loud at this table, ever. We laughed behind closed doors, in our bedrooms, in the bathroom, never before my father. We laughed sometimes with my mother, on those glorious days when he would be off on a trip—

But Kaitlin is not laughing. She is trembling; her face is turning red.

"Why were you always so angry?" Kaitlin cries out in a strangled voice. It is the question she has waited thirty years to ask. "Why were you so angry?"

There is a shocked silence. My father looks weary and embarrassed. He smiles wanly and shrugs his thin shoulders.

"No really." Kaitlin insists. "All those years. With Mama. Why?"

"I don't know," my father murmurs. "People get angry."

And I know, in that moment, that he doesn't have an answer. He literally doesn't. It's as if anger was this chemical which reacted on him for twenty years. Who knows why, but like some kind of spirit, it has left him now. The rage is spent. He is old now. He is old.

Dusk has fallen, and long shadows fall across the worn parquet floor of the dining room. After a moment of silence, my father asks Zhou Ping to sing a song. The hausfrau from Qang Zhou opens her mouth and with an odd dignity, sings simply and slowly. My father translates.

> From the four corners of the earth
> My lover comes to me
> Playing the lute
> Like the wind over the water

He recites the words without embarrassment, almost without emotion. And why shouldn't he? The song has nothing to do with him personally: it is from some old Chinese fable. It has to do with missing someone, something, that perhaps one can't even define any more.

As Zhou Ping sings, everyone longs for home. But what home? Zhou Ping—for her bitter winters? My father—for the Shanghai he left forty years ago? Kaitlin and I? We are even sitting in our home, and we long for it.

Crazy Life

Lou Mathews

CHUEY CALLED ME FROM THE JAIL. He said it was all a big mistake. I said, Sure Chuey, like always, *que no?* What is it this time, weed or wine? He said it was something different this time. I said, You mean like reds, angel dust, what? Chuey says, No Dulcie, something worse.

I said, So? Why call me? Why don't you call that Brenda who was so nice to you at the party. He said Dulcie. Listen. It's a lot worse. I got to get a lawyer. Then he like started to cry or something. Not crying—Chuey wouldn't cry—but it was like he had a hard time breathing, like he was scared. I couldn't believe it. I didn't do it, Dulcie, he told me. I didn't do nothing. I was just in the car.

I got scared then. Chuey, I said, Can anybody hear you? He said there was a *chota*—a cop—around and some dude from the DA's office, but not close. I told him, Shut up Chuey. Just shut up. Don't say nothing to nobody. I'll come down. Chuey said, I don't know if they'll let you see me.

They'll let me, I said, Hang on.

I skipped school, fifth and sixth periods, just gym and home wreck, and hitchhiked up to Highland Park. I been there before, the Highland Park cop shop. Chuey's been busted there three or four times. Nothing bad, just drunk and one time a joint in the car.

This time it looked bad. They had a bunch of reporters there. This TV chick was on the steps when I come up, standing in front of the bright lights saying about the police capturing these guys. She kept saying the same words, Drive-by murders. Drive-by murders. There was these two kids, brothers, and one was dead and the other was critical.

I walked up the steps and all these people started yelling. This one guy tells me, You can't come up here while we're shooting. I told him, You don't own the steps. The TV lights go out and the chick with the microphone says, Fuck. Then she turns around to me, real sarcastic and says, Thanks a lot honey. I told her, *Chinga tu madre*, Bitch, I got rights too. My boyfriend's in there. I got more business here than you. She gave me the big eyes and went to complain.

I went on inside, up to the desk and said I'm here to see Chuey Medina. Who? he says and he looks at the list, We got a Jesus Medina. That's Chuey, I tell him.

He looks at me, up and down, this fat Paddy with the typical little cop moustache. What's your name, he says. Dulcie Medina, I tell him. It's not, but if they don't think we're related they won't let me see Chuey. Dulcie? he says, does that mean Sugar? Sweet, I tell him it means sweet.

You related? he says. What the hell, I'm thinking, God can't get me till I get outside. I tell him, I'm his wife.

Well, sweetheart, he says, nobody gets to see Jesus Medina until he's been booked. He says it Jeezus, not Hayzhoos the way it's supposed to be pronounced, like he's making a big point.

He's *been* booked, I say. He called me. They wouldn't have let him call me if he hadn't been booked already. The cop looks real snotty at me but he knows I'm right. Just a minute, he says. He gets on the phone. When he gets off he says, You'll have to wait. You can wait over there.

How long? I say. He gets snotty again, I don't know, sweetheart. They'll call me.

Cops, when they don't know what to do, they know to make you wait. I hung out, smoking, for awhile. Outside on the steps, the lights are on and that same blonde TV bitch is holding a microphone up to a guy in a suit; he's banging his briefcase against his knee while he talks. I come out the door as the guy is saying about We have to send a message to gang members that we will no longer tolerate—blah, blah, blah, like that—and then all this stuff about the Community.

Hey, I tell him, are you the DA? They won't let me see my husband, Chuey Medina. He turns around. The blondie is mouthing at me GO AWAY. I tell the DA guy, They won't let him talk to a lawyer. Isn't he entitled to legal representation? Those are the magic words. He grabs me by the arm, Mrs. Medina, he says, let's talk inside. The blondie jerks a thumb across her throat and the lights go out. She looks at me and thinks of something. Keep rolling, she says, and the lights go on again. Mrs. Medina, she says, Mrs. Medina. Could we talk with you a moment? The DA still has hold of my arm and he pulls me through the door. She gives him a nasty look and then turns around to the lights again, I can hear her as we're going through the door.

In a dramatic development, she says, here at the Highland Park Police Station, the wife of alleged drive-by murderer Jesús Chuey-Medina has accused the district attorney's office....The DA says, Goddammit. I don't hear what she says after that, my legs get like water and he has to help me over to the bench. Chuey didn't kill nobody, I tell him, he wouldn't. He looks at me funny and I remember I'm supposed to already know everything. I straighten up and tell him, Chuey wants a lawyer.

That's simply not a problem, Mrs. Medina, he tells me, an attorney will be provided. I *know* Mr. Medina has been offered an attorney.

No, I say, he wanted a certain one. He told me on the phone, but your *chingadera* phone is such junk that I couldn't hear the name. I have to talk to him.

He gives me another funny look and goes over to the guy at the desk. Look, he tells the cop, I don't know what's going on here, but I don't want *any* procedural fuckups on this one.

The cop says, Big case huh? and the DA tells him, This is the whole enchilada, Charlie. Where are you holding Medina?

Second floor tank.

Okay, he says, We'll use the conference room there. Call ahead. The cop looks at me and tells the DA, We'll need a matron.

I know what that means. One time before, when I went to see my brother Carlos in jail, they gave me a strip search. It was some ugly shit. They put their fingers everywhere, and I mean everywhere, and the lady who did it, she got off on it. You could tell. My ass was sore for a week. I swore to God then that I'd never let anybody do that to me again.

Bullshit, I yell. No strip search. The DA guy whirls around. The cop says, If it's a face-to-face meeting with a prisoner, the Captain says skin search. That's the way we play it.

The DA tells him, I'll take responsibility on this one. We'll do a pat search and I'll be with her every step after that. I'm going to walk this one through. He holds the cop on the arm, We got cameras out there Charlie, he says.

The matron is waiting for me in this little room. Undo your blouse, is the first thing she tells me. I already told them, I say, I ain't going to strip. Just the top two buttons, she says, visual inspection, honey. I have to make sure your bra's not loaded.

I undo the buttons and hold the blouse open. Just some kleenex, I tell her. She checks me out and then pats me down. Then she starts poking in my hair. They always do that. Some *pachuca* thirty years ago supposedly had a razor blade in her beehive and they're still excited about it. They never do it to any Anglo chicks.

The DA guy meets me outside and we walk through the first floor jail. It's like walking through the worst party you ever been to in your life. All these guys checking me out.

Putting their hands through the bars and yelling. *Ola, Chica.*
Hey, *Chica*, over here, they keep saying, and worse stuff. This
one dude keeps making these really disgusting kissing nois-
es. Guys can be weird. I give the dude making the kissing
sounds the finger and make my walk all sexy on the way out,
shaking my ass. They all go wild. Serves them right.

Chuey is in this big cell, all by himself except for one
other guy. When I see who that is, I know why Chuey's in
trouble. Sleepy Chavez is sitting next to him. I don't know
why they call him Sleepy. He's wired most of the time. I
think he might have been a red freak once. Sleepy is one *vato
loco.* The craziest I know. Everything bad that happens on
42nd Avenue starts with Sleepy Chavez.

There's this guy that shines shoes outside Jesse's Barber
Shop. I thought he was retarded but it turns out he got in a
fight with Sleepy in like sixth grade and Sleepy kicked him
so hard in the *huevos* that the guy ain't been right since. And
what's really sick is that Sleepy *loves* getting his shoes
shined there.

Chuey doesn't look so good. He's got bruises on his
checks, a cut on his forehead and his hand's bandaged up.
He looks like what the 42nd Flats, that's his gang, call resisting arrest. He looks sick too, pale and his eyes are all red.
Sleepy sees me first. He's chewing on his fingers, looks up
and spits out a fingernail. Sleepy can't leave his fingers
alone. When he was little, his sister told me, his mom used
to put chili juice on them. He's always poking them in his
ears or picking his nose or something. You don't want to be
alone with him.

Chuey stands up while the cop is unlocking the door. He
just looks at me and his eyes are so sad it makes me feel sick.
He looks worse than when his father died or even when the
guys from White Fence burned his car and laughed at him.
Sleepy Chavez looks at me and chucks his head at Chuey.
Watch your mouth, Medina, he says.

They take us in this big room. The cop stands by the
door. The DA guy sits down at the end of this long table and

we go down to the other. Chuey reaches out and touches my face. Dulcie, he says, *Mi novia*. Chuey only calls me that when he's really drunk or sentimental, he never has asked me to marry him. No touching, the cop says. Keep your hands on the table. I figure Chuey needs cheering up so I slip off my shoe and slide my foot up on the inside of his leg and rub him under the table.

Aye, Chuey, I tell him, all happy, *que problemas* you have, Chuey. My toes are rubbing a certain place, but Chuey surprises me he doesn't even push back.

Dulcie, he says, They think I was the shooter.

Keep your voice down, I say, What did you tell them? *Exactamente.*

We didn't say nothing. We got to stick together like Sleepy says. They haven't got any witnesses.

Chuey, I say, one of those guys is still alive.

He sits up when I tell him that.

It doesn't matter, Chuey says, neither of them saw us. All the cops got is Sleepy's car. They ain't got the gun. Sleepy threw it out when they were chasing us. Chuey, I said, were you driving? He just looks at me for awhile and then he says, yeah. I ask, How come you were driving?

He had the shotgun, Chuey said, I had to drive.

I can tell when Chuey's lying, which is most of the time; I think he was telling the truth. Chuey, I said, you're crazy. They'll put you both away. You don't owe Sleepy nothing.

Chuey looks mean at me, his eyes get all skinny. It was my fault we got caught, he says. We should have got away. I hit another car and wrecked Sleepy's Mustang. We tried to hide and the cops found us. I owe Sleepy, so just shut up Dulcie.

It's hopeless to argue with Chuey when he gets like this. *Muy macho.* You can't talk to him about his friends, even the jerks. He won't believe me over them. Chuey says, I'm gonna need a good lawyer. Get me Nardoni.

Tony Nardoni is this big lawyer all the drug dealers in East LA use. Chuey I say, I don't think Nardoni does this kind of stuff. I think he just does the drugs.

Yeah he does, Chuey says, he's a lawyer isn't he? Sometimes Chuey can be just as dumb as his friends; it's not even worth telling him. Now he's all puffed up. You call Nardoni, Chuey says, Tell him I'm a *compañero* of Flaco Valdez. Tell him we're like this, Chuey holds up two crossed fingers, Tight. Flaco Valdez is like the heavy-duty drug dealer in Highland Park and Shaky Town. As usual, Chuey's bullshitting. Flaco never ran with 42nd Flats and he deals mostly smack, so Chuey isn't even one of his customers. It's just that Flaco Valdez is the biggest name that Chuey can think of. OK, I tell him, I'll call Nardoni. Now what about your mom?

Don't call her, Chuey says, all proud, I don't want her to know about this. Chuey, I say, Chuey you big *estupido*, she *is* going to hear about this. It's going to be in the papers and on TV.

OK, Chuey says, like he's doing me this big favor, You can call her. Tell her they made a big mistake. Right Chuey, I'm thinking. Smart, Chuey. Pretend it didn't happen, like always. That's going to be a fun phone call for me. His mom is going to go crazy.

I know better, but I have to ask. Chuey?, I say. Why did you do such a stupid thing?

They was on our turf!, Chuey says. They challenged us. Like we didn't have any *huevos*, Chica. We got *huevos!*

And whose smart idea was it to shoot those boys? As if I didn't know. Chuey just looks at me, he doesn't say nothing.

Chuey, I say, was you high? He looks down at the table, when he looks up again, I can't believe it, his eyes are wet. He sees me looking so he closes them. He just sits there, with his eyes closed, pulling on his little chin beard. God, he's such a pretty dude. Ay, Dulcie, he says. His eyes open and he gives me that smile, the one I have to argue to get, the one I love him for. What can I say?, Chuey tells me, *La Vida Loca*, no? *La Vida Loca.*

Right Chuey, I think, *La Vida Loca.* The Crazy Life. It's the explanation for everything on 42nd Ave.

The DA knocks on the table. Time, he says. I look right at him, I got to talk to you. Chuey cuts his eyes at me but I don't care. I never done anything like this, I never gone against him but now I have to. Sleepy Chavez could give a shit if Chuey takes the fall. Chuey doesn't get it, he thinks he's tough. If he goes to a real jail, they'll bend him over. They'll fry those *huevos* of his that he's always talking about.

I walk over to the DA and sit down. I tell him, Sleepy Chavez was the shooter. Chuey was driving and he was stoned. If Chuey testifies what will he get? That DA sees me for the first time. The numbers turn over in his eyes like a gas pump.

Mrs. Medina, he says, You are not a lawyer, I cannot plea bargain with you. If you were a lawyer I would probably tell you that your client is guilty and that we can prove it.

You got some witnesses? I tell him. He doesn't say nothing but the numbers start rolling again.

Chuey stands up and yells at me, Dulcie you stupid bitch, just shut up. He's all pale and scared. The cop walks over and sits him down.

I'm going to get him a lawyer, I say. The DA tells me, If you get a lawyer, we will talk. I would say better sooner than later—he has this little smile—before a witness shows up.

One other thing, I tell him, if I was you I'd put Chuey in a different cell from Sleepy Chavez.

Chuey won't kiss me goodbye. He pushed me away, all cold. He won't look at me. Out in the hall, he won't look at Sleepy Chavez either. Sleepy checks that out good and then when he sees that the cop is taking Chuey someplace else, he starts banging on the bars and screaming in Spanish. *Hombre muerto*, he's screaming, *Hombre muerto*. The DA looks at me and asks, What's he saying? Dead man, I tell him, he says dead man.

The DA walks me back downstairs to the desk and shakes my hand. Thank you Mrs. Medina, he says.

I tell him, Look, don't call me Mrs. Medina no more. OK? They're going to check and find out anyway and it doesn't make any difference. It's not Mrs. Medina, I tell him, It's Dulcie Gomez. I'm only married in my mind.

I got what I wanted, I guess. Chuey's lawyer who was this woman from the Public Defender's office, and Chuey's mom, and me, we all worked on Chuey. We worked on him real good. Chuey testified against Sleepy Chavez. We talked him into it.

The DA wouldn't make any deals. The brother that was on the critical list recovered but he never came to court. He hadn't seen nothing and they didn't need him anyway. They done this test that showed Sleepy fired a gun and then they found the gun. Some tow truck driver brought it in. It was under a car he towed away. Sleepy's fingerprints was all over it. The only thing the DA said he would do, if Chuey testified, was talk to the judge when it was time for the sentencing. Ms. Bernstein, Chuey's lawyer, said it was probably as good a deal as we could get.

Chuey had to stand trial next to Sleepy. Every day Sleepy blew him kisses and told him he was a pussy and a *maricón*. Ms. Bernstein never complained about it. She said it might help with the jury.

I was surprised at the judge. I didn't think she would let that stuff go on. Every day Sleepy did something stupid. There was all this yelling and pointing, and she never said nothing. The judge was this black chick about forty. She wore a different wig and different nails every day. She sat there playing with her wooden hammer. It didn't seem like she was listening. If you ask me, she was losing it. She called a recess once when one of her nails broke. Ms. Bernstein was real polite to her. She said this was the best judge we could get because she was known for her light sentences.

Ms. Bernstein didn't even try to prove that Chuey was innocent. All she did was show that he didn't know what he was doing. She said that he was stoned that day and she said that he was easily led. Even Chuey's mom got up and said that Chuey was easily led, from when he was a little boy.

It was weird to watch. They talked about him like he wasn't there. Ms. Bernstein would show that Chuey was a fool and then Sleepy's lawyer would try to show that Chuey wasn't a fool. He couldn't do it. Everybody in that court-room thought Chuey was a fool by the time they got done. Chuey sat at that table listening and he got smaller and smaller, while Sleepy Chavez kept showing off for all the *vatos locos* and got bigger and bigger.

The jury said that Sleepy Chavez was guilty but they couldn't make their minds up about Chuey. They didn't think he was innocent but they didn't think he was guilty either. They didn't know what to do. The judge talked to them some more and they came back in ten minutes and said Chuey was guilty but with like mitigating circumstances.

The DA did stand up for Chuey when it came to the sen-tencing. The judge sent Sleepy Chavez to the CYA, the California Youth Authority, until he turned twenty-one, and then after that he had to go to prison. The judge said she wanted to give Sleepy a life sentence but she couldn't because of his age. She gave Chuey probation and time served.

The courtroom went crazy. All the gangs from Shaky Town were there. 42nd Flats, The Avenues and even some from White Fence. They all started booing the judge, who finally bangs her hammer. Sleepy Chavez stands up. He makes a fist over his head and yells, Flats! *La Raza Unida*, and the crowd goes crazy some more.

I couldn't believe it. Sleepy Chavez standing there with both arms in the air, yelling, *Viva!*, like he just won some-thing and Chuey sits there with his head down like he was the one going to prison.

I go down to kiss Chuey and Sleepy spits at my feet. Hey, *Puta*, he tells me, Take your sissy home.

I can't stand it. I tell him, Sleepy, those guys in prison are gonna fuck you in the ass and I'm glad.

Sleepy says, Bullshit. I'll be in the Mexican Mafia before
I get out of CYA. I'll tell you who gets fucked in the ass, *Puta*,
your sissy, li'l Chuey. He yells at Chuey, Hey *maricón*. *Hombre
muerto*. Chuey don't never raise his head.

I talked to the DA afterward. I said, You saw those guys.
Chuey needs help. He helped you, you should help him.
What about those relocation programs? The DA could give a
shit. He cares for Chuey about as much as Sleepy Chavez. He
just packs his briefcase and walks away, shaking hands with
everybody. The TV is waiting for him outside.

Ms. Bernstein says she'll see what she can do about police
protection. I tell her that ain't going to make it. The only thing
that will make it is if Chuey gets out of East LA. She says
there's nothing to keep Chuey from moving, as long as he
tells his probation officer and keeps his appointments. She
doesn't understand, the only way Chuey will move is if they
make him. She says they can't do that.

I tried to make him move. I tell him, Chuey, they going
to kill you. Sooner or later. He doesn't want to talk about it,
all he'll say is, Forget it. Flats is my home.

The night he got out, Chuey came to my sister's house
where I was babysitting. I wanted him so bad. After I put the
kids to bed we made love. He looked so fine, even pale and
too skinny, but it wasn't any good. It wasn't like Chuey at all.
He hardly would kiss me. It was like I could have been anyone. After we made it all he wanted to do was drink wine
and listen to records. Every time I tried to talk he got mad.

On the street, the first month after the trial, the cops were
doing heavy duty patrols. It seemed like there was a black
and white on every corner. They sent the word out through
the gang counselors that Shaky Town was going to stay
cool or heads would get broken. They busted the warlords
from the 42nd Flats and The Avenues for like jay-walking
or loitering.

None of the 42nd Flats would talk to Chuey. They
cruised his house and gave him cold looks but there was too

many cops to do anything. Chuey went back to work at Raul's Body Shop. Raul said he didn't care about the gang stuff and Chuey was a good worker, but then things started happening. Chuey was getting drunk and stoned every night and then he started smoking at work too. Plus windows got broken at the body shop, then there were fires in the trash cans and over the weekend someone threw battery acid on a bunch of customers' cars. Raul told Chuey he'd have to let him go. He didn't fire Chuey, he just laid him off so Chuey could collect unemployment.

The night that he got laid off I took him to dinner and a movie, Rocky something, I forget the number. I didn't want him to get down. After the movie I took Chuey to the Notell Motel in Eagle Rock. It cost me all my tips from two weekends. They had adult movies there and a mirror over the water bed.

Chuey got into it a little. He'd been smoking weed at the movie and he was real relaxed. He lasted a long time. It wasn't great for me. I was too worried about what I wanted to ask and also he wasn't really there. Maybe because of the weed, but it was like that time when he first got out of jail. I could have been anyone.

When he was done I turned off the TV and laid down next to him with my head on his chest. We had a cigarette. When I put it out, I kissed his ear and whispered, Chuey, let's get out of this place. You got a trade, I said. We could move anyplace. We could get married. We could go to San Francisco or San Diego. We could just live together if you want. I don't care. But we got to get out of here.

Chuey sat up. He pushed me down off his chest. Flats is my home, he said. Chuey, I said, They're going to kill you. He looked at me like I was a long way away and then he nodded and his eyes were just like that DA's. With the numbers. That's right, Chuey said. They're going to kill me. The numbers flamed up in his eyes like a match. You did this to me, bitch.

Chuey, I said, I love you. He said it again, You did this to me, bitch, and after that he wouldn't talk. We didn't even spend the night.

After he got on unemployment, he filled up his day with weed and wine. I seen him walking right on the street with a joint in one hand and a short dog of white port in the other. Chuey's color TV, he calls it. I had to be in school, I couldn't babysit him. On the street, none of his old friends would talk to him and there was no place he could hang out. Even people who didn't know him didn't like him around. White Fence had put out the word that they were going to do him as a favor to 42nd Flats. No one wanted to be near Chuey in case there was shooting.

When I got out of school every day, I'd go find him. I tried to get him interested in other stuff, like school, so he could get his high school diploma, or a car. I was even going to front him some of the money, but he didn't want it. All he wanted was his weed and his wine. I even set him up for a job with my cousin who's a plumber but Chuey said no, unemployment was enough. He just kept slipping, going down, and I couldn't pull him up. There wasn't nothing I could do.

He started hanging out with the junkies. They were the only ones, except his family and me, that would talk to him. The junkies hang out in this empty lot across from Lupé's Grocery Store. A Korean guy owns the store but he's afraid to change the name. He's afraid of the junkies too. They steal him blind and shoot up in his alley. They got some old chairs and a sofa in the lot and they sit there, even when it rains. It wasn't too long before Chuey started doing reds. If you ask me, reds are the worst pill around. Red freaks are like zombies. They talk all slurred and spill things. The only thing that's good about them is they don't fight too much, like a white freak, and if they do, they don't hurt each other.

It was hard to be around Chuey once he started doing reds. He'd want to kiss me and his mouth was always full of spit and then he'd try to feel me up right in front of other guys. I hated it, even if they were just junkies.

Then I heard he was doing smack. Chuey didn't tell me, his uncle did. They were missing money from the house and a stereo. They found out Chuey had done it and they found his kit. The only thing I'd noticed was that he wasn't drinking so much and he was eating a lot of candy bars.

The weird thing was that once he got to be a junkie, the 42nd Flats stopped hassling him so much. Gangs are funny that way. They treat junkies like they was teachers or welfare workers. They don't respect them. It's like a truce or like they're invisible. I don't know now whether they're going to kill him or not. Maybe they think the smack will do it for them or maybe they're just waiting for the cops to go away or maybe they're saving him for Sleepy Chavez's little brother who gets paroled out of Juvie next month. I don't know. They still come by the junkie lot. We'll be sitting there and a cruiser will pull up with like four or five dudes inside and you'll see the gun on the window. They call him names, *Calavera*, which is like a skeleton, or they whisper *Muerto, hombre muerto*. But it's like they're playing with him. The other junkies think it's funny. They started calling him Muerto Medina. Chuey don't care.

Sometimes I skip sixth period and come down and sit with him. That's the best time of day. He's shot up and mellow by then. I cut out coming by in the morning 'cause he'd be wired and shaky and if he'd just scored he'd want me to shoot up with him. But by late afternoon he's cool. It's real peaceful there in the lot. The sun is nice. We sit on the sofa and I hold his hand. I like to look at him. He's getting skinny but he's still a pretty dude. Chuey nods and dreams, nods and dreams, and I sit there as long as I can. It's what I can do.

Winter in Los Angeles

Tom McNeal

ALREADY MARCY HAS A BAD FEELING about what she has done and what she's about to do. She is awake, but pretending not to be, when Randall rises an hour before dawn. It's autumn in Nebraska, already cold. Randall's getting ready to go hunting, and for once in his life he's being quiet about it. He sounds almost like a prowler, in fact—the slow, cautious way he moves through the dark trailer-home, setting out his coat and gear, wrapping up sandwiches, feeling in the closet for a gun. When he steps outside, he sets the front door softly to behind him. There is a clinking sound as he eases open the metal kennel gate, and the tinkling of collars as the dogs cross the yard and bound into the truck. The truck door opens and closes, the engine starts and idles.

Marcy lies in bed and listens as the truck door opens again, and then the front door to their trailer. Randall moves slowly along the dark, narrow hallway toward their bedroom—under his boots, the trailer trembles slightly on its piers—then stops at the open door. Marcy is turned from him, but she can feel him there staring in. Finally he comes near and touches his hand to her neck. She doesn't move. When he speaks, his voice is gentler than usual. "Guess you know I'm sorry I hit you," he says. "I lay there in bed all night trying to figure out how I could've done that." A moment passes. "Marcy?"

She still doesn't move.

His voice is low and serious. "Well, I just want to say that I love you, no matter what. Even if I wanted to, that's something I couldn't ever change."

Marcy opens the one good eye and turns over in bed without speaking. They try to see each other in the darkness, but she can only guess at what is in his face. It is a little while in fact before she can see that he's brought one of his long guns into the room with him. "What's that for?" she says. Her voice is sleepier, softer than she wants it.

"It's the wrong gun. I'm putting it back for something else." He forces a little laugh. "Shoulda turned on the light, I guess." She doesn't say anything. With three fingers she's carefully exploring the edges of the bad eye. He says, "If you want, Marcy, I won't go. I'll call Leo and tell him...." This is a sticking point for Randall—lying is something he prides himself in not doing. "I'll tell him we both feel punk and I need to lay low."

"No," Marcy says, "it's nice to offer, but it wouldn't help that much."

"Truth is, I'd rather stay," he says and stands waiting. The silence lengthens. In the darkness his face seems like a sad, ghostly mask of his face. At last he says, "Okay, then, Marcy, Sugar. I'm going now."

He does. He goes, Randall and his dogs.

After he leaves, Marcy dresses and moves in a daze back and forth from the trailer to the car, not thinking, just taking what she can and piling it into the trunk and back seat. She keeps at it until the sky begins to lighten. Not too far off, a tractor cranks and starts. From somewhere the metallic sound of pigs rooting a creep feeder carries in the still cold air. Across the street, in another trailer, a light goes on. Marcy puts on her dark glasses. She doesn't write a note. She doesn't consider what more she ought to take. She gets into the old Mercury Cougar and slowly drives away from her home and hometown, her parents and her husband.

She drives east out of Goodnight, through Rushville and Gordon, toward Valentine, where, beyond her range of acquaintances, she will swing south, and then, when she hits I-80, turn the Mercury west, toward California.

Once she settles into the drive, a low-grade melancholy overtakes her. Old sights put her in mind of Randall, and old songs, so while she drives she listens instead to call-in shows, people with terrible-sounding lives talking to announcers who in Marcy's opinion believe they have all the answers even though they pretend not to. Every now and then Marcy glances at the radio and says, "Well, that's one theory." Her favorite thing to say to a caller is "Join the club, Lady." But, once, when a woman doctor leaves a caller speechless by saying, "Look, Elaine, desires affect decisions and decisions have consequences and you have to take responsibility for those consequences," Marcy, on I-80 out of Cheyenne, can see nothing but the caved-in look of Randall's face when he comes home and finds her gone. What would he do? What in the world would he do? He would swallow it whole, she knew that. He would tell no one. Would answer not one question from one friend. He would swallow it whole and bear it alone. He would become one of those thin, still men with gray eyes and stubbled beards and stained coats whose insides are not right, whose sadness makes a perfect nesting place for cancers.

It takes two days, driving like this, to make the desert. Late at night, she crests the Cajon pass and drops into the San Bernardino Valley, a vast blackness dotted with what seems like a million million shimmering lights. Marcy, in that jangly state of hope that sometimes comes from travel alone across wide-open spaces, sees each dot not as a light but as a person, a single person, suddenly come to life and made bright and brand-new. That is one moment. In the next, she wishes more than anything that Randall were here, too, so they could both start new.

On her first morning in LA, Marcy drives along Sunset Boulevard, past places she's only heard of—Frederick's, Grauman's, The Roxy, The Whiskey. To her surprise, there are frightening people everywhere. When a muscular man in black leather pants, no shirt, and lemon yellow hair glances at her license plate, steps out of the crosswalk and, leaning into her window, drawls, "Miss Nebraska, I'd like you to meet Mr. Peanut," Marcy winds up the window and doesn't lower it again until the street turns residential.

Farther on, in a normal-seeming commercial section of town, Marcy goes into the first realty she likes the looks of. It's a big, oddly formal office with thick gray carpet and, on each of the many white desks, a small vase of bright flowers that Marcy's never seen in Nebraska. She asks about rentals and gets passed around. The men in the office wear blazers and ties. The women go for skirt suits, a nice look, Marcy thinks, though it's hard to tell exactly because she doesn't want to take off her dark glasses.

One man in the office seems to change the way everyone else acts. He is a stiff, frail-seeming man in wire-rimmed spectacles, white shirt, and burgundy bow tie—the man, Marcy realizes, who is the source of the office's formality. A trim secretary follows behind as he goes through the office desk to desk, chatting briefly with different agents. Each stiffens slightly at his approach. "A rental, sir," the agent helping Marcy tells the man, and they pass on, the frail man, his secretary, and her perfume.

"Whew!" Marcy says in a low voice of the perfume, and in the same low voice the agent, still clacking away at his computer, says, "It's not that Mr. Realty likes it potent. It's that Mr. Realty's got no sense of smell."

Marcy laughs. In a funny, happy way, this is what, without ever having put a finger on it, she had wanted from Los Angeles. This fancy office. The muttering help. The frail, feared executive. Marcy keeps her eye on him. He's talking on the telephone while filling his briefcase with papers. When he looks her way, Marcy does something that surprises her. She tilts her head and combs her fingers through her long hair, a method of flirtation she developed in high school but which, here and now, seems suddenly klutzy. The man snaps closed his briefcase, hands the phone to his secretary, moves through the office in stiff strides, past Marcy and her agent. But he stops, turns back.

"Look, Miss," he says, "I know of a place that's not listed, a nicely old-fashioned studio. May I ask if you smoke?"

Marcy, looking up at him, knows this is the moment when anyone with an ounce of politeness would take off her sunglasses, but she doesn't. "No," she says.

"Pets?"

"Nope."

"Drugs?"

Marcy stifles a laugh. "Hardly."

The man asks a few more questions. His glasses are coke-bottle thick and, behind them, his eyes are hard to read. Quiet? he asks. Responsible? Employed, or soon will be? Marcy smiles and says yes to each.

For a moment she can almost hear him thinking her over. "Okay," he says, "why don't I just run you up there and show you the place."

The car they drive away in is white, enormous, and deeply quiet. "This is like driving in a new refrigerator," Marcy says, going for a joke, but the man merely responds by turning down the air conditioning. "Two stops to make," he says, almost to himself. With one hand he unsnaps the briefcase lying on the leather seat between them and brings out a roll of chocolate toffees. Before partaking himself, he offers one to Marcy, who wants to accept, but doesn't.

The first stop is at a place called Prestige Motors on Melrose Avenue. The man leaves Marcy in the car while he goes inside, where the salesmen treat him a lot like the people in the real estate office had. They smooth their clothes and work their faces into smiles. It's funny to watch. Also funny to watch is the way the man walks. He is so stiff that Marcy imagines that someone has just wound him up and pointed him her way. When he gets back in, she says, "That where you bought this car?"

He stares at the car agency. "This car is a little newer than those."

The man accelerates the car smoothly into traffic, and Marcy says, "You left me and your keys in the car."

He says nothing, makes a lane change, turns up a narrowing canyon road.

"I could've stolen this big, fancy, newer car of yours."

"It's part of my tenant screening process." A tiny smile seems to form on his lips. "You irrefutably passed." For the first time, Marcy senses something playful in the man's formality. And he has the right voice for it. Besides his brains and expensive clothes, it's the voice, Marcy decides, that's gotten this man up in the world. It is a clear, pure voice that goes into your ear in a ticklish way. Marcy gives him another look. Forty to forty-two, she decides. Marcy has just turned twenty-three.

Their second stop is at the man's home, perched on a cliff out among tall, slender, smooth-barked trees. Marcy waits in the car. As the realtor approaches his house, a male gardener very slightly picks up the pace of his clipping, but a woman in gardening clothes merely pushes back her dark red hair with the back of a hand and says something before she resumes puttering with the potted flowers along the walk. Marcy picks up the tube of toffees. *Callard & Bowser*, it says on the foiled outer wrap, *Made in Great Britain*. Inside, each toffee is neatly wrapped in wax paper. She slips one into her mouth, fiddles with the radio, then the car windows. They slide quietly down, and the car fills up with a pleasant menthol smell from the outside air. She asks about it when the man returns.

"Eucalyptus." He points to the tall trees.

The man drives slowly, the road spiraling upward. He starts to set the toffees back into his briefcase, but pauses to hold the roll out to Marcy. "Another?" he says, and she says, "Nope, one was fine."

A turn in the road affords a sudden, sweeping view of the city. The car slows just a little. "That's the way it used to be," he says. "You could see Catalina Island almost every day. It was a wide-open world then." He looks off into the haze. "One day, when I was ten or eleven, I walked into the Sav-On drugstore at Ventura and Laurel Canyon and found myself standing at the candy counter not far from a man who seemed dimly familiar. I was nearsighted even then, so, without much awareness I was even doing it, I began edging closer and closer to this man, squinting up at him until I was so close I could smell his heavy tobacco smell. At the exact moment that I realized that he was in fact Bela Lugosi, he curled his lip and issued a hissing sound that seared the pea-wadding out of me." A small, self-mocking chuckle slips from the realtor. "I hastily retired. But as I was climbing onto my bicycle, a clerk caught up to me with a box of Callard & Bowser Toffee. There was also a note, which I still possess, that said, 'With this gift Mr. Bela Lugosi wishes to commemorate the pleasant occasion of your acquaintance.'"

The realtor glances at Marcy. "This reminds me that we haven't been formally introduced." He keeps his left hand on the wheel, short-arms his right toward her. "I'm Harmon Martin."

That was what the sign had said in front of the realty: *Harmon Martin's Mr. Realty*. Marcy decides to slip a small one by him. "Marcy Marlene Lockhardt," she says, "but everybody calls me Lena." Lockhardt is her maiden name and nobody in her lifetime has called her Lena.

Harmon Martin releases her hand, "Lena then," he says. More tall eucalyptus trees pass by, more snug bungalows. "So where are you from, Lena?"

Marcy considers lying about this, too, but worries that the man might've seen the plate on her Mercury. "Nebraska." She expects him maybe to ask what part of Nebraska, but he doesn't.

"I've been a lot of places," the man says, "but I've never been to Nebraska. In fact, I think of Nebraska as a kind of

English-speaking foreign country. All that *swaggering* and *roping* and *branding*."

"They don't brand so much anymore," Marcy says. "Mostly they just tag their ears."

"Darn," Harmon Martin says softly. "No more hiss and sizzle."

"Not so much anyway," Marcy says.

They fall silent. Marcy leans out the window, stares up at the slender, smooth white trees, takes into her lungs this new, mentholated air.

After a while she says to the man, "Your wife's pretty."

He looks at her in surprise. "Yes, she is." Then, "How did you know she was my wife and not, let us say, a fetching Hollywood Hills gardener?"

Because she wasn't like all the others. She treated Harmon Martin like just another human being. "I could just tell," Marcy says, and as they drive along a fact presents itself like a utensil she has no use for, namely that if a woman wanted to get to Harmon Martin, the way to do it was to force him to imagine everything, and allow him to touch nothing.

Marcy loves the studio. It has hardwood floors, white walls and, beyond the parted French doors, an enamelled deck with solid siding. "For total privacy," Harmon Martin says in an abstracted voice, as if he's saying one thing and thinking another. She asks about rent, is shocked at how high the figure is. "You're kidding," she says.

"I know. It's a very good deal. The owner could get quite a lot more, but won't advertise. She's afraid of the riffraff." He gazes down the canyon toward the freeway. "You'll get a nice view at night."

She stares out.

"This is a Los Angeles address or Hollywood or what?"

"You're in the city of LA, but the mailing address is Hollywood." He glances at her. "Have you by any chance heard of Tom Hulce?"

"*Amadeus.*"

Harmon Martin seems pleased. "Yes. A good young

actor, I'd say. He lived here nearly two years, until his salaries grew. He has a reputation, but he left the place neat as a pin."

Marcy knows she shouldn't take the apartment, but says she will. She takes out her folded cash, counts out the first two months' rent, and presents it to Harmon Martin, who, moving close as if to take it, instead reaches forward and gently slides off Marcy's sunglasses. In the change in his face, she sees what he sees: a swollen eye—almost the color of eggplant with a yellowish subsurface. He slides the glasses back and steps away. "Who's the party responsible for this?"

Marcy answers quickly, as if there is only one answer. "A guy." She looks away. "My husband actually."

Harmon Martin makes a smile so small that Marcy wonders if she imagines it. "This isn't, I hope, an accepted form of husbandry out there in the hinterlands."

"No," Marcy says, pinkening a little, she isn't sure why. She also isn't sure what Harmon Martin is up to. He still hasn't taken the money.

"So is this imbecile husband going to be a problem?" he asks.

Marcy feels funny, letting this man call Randall an imbecile, which Randall is not, but she shakes her head certainly. "No," she says, "no problem whatsoever."

Marcy's new neighborhood, a curving line of smooth-plaster cottages nestled into the hillside, is as different from Nebraska as different could be. She has painted the mailbox blue and nearly finished stencilling L. Lockhardt in yellow when a dog arrives, a small, bowlegged Doberman mix with a frisbee in his mouth. He drops it at her feet and looks up expectantly. She throws it, it wobbles off, the dog retrieves it. They do this several times. The dog's focus on the frisbee is absolute. Marcy can make him shake or nod his head by either waving the frisbee side to side or up and down. She kneels down, holds the frisbee overhead, and in a low voice says, "Will I find a job in television?"

The dog nods a slow yes.

"Will Randall find me?"

No.

"Will I find someone?"

An even more definite yes. Marcy laughs.

"Am I the fairest in the land?"

Yes.

Marcy laughs and tosses the frisbee a few more times, until it gets too slobbery to throw. The dog takes no offense. He merely picks up his toy and trots away, looking surprisingly businesslike. He knows what he wants and how to get it. He visits strangers, drops this plastic disc at their feet, and gives them the chance to make him happy. It seems so simple.

A few days later, Marcy sits in the sun on the private deck hugging her knees. She's come to LA with the idea of working in television, but the truth is, except for a friend's cousin who is an assistant director on *The New Price is Right,* and who, it turns out, left yesterday for Berlin, Marcy knows no one in LA. She thumbs through a *Variety* with her right eye closed. Something is still wrong with that eye. The shiner has healed, but the eye floats, feels unhinged. It weeps and blurs her vision.

She puts down the paper and doesn't know how many minutes have gone by when she realizes that, in this space of time, however long it's been, all she's done is look at her feet. There is so much *time* here. In Goodnight, there were tons of ways to keep yourself busy, but here it is like a vacation, except with all the fun drained away because there's no stop to it.

Somewhere a dog barks, but not the frisbee dog—she knows his bark by now. It is seventy-nine degrees, mid-November. Marcy lies back on her towel, closes her eyes, and tilts her face to meet the angle of the sun. What she wants is something in the television or movie business, not in acting or anything big. Just something that helps keep things going day to day.

She tells Harmon Martin this the next time he telephones, which he does fairly often. Just checking in on the newest leaseholder, he will say dryly. "Sure you wouldn't like to shoot a little higher?" he says today.

"Naw. I like to shoot at things I have a chance of hitting."

Harmon Martin makes a little humming sound, then says he'll do some asking around, see what he can turn up.

Thanksgiving Day, Marcy calls home and is swarmed over by questions. "Where are you?" her mother asks. "Are you okay? Do you have enough money? What're you doing? Are you coming home?"

"Not for a while yet," Marcy says, "but I'm fine, Mom. I am."

"But where—"

"Someplace warmer," Marcy says. "Has he been asking, do you know?"

"Not that I know of. His friend Leo was asking around for a while, but I don't know if that was on his own or for Randall."

Marcy doesn't know what to say. "Is Dad okay then?" she asks finally.

"He'll be better now, knowing you're okay. Provided you are."

"I am, Mom. I really am."

After a little silence, her mother says, "We heard he hit you."

Marcy doesn't say anything.

"Why would he want to do that?"

"He had it in his head that I was running around, Mom."

"But you weren't."

"Nope. But I couldn't convince him, he had it so much in his head."

This much is true, but the larger truth is that Marcy had concluded she'd married the wrong man. She didn't want to spend her life with an ingrown man who wouldn't be happy until she was ingrown, too. Marcy wanted out. And she needed Randall to give her a good enough reason to go, so she invented and told him a story instinctively shaped to organize his anger. At the moment Randall struck her, he was more surprised than she was. Marcy knows this. And for this entrapment of Randall's pitiful worst self, Marcy is beginning to believe, she can never be forgiven.

Marcy in a soft voice says, "So do you think Randall's doing okay?"

"I wouldn't know. He doesn't call and he hardly speaks when spoken to. He still goes to work, I guess, but he stays mostly now in Scottsbluff. People say he's hardly been at the trailer. It's a mess, they say."

A silence, then Marcy says, "I'll call soon, okay? I love you, and tell Dad I love him, too."

Later that day, Marcy cooks herself Thanksgiving dinner for one—a Cornish game hen, fresh peas, and a yam—then sits looking at it. She takes a few bites, wraps the rest in foil for the dog, and goes outside, but he's nowhere to be found. She climbs a winding set of public stairs to the top of a knoll where a public lawn is maintained, and where the dog lies sleeping. He stretches, wags his nubby tail. "Happy Thanksgiving," Marcy says as he greedily bolts the food. Marcy is gazing down at the city when—a slight shock—she realizes that from here there is a narrow line of downward sight to Harmon Martin's house. She stands looking into the brightly lighted kitchen where guests are milling. She can pick out Harmon Martin from among the men—he is mixing drinks, measuring things very carefully—but she can't be certain which of the women is his wife. From a distance, all of them look elegant, handsome, and happy.

———

Harmon Martin has lined up three job interviews for Marcy, all on the same day. "Trial by fire," he says. "But my advice is not to commit to anything. Say you have another offer pending, that you will tell them something definite within seventy-two hours."

"Three days."

"But you might say hours." His little smile. "In order to create the impression that your time units are small, compressed, and important."

The interviews are a nightmare. Marcy wears a simple beige-and-black dress that she hoped would seem elegant, but, she realizes, is made to be overlooked in. The men who interview her wear more color than she does. They ask questions like, What unique talents can you bring to this job? Marcy sweats, stammers, and introduces to the room the kind of awkwardness that infects others. At the final interview, the man breaks a long, horrible silence by picking up her application and reading through it. "What's KDUH?" he says finally.

"It's Channel 4 in northwest Nebraska." She daubs at her eye to keep the liquid in its pink sac from spilling down her cheek. "For about six months I read the weekend news."

What's the ENG capacity there?" the man says and then, when he sees her confusion, says, "The electronic newsgathering capacity."

"Oh. I really don't know. I guess I should, but all I did was read the news." She pulls out another tissue from her purse.

Later, when Harmon Martin telephones to find out how the interviews went, Marcy says, "Not that great." She thinks about it and says, "Thinking about it makes me kind of tired."

"You might be wrong. You might be pleasantly surprised. But it doesn't matter. Those folks were flyweights, they couldn't carry your bags. So let's say we keep looking around until we find just the right fit."

The right fit, Marcy thinks. Fitting in. When she realizes she might begin to cry, she makes a quick excuse and says goodbye.

Another sunny day. Where she has come from, weather dictates activities and affects moods, and Marcy misses the little indicators. The smell of burning leaves, the creak of frozen porchboards, Randall carrying the fresh smell of winter with him into a warm room. But December in southern California is relentlessly green, leafy, and bright. There is only the changing angle of the sun as it streams onto the deck, where Marcy spends her afternoons reading and tanning.

Marcy has been offered a job. She can work as a cocktail waitress at a country-western place called The Palomino. Harmon Martin had nothing to do with this. Marcy saw the ad, called up, drove out to the valley. A woman looked her over the way a man would and said, "The one position is filled. But there's another in mid-January. Can you wait that long?"

Marcy said yes she could, but in truth she's not so sure about the job. The money would be good, and she wouldn't mind the get-up, but it seems so different out here. In Goodnight, she knew how to say no to men because she knew who they were and they knew who she was.

A crow glides past Marcy's deck. Marcy blinks, realizes she's been thinking of Randall. Of the tons of things she knows she shouldn't do, the one she knows she shouldn't do most of all is think about Randall, but she can't always help it. Usually she hopes Randall is with somebody, but today, a bad sign, she hopes he isn't. She sits down and writes Randall a long rushing letter full of explanation and questions and soft thoughts. Without reading it over, she seals it and means to walk it down the canyon to the mailbox before the last pickup, but when she opens the door, Harmon Martin is standing there about to knock. He hasn't saved her, not in any real sense, but when she awakens the next morning with the letter still in her purse, she will allow herself to think of it in almost that way.

Harmon Martin has come to the door because he has news. "Something quite remarkable." His little, self-knowing smile forms. "An interview, in January."

"Who with?" she says, but he merely winks. He's brought makings for what he calls "a celebratory gimlet." He mixes it precisely, savors his first sip. "Well," he says, seating himself. "I put in a word with a colleague. The colleague put in a word for me." He takes his handkerchief from his suit pocket, fogs and cleans his thick glasses, holds them to the light, gives them a finishing touch. He slides them on, looks beamingly at Marcy. "You have an interview on Tuesday, January 17th, 10:00 A.M., with Universal, for the position of personal secretary to Steven Spielberg."

Marcy stands frozen for a moment. "This isn't some kind of joke?"

"That's correct," Harmon Martin says. "It is not."

Marcy gives him a quick kiss on the cheek before walking about the apartment in a state of real agitation. "You did it," she says, as much to herself as to him and then, beside herself, she whoops, *"Hot chaw!"*—a phrase that makes Harmon Martin actually chuckle, a phrase that Marcy has never used before, a phrase that until now had been exclusively Randall's. She dances up to Harmon Martin, slips off his glasses, puts them on herself, keeps dancing. She takes his hand and, against his protests, pulls him up to dance. He moves mechanically for a minute or so, then retreats back to his chair. It's an endearing surprise, this rich man's embarrassment. When his blushing recedes, he makes a little smile. "I'm not much of a dancer," he says. "If I'd thought it was pertinent, I'd have told you sooner."

On Christmas morning, Marcy dials her old number in Nebraska, imagines the telephone on the coffee table in the living room of the trailer as it rings and rings. Finally she gives up and tries her parents' number. Her father answers on the second ring. *"Ha!"* he says when she says hello. "I *knew* it was you. It's the sixth time it's rung today, but this time I said to your mother, 'This one's her,' and, sure enough, here you are."

They talk amiably for a while, her father relying mostly on local crime stories to avoid touchy subjects. After telling about the stolen tractor discovered hidden in Raymond Fales's haymow, he says, "Okay, okay, I better give the phone to your mother before she turns blue."

"Hi, Polkadot," her mother says and, following a rush of questions, she takes a breath and says, "I was hoping you'd be home by now."

"I think I'm here to stay, Mom. The people are nice to me and I'm beginning to like it." Then, "Did you get my presents okay?"

Marcy has sent presents anonymously through a mail-order catalogue, a doe and fawn in a snow-globe for her mother and a set of nesting presidents for her father, who'd always taken pride in his ability to tick off all of them in order. To Randall she'd sent a pair of flannel boxer shorts in a duck-hunting pattern and a plaid electric blanket. She mentions this and her mother says, "I don't know that he'll receive those kindly."

"Why is that?" Marcy says. She can tell her mother is thinking something over. "What?"

"Oh, a story," her mother says.

"About him and somebody else?"

"No, but how would you feel about that?"

"Fine. I want him to be happy, is all I want."

"Well, I don't think he's so happy."

"What makes you say so?"

Another pause, then, "Well, the story, according to Flossie Boyles, is that about two weeks ago Randall took all your clothes out onto the carport by the trailer and heaped them up and burned them. Then he swept the ashes into a neat pile and put them in a Tupperware container and, the story goes, he consumes a teaspoon at a time by spreading it over his meals."

Marcy feels actually sickened. "Mom?"

"What, Polkadot?"

But Marcy catches herself. The story she was about to tell would've just played into her mother's hands. "I love you," she says, "and just tell Dad it's warm here and the people are nice to me and I miss him."

What she had thought to describe to her mother was the recurring dream she'd been having. In it, she brings Randall to the edge of a bluff overlooking the beach. They are both younger, in high school, happy, unsteady with laughter, trying to catch with their mouths black jelly beans they lob into the air. From the overhanging bluff face there is a steep, red-dirt channel, made by erosion, that is like a long chute down to the beach. There is sheer happiness in Randall's face when Marcy brings him to it. He plunges down at once, on the seat of his pants, whooping at first, but the moment he turns a corner, beyond Marcy's view, his voice stops and there are loud sickening thuds as his body bumps its way down the rocky slope. Marcy runs for the stairs, but cannot go down to look.

The first week of January, Marcy browses department stores for the right thing to wear to her interview (no luck) and reads everything about Steven Spielberg she can lay her hands on (the East Hampton inside-out barn in *Architectural Digest*, the money to Harvard for an extraterrestrial scanner in *Physics Today*, the rumors about Kate Capshaw in *People*). "Steven is boyish," says Richard Dreyfuss in *Life*, "and financially canny, but the word that really nails him is adventurous." In the background of one photograph, Marcy finds his secretary. She is dark haired, too. Like his first wife. Like Amy Irving. Like Kate Capshaw.

The next morning Marcy spends seventy-five dollars on tinting her hair. "That color," she says to the hairdresser and points to a photograph of Kate Capshaw she's torn out of a magazine.

This is the first of two changes Marcy makes. The other is a molded leather eye patch she finds in a costume shop. It stops the double vision and the weeping, but she's not so sure about it. The first time she wears it outside the house, she turns away when a car passes. She whistles and before long the little bowlegged Doberman trots smartly around the corner carrying a new red frisbee. He drops it at her feet. She picks it up, holds it close to her head. "Shall I wear the eye patch?"

Yes.

No.

She tosses the frisbee into the empty street. It skips off the pavement and floats over the hillside. The dog leaps out into the air, disappears over the side. For a moment, time stands still, then the dog reappears, grinning around his red frisbee.

Whether she'll wear the eye patch, Marcy decides, will depend on the outfit she buys for the interview, but the days go by without finding the right thing. Finally, the day before the interview, she begins to cry in the dressing room of Bullocks Wilshire. Everything that looks good on the rack looks horrible on her. She takes off what she has on, goes to the most stylish saleswoman on the floor, and says, "I'm looking for something for a job interview at Universal, nice, but with a sense of adventure."

When Marcy arrives for the interview, she is directed to a large, tightly quiet room where about a dozen applicants are already waiting. Most of the women are wearing tasteful coat dresses in navy or cream, expensive but not too expensive. Marcy's outfit, she realizes, is just foolish. A semi-safari look, the saleswoman had called it. A khaki skirt, a Chinese peasant coat worn open to a tight, stretchy top in an orange color the saleswoman called quince. With suede flats, long, dangly, costume-gold earrings, and a brimless red hat, the total was $625, more money than Marcy had, so she opened an instant charge account.

"I heard the job was an aide to Steven Spielberg," Marcy says to the woman closest to her.

Several of the women glance toward her. One of them, before turning just slightly away, says, "I hope you're right, Sweet Pea."

At a little past noon, Marcy is given a brief interview by a man—it goes fine—and then is shown into a round, windowless room where she is left alone. The walls are meant to be funny, Marcy guesses, but they scare her a little. White Roman columns have been painted on every wall and door, with dark vines trailing from one to the other. Walking among the columns is an odd cast of creatures—browsing zebras, penguins with parasols, grim-faced businessmen in bowler hats. Two black chairs and a white, glass-topped table are the only furniture in the room. Sitting on top of the table are a typewriter, a loud windup clock, a telephone, and a shrink-wrapped leather book. She is staring at the telephone when it rings. Marcy answers and a woman's voice says, "Miss Lockhardt, kindly check Mr. Spielberg's daybook, confirm for Lafcadio's and with Miss Wittenburg at CBS, cancel everything between 1:15 and 3:25, and if Mr. Wallace, White, or Wilson calls, advise them that Mr. Spielberg will be out of the office until tomorrow."

Marcy does these things, politely and as far as she knows, correctly.

Shortly thereafter, as if of its own, a door Marcy, hadn't seen swings open, cleanly sweeping out most of a Roman column. A woman rides into the room on a wave of confidence and energy, gives her name as Connie DeVrie, and, after a glance at Marcy's outfit, says, "What a *dramatic* coat!"

Connie DeVrie is wearing a dark, executive-looking skirt suit.

"First a five-minute typing test," she says and sets the clock.

The text concerns itself with the stress capacities of concrete. Moments after Marcy starts typing, the telephone rings. At the instant that Marcy picks it up, Connie DeVrie suspends time on the test. "Mr. Spielberg's office," Marcy says as briskly as she can.

A woman says, "Mr. Wade's office for Mr. Spielberg please."

Marcy, uncertain, says, "Your name again?" and the woman at the other end hangs up without a word. Connie DeVrie starts time running again and Marcy tries to concentrate on the typing. There are numbers and fractions everywhere. Marcy's fingers move unsurely over the top row of the keyboard. The last minute of the test, she tries to think up something worth saying to excuse her performance, but can't. She fights off the impulse to cry.

There are other tests, too, not quite as horrible, but almost.

When they're all completed, Connie DeVrie disappears through the swinging door, tests in hand. From the inner sanctum beyond the wall, Marcy can hear rich male laughter, and then laughter from men and women together, until finally the wall swings open again, but not completely. Connie DeVrie uses it like a shield, around which only her head appears. She says she'll call Marcy when all the interviews are completed and then, before Marcy can say a word, Connie DeVrie closes the door that wasn't a door.

When she returns to her bungalow, the dog is asleep on her stoop. The door is also ajar. Through the window she can see Harmon Martin in shirt sleeves, wearing an apron, standing at the kitchen sink washing spinach leaves one by one. Marcy, stepping inside, asks how he got in.

"Key," he says, with enough unconcern to annoy Marcy. He doesn't look at her. He nods toward the sinkful of carrot peelings. "You know if you keep eating nothing but carrots, you will actually turn yellow."

She thinks of telling him that the reason Howard Hawks wanted Lauren Bacall for *To Have and Have Not* was her yellow complexion, which looked good on film—it's the kind of story that interests Harmon Martin—but he turns and is brought up short.

"*Good grief,*" he says.

He's never before seen the eye patch, the peasant coat, the quince-colored top. Marcy's shoulders drop. "I know, I know," she says.

He lays down the spinach leaves. "Look, Lena," he says, "I knew you were very attractive, but I didn't know that you could be so...fetching."

Marcy wonders if he's joking.

"I spoke to my colleague. He said the interview didn't work out so well. I was going to make you dinner as a way of...*condoling,* but, just for the record, whoever turned you down ought to have had his head examined."

Marcy stares at him. "You're not joking, are you?"

"We're going out, Lena Lockhardt. I'm taking you out. That much you owe me."

They go to a place called Sports. She orders crab and a flaming dessert. She enjoys every bite. "I'll pay my half," she says while he's sipping coffee. He smiles. Half, rounded off, is seventy-two dollars.

She pays it. She pays it so that after he drives her home, she can give him a quick kiss, say goodnight, and feel virtuous even while experiencing the strange pleasure of watching his appetite grow.

Last night Marcy worked her first shift at The Palomino. Joe Ely played, she made a couple of mistakes on drink orders, but still took home over ninety dollars. Except for a couple of unfunny remarks, it was okay, so this morning, a Saturday, Marcy feels just fine. She has gone out to sit in the sun on the deck, but as the sky clouds over she puts on a T-shirt and, a while later, sweat pants. When she hears Harmon Martin's peculiar knock on the door, she sings out, "It's unlocked! I'm out on the deck!"

He sets a grocery bag on the drainboard, slides open the door to the deck. "I've been wondering if you got mauled last night?"

She laughs. "No real bruises."

Harmon Martin regards her, then goes to the deck rail and looks out.

"Rain," she says. "Or would be if this was Nebraska."

He stares off. "It's coming up from the gulf. It's the kind that can really open up."

It's quiet except for the drone of an airplane. For the first time, Marcy wonders where Harmon Martin's wife thinks he is.

"Did I mention the hotel project we've begun in St. Martin?" he says, still looking off. "It's quite reckless, four hundred rooms, on the Dutch side." He turns around. "I have to go over there this week."

"How nice," Marcy says. It *does* sound nice, actually.

"Yes, well, I've been thinking," Harmon Martin says. "Do you remember the car dealership I went into the day I showed you this place?"

"The place with the old cars."

"*Vintage cars*, we call them, but yes. I own that agency. We sell pre-'68 Rollses, Mercedes, Porsches, Bentleys, and Bugattis that we bring over from Europe. We restore them to mint condition, guarantee them, and sell them as invest-ment-quality classics, which they are."

Since when, Marcy wonders, does Harmon Martin fill her in on his work? "That's interesting," she says.

"There are three salesmen, but one will soon be leaving."

Marcy doesn't say anything.

He says, "What got me thinking were those clothes you wore the other night, the Asian coat and red top. Tasteful, but somewhat...sportive." He smiles his subdued smile. "I think you'd be, as they say, a selling fool."

On the freeway below, loose lines of traffic flow smooth-ly along.

Gently he says, "Six figures is not out of the question."

Marcy tries to keep her voice calm. "I don't know beans about cars."

"I'd be happy to teach you—history, horsepower, appreciation potential, that kind of thing." He snugs his glasses to the bridge of his nose. "Which is why I mention St. Martin. I'll have meetings, but there will be dead times. We could put them to use. Probably we'd just start with Mercedes and Bentleys for now, and work on the rest later on."

Marcy feels lightheaded. She needs to say something. "I never thought I was coming out to Hollywood to sell used cars," she says.

"*Vintage,*" he says, with his smile.

Then Harmon Martin half-closes his eyes, a few moments pass, and his lids slowly open. "Look, Lena," he says. "In a way it *is* part of the business. Take the day before yesterday. Alec Baldwin came in and used his American Express for a Porsche roadster, the '58 Super Speedster, eighteen thousand dollars. Last week Randy Quaid purchased a three-wheel Morgan. We sell to anybody, but it's amazing how many of the buyers are recognizable. Julie Newmar bought a '31 Bentley, and before he died Steve McQueen bought his 356 from us." Harmon Martin spreads his hands, looks at them, spreads them wider. His voice grows almost melodious. "Both of John Wayne's sons. Dwight Yoakam. Rita Moreno." It is a surprise and not a surprise, this new use of his fine, pure voice. Far away a car horn sounds. Harmon Martin slows his pace. "Fernando Lamas," he croons. "Whit Bissell...Strother Martin...John Cassavetes." Marcy grins dreamily. "Sterling Holloway...Elizabeth Ashley...Lou Diamond Phillips...." One after another, the names, the dreamy, beautiful, expensive names, hover close by, floating, then on the updraft rise overhead.

"We'll need to leave by four P.M. Tuesday," Harmon Martin says. "You can pack light. We're building on the Dutch side, but staying on the French, where dress is informal, especially on the beach."

Slowly and with real effort Marcy brings the room back
into focus. She has to say no, thanks but no thanks, and she
has to say it now. Thanks but no thanks. Say it.

Harmon Martin is at the door, looking as lightheaded as
Marcy feels, and then he is gone.

The storm takes hold that night and doesn't let go. The
weatherman Marcy watches is called Dr. George by the
cheery co-anchors. Dr. George runs a clip of two women in
rain-drenched bikinis rollerskating in Santa Monica, then
shoves his face muggingly into the camera and says that
what we have here, folks, is a good old-fashioned gully
whumper. Marcy spends the day reading and watching TV,
eating popcorn and thinking of spending similar days when
snow floated idly down in Nebraska. She puts on her swimming suit and stands on a stool to look at herself in the mirror. She tries it with the top off and actually laughs. If
Harmon Martin thinks she'd go out on a public beach like
that, he can think again. She wishes he would call so she
could remember how his voice made her feel while he was
saying those names, but he doesn't. By Sunday afternoon,
whenever she looks at a clock, Marcy converts it to Nebraska
time. That evening, for the first time since the storm moved
in, she thinks of the dog. She opens the front door, calls into
the sheets of slanting rain, but her voice is swallowed in the
gurgling throat of the storm. Through the night she imagines
hearing the dog scratching at the door, but when she shines a
flashlight out, he isn't there. There is only the splash of water.

The storm is supposed to let up Tuesday morning, but
doesn't. Marcy packs her suitcase in hopes that her feelings
will catch up with her actions. She packs perfume, lingerie,
diaphragm. But Harmon Martin's knock on the door makes
her do something surprising. She slides the packed suitcase
under the bed and opens another one on top, empty.

Harmon Martin shakes out his umbrella at the door and
enters uncertainly. He doesn't seem completely surprised
when Marcy leads him to the empty suitcase. "I'm not
going," she says. He frets and coaxes, growing smaller by the

minute. Beneath his linen jacket, he wears a pale pink long-sleeved shirt that seems to Marcy unpleasantly showy. While he walks stiffly about the room, he fusses with the pale pink cuffs, tugging them down on his too-thin wrists. When finally he sits down and pleads, Marcy says, "No. Once and for all, no."

Moments later, clouds outside part to a startling blue and the entire room lightens. Harmon Martin writes something down. "This is my home number. I'll be there another hour, in case you change your mind." He taps his glasses. "If my wife answers, just say, 'About the leak in the studio on Ione, tell Harmon never mind it's been fixed.'"

After he leaves, Marcy goes outside and is surprised that his car is actually gone. The sun glares down; vapor rises from the wet asphalt. Everywhere on the ground there are worms, and snails, and soaked newspapers. People begin popping out of houses. From a distance, a dog barks, her dog, his sharp clear anxious barking. Marcy follows the sound down the hillside streets, along Ione, down finally to Cahuenga. In the traffic, the barking is lost, or perhaps it's stopped. Marcy keeps walking, farther from her studio, farther from Harmon Martin's house, taking deep breaths of the new clean air. In Goodnight, after a storm like this, there would be careful appraisal of crops and stock, but here there is nothing but a general sense of freedom after long constraint. Joggers appear. Bicycles whiz by. Music carries from open car windows.

The clearing, however, is a false one. The skies again turn dark, car windows slide up, fat raindrops spatter, and the sweep of windshield wipers begins again. Marcy, coatless, keeps walking, following the flood control channel, watching the water pour by, branches and bottles and plastic containers all rushing along on the fierce current.

It is from a bridge spanning the channel that she sees the dog. He is down below, to the right, in a muddy lot within the fence enclosing the channel, an area used to park orange government trucks, where neither the dog nor the group of boys surrounding him should be. The boys are bickering over whose turn it is to throw the frisbee next. When finally one of them throws it, the dog seems to skate above the mud, and to rise out of it for the long moment needed to pluck the frisbee from the air. Marcy can hear the boys' shrill voices. *"Whoa!* Check it out! This canine can *fly!"*

The cars splash past Marcy on the bridge, but the pedestrians and bicyclists have disappeared. The rain turns hard and finally the boys notice it, too. They hunch their shoulders, look up at the sky, and move toward their bikes. One, however, lags back and, as he sees the others mount their bikes, this last boy picks up the frisbee for one last throw.

What is this like? Like watching one of those TV nature shows and knowing that the snow rabbit or the lame gnu is going to get it and not turning the channel. Marcy wants to call out to the dog, to retrieve him from danger, but she doesn't. She stands mute as the boy turns toward the storm channel and without a moment's hesitation flicks the frisbee toward it. The dog races after the frisbee, pitches forward when the level ground gives way beneath him, then tumbles and skids down the concrete bank into the rushing current. His neck stretches up out of the water for a moment before he is swept away.

Marcy feels suddenly boneless. There are so many ways to act cowardly. There are just so many ways to do it. She could've yelled at that boy and saved the dog. She could've done that little bit. And she could've given Harmon Martin, a married man, nothing whatsoever to think about. And she could've told Randall that for reasons she didn't get and couldn't explain, she had to change her life or go crazy. She could've done that instead of telling him lies and making him hit her, making him feel and look to all of Goodnight like a brute. She could've done these things, if she were only not such a coward, and then besides saving that dog's life and saving Randall and Harmon Martin a lot of trouble, her life would now have more of the decency she always meant it to have. It was like that boy who threw the frisbee. That boy knew what that poor dog would do. Probably that boy would grow into someone worthless, and then the dog wouldn't matter. But it would matter if that boy somehow began to turn into somebody decent. Then his carelessness with that trusting dog would nibble away at him and he would learn that, no matter who said what to you, it was the kind of sin that only you who committed it could forgive yourself for, except that you never could unless you began scaling back your ideas of what makes a wrongful act. Marcy begins to walk. Water streams from her hair into her face. Her pant legs and sweater soak up the rain and grow heavy. She walks and walks, along Cahuenga, up the canyon toward Ione, past Harmon Martin's house, soaked through, not thinking, just walking in her own water world.

Marcy is at her gate when it dawns on her that the green Dodge pickup she has just passed seems familiar. Marcy turns and stares in disbelief. It is Randall's truck. The shadowy form slouched behind the steering wheel must then be Randall. Marcy moves toward him. In the truck bed there is a dark, wet canvas tarp roped over odd shapes that suggest furniture. Scattered on the dashboard are a seed cap, a road map, a box of Good & Plentys. A feeling of relief and perhaps even affection swells within Marcy. What kept you? she thinks of calling out when he rolls down the window, but he doesn't. He doesn't move at all, an indication, she guesses, of sullenness or mean satisfaction, and all at once Marcy has no real idea what she is feeling, what she will say. But she doesn't have to say anything. Behind the fogged windshield, behind the streaming rivulets of water, in a tightly closed cab that Marcy doesn't actually have to smell to know its wintry mingling of licorice and boot leather, coffee and flannel, Randall is fast asleep.

Traffic

Rubén Mendoza

I HAD TOLD NANETTE I would pick her up at 7:30. It was already 7:42. She had just moved into a new condominium in the Hollywood hills, and I had to take Sunset to get there. I knew she would probably be angry with me for making her wait, but I really couldn't decide if this worried me or not. As I began to speed through a yellow light at Highland Avenue, something strange caught my eye on my left-hand side. I hit the brakes and slowed to a stop to let the light turn red.

On the sidewalk in front of Dally's Burgers, I watched a huge, floppy king-sized mattress move toward the intersection. The mattress turned to move into the crosswalk, and the two men carrying it came into view. The mattress had no handles, and the taller of the two men, a hunchbacked white guy, kept dropping his end of it. Every time he did this, the other, a short black man, would yell at him. I watched while they crossed the street in front of me. My window was halfway down, and as they came closer, I turned down the radio to listen.

"Hold it up, you're getting it wet," the black guy said. The street was still slick and soaked from an earlier rainstorm, and I could see that the corner of the mattress that kept getting dropped was indeed becoming more and more visibly wet. A dark stain of dirty water was spreading there.

"I can't hold it up anymore. My hands hurt," the white guy said. Again, the mattress slipped out of his hands to the ground and he scrambled to pick it up by its edges. As they came closer, I could see that the mattress was in a very sorry state. It had brown and yellow stains, holes with yellowish stuffing and rusted springs poking out, and rips and tears all along the edges. It was a thin, worn mattress, the kind you find in cheap motels with bent, burned spoons and used hypodermic needles hidden underneath.

When they were right in front of me, the white guy with the hurting hands let the mattress fall and twist onto the hood of my car. He held his left wrist in his right hand, then his right wrist in his left hand, alternating nervously every few seconds, and I could see tears streaming down his face. He looked dazed, and I realized he was on something.

"Pick it up, man," the black guy said, and his big eyes darted quickly in my direction as the cross-traffic light turned yellow and my light prepared to turn green.

"I can't, Eddie. My hands hurt." In my headlights I could see now that he was very dirty, with long matted hair, soiled, torn pants, and a tattered, stained powder-blue bathrobe which came down to his knees. He had a scraggly beard. Holding his raw, red hands out in front of him and watching Eddie with glazed eyes, he looked like some kind of crucified Jesus.

The black guy, Eddie, was also dirty. He wore endless layers of what looked like filthy shirts, jackets, polyester pants, aerobic leggings, knit sweaters, multicolored scarves, torn fishnet stockings. He began yelling at the Jesus guy again as my light turned green. "C'mon man, help me move this thing," he said, but the Jesus guy just stood there and stared at the mattress on my hood, holding out his hands. The cars behind me began to honk, then started pulling into the lane next to mine to pass us. As they drove by, I could hear them yelling at us. I turned on my hazard lights and wondered what to do.

I stuck my head out the window and said, "Hey, c'mon, get your mattress off my car," and Eddie said, "Yeah, c'mon asshole, let's go," as he pushed the Jesus guy's shoulder. I thought maybe he was afraid I would run them over or something, and I gunned my engine lightly.

"But my hands hurt, Eddie," the Jesus guy said. He did not move, even when Eddie pushed him, but instead just stood there in front of my car, staring at the mattress and the headlights like a catatonic deer.

"Shit!" Eddie said. "Man, this was your stupid ass idea, now I gotta carry this shit by myself." Eddie began pulling on the mattress and trying to lift it. It slid off the hood and flat onto the wet ground in front of my car, then lay there like some uncooperative, rotting animal carcass that refused to be moved. He kept trying to pick it up, but it was too high for him to hold up off the ground without the help of his taller friend. Finally, I got out of my car and walked over to him. The Jesus guy had wandered off toward Hollywood High School, still holding his wrists and crying.

"Here, let me help you get this onto the sidewalk," I said, but Eddie just stood there.

"What for?" he said. "I can't take it anywhere by myself. I'll have to leave it there."

"Well, I'm sorry, but it's blocking the street," I said, as people continued to pass, staring out their windows and yelling obscenities at us.

"Listen," he said, grabbing hold of my sleeve and leaning forward so I could see his black, rotting teeth. "Help me out, man. We were taking this just up the street here behind the gas station on Franklin so we could have something to sleep on, you know? We could put it on top of your car and just drive it up there. It won't even take five minutes. You don't know what this would mean to me."

I considered helping him out. It really wouldn't be too much trouble, and it was raining. I mean, it wasn't like he was asking for money to buy drugs or something. He just wanted something comfortable to sleep on. It was a chance to actually, really help. I thought about his situation. I wondered what awful circumstances had led him to this pass, this pathetic situation in the middle of a rain-soaked street at night, and thought about the way I always refused to give panhandlers money because of what I thought they might do with it. He just wanted a bed to sleep on.

But I could smell the alcohol and body odor on him, and I began to imagine him sitting in my newly washed car, the mattress on the roof, his smell seeping comfortably into the fabric of my seats and then lingering there for weeks. I had a date to pick up, and I was already late.

"No, I don't think so," I said. "Here, I'll put it on the sidewalk for you, but you're on your own after that." I started pulling the mattress toward the sidewalk. The edges rubbed my fingertips and made them feel raw as I tried to get some kind of grip on the mattress. I could smell urine and sex on it. I tried to hold it away from my clothes, and this made it even harder to move. Eddie just stood there, scowling, shaking his head, and watching me drag the mattress off the street.

"White bastard," he said, as I lifted the edge onto the sidewalk corner. There was a Middle Eastern restaurant in the strip mall there. Above the restaurant was a green neon sign that made the mattress glow like Kryptonite in a sick lime-green color. "You're a real big man, with your fine clothes and big fancy car. Real big man," he said in a rough, husky voice. I didn't look up at him. I let the mattress fall to the sidewalk and rubbed my burning hands on my pants, then sniffed them quickly, hoping he wouldn't notice. He let out a disgusted grunt.

It began to rain again, lightly, as I walked back to my car. He stood on the corner next to the Kryptonite mattress, staring at me, and I could feel his eyes on my back as I walked in front of my headlights. My neck was burning, and my shirt felt damp and sticky under my arms. I got into my car and shut the door, and as I began to drive off, out of the corner of my eye, I could see him walking away up Highland Avenue, cursing to himself and shaking his head, maybe looking for the Jesus guy, the mattress left hanging partly off the curb as the rain began to fall harder.

Later, when I finally picked up Nanette, she was angry that I had taken so long. I said, "I'm sorry, but I ran into some traffic on Sunset," and we went out for sushi and plum wine.

The Thief

Walter Mosley

Iula's grill sat on aluminum stilts above an open-air, fenced-in auto garage on Slauson. Socrates liked to go to the diner at least once a month on a Tuesday because they served meat loaf and mustard greens on Tuesdays at Iula's. The garage was run by Tony LaPort, who had rented the diner out to Iula since before their marriage; it was a good arrangement for Tony so he still leased to her eight years after their divorce.

Tony had constructed the restaurant when he was in love and so it was well built. The diner was made from two large yellow school buses that Tony had welded together—side by side. The front bus held the counter where the customers sat, while the back bus held the kitchen and storage areas. The banistered stairway that led up to the door was aluminum also. When Iula closed for the night she used a motor-driven hoist to lift the staircase far up off the street. Then she'd go through the trapdoor down to Tony's work space, let herself out through the wire gate, and set the heavy padlocks that Tony used to keep thieves out.

If the locks failed to deter an enterprising crook there was still Tina to contend with. Tina was a hundred-pound mastiff who hated everybody in the world except Iula and

Tony. Tina sat right by the gate all night long, paws crossed in a holy prayer that some fool might want to test her teeth.

She was waiting that afternoon as Socrates approached the aluminum stairs. She growled in a low tone and Socrates found himself wondering if he would have a chance to crush the big dog's windpipe before she could tear out his throat. It was an idle thought; the kind of question that men discussed when they were in prison. In prison studying for survival was the only real pastime.

How many ways were there to kill a man? What was more dangerous in a close fight—a gun or a knife? How long could you hold your breath underwater if there were policemen looking for you on the shore? Will God really forgive any sin?

Thinking about killing that dog was just habit for Socrates. The habit of twenty-nine out of fifty-seven years behind bars.

As he climbed the aluminum staircase he thought again about how well built it was. He liked the solid feeling that the light metal gave. He was happy because he could smell the mustard greens.

He could almost taste that meat loaf.

"Shet that do'!" Iula shouted, her back turned to Socrates. "Damn flies like t'eat me up in here."

"Shouldn't cook so damn good you don't want no notice, I." Socrates slammed shut the makeshift screen door and walked up the step well into the bus.

The diner was still empty at 4:30. Socrates came early because he liked eating alone. He went to the stool nearest Iula and sat down. The musical jangle of coins rose from the pockets of his army jacket.

"You been collectin' cans again?" Iula had turned around to admire her customer. Her face was a deep amber color splattered with dark freckles, especially around her nose.

She was wide-hipped and large-breasted. Three gold teeth
decorated her smile. And she was smiling at Socrates. She
put a fist on one hip and pushed her apron out, making an
arc that brushed her side of the counter.

Socrates was looking at those breasts. Tony had once told
him that the first time he saw those titties they were standing straight up, nipples pointing left and right.

"Yeah, I," he said, in answer to her question. "I got me a
route now. Got three barmen keep the bottles an' cans on the
side for me. All I gotta do is clean up outside for them twice
a week. I made seventeen dollars just today."

"Ain't none these young boys out here try an' take them
bottles from you, Mr. Fortlow?"

"Naw. Gangbanger be ashamed t'take bottles in a sto'.
An' you know as long as I got my black jeans and army
green I don't got no color t'get them young bulls mad. If you
know how t'handle them they leave you alone."

"I'ont care what you say," Iula said. "Them boys make
me sick wit' all that rap shit they playin' an' them guns an'
drugs."

"I seen worse," Socrates said. "You know these three
men live in a alley offa Crenshaw jump me today right after
I got my can money."

"They did?"

"Uh-huh. Fools thought they could take me." Socrates
held out his big black hand. The thick fingers were the size
of large cigars. When he made a fist the knuckles rode high
like four deadly fins.

Iula was impressed.

"They hurt you?" she asked.

Socrates looked down at his left forearm. There, near the
wrist was a sewn-up tear and a dark stain.

"What's that?" Iula cried.

"One fool had a bottle edge. Huh! He won't try an' cut
me soon again."

"Did he break the skin?"

"Not too much."

"You been to a doctor, Mr. Fortlow?"

"Naw. I went home an' cleaned it out. Then I sewed up my damn coat. I cracked that boy's arm 'cause he done ripped my damn coat."

"You better get down to the emergency room," Iula said. "That could get infected."

"I cleaned it good."

"But you could get lockjaw."

"Not me. In the penitentiary they gave you a tetanus booster every year. You might get a broke jaw in jail but you ain't never gonna get no lockjaw."

Socrates laughed and set his elbows on the counter. He cleared his throat and looked at Iula watching him. Behind her was the kitchen and a long frying grill. There were big pots of beef-and-tomato soup, mashed potatoes, braised short ribs, stewed chicken, and steaming mustard greens simmering on the stove. The meat loaves, Socrates knew from experience, were in bread pans in the heating pantry above the ovens.

It was hot in Iula's diner.

Hotter under her stare.

She put her hand on Socrates's arm.

"You shouldn't be out there hustlin' bottles, Mr. Fortlow," she said. Her voice was like the rustling of coarse blankets.

"I got t'eat. An' you know jobs don't grow on trees, I. Anyway, I got a bad temper. I might turn around one day an' break a boss's nose."

Iula laid her finger across his knuckles.

"You could work here," she said. "There's room enough for two behind this here counter."

Iula turned her head to indicate what she meant. In doing so she revealed her amber throat, it was a lighter shade than her face.

He remembered another woman, just a girl really, and her delicate neck. That woman died by the same hand Iula stroked. She died and hadn't done a thing to deserve even a bruise. He had killed her and was a little sorrier every day; every day for thirty-six years. He got sadder but she was still dead. She was dead, and he was still asking himself why.

"I don't know," he said.

"What?"

"I don't know what to say, I."

"What is there to say?" she demanded. "All you could say is yeah. You ain't got hardly a dime. You need a job. And the Lord knows I could use you, too."

"I got to think about it," he said.

"Think about it?" Just that fast Iula was enraged. "Think about it? Here I am offerin' you a way outta that hole you in. Here I am offerin' you a life. An' you got to think about it? Look out here in the streets around you, Mr. Fortlow. Ain't no choice out there. Ain't nuthin' t'think about out there."

Socrates didn't have to look around to see the boarded-up businesses and stores; the poor black faces and brown faces of the men and women who didn't have a thing. Iula's diner and Tony's garage were the only working businesses on the block.

And he hated bringing bottles and cans to the Ralph's supermarket on Crenshaw. To get there he had to walk for miles pulling three grocery carts linked by twisted wire coat hangers. And when he got there, they always made him wait; made him stand outside while they told jokes and had coffee breaks. And then they checked every can. They didn't have to do that. He knew what they took and what they didn't. He came in twice a week with his cans and bottles and nobody ever found one Kessler's Root Beer or Bubble-Up in the lot. But they checked every one just the same. And they never bothered to learn his name. They called him Pop or Old Man. They made him wait and checked after him like he was some kind of stupid animal.

But he took it. He took it because of that young girl's neck; because of her boyfriend's dead eyes. Those young people in Ralph's were stupid and arrogant and mean—but he was evil. That's what Socrates thought.

That's what he believed.

"Well?" Iula asked.

"I'd...I'd like some meat loaf, Iula. Some meat loaf with mashed potatoes and greens."

From the back of her throat Iula hissed, "Damn you!"

Socrates was heavyhearted over the thoughts he had. He was sad, even depressed, over the guilt he could not escape.

But that didn't affect his appetite. He'd learned when he was a boy that the next meal was never a promise and that only a fool didn't eat when he could.

He laced his mashed potatoes and meat loaf with pepper sauce and downed the mustard greens in big noisy mouthfuls. When he was finished he looked behind the counter hoping to catch Iula's eye. Because usually Iula would give Socrates seconds while smiling and complimenting him on the good appetite he had.

"You eat good but you don't let it turn to fat," she'd say, admiring his big muscles.

But now she was mad at him for insulting her offer. Why should she feed the kitty when there wasn't a chance to win the game?

"I," Socrates said.

"What you want?" It was more a dare than a question.

"Just some coffee, babe," he said.

Iula slammed the mug down and flung the Pyrex coffeepot so recklessly that she spilled half of what she poured. But Socrates didn't mind. He was still hungry and so he finished filling the mug with milk from two small serving pitchers on the counter.

He had eleven quarters in his right-hand jacket pocket. Two dollars and fifty cents for the dinner and twenty-five cents more for Iula's tip. That was a lot of money when all you had to your name was seventy-two quarters, four dimes, three nickels, and eight pennies. It was a lot of money but Socrates was still hungry—and that meat loaf smelled better than ever.

Iula used sage in her meat loaf. He couldn't make it at home because all he had at home was a hot plate and you can't make meat loaf on a hot plate.

"Iula!"

Socrates turned to see the slim young man come up into the bus. He was wearing an electric-blue exercise suit, zipped up to the neck, and a bright-yellow headband.

"Wilfred," Iula said in greeting. There were still no seconds in her voice.

"How things goin'?" the young man asked.

"Pretty good if you don't count for half of it."

"Uh-huh," he answered, not having heard. "An' where's Tony today?"

"It's Tuesday, ain't it?"

"Yeah."

"Then Tony's down at Christ Congregational settin' up for bingo."

Wilfred sat himself at the end of the counter, five stools away from Socrates. He caught the older man's eye and nodded—as black men do.

Then he said, "I done built me up a powerful hunger today, Iula. I got two hollow legs to fill."

"What you want?" she asked, not at all interested in the story he was obviously wanting to tell.

"You got a steak back there in the box?"

"Shit." She would have spit on the floor if she wasn't in her own restaurant.

"Okay. Okay. I tell you what. I want some stewed chicken, some braised ribs, an' two thick slabs'a meat loaf on one big plate."

"That ain't on the menu."

"Charge me a dinner for each one then."

Iula's angry look changed to wonder. "You only get one slice of meat loaf with a dinner."

"Then ring it up twice, honey. I got mad money for this here meal."

Iula stared until Wilfred pulled out a fan of twenty-dollar bills from his pocket. He waved the fan at her and said, "Don't put no vegetables on that shit. You know I'm a workin' man—I needs my strength. I need meat."

Iula moved back into the kitchen to fill Wilfred's order.

Socrates sipped his coffee.

"Hey, brother," Wilfred said.

Socrates looked up at him.

"How you doin'?" the young man offered.

"Okay, I guess."

"You guess?"

"It depends."

"Depends on what?"

"On what comes next."

When Wilfred smiled Socrates could see that he was missing one of his front teeth.

"You jus' livin' minute t'minute, huh?" the young man said.

"That's about it."

"I used to be like that. Used to be. That is till I found me a good job." Wilfred sat back as well as he could on the stool and stared at Socrates as if expecting to be asked a question.

Socrates took another sip of coffee. He was thinking about another helping of meat loaf and his quarters and Iula's nipples—and that long-ago-dead girl. He didn't have any room for what was on the young man's mind.

Iula came out then with a platter loaded down with meats. It was a steaming plate looking like something out of the dreams Socrates had when he was deep inside of his jail sentence.

"Put it over there, Iula." Wilfred was pointing to the place next to Socrates. He got up from his stool and went to sit behind the platter.

He was a tall man, in his twenties. He'd shaved that morning and had razor bumps along his jaw and throat. His clothes were bulky and Socrates wondered why. He was thin and well built. Obviously from *the 'hood*—Socrates could tell that from the hunger he brought to his meal.

"What's your name, man?" Wilfred asked.

"Socrates."

"That's somebody famous right?"

"Long time ago."

"In Europe right?"

"I guess."

"You see?" Wilfred said, full of pride. "I ain't no fool. I know shit. I got it up here. My name is Wilfred."

Socrates breathed in deeply the smells from Wilfred's plate. He was still hungry—having walked a mile for every dollar he'd made that day.

His stomach growled like an angry dog.

"What you eatin', Socco?" Wilfred asked. Before giving him a chance to answer he called out to Iula, "What's my brother eatin', Iula? Bring whatever it is out to 'im. I pay for that, too."

While Iula put together Socrates's second plate, Wilfred picked up a rib and sucked the meat from the bone.

He grinned and said, "Only a black woman could cook like this."

Socrates didn't know about that, but he was happy to see the plate Iula put before him.

Socrates didn't pick up his fork right away. Instead he regarded his young benefactor and said, "Thank you."

"That's okay, brother. Eat up."

Halfway through his second meal Socrates's hunger eased a bit. Wilfred was almost through with his four dinners. He pushed the plate back.

"You got some yams back there?" he called out to Iula.

"Yeah," she answered. She had gone to a chair in her kitchen to rest and smoke a cigarette before more customers came.

"Bring out a big plate for me an' my friend here."

Iula brought out the food without saying a word to Socrates. But he wasn't worried about her silence.

He came around on Tuesdays, when Tony was gone, because he wanted Iula for something; a girlfriend, a few nights in bed, maybe more, maybe. He hadn't been with a woman since before prison when, in a blind rage, he'd slaughtered a man, raped that man's girlfriend, and then broke her neck for whining about it.

When the judge asked him for an explanation he couldn't give it. What was there to say? That he'd been mad as hell every day of his life and then that one day it all fell into place?

He had the right amount of Jim Beam and reefer, he was in the man's house, and the man's girlfriend was giving him the eye. When Socrates looked back at her the boyfriend wanted to fight.

Fight him! When it was his woman smiling and flirting like some whore.

It just all fell into place like a royal flush, like a perfect left hook.

And when it was over he didn't even know what he had done. He woke up the next morning with barely a notion of the crime. He'd hit the man pretty hard. He choked the girl till she stopped that crying.

But it wasn't till the prosecutor showed the police photographs in court that he knew for sure what he'd done.

He wanted to tell the judge that he didn't mean it, that he was sorry, but the words didn't come. They didn't come for a long time. When they finally came out, he'd been in prison for a dozen years.

And when they'd let him out of jail, because it was his birthday and because he hadn't killed anybody white, he was afraid; afraid of his hands on a woman. Afraid of the photograph of that girl.

Iula was petulant, but she didn't understand how scared he was even to want her.

But he did want her; partly because she wanted him. She wanted a man up there on stilts with her to lift tubs of shortening that she couldn't budge. She wanted a man to sit down next to her in the heat that those stoves threw off.

If he came up there he'd probably get fat.

"What you thinkin' about, brother?" Wilfred asked.

"That they ain't nuthin' for free."

"Well...maybe sometime they is."

"Maybe," Socrates said, "but I don't think so."

Wilfred grinned.

Socrates asked, "What kinda work you do, Wilfred?"

"I'm self-employed. I'm a businessman."

"Oh yeah? What kinda business?"

Wilfred smiled and tried to look coy. "What you think?"

"I'd say a thief," Socrates answered. He speared a hot yam and pushed it in his mouth.

Wilfred's smile widened but his eyes went cold.

"You got sumpin' against a man makin' a livin'?" he asked.

"Depends."

"'Pends on what?"

"On if it's wrong or not."

"Stealin's stealin', man. It's all the same thing. You got it—I take it."

"If you say so."

"That's what I do say," Wilfred said. "Stealin's right for the man takin' an' wrong fo' the man bein' took. That's all they is to it."

Socrates decided that he didn't like Wilfred. But his stomach was full and he'd become playful. "But if a man take some bread an' he's hungry, starvin'," he said, "that's not wrong to nobody. That's good sense."

"Yeah. You right," Wilfred conceded. "But s'pose you hungry for a good life. For a nice house with a bathtub an' not just some shower. S'pose you want some nice shoes an' socks don't bust out through the toe the first time you wear 'em?"

"That depends, too."

"'Pends on what? What I want don't depend on a damn thing." Wilfred's smile was gone now.

"Maybe not. I mean maybe the wantin' don't depend on nuthin' but how you get it does, though."

"Like what you mean?"

"Well, let's say that there's a store sellin' this good life you so hungry for. They got it in a box somewhere. Now you go an' steal it. Well, I guess that's okay. That means the man got the good life give it up to you. That's cool."

"Shit," Wilfred said. "If they had a good life in a box you know I steal me hunnert'a them things. I be right down here on Adams sellin' 'em for half price."

"Uh-huh. But they don't have it in a box now do they?"

"What you tryin' t'say, man?" Wilfred was losing patience. He was, Socrates thought, a kind benefactor as long as he didn't have to see a man eye to eye.

"I'm sayin' that this good life you talkin' 'bout stealin' comes outta your own brother's mouth. Either you gonna steal from a man like me or you gonna steal from a shop where I do my business. An' ev'ry time I go in there I be payin' for security cameras an' security guards an' up-to-the-roof insurance that they got t'pay off what people been stealin'."

Socrates thought that Wilfred might get mad. He half expected the youth to pull out a gun. But Socrates wasn't worried about a gun in those quarters. He had a knife handy and, as he had learned in prison, a knife can beat a gun up close.

But Wilfred wasn't mad. He laughed happily. He patted Socrates on the shoulder, feeling his hard muscle, and said,

"You got a good tongue there, brother. You good as a preacher, or a cop, when it comes to talkin' that talk."

Wilfred stood up and Socrates swiveled around on his seat, ready for the fight.

Iula sensed the tension and came out with a cigarette dangling from her lips.

Wilfred stripped off his exercise jacket and stepped out of the gaudy nylon pants. Underneath he was wearing a two–piece tweed suit with a suede brown vest. His silk tie showed golden and green clouds with little flecks of red floating here and there. His shirt was white as Sunday's clothesline.

"What you think?" Wilfred asked his audience.

Iula grunted and turned back to her kitchen. He was too skinny for her no matter what he had on.

"Come here," Wilfred said to Socrates. "Look out here in the street."

Socrates went to the bus window and crouched down to look outside. There was a new tan car, a foreign job, parked out there. Socrates didn't know the model, but it looked like a nice little car.

"That's my ride," Wilfred said.

"Where it take you?" Socrates asked, but he already suspected the answer.

"Wherever I wanna go," Wilfred answered. "But mostly I hit the big malls an' shoppin' centers up in West Hollywood, Beverly Hills, Santa Monica, and what have you. I get one'a my girlfriends to rent me a car. Then I get all dressed up like this an' put a runnin' suit, or maybe some funky clothes like you got on, over that. An' I always got me a hat or a headband or somethin'. You know they could hardly ever pick you out of a lineup if you had sumpin' on yo' head."

Socrates had learned that in jail, too.

"I grab 'em in the parkin' lot." Wilfred sneered with violent pleasure. "I put my knife up hard against they necks an' tell 'em they dead. You know I don't care if I cut 'em up a li'l bit. Shit. I had one young Jap girl peed on herself."

Wilfred waited for a laugh or something. When it didn't come the jaunty young man went back to his seat.

"You don't like it," Wilfred said, "too bad."

"I don't give a damn what you do, boy," Socrates answered. He sat back down and ate the last piece of meat loaf from his plate. "I cain't keep a fool from messin' up."

"I ain't no fool, old man. I don't mess up, neither. I get they money an' cut 'em up some so they call a doctor fo' they call the cops. Then I run an' th'ow off my niggah clothes. When the cops come I'm in my suit, in my car comin' home. An' if they stop me I look up all innocent an' lie an' tell 'em that I work for A&M Records. I tell 'em that I'm a manager in the mail room over there. No sir, I don't fuck up at all."

"Uh-huh," Socrates said. He put a yam in his mouth after dipping it in the honey-butter sauce at the bottom of the dish; it was just about the best thing he had ever tasted.

"Motherfuckah, you gonna sit there an' diss me with yo' mouth fulla the food I'm buyin'?" Wilfred was amazed.

"You asked me an' I told ya," Socrates said. "I don't care what you do, boy. But that don't mean I got to call it right."

"What you talkin' 'bout, man? I ain't stealin' from no brother. I ain't stealin' where no po' brother live. I'm takin' the good life from people who got it—just like you said."

"You call my clothes funky din't ya, boy?"

"Hey, man. I din't mean nuthin'."

"Yes you did," Socrates said. "You think I'm funky an' smelly an' I ain't got no feelin's. That's what you think. You don't see that I keep my socks darned an' my clothes clean. You don't see that you walkin' all over me like I was some piece dog shit. An' you don't care. You just put on a monkey suit an' steal a few pennies from some po' woman's purse. You come down here slummin', flashin' some dollar bills, talkin' all big. But when you all through people gonna look at me like I'm shit. They scared'a me 'cause you out there pretendin' that you're me robbin' them."

Wilfred held up his hands in a false gesture of surrender and laughed. "You too deep for me, brother," he said. He was smiling but alert to the violence in the older man's words. "Way too deep."

"You the one shovelin' it, man. You the one out there stealin' from the white man an' blamin' me. You the one wanna be like them in their clothes. You hatin' them an' dressed like the ones you hate. You don't even know who the hell you is!"

Socrates had to stop himself from striking Wilfred. He was shaking, scared of his own hands.

"I know who I am all right, brother," Wilfred said. "And I'm a damn sight better'n you."

"No you not," Socrates said. A sense of calm came over him. "No you not. You just dressin' good, eatin' like a pig. But when the bill come due I'm the one got t'pay it. Me an' all the rest out here."

"All right, fine!" Wilfred shouted. "But the only one right now payin' fo' somethin' is me. I'm the one got you that food you been eatin'. But if you don't like it then pay for it yourself."

Iula came out again. Socrates noted the pot of steaming water she carried.

"I do you better than that, boy," Socrates said. "I'll pay for yo' four dinners, too."

"What?" Wilfred and Iula both said.

"All of it," Socrates said. "I'll pay for it all."

"You a new fool, man," Wilfred said.

Socrates stood up and then bent down to pick up Wilfred's stickup clothes from the floor.

"You always got to pay, Wilfred. But I'll take this bill. I'll leave the one out there for you."

Wilfred faked a laugh and took the clothes from Socrates.

"Get outta here, man," Socrates said.

For a long moment, death hung between the two men. Wilfred full of violence and pride and Socrates sick of violent and prideful men.

"I don't want no trouble in here, now!" Iula shouted when she couldn't take the tension anymore.

Wilfred smiled again and nodded. "You win, old man," he said. "But you crazy, though."

"Just get outta here," Socrates said. "Go."

Wilfred considered for the final time doing something. He was probably faster than the older man. But it was a small space and strength canceled out speed in close quarters.

Socrates read all of that in Wilfred's eyes. Another young fool, he knew, who thought freedom was out the back door and in the dark.

Wilfred turned away slowly, went down the stairwell, then down the aluminum staircase to the street.

Socrates watched the tan car drive off.

"You're insane, Socrates Fortlow, you know that?" Iula said. She was standing on her side of the counter in front of eighteen stacks of four quarters each.

"You got to pay for your dinner, I."

"But why you got to pay for him? He had money."

"That was just a loan, I. But the interest was too much for me."

"You ain't responsible fo' him."

"You wrong there, baby. I'm payin' for niggahs like that ev'ry day. Just like his daddy paid for me."

"You are a fool."

"But I'm my own fool, I."

"I don't get it," she said. "If you so upstandin' an' hard-workin' an' honest—then why don't you wanna come here an' work fo' me? Is it 'cause I'm a woman? 'Cause you don't wanna work fo' no woman?"

Socrates was feeling good. The food in his stomach had killed the hunger. The muscles in his arms relaxed now that he didn't have to fight. There was an ache in his forearm where he'd been cut but, as the prison doctor used to say, pain was just a symptom of life.

Socrates laughed.

"You're a woman, all right, I. I know you had that boilin' water out there t'save me from Wilfred. You a woman all right and I'm gonna be comin' back here every Tuesday from now on. I'm gonna come see you and we gonna talk too, momma. Yeah. You gonna be seein' much more'a me."

He got up and kissed her on the cheek before leaving. When his lips touched her skin a sound came from the back of her throat. The sound of satisfaction that takes a lifetime to understand.

Socrates only had four dimes, three nickels, and eight pennies left to his name. If he took a bus he'd be broke, but he was just as happy to walk. On the way home he thought about finding a job somewhere. He thought about making a living from the strength of his hands.

Girl on Fire

Yxta Maya Murray

I TOLD MANNY THAT THERE'D BE TROUBLE between the *Juelos* and the C-4s, but he didn't listen to me. You know how these men are—he just pats me on the ass—"Yeah, baby."

Me and my girls belong to the Juelos. It's not that we have jackets or nothing. We just juice them, most times. It's a good arrangement. In return they take care of us, protect us and our babies. Manny told me it would be OK if I dropped out of Millikan. If there are ever any big problems, I can just run my own deals on the side. He's got the connections.

We come from Long Beach, about an hour away from East LA and not that much different. Manny's people run the eastside. A lot of our parents settled here from Oaxaca, doing the seasons, oranges mostly, some travel to the desert to do dates. I've seen them, breaking their backs over baskets of fruit. Only this generation got it straight. We found out where the money is.

We don't do big drugs at my house, just a little pot and coke. I need the hit sometimes to keep it going, be a good screw. Sex here, it's like a contest. Even when you don't feel like doing it, you have to bash around like some horse. The men say that they don't need white women because their girls are hot!!!, but they still keep looking at that blond hair.

I smoke a little to get it jumping, try to make enough noise like a cat, be the little tamale. It keeps me on the in, because outside, there's rough.

Sometimes I live with my mama and she's bringing me down. "*Chique*," she'll say, "I didn't travel all this way so that you could be some bastard's *puta*, no school and the drugs, your friends having babies when they're 15." She'll tell me this even when I give her money. Where does she think it comes from? She eats regular, but that doesn't stop her from complaining all the time. She gets on me about the way I look, but I look good, like my girls.

It's not easy. We got that dark brown hair, so we get some Sun In, turn it red color. I fry my bangs so they get a nice wave, then tease it all the way. Get our faces rose-colored and lips glossy, and we are *pumped up*. Besides belonging to the Juelos, we got our own thing going. We're called Girls on Fire.

There's me, Carla and Susanna. Hangin' since eleven. Playing Barbies before we knew what was out there. Now we babysit for each other, I'm the only one with no kid. Susanna says it's because I'm dry. If I'm not in my mama's house or with Manny, I'm over at one of their houses, playing with those boy babies and making dinner. When I stay over it Susanna's, we'll even sleep in the same bed together, rolled tight under all her blankets, feeling safe. We laugh about it and she'll say, "Don't let the men know about it. They'll think we're off!"

But we don't just sit around. To keep our end fresh, we have to help out with the business. The three of us will keep watch over a deal, sitting in a car at the end of the block, with our phones, in case of an emergency. Manny even made sure we got our own guns with a big *pop*. Bought them from some redhead my age who sells to us out of the back of his daddy's store. What does he care?

We'd been sticking tight for six years now, with the same crew of men usually. It can get a little wild, but I always thought you need to build yourself a family, to find out where you really are.

It was Carla who jumped that stupid war with her C-4 Jaime. Pissed off Beto and got the whole thing started.

Whereas the Juelos got the east, the C-4s deal on the west end. It keeps pretty separate, but sometimes there's turf problems or the women will mix.

Carla was with Beto for more than two years, had his baby at Kaiser, Beto made sure the whole thing was paid for. Told her to get clean when he knew that she was pregnant, got her milk and meat and didn't even seem to care that much when she got all fat. He screwed around, but so what? To men it's a party, but the women have to keep it together, they have to make sure the lid stays on when everything goes all crazy. Not Carla. She meets Jaime, I don't know how, the 7-Eleven?

I go over to her house, Jaime is sitting on the couch like it's his. They're watching TV with the baby, she's sitting next to him all big with her red fried hair, some wild purple eye shadow, done up for her prince. Stretching out those new pink jeans.

I said, "Girl, you know that Beto's gonna get pissed he finds out about this. He thinks that you belong to him, especially with that baby. And the money he paid for the hospital!"

She told me to shut up. "I don't belong to no one," she says. "I found out that Beto's screwing some junior white girl named Donna, thinks he's Mr. Latin Lover. Jaime's good to me. Bought me this." Carla shows me this sparkly new ring, tiny diamonds shaped into a heart.

I knew when I told Manny that they'd just *loco*. They try to hold us to their code, but don't understand that we just keep with them out of love. So sometimes, since it's the heart and not the boys' rules talking, girls will just switch over. It's not a Juelo/C-4 thing, but they don't get it and start taking out their guns.

Manny explained it to me once. Only thing I knew afterwards was that I wasn't going to be doing anyone but a Juelo.

"*Vieja*," he said, and he knew I hated it when he called me that name, "that's just the way the world works. This side and that side, ours and theirs. When we see them taking from us, we have to do something or else it'll never stop. They'll cover our deals. They'll steal our streets."

I tried to tell him sense. "But, Baby, you know that the heart don't work on lines, and sometimes girls will move around a while and then come right back."

He looked at me real hard. "Whoever does that will make a big mistake."

I didn't say anything after that, because in this place it's hard for a woman to get her mind heard. You've got to plan what you say ahead of time, make sure it won't get you into trouble. But saying what you think, it feels good, just like breathing.

The C-4s started in '85, when some grouper named Hi-C cashed in what he'd earned in jail and got some distribution deals going. He had three others for a crew, which is why it's called the C-4. It's lots bigger now.

My mama grew up with his family in Oaxaca, and so I know that his real name is Pepe. He's short, with spiky greaser hair under his baseball cap, 5'2" trying to act tall. Back inside now since he popped a cop last year.

Hi-C and his crew ran the stream for all of Long Beach until 1988, when Manny got the Juelos together with money they'd stolen from liquor stores. Small stuff, but like the C-4s Manny used the people he'd met in jail and somewhere down the line there was a good source. He tried to talk things out with Hi-C's gang, but there were a lot of drive-bys over who got a street. Things are worked out now, but stunts like Carla's could really mess it all up.

I wound up with Manny, because I went to Millikan High, which is strictly eastside, and he'd cruise the school looking for the cherries ditching class and smoking.

A week after I caught Carla with Jaime, Beto found out. There was a couple of meetings, grease boys sitting on park benches with their man talk. To decide if it's big enough to do some shooting, or what. If there should be some kind of trade. Manny started coming home mad, shaking his head. "I told you we take this serious. Get your girls straight!" We knew that there'd be some action, anyhow, so we started shaking things together.

Me and Susanna went over to see the redhead, Scott, to do a buy. Manny gave us his number a couple of years ago. "Just for special occasions."

His dad's shop was called Gun World, and we had to go around to the back door and into this little room, all nice and clean, where their secret deals went down. We'd moved up from those late-eighties specials, two tin cans tied together that could take off your face on misfire. Susanna was the expert; I just hung back.

"I think just all Glock," she said. I don't know why we were buying the super expensive, but I guess with the new money we were going glamour.

She was seventeen, copper hair stringy, and she'd do these serious eyelashes. Next to her left eye was the Juelo tattoo, a small black star. She'd grown up two blocks from me and dropped out of school early to have Enrico's kid, Carlito. She was usually stay-at-home.

Scott was Mr. Business twitchy face. "17 or 17L?" He pulled out these two guns, one bigger than the other.

She did her James Bond coupon, pretending to shoot me with that empty gun. BAM! BAM! and I put my hands where my heart is, like I'm hit. She goes quiet and says, "Front and rear sight. How about a deal on extra magazines?" Smiling, fluorescent light bouncing off her shiny lips.

Afterwards we brown-bagged it and walked back to our car, looked like a couple of old ladies shopping. These blond boys called from across the street. Little button-down shirts. "*Chola!* Hey, *Chollllla!* Ha, HA!"
We didn't do anything. Our groceries were just too hot.

Carla's the crazy one, Susanna's real stable, and I used to try to tell them what to do. We were pretty bored when we were all in school, never did all that reading. Sit in the back row, wearing our black pants, staring out the window. Didn't make any trouble, we stayed put until our boyfriends would pick us up at lunchtime.

Before Susanna had her baby, she talked about being a teacher: "I can sit and talk at kids as good as Mrs. Klegg does. Klegg just hands us those magazines and feeds us Shakespeare videos, no big deal, she's waiting to retire. I bet she's shut down since we started moving in here, only dealing special with those two bus girls in the front row. She just wants to keep the Mexicans and the black kids quiet, doesn't think they know anything. I could graduate and get a teacher's credential, teach Spanish. My own money and not get all dragged down."

Still, she was the first one to quit. All the talk about teaching stopped as soon as she met Enrico and got pregnant. Fifteen years old.

Carla moved here from Mexico after her father died and her mom hooked on with some guy from the States who brought them both over. When she first came to the neighborhood, she was a little string bean running around laughing. She'd caught the English quick. Probably the smartest one, but who could know now. Dancing and singing Madonna songs, like some fat girl on *Soul Train*.

I was born here, same as Susanna. Nothing much to say. My dad worked the seasons, but we just lost track and haven't seen him in five years. My mom is on welfare, but cleans houses, too. I've been with Manny since I was 14. His eyes are as black as a bad night.

"*Chique*," Mom will say to me when I come home, "God is watching you. He knows everything in that little *cucaracha* brain of yours."

Sometimes when we all together, we'll smoke and watch the *novelas*. Stupid Old World love stories. We feel just like housewives. Should be wearing those little polyester dresses and crying over chicken dinners.

I heard about the decision meeting later, with Beto firing all the boys up, Manny trying to keep the cool. Manny's the leader, since he taps into the sources and he's got a head for business. Does the numbers.

Gangs are like a little country and Manny's the king. There are about 50 boys. They do the deals he tells them to, and then he'll give them a cut. Anyone gets out of line, steals some money from a take, there'll be the discipline. Once there was this Francisco, bought some bags and then sold them himself on the street. When Manny found out, he had Cisco bloodied. He's got some scars now over his eyes and his mouth's a little funny, but he took it all right. They just went right back to normal after.

But sometimes Manny has to step out of the way, because things can get too hot.

Beto had seen Carla as an attack on the Juelos, since Jaime was a pretty high ranker in the C-4s. He'd told them, all standing around this kids' park in the neighborhood, "We fought so hard for this side, doesn't anyone remember '88?

And they take it from us in pieces, moving in on my family. If they find out they can do this, then the bigger things will come and we'll be fighting for Hawaiian Gardens again." The Gardens, that's my town.

For all of Manny's talk to me, I think he understood that it was just about a little sex. Nothing about streets. He'd told Beto to give it some time, let their thing slow down. "We have to wait for the important stuff before we get shooting. She's just squeezing a little cheese, giving you back some." He was talking about that Donna.

But with all those guns and drugs around, it's any excuse, and Manny came back that night tense. "They want to take out Jaime, I think it's stupid, but I had to let them go ahead. Otherwise they just do it behind my back." Since it wasn't my place, I didn't say much.

Girlfriends don't care about who owns what, just as long as things are fine at home. Still, I let out the word to Carla and Susanna just in case things got too close, and I guess that Carla warned Jaime.

It turned out that the C-4s tried to make the hit first, putting all of these bullets in Manny's house the night after the meeting. We didn't have any kids, running around, getting their little butts shot off. I mean, someone could have gotten hurt, but the news makes it sound like the gangbangers really work it. It's not Mafia, no front face attacks. Our boys are too scared; they just want to make the show from the car, screeching their tires and making their guns go boom. If someone buys it, then all the better. More often, they tag babies and grandmas who are sitting outside.

We were asleep. It sounded like rockets were landing in the living room. I was still waking up when Manny was yelling "DOWN DOWN DOWN!" and pushing my head onto the floor. There was breaking glass and everything got hotter. I'd never been in gunfire before, so I crawled under

the bed and hid under my hair, crying so hard I drooled pud-
dles on the floor. Big sounds in my ears and Manny screaming out into the street. I forgot all about that big fancy gun
that Susanna and I had bought. No balls. They drove off after
a couple of minutes, but Manny caught one in the shoulder
and I had to drive him to the hospital, blood running down
his arm, smears of it on the dash and the windows, his head
drooping back onto the seat. "I'll KILL those fucks!" he kept
saying and me going ssshhhhh. I don't know why they hit
us, when it was Beto who was yelling his head off.

The whole way in the car I kept thinking about how
Susanna had talked when we were in high school. Braver
than this.

Carla wound up staying with Jaime. We were still friends,
the three of us, but I couldn't help being mad at Carla and
her ways that almost got me killed. "Think *above* the waist,
girl," I'd say, not looking at anybody. Susanna felt bad, but
she kept tight with Carla, since no guns had come to her
door. I guess I did break apart from them. It was grow-up
time.

Susanna helped me with Manny, driving him around,
listening to him get mad. His arm wasn't working. One day
we were doing his laundry, folding shirts in her kitchen, and
she said, "You know I'll always be there for you. *Hermanas.*"
She knew what was up. I watched her face with that little
star and tried to remember how I liked to feed her baby. How
I felt safe, curled up under her blanket. But I closed my ears
a little bit. One slip could hurt you a lot later on.

When we were all in the eighth grade and our science
teacher got these school buses together, we went on a field
trip to a park out of town. Everyone had a glass jar to put

nature things in. Me and Carla and Susanna found a little hill with all these yellow flowers on it, yellow daisies and green grass, with sun.

Carla and Susanna got excited and ran fast over the hill, laughing like little rabbits. I stayed behind and watched them get swallowed up by the blue air. Listened for birds in trees that had Latin names.

There was so much sky.

Los Angeles
Here and Now

Ann Nietzke

MID-MORNING THE ASHES of her neighbor's son arrive still warm from somewhere in the Valley. The boy who delivers them may or may not realize the nature of his cargo, having no command of English and appearing to expect a tip. He offers no receipt to sign, and Fran doesn't bother to steer him next door, simply transferring the blond, fake-wood case directly from his hands onto the red canvas chair inside her narrow hallway. She knows that Carol is off to a doctor in search of a drug that will make her stop weeping.

Carol hasn't lived here long, having moved in from the beach to take an office job downtown (in from the beach and away from Joey). At twenty-two the boy was still an ardent surfer, much too adept, even at riptide, to snap his neck and drown, though this is what he did. Fran has seen pictures of Joey at every age on his mother's walls but never actually met him, which complicates her feelings now as she clears off the small oak table in her breakfast nook and carefully centers the tepid box, less with sadness than a cloying sense of awe. She hears a starched and solemn voice from her grandfather's funeral years ago: *We brought nothing into this world, and it is certain we can carry nothing out.*

Fran and Carol are the same age and friendly, take in an occasional movie together, toured the Frank Lloyd Wright house at Barnsdall Park one extra-smoggy Sunday afternoon. They keep track of neighborhood graffiti and gunshots and abandoned cars and share lists of toll-free numbers for futile complaints to the city. Carol has always talked more about Joey than about herself, a habit that has intensified in the week since his death. There is never a mention of the father, and Fran has run out of impotent, comforting words. She moves to the sink to wash her hands and stares at a framed lunar postcard of Earth. Fran spent the first moon landing (her first honeymoon) making love on the floor of an empty house, empty, that is, but for TV and mattress. For years she viewed the famous photos through that fleshy, myopic memory, though of late the blue-black image has widened, beyond the whirl of days and months.

She should be at work, but it gusted rain all night and drowned her car, soaking wires past any hope of ignition. Nate at Old Volks advised her to remove the distributor cap and blow on the connectors, which Fran has done, plus wiped everything with paper towel. She put a garbage bag over the engine, beneath the stupidly vented hood, and has come upstairs to wait for evaporation. On this first day of mandatory rationing, well into a five-year drought, water has burst through her living room ceiling. She's been half watching a talk show on osteoporosis, trying not to hear the drips in the bucket, but now she turns the TV off to listen for the click of Carol's key next door. Once it comes, she waits a bit before calling.

"Carol?" she says. "Listen. There was a delivery while you were gone."

"A delivery?" Carol says vaguely.

"From the Valley," Fran says.

"Oh, God," Carol says. "They told me afternoon. Not before three."

"Yes, I think they were supposed to wait," Fran says, unable, quite, to mention temperature. "But anyway, I'll be right there."

As it happens, once over the tactile shock—Fran sees it register in her weary gray eyes and thin twist of mouth— Carol seems to take comfort in the heat, snuggling up to the tin-lined box as she curls herself onto the couch.

"Do you want me to call your brother?" Fran asks. "Maybe your sister-in-law can come and stay a couple more nights."

"They're back in Vegas now," Carol says. "They've got problems of their own."

"Well. Do you want anything before I go?" Fran eyes what looks like half a pound of pale blue oval tablets spread out on the hardwood floor.

"I took two and spilled the rest," Carol explains, both hands on the box against her belly. She is a lanky woman, the palest kind of blonde, her skin translucent now with days of grief.

"Where did you find this doctor?" Fran asks.

"West Hollywood," Carol says. "He was really nice. He said this is the worst thing that can happen to a person, to lose a child. He went ahead and wrote refills, too."

"Hmm," Fran says, bending to scoop the pills back into their bottle. "I'm going to put these in the bathroom. I'm going to put them inside your medicine chest. Then I'm going on to work if the car will start. And check back with you when I get home." Carol responds to none of this, so Fran lets herself out, locking the knob.

Traffic is jammed and detoured onto Beverly due to a fallen palm across Wilton, but nobody's honking. Pedestrians seem frisky in the rain, parched souls sprung to life like those flattened sponges. Fran's engine dies at every light but reignites with little strain. At Crenshaw and Venice she pulls up behind a tiny, white-haired lady wearing gossamer wings that project higher than the car seat, higher even than her head. Her bouffant appears to float back and forth in time with her windshield wipers, and as she leans forward to execute her turn, she makes ascension look accessible. Fran considers skipping the workday afternoon to follow this battered green Mercury wherever it might lead. She sees herself slipping into the rear pew of a white frame church, privy to a winged pageant. *Cremains* is the word for what's in the box, a word Fran has seen in print before, surely a mortician's word and not a word that people speak. *Cremains.* Her eyes fill up over this word, obviously devised to squelch emotion. Some weeks ago in a grocery store she quietly burst into tears when a man accused his wife of being on the rag. Early menopause is warping her nerves toward some eccentric clarity. On the radio Van Morrison still believes it's a marvelous night for a moondance, is begging to make some more romance.

"No," Fran thinks. "No more romance. Thank you very much." She's been alone since Kathryn, nearly two years, and feels like a wise old virgin, as wary of women's determination to merge as of men's determination not to.

On the porch of the shelter Capricia stands waiting, a cigarette in each hand. "You late, Miss Fannie May," she says. "You get you butt fired like that. That's what they tell me. You the secatary, you got to be here don't mean maybe."

"I couldn't help it," Fran says. "I was at the mercy of the rain. Or at the mercy of my distributor cap."

Capricia tosses both smokes into the waterlogged bushes that frame the sidewalk and follows Fran inside. To stay at the shelter the residents have to see a psychiatrist but by law can't be forced to take the meds he prescribes. Capricia's paranoia has been on the rise, and with it her rambunctiousness, so Fran is hoping not to get cornered alone in the downstairs office.

"At the mercy of that distributing cap," Capricia says. "I heard that. I'm at the mercy of dogshit." Fran keys into the familiar undertone of rage that keeps her from laughing at this and does not invite elaboration. "Every time I go to McDonald's some big ol' dog is out there in the parking lot taking a shit, and people start to laugh at me. Every damn time." Capricia pauses to watch Fran lock her purse away in the filing cabinet. "I'm sick of it, too." Her voice rises in pain. "They look at that dogshit, and then they look at me and laugh. Don't tell me they don't."

Fran doesn't doubt that people might be laughing at Capricia, who at five-three weighs well over two hundred pounds and wears bulge-hugging elastic skirts above her knees. "Maybe they're laughing at something else," Fran says. "You never know what people are laughing at. It doesn't have to be at you, just because you see them laughing."

"They laughin' at me all right. And that damn ol' dog follows me to these restaurants so they can humiliate me. It's very precise, believe me. It's not some accidental recurring dream, or whatever you want to call it. It's all to the purpose, but I don't know what the purpose is. I'd like just once to be left alone."

"Well, I'll leave you alone," Fran says. "I've got charts to Xerox upstairs."

"They say to let your little light shine, though," Capricia advises. "Might be somebody down in the valley tryin' to get home."

"I drove in behind an angel," Fran tells her from the steps. "I mean, a little lady was wearing wings and driving."

"M-hm," Capricia says. "I heard that. I heard that one, but good."

"Come on up later if you want me to help you go through the closet and look for a longer skirt," Fran says. "There could be something in there that would fit."

"I don't want no long skirt," Capricia says.

"Remember Dr. Berman suggested you find something more appropriate to wear?" Fran issues this reminder as gently as possible. "He thought you might feel better in something more modest. You might not get hassled so much on the street. You know what I'm talking about."

"He's tellin' me what to wear and him wearin' that skullcap," Capricia says. When she laughs her eyes shut tight while her mouth expands to astounding width. "He got it so far back on his head he have to wear bobby pins to keep it from fallin' off. But Jesus said the circumcision wouldn't do them any good. He sendeth rain on the just and the unjust alike, and that include Mr. Get-Back-Honky-Cat George Heebie-Jeebie Bush."

"Well, let me know if you change your mind," Fran says. "Or I can give you a note for the thrift shop."

"You go with me, I'll go," Capricia says. "I done told you that yesterday."

"I can't go with you," Fran says. "One of the counselors can go with you. Dennis can go with you."

"He laughs out both sides of his mouth," Capricia says. "If he thinks he's on a pedestal, he ought to think again. It's all he can do to keep from pullin' his dick out every time he sees me, anyway. Let him that thinketh he standeth take heed lest he fall."

"I wish you'd give the Haldol another try," Fran says.

"You try it, I'll try it," Capricia says. "See how you like it for a change. The only thing drivin' me crazy is this dogshit business. Ain't no medicine about to fix that."

"It might," Fran says. "It might make things seem different to you."

"So would her-oin," Capricia says. "And be a lot more fun, too." She pulls a pack of Eve cigarettes from a pocket tight beneath her armpit and turns toward the exit. "If He shall give thee the desires of thy heart, then it means He'll give me you. The rain has no father and it has no mother, and neither do I." She closes the door softly behind her.

"How's your girlfriend?" Dennis is grinning his handsome young grin at the top of the stairs. "If you'll go to the bathroom, I'll go to the bathroom."

"It's charming the way you amuse yourself," Fran says dryly, grabbing his chiseled upper arm. "Maybe someday you'll amuse others, too."

By four the rain has slowed to mist, and on her way home Fran pulls into Ralph's as close to the exit as she can get. People often toss receipts into the trash bin there, and on the back of some of these are coupons for free frozen yogurt at the mini-mall across the street. She lifts an address book from her purse and uses it to fan herself. So far she can discern no pattern in what sets off the flashes of heat. Having to call the car shop seemed to do it, and having to change the Xerox toner. The thought of Joey's ashes has brought on more than one today, along with the image of being smothered in Capricia's mass of flesh. At night it may be dreams, though when she wakes up with the burning that turns to cold sweat, it feels merely thermal, untied to sex or the usual terrors. Most likely the heat flares up in cycles, controlled by hormones rather than life. She's as weird as Capricia, determined to fix a causal link between defecating dogs and random laughter. In any case, the weather has helped, but still Fran is craving something cold. A young woman with an infant strapped to her belly unloads a basket two cars down and doesn't bother to retrieve the curled receipt that rolls out from one bag. Fran waits a discreet amount of time before she lifts the thing from a shallow puddle.

The tiny shop is deserted except for the somber, teenaged Korean in charge, who quickly serves Fran and silently accepts the soggy ticket, then resumes her seat at the table up front and continues to read her Bible, printed in vertical rows of delicate black. The whole side wall is mirror, and Fran chooses the only spot in the place where she won't be forced to watch herself eat. The creamy chocolate and toffee yogurt soothes the back of her head and chills the base of her throat, where fire concentrates at times. These vivid flavors neutralize the shelter odor on her clothes, a faint combination of smoke and must. Somewhere in her daze of pleasure she becomes aware that the cashier has cozied up to the mirror, examining zits. Fran watches, incredulous, as the young lady begins to squeeze her chin, not once, not twice, but on and on, even as Fran walks past and out the door. She's been scavenging freebies for weeks now at two bucks a slap, and here's retribution (from a girl at the mercy of hormones herself). Fran finishes her treat in the car with the radio up. Astonishingly, Bob Dylan is turning fifty, and some phony DJ wag is playing "Knockin' on Heaven's Door" in honor of his birthday and "Hard Rain" in honor of precipitation.

Her mailbox is so stuffed with junk mail that Fran tears the cover off *Newsweek* getting it out. Once for an old friend's birthday she ordered a Thomas Merton tape, so she's been slotted into numerous religious and New Age mailing lists. She is now invited to purchase subliminal cassettes of magical affirmations (*My mindpower rejuvenates me. My body remolds into perfection. My mental abilities sharpen with the years. I am a powerhouse of boundless energy.*) Deep weariness settles behind Fran's knees as she reads and climbs the steps into her building. There are two identical bright blue envelopes from Servants of the Paraclete requesting that she send fifty dollars to relieve the poignant plight of priests who suffer spiritual emptiness. Fran might, if she had the cash, send twenty-five to the Union of Global Women to eradicate clitoridectomies.

She dials Carol's number before stretching out for a nap. "So how's it been?" she says.

"At least I'm not crying," Carol answers hoarsely, over-enunciating through the drug. "There was a moment when I could almost believe what's happened, but it passed. I'm afraid if I take down my garbage, somebody will break in here and steal him."

"I'll take it out later," Fran says. "I'll come over and see what needs doing." A pause elongates the space between them. "A mourning dove has built a nest in the signal on

Serrano," she offers. "It blocks the whole green light when the bird is there."

"I have to lie back down," Carol says, "before sunlight starts hitting this bed and throwing shadows on my mirror. Lately that really gives me the creeps."

It is nearly eight when Fran taps next door for garbage, taking her own down as well, having to pour water off the flat barrel lids out back. Another storm is gathering, due in before midnight. She carefully redrapes her VW engine in plastic. Carol's apartment is still dark behind her when she answers the door again, though she's semi-dressed, and Fran smells burnt toast. Carol clicks on the muted hallway bulb, then leads Fran to the living room and fumbles for lamplight. She is wearing a pale green cotton robe with jeans on underneath. The low lilt of a radio drifts in from the bedroom on heavy air, and in one corner the unlovely blond box occupies a stuffed chair, the comfortable chair, beneath a long-chained bamboo swag light. The women settle on the couch, not quite facing each other.

"More rain," Fran says. "The sound is so soothing. Except in my living room, where it's a drip at a time."

"I hope it stays cloudy," Carol says. "I couldn't bear a sunny, blue-sky day right now. I hope it clouds over for a month."

"Ever hear Willie Nelson sing 'Blue Skies'?" Fran asks. "The words are happy, but he sings it so slow, it wrings you out." She accompanies herself on imaginary guitar. "Blooooooo skiiiiiiiiiiiiiiies, smiiiiiiiiiilin' at me, nothin' but blooooooo skiiiiiiiiies do I see. Deer-neer-neer." Carol reaches into a pocket for Kleenex, sinking Fran's heart. "God, I'm sorry," she says.

Carol waves this off but sniffles on for a while before getting up. "I'm past time for a pill is all," she says. "Please stay till it kicks in. Sing me something else."

"I guess I won't sing," Fran says. While Carol is in the bathroom the Beach Boys glide through on the radio. She snaps them off on her way back in.

"I never wanted him on the boards," she says. "I worried myself sick all the way through his childhood, but there we were, and there seemed to be no stopping him, the way he loved the water. Quite obviously I should have stopped him. I should have never let it get started in the first place. So now here we are." She looks toward the shadowed corner, but her face doesn't break.

"You mustn't think about it that way," Fran says softly. "He could as easily have been taken doing something else. It was his life to live."

"His life to live and his death to die," Carol says with an edge. "I can't believe he would leave me like this."

The moment grows long and silent except for the hollow sound of slow rain hitting palm fronds. Fran has heard suicide called the ultimate declaration of independence, and maybe any death is that. Fran can't imagine either having a child or losing one. She feels herself blush with heat and shifts on the sofa, takes a deep breath as if that will help. She thinks of mentioning the driving angel but decides against it. In *Wings of Desire* there were all those beautiful male angels in business suits, hovering in the library.

Carol picks up the remote control and begins pushing buttons. Flooded streets in Van Nuys cut to fire in San Francisco, cars in pursuit, a couple in bed. "Joey calls this channel surfing."

"Clever," Fran says, uneasy with the tense, which Carol lets stand without a blink. Fran feels a perfect circle of sweat break out around the crown of her head. *Fontanelle*, they called it, in her baby-sitting days, the soft spot. What yarmulkes cover up. Carol finally lands for a moment on Marlon Brando, defending his bail-freed son in a most humble voice. His loose black raincoat makes him much, much fatter than surely he can be. Fran remembers him not so much in the T-shirt in *Streetcar* as in the camel coat in *Tango,* putting it to Maria Schneider standing up. It is painful now to look at him, the way his body's become such a burden.

Carol flips to PBS, which is rerunning Bill Moyers on "Amazing Grace." *'Tis grace that brought me safe thus far, and grace will take me home.*

"Oh, puh-lease," Carol nearly shouts at the screen. Her eyelids are pulled unnaturally wide, and it occurs to Fran that she has popped the wrong pill or too much of the right one or maybe something else altogether. She stands up and surfs from 28 to 56 with several audible intakes of breath, rhythmically waving the remote at arm's length as if to keep her balance. "Here we are, here we are," she says. "This shopping thing. They talk until you're hypnotized, and then they toot a little horn to break the spell." Gingerly she lays the remote on the glass coffee table and arranges herself back on the couch. "Feet up," she tells Fran. "We can both fit our feet up if we work it right." Her robe has slipped sideways so that one breast is nearly exposed, a dishevelment startling in a woman prone to turtlenecks and three-piece office suits. "Because this is the only show that won't make it worse," she adds, as if Fran had asked for an explanation.

A perky organ rendition of "California Dreamin'" reminds Fran that she never learned to skate, while a gaudy piece of jewelry spins slowly in the center of the screen. An overly enthused male voice announces that this is a Cubic Zirconia Diamond Spectacular Pendant, which retails for $299.95. At the moment, however, it's a CZ Special, running not at $150, not at $140 and not at $130. Not even at $119.95, but at $99. "No," he says. "Tell you what. We're going to let you have it for $74.25. No, wait, ladies and gentlemen. Can you believe this? We'll run it for eight minutes only at the incredible price of $29.75. Look at that. As that pendant revolves around and catches the light, you can perceive its heavenly beauty."

The weariness is back, behind Fran's knees. Her nap after work was an anxious one with an outlandish dream involving stolen shoes, a black Ferris wheel, and flammable cotton candy vomit.

"See?" Carol says. "What did I tell you? Isn't this amazing?"

"It is amazing," Fran says. Her right calf feels seared where it's been touching Carol's, and the heat now shoots up her thigh, then up her spine and into the base of her throat. "If you're feeling steady for a while, I think I'll go on home," she says, but before Carol can respond there's a sudden banging next door.

It's a long gaze through the peephole before Fran lets register the fact that Capricia is standing patiently in the corridor with a very long-stemmed bird-of-paradise tucked beneath one arm. If Fran could get away with it, she might retreat on tiptoe and try to ignore the knocking. Her experience with Capricia, however, has been that she's not a woman easily ignored.

"Just a minute," she calls through the door. "I'll be out in a minute. Just hold on." Quickly, and without consulting Carol on the couch, Fran dials the shelter for Bayne, the evening counselor. "Capricia Laidlaw is knocking at my door right now," she tells him. "What the hell is going on?"

"She's been discharged," Bayne says. "That's all I know. Dennis found her in the office before shift change, going through the Rolodex. Maybe she got your address out of there. She threw the thing at him on her way out, along with a few choice words. He smelled booze on her, too. You know she's been pushing limits all week and riling all the women up. So she finally managed to get herself kicked out."

"Well, can somebody come and get her?" Fran says. "She can just as well set off again in the morning if she'll go back."

"Nobody here but us chickens," Bayne says. "I mean, this chicken. I'm the only chicken here because Gary called in sick. Dennis gave Capricia bus tokens to get to the Sundown Mission, anyway."

"Wonderful, Bayne, you are all such a help."

"Must be love." He laughs a hearty, resonant laugh.

"And you must be jealous," Fran says. Bayne is a gentle, small-boned black man, perhaps one-half Capricia's width.

"Oh, I am jealous," he says. "I'm ate to pieces by the green-eyed monster. But really, Fran?"

"What?"

"Don't hesitate to call the police if you need to."

"I'll just drive her to the mission myself," Fran says. "Or somewhere. It's already pouring rain over here."

She retrieves her keys from the living room. "It's a client from the shelter," she tells Carol, who remains wide-eyed but impassive. "I've got to take her somewhere to sleep. Or at least to Pico for a bus."

"There was thunder," Carol says. "It sounded like those guys on radio used to do it with sheets of aluminum. Joey's terrified of lightning, but he never would admit it." She gets up and follows Fran to the door.

"Hello, Capricia," Fran says as neutrally as possible.

"There you are!" Capricia grins. "I knew I'd make it. I told you I would, didn't I? How come you to live way over here in Mexikorea?" At thirty Capricia has been homeless on and off for years but prides herself on keeping to westside streets. She stands teetering on bright red, tiny-heeled slingbacks that match her damp and frilly acetate blouse, cut for cleavage down the belly. Fran can't help but think the word *bazooms*.

"How did you even get here?" she asks.

"I took the 33," Capricia says. "I took it to Western, but then I got me a ride."

"I bet you did," Fran says. "I thought you weren't doing that anymore."

"He was nice," Capricia says. "The body is not for fornication but for the Lord. He didn't want nothin' but a little gladhand. Then he drop me off over here at Taco Bell. Which is when the trouble started back with that dogshit."

"I'm going to give you a ride to the Sundown Mission," Fran says. "Or else to a bus stop so you can go where you want."

"Don't be cold now, Miss Fannie May. Lookie here what I got. You already said these bird-of-paradises was your favorites. I heard you say that, and here it is."

Fran hangs back, reluctant to accept the gift, dripping wet and obviously torn from a nearby yard.

"I've got the perfect vase." Carol steps from behind Fran to extend a long, pale arm for the flower, then disappears with it.

"See?" Capricia says. "You friend not near as cold as you try to be. If she you love-sister, she might not like me checkin' up like this."

"Don't mess with me," Fran says. "You're already in trouble enough. You'll be lucky if the mission has a bed this late."

"I heard that," Capricia says, "Why you think they call it Sundown? They lock you in that place at dark and kick you butt out in the crack of dawn. Don't nobody get in or out this late."

"Shit," Fran says.

"Shit is right, girl. Look at this knee." She lifts her leg delicately for Fran to see, miraculously maintaining her balance. There is an ugly gash with blood caked all around.

"I'll have to put some peroxide on that," Carol announces from the doorway. "Come in here." Fran shoots what's meant as a warning look, but Carol is already on her way to the bathroom with Capricia at her heels, trailing a yeasty whiff of wine.

"One of these big ol' red dogs," Capricia says. "What you call these big ol' red dogs? I could already see this ol' dog at the Taco Bell about to take a shit right where I was to be walkin' by. So I told this man to keep him away from the door till I got in, but he got right up in my face to laugh and somethin' told me to push him back. There was already dogshit under one of the cars, and this big ol' red dog made me twist my ankle, so I'm limpin' all the way over here. That's what they wanted to see, and that's what they got. It's not just here, either, but everywhere I go at."

Fran leans out the screenless window at the end of the corridor, catching rain in her palms and patting her face and neck, nearly inspiring a chill. The drag in her back means soon she'll bleed, a sporadic blessing that should bring relief. This intricate day seems to have wound itself past all reason into night. She stretches to touch the top of the window frame, then down to touch her toes. Every light is lit in the dilapidated cottage across the street, and the black-robed, elderly Mexican man who lives there is being helped into bed by a young female Sikh in luminous white. Fran will gather up imaginary energy, load Capricia into the Bug, and deliver her to Bayne for the night.

In the bathroom Carol and Capricia sit smoking long, brown Shermans, Capricia on the closed commode with an elaborate white gauze bandage around her knee, Carol on the edge of the bathtub, flipping ashes into the sink.

"Ashes to ashes and dust to dust," Capricia is saying. "But why you burn him up like that? You crazier than I am. How he spose to get up and dance in Heaven? He got to have some bones, at least. How come you to burn him up?"

"Capricia!" Fran says, but Carol is laughing.

"He told me to when he was in junior high school," she says. "He told me to burn him up and toss him into the waves. So that's what I'll do."

"We shall see the dead, small and great, stand up and dance before God," Capricia says. "I guess if the Lord can raise up the dead He can build back some bones if He has to. He delightest not in burnt offerings, though. The scriptures certify to that."

"Apparently he delighteth in killing off young boys before their time," Carol says. Her face has regained its hurting edge.

"Oh, it was that boy's time, all right," Capricia says. "You needn't to worry about that. You can rest assured it was that boy's time."

"How do you know it was his time?" Carol demands, in earnest but not with anger. "Just how do you know it was his stupid time?"

"He went, didn't he?" Capricia says. "That's the only time you go, when it's your time. You can't go no other way. If you go, it's your time, and if it's your time, you go. Ain't no use to quarrel over these truths we hold to be self-evident. Now he's baptized by fire among the children of the resurrection. An' he don't want his gorgeous mama sittin' here in the toilet bawlin' her eyes out, either."

"Well, that's true, he hates that," Carol says.

"Somethin' I always wanted to learn how to do was to learn how to surf," Capricia says, lifting the bad knee with one hand to guide it atop the good one. "I can just see me up there, shootin' them curls."

"Joey would teach you, too," Carol says. "He's that kind of kid. He wouldn't think a thing about taking you down to the water with him and getting you up on a board. You wanna do it? He says let's do it."

Fran has begun to feel like a chaperone, irrelevant at best, intrusive at worst. "Before you get ensconced here, Capricia, I have to call Bayne and tell him I'm bringing you back."

"I'm not goin' back to that Dennis the Menace," Capricia says. "He ack like I got dogshit on both shoes. He too enthralled with his own self to care who be who or what be what." This is an accurate appraisal of Dennis, narcissism having driven him, perversely, to "help those less fortunate than himself." Fran tries not to laugh. "And that Bayne a little sparrowfart," Capricia adds. "He look like one good sneeze blow him away. These mens. You think it's the mens or the womens that break your heart the worst? Which one the worst ones to fall for?"

The question hangs suspended in the space between Fran and Carol, like a high lob in doubles that no one calls.

"I don't think it matters," Fran finally says. "Maybe we're all more trouble to each other than we're worth."

"It's just that you expect better of women," Carol says.

"I heard that," Capricia says. "The flesh lusteth against the spirit and the spirit up against the flesh. No fountain yields both salt water and fresh." As she reaches backward to flick her ash, she knocks a flattened saucer of soap off the back of the toilet. The shattering reverberates on inlaid tiles and jolts Capricia into begging forgiveness.

"I don't even care," Carol says. "Let's break something else." She picks up a thin pink drinking glass and tosses it into the tub for a high, crackling smash.

"Let's break this, then," Capricia says, reaching for a Mason jar full of drooping freesias.

"How about let's not," Fran says, stopping her hand. Suddenly the bathroom feels close as an elevator.

"You always so proper, Miss Fannie May. That's what I like. You always aimin' for the up-and-up."

"So let's go," Fran says. "Let's let Carol get some rest." She steps back and sees through the living room door that the bird-of-paradise stands in a lovely, tall vase on the floor in front of Joey's ashes.

"Capricia can stay here tonight if she likes," Carol says.

"That may not be such a good idea," Fran answers quickly. "You don't know Capricia, really. It might not be such a good idea."

"Do not forget to entertain strangers," Capricia says, "whereby some have entertained angels unawares. Hebrews, chapter 13, verse 2." Fran suspects this reference has been used to past advantage.

"I want her to stay if she wants to," Carol says.

"I cook the best spaghetti," Capricia declares. "And Carol has got to fatten up. All I need is a glass of wine and a jar of Ragu. This woman's belly has drawn up to her backbone. Eyes all sunk in. I got to call it a halt. Them that putteth their trust in the Lord shall be made fat."

"You wanna do it?" Carol says. "Let's do it."

Often when Fran awakes in a blast of heat she has the feeling she's burned through something that was in her way, but tonight the sound of rain confuses her. The wind has picked up, and she rises in darkness to spread newspapers beneath wide-open French windows throughout the apartment. She dips one hand into the living room bucket, not yet quite a whole inch full, then pulls on a pair of jeans. From the canvas chair in the breakfast nook she can watch rain angling through pale orange streetlight. As she leans forward her nipples come to rest on the tabletop, and she hears Brando warning Schneider that she'll get old like him and play soccer with her tits.

Before Fran woke up sweating she was at a party with her second husband, whose yelling drove her coatless down outer stairs and into a wintry parking lot. She could still hear him from there, though the words were indistinct, the whole situation more memory than dream. She had been dancing wrong with a guy, as she was inclined to do throughout that marriage. What strikes her now is the way Sam continued to yell long after she had quit the scene. She can't recall the dénouement. It took her three Wisconsin marriages to realize men bored her except for sex. At the sink she wets a washcloth and sponges neck and shoulders, belly and breasts. Flashes of lightning and occasional headlights illuminate Earth above the faucets. There is a crash next door, followed by whoops of laughter from Capricia, then Carol. Something is definitely cooking, garlic wafting thick on saturated air.

Fran winds her way back to the living room, turns on the end-table radio and stretches out on the couch, listening idly until Creedence gets into "Heard It Through The Grapevine." A surge of energy rolls through her bare feet and along her legs until she is up and moving. *Honeyhoney, yeah.* Soon she is sweating from exertion as much as from a thermostat gone awry. *There must be some kinda way outta here.* Get up in the dark and dance while you got bones. *We are stardust, we are golden.* Suddenly, except for this music, whole decades seem to have gone up in flames behind her. *Gimme, gimme shelter.* Fran rushes to the bedroom for the stereo effect of a second radio, louder than is decent for the hour. She begins to pick an extremely mean guitar. *Rejoice, rejoice, we have no choice but to carry on.* She can feel a release of blood imploding deep in her swollen belly. Old moons and tides and women who bleed. *The lunatics are in my hall, I'll see you on the dark side of the moon.* Waves of sound keep swelling beneath her, curving out beyond the rain. *She's as sweet as Tupelo honey, she's an angel of the first degree.*

The Court Interpreter

Ty Pak

I was at our Anaheim flower shop, cleaning up after my wife as she designed, when the phone rang. It was Bill Samuels, the attorney defending Mrs. Moonja Joo, the Korean grocer, accused of shooting to death a black teenager for stealing a bottle of orange juice. The case had become a cause celebre with the whole of black Los Angeles clamoring for their pound of flesh. As a certified court interpreter I had been mildly curious who had been appointed to interpret for the defendant, as she plainly needed this help, but had not given the matter much further thought. Los Angeles, insulated from Orange County by the sclerotic 5 or 405, held very little professional interest for me.

"How is it going?" I asked, recognizing his name from the papers.

"Not as well as it should. Not the least of my problems is finding a decent Korean interpreter. I have looked high and low in vain, when your name has been suggested to me."

"Can't you find somebody qualified in Los Angeles?"

"No, not the type we want, someone classy with the right diction and style to project my client as an educated, refined person, not some callous killer from a backward culture as the media has been portraying her. It's not just her who has this image problem. Every Korean immigrant is affected."

I knew without his telling me in so many words. It was so unfair. In total disregard of our shame and outrage over the seemingly senseless killing by one of our number, we were all being lumped together as a bunch of blood-thirsty mercenaries who didn't hesitate to kill our hosts just to make a buck. One Korean pastor I knew had even suggested that he and I collaborate on a letter to the *Los Angeles Times*, apologizing to the victim's family and friends, to the American society at large, explaining that as a people we were not given to such violence, that few of us knew how to use firearms, let alone carry them. We certainly didn't want the garden variety of muggers and robbers, be they black, white, or otherwise, to shoot us first, thinking we were all well armed and ready to fire.

Our corporate guilt, remorse, concern soon gave way to dismay and anger as the smear and hate campaign against Koreans escalated. Not content with closing down the Star Market by blocking its access and smashing its windows, the blacks marched the streets waving banners and placards that read, singular shifted to plural, "Go Home Killer Korean Grocers," "Deport Murderer Immigrants." Rap lyrics, recorded by popular black singers and sold in the millions, ridiculed and denigrated "Gooks, not born here, not speaking English, looking down on us, killing our kids." And the media lapped it all up, faithfully reporting their daily demonstrations, depicting us as pushy, crass materialists, holding human life cheap, obsessed with the goal to get rich quick, taking, never giving. The incumbent District Attorney, up for reelection and with political sights set on mayorship and beyond, ordered his deputies to get a life sentence, if not the gas chamber, for the reprobate. Other opportunists jumped on the band wagon, endorsing and encouraging the black hysteria. After all, the blacks had the head count, the votes. By now it had definitely become a matter of our national reputation, our survival, let alone our acceptance and advancement in the American mainstream, the dream of all of us with children born here, going to school, and making headway in their various professions and occupations. The victim was no longer Natasha Brook, but Moonja Joo and the entire Korean American community.

Coupled with this sense of threat was our revulsion and indignation as more facts about the Brooks filtered through the Korean language press, though unmentioned by its American counterpart. In fact, the grief of the family and friends, so telling on TV screen, appeared positively repulsive and obscene. The minister of the church the Brooks had been members of allegedly, who had displayed such genius in orchestrating the heartrending memorials and vigils for the young victim, hardly knew her. The loudly keening mother, the epitome of crushing maternal sorrow, had beaten and abused her daughter and turned her out of her house many years ago. Natasha herself, at the tender age of fifteen, was the mother of two children already, and had been living with her current boyfriend. Instead of pity for her or her orphaned children, she evoked with her enormous weight of two hundred and fifty pounds orgiastic images of eating, mating, and breeding destined to unbalance global ecology.

We had to exonerate the accused, who had by now become a folk hero, especially among our small business owners, continually plagued by black shoplifters and other predators, for showing to the whole world that Koreans were no pushovers at their mercy. We had to fight back and reclaim our tarnished national honor. But how? We could only wring our hands in helpless fury, realizing that we didn't come across as eloquently and effectively as the blacks, that we didn't have their native English, their orators, artists, athletes, politicians, TV personalities, and other resources.

"We would like to have your services, Professor," said Samuels.

He must have gotten my credentials from his Korean friends. Lately the Korean language papers had written me up, praising my fiction. I had resigned from the University of Hawaii where I had taught for twenty years. Both faculty and students had always looked on me askance, a non-native with an accent daring to teach English to the natives. Then there were the subtle barriers, the hesitations, double takes that made me self-conscious, ill at ease. In the two decades of my employment, I hadn't made a single friend in the Department. A few years before I quit, Yoonhee and the children were already in California, a move felt necessary to send the children to the schools in Lemon Heights, Orange County, where my physician brother lived. Public schools in Hawaii left much to be desired, and Punahou and Iolani, the prep schools that produced Ivy League material, were forever out of our reach. In the meantime the first flower shop Yoonhee had set up at Larwin Square near Lemon Heights was doing phenomenally well. It made more sense for me to stop commuting between California and Hawaii and become her full-time assistant. We sold and bought other businesses, went to live in Boston for a year to be with Brigette and Woodrow when they went to Harvard and MIT, and invested in commercial properties. Financial independence seemed just around the corner, when the recession struck, forcing foreclosures on us. With judgments hanging over our heads, we had to open our current flower shop, Orient Florist, in our daughter Brigette's name.

"Thank you for the confidence, but Los Angeles is just too far for me."

"We are prepared to more than double your normal fee to $1,000 a day."

The figure, though a fraction of what he must be charging for himself, made my heart skip a beat. I hadn't been making that kind of money since I left Hawaii, where indeed I could write my own ticket, up to $200 an hour for depositions. In a conference call with Korea I was paid $500 for translating one phrase. But in California the courts and lawyers treated interpreters like trash they could kick around at will, for $200 a day at most. For one thing, to service the huge ethnic populations with their aptitude for getting into trouble, an army of certified interpreters had to be maintained, on a pay scale palatable to the taxpayer, which was minimal, lower than a laborer's. A profession, financially unrewarded, was no profession. In the popular conception bilingualism was a social problem, like poverty, endemic to the ethnic ghettos, to be overcome with tax money by harassed school districts and welfare agencies, not an art to be cultivated by lifetime study and dedication. Consequently the really qualified people, scholars, doctors, lawyers, and other professionals, stayed away from the demeaning role of interpreter or translator. I myself had also snubbed the state certification examinations of California for a long time. Apart from the lowly pay, the very thought of examination by some bureaucrats, novices and amateurs in the niceties of the vocation I had held sacred all the adult years of my life, was repugnant. What would they know about the agony of search for the exact equivalent in English of a Korean expression or vice versa and the ecstasy of discovery when the miracle was accomplished? It was every bit as artistic and creative as the poet's or musician's labor for the perfect line, perfect note. In time, however, I had to yield to Yoonhee's insistence on my getting the certification: it might come handy someday. It did, becoming the mainstay of our livelihood during the recession. With any luck, if the trial should last any length of time, I could earn enough to make our mortgage payments for some months without dipping into our ever-dwindling savings.

"But who pays?" I asked, knowing too well that the Joos must be bankrupt by now.

"The insurance company does, which also pays me," Bill said, guessing my thoughts. "Yes, she has been provident enough to maintain a sizable liability insurance for her business."

"But doesn't the court appoint the interpreter?"

"Not the ones the defendant pays for. Of course we need court approval, which is automatic in case of an active certified interpreter like yourself. The one we now have, certified and court appointed, is so bad that the court will be more than happy to see replaced."

"There is just one thing, the interpreter's fundamental duty of fidelity to the original. What is your client like?"

"She may not be the classiest lady, but then who is? Personally I don't believe one is intrinsically this or that, except as packaged and presented. She has had her hard knocks, even before this, but is quite a woman. She and her husband could get together a million dollars to qualify under the new US immigration policy for foreign investors. That's quite an accomplishment anywhere but especially in Korea. They could live comfortably there but decided to emigrate during the reign of terror under Doohwan Jun's Combined Investigative Board following President Junghee Park's assassination."

"You seem to know a lot about Korea."

"My wife is Korean."

So he had a personal stake in this beyond just the money he made as defense lawyer. His talk about the insult to the Korean pride, before mentioning my substantial fee, which would have been motivation enough for me, hadn't been just a line to bait me.

"I met Sunhee in Seoul where I was goofing off from college as a Peace Corps volunteer. Her father, a lawyer, was looking for an American tutor for her English before she went to the States to study voice. After threatening to deport me to stop our romance, her family finally consented to our marriage on condition that I go to law school and pass the bar."

"Fascinating! You should write a story about it."

"I haven't got the talent. Why don't you? We read your story, "GI Orphan." Interracial marriage is your favorite theme, isn't it? Sunhee will give you all the material you need in full detail. You have quite a fan in her. She was the one who went out and got a copy of your short stories after reading about you in the *Korea Times*."

"Thank her for me. Does she sing still?"

"No, I plead guilty to preempting her career and turning her into the world's champion wife and mother. We have three children, all musical like their mother."

"And will all pass the bar like their father," I said, with genuine envy. I had been trying in vain to persuade my offspring to do the same, instead of just becoming educated bums with doctorates in public policy or history of art.

"Just out of curiosity, how did you master English as you did? You write as well as our best writers, with no hint of foreignism...."

"But in speech I can't get over this accent. I was wretched about it for a long time but am resigned to it now."

"One has to really listen for it and, when discovered, it is pleasing, like patina to sterling."

"You are a great flatterer and we'll get along famously."

Bill had argued for the bail of his client, a propertied businesswoman who posed no danger of flight, but his adversary, Assistant DA John Moss, had his way. The magistrate set the bail prohibitively high, $2 million, to make sure that she stayed in jail for her trial. The mob wouldn't have forgiven them in case of her flight to Korea, a hinterland sanctuary for hardened criminals to the popular American mind, in spite of Korea's efficient police and extradition treaty with the US. But perhaps they did her a favor: the mob would have torn her to pieces, if only they could lay their hands on her through the protective jail walls. As a result, for her daily court appearances, she had to be transported in a police van under armed escort with other custodies, handcuffed and sometimes leg-ironed, in jumpsuits stamped LA County Jail on the back. From the loading dock at the basement level of the Superior Court building, they were herded to a barred elevator, remotely controlled, that took them to the holding areas on the different floors. From there the individual custodies would be taken via a maze of narrow passages to the smaller holding cages next to the courtrooms where they were to be produced. At this point, before entrance, the handcuffs or leg irons would be removed, unless there was reason to fear physical outbreak. Also some considerate lawyers would provide their clients with a presentable change of clothes for a better impression on the jury.

The custody defendants then emerged, one at a time through the side door, walking before the conspicuously armed bailiffs, who kept a wary eye on their every move.

My first meeting with Mrs. Joo was in the passageway by the holding cage for Department 72 before her pre-trial hearing. We spoke through the inch-thick bars. She had just changed to a blue two-piece dress, her discarded jumpsuit folded in a pile on a shelf. The ordeal had taken a toll on her, dark rings around her eyes and a visible loss of weight.

Samuels presented the prosecution's offer: her guilty plea for life sentence with the possibility of early parole instead of the gas chamber.

"No, let's fight it," she said without a moment's hesitation. "I believe in the justice of this country. We wouldn't have come here without this faith."

"But it is human and errors are made," Samuels said. "Just suppose a mistake is made and we lose."

"We'll win," she said with finality. "I have full confidence in your ability."

Jury selection began. If guidelines existed about this business, such as the prosecution favoring the prosperous and conservative and the defense the poor and liberal, they flew out the window in deference to another overriding principle: racism. Both sides were intent on eliminating those who belonged to the race of the opposite party. Samuels ruthlessly weeded out blacks and Moss Asians or recent immigrants. However, to keep up the semblance of a search for an impartial and fair-minded panel, they routinely asked the prospective jurors whether they had heard or read about the case and formed an opinion, predisposing them to such a degree that they would vote in a certain way regardless of the evidence presented to them, which was followed by the predictable answer: emphatic denial.

Nobody would own up to being duped and manipulated by the media or being a racist. Amazingly in the first panel selected from the juror pool there were two Koreans, both first generation, one a mechanical engineer with

McDonnel Douglas and the other a computer scientist with Hughes, both peremptorily avoided by Moss for inadequate comprehension of English, though in fact their English was quite good. The fourth or fifth replacement was a Japanese lady, Julia Tanaka, born and raised here, and wife of a police detective, with whom Moss found nothing wrong, obviously aware of the enmity between the two races, Japanese and Korean. It was Defendant Joo herself who told Bill to avoid her. The last survivors were fourteen people, two of them alternates, nine women and five men, all white, Anglo white, not even a Latino among them. So this was the secret of white success in the US. By default, because the minorities could not trust each other.

Trial began immediately that afternoon. In his opening statement Moss exulted in the overwhelming proof that convicted the defendant of murder. His first witnesses were the various law enforcement personnel. A firearms expert from LAPD verified that the bullet and the casing, recovered at the scene, matched the caliber of the pistol used in the shooting. The Deputy County Coroner, who had examined the victim's body, described, with the help of charts, the entry of the single fatal bullet in the victim's back a few inches below the collar bone to the left of the spinal column, between the fourth and fifth ribs, and its exit through the left ventricle and at the base of the left breast.

One of the prosecution's coups was the cassette tape extracted from the video camera installed at the ceiling over the counter to document shoplifts and holdups. Telling though it was, the evidence turned out a two-edged knife. Moss wanted to show just the portion where the defendant shoots the victim, "the relevant part, not to take up the court's valuable time," but Samuels wanted to be shown the whole three-hour reel, "not to take anything out of context." All or nothing it had to be. Judge Janice Wilson asked Moss if he still wanted the showing. Moss had to agree: if he refused, the jury would think he had something to hide in the rest of the tape. Lamenting its undue imposition on the court's calendar, already squeezed by this trial that promised to be long, the Judge ordered continuance to the next morning, since it was already past three, the rest of the afternoon to be taken up in the disposition of other calendared matters, motions, sentencings and such like that went off in quick order.

The TV set and VCR were wheeled out on a cart and placed next to the witness stand. An audiovisual technician from the Sheriff's Department inserted the cassette into the VCR slot and pushed the play button. It was a typical afternoon at a neighborhood grocery store, uneventful and boring, with customers coming in and out, picking up their merchandise and paying at the counter. One juror sitting at the opposite end of the box from the judge's bench decided to create some diversion. He folded a sheet torn out of the pad provided by the court into an airplane and sent it flying to the middle of the courtroom, incurring a severe frown from the judge.

Then it happened. The lower right corner of the screen showed a hulking figure, tall and big, heading for the door with a gallon bottle of orange juice hooked in a finger, a loaf of bread, a bag of apples, and other packages under her arms and in her hands. Noticing, Moonja called to the exiting figure. The would-be shoplifter stopped in her tracks, hesitated, then strode over to the counter and confronted her accuser. Down came the gallon jug of orange juice over Moonja's head. A punch quickly followed, sending her to the floor behind the counter, invisible to the camera. Natasha turned to walk off like a gladiator who had just vanquished her opponent, when Moonja's head inched up from behind, followed by a flash of gunfire. Natasha tottered a few steps toward the front door, then fell to the floor. The whole sequence had taken exactly two minutes.

The prosecutor paraded a legion of eyewitnesses, twelve, all black, swearing to have witnessed the defendant shoot point-blank in the back of the victim. If allowed, the whole town of South Central Los Angeles would have queued up to swear to the same, but the prosecutor wisely held the line at a dozen. Each time Samuels objected, on the

ground that the defense had stipulated to the act of shooting
and the trial should move on to the issue in dispute, namely,
the defendant's psychology in so acting. The prosecution
countered that they were about that very point, because the
psychology of an action could not be determined except by
examination of the manner in which it was performed. The
judge overruled the objection and permitted the redundant
litany to go on, though not without Bill's skillful puncturing
of its effect. For example, one eyewitness claimed to have
been at the counter when the victim fell at his feet.

"Were you in line already to pay for your purchases
when the victim came over?" Bill asked.

"No, I was still shopping elsewhere in the store."

"Exactly where?"

"It's been a while and I don't remember every square
inch I trod. Do you?"

"Just answer the question."

"I suppose I was somewhere in the middle where the
chips are."

"So you walked from there to the counter area?"

"Yes."

"Why?"

"There was some disturbance."

"Shouts and screams as the victim beat and mauled the
defendant?"

"Objection!" Moss interjected. "Leading the witness."

"Sustained," the judge said.

"You don't have to answer the question," Moss told the
witness.

"No, I don't mind answering. I didn't see any of that stuff."

"What stuff?"

"Beating and mauling you mentioned."

"Do you swear to that?"

"Yeah."

"Even though there is a videotape showing the attack?"

"Maybe the camera saw something I didn't," was the
somewhat less strident answer.

"Would you be able to identify yourself among the onlookers if the tape were shown?"

"I can't tell until I see it."

Samuels did not press the issue further, however. The majority of the so-called eyewitnesses likewise swore only to the shooting part, not the battery and mayhem preceding it. One person was willing to admit seeing the antecedent attack by the victim, but when asked why he didn't think of intervening, he said he was "no bloody cop and minded his own business."

Bill called the defendant to the stand. My hour had come. Up to now, seated next to Moonja, I had been whispering a blow-by-blow report in Korean for her benefit alone. Now the whole world would hear her side of the story through my voice. This was the supreme moment, the culmination of my years of obsession with English ever since I was seven years old when Korea was liberated. English, the language of the Americans, the liberators, was the open sesame, and the interpreter, the high priest dispensing sacred rites. During the war years of the early 50's it literally meant the difference between eating and starving, between life and death. I still recall the time when Seoul was retaken by MacArthur's Marines after Communist occupation, three months of hunger and unspeakable horrors. A group of GI's sat by the roadside near our house eating C rations. Screwing up my courage I said, "I am hungry." One of them handed me a can of pork and beans. I ran with it to my house to share it with my starving family, younger brother and sister, mother, and dying father, a professor of English at Seoul University just home from Communist prison where he had been tortured beyond repair. Only if he could get up and tell the Americans in his fluent English that we needed food, clothing, and so many other things, and we would have everything, as in the good old days when Father got the big house we had lived in, the car, piano, and other luxuries. Despite our fervent prayers he died the next day. I had to master English, recover what he had lost. I had to make

Moonja Joo credible, show her as the victim, not assailant, a law-abiding, hardworking individual outrageously and brutally attacked and abused, who had struck back as the last resort, to save herself. But how explain her shooting someone in the back?

Bill Samuels asked her name, address, date of birth, occupation, date of entry to the US, and motive for immigration.

"We had come to South Korea from the north and always felt like strangers anyway. We hated the division, war, fratricide, narrowness, dog-eat-dog of Korea and wanted our children to grow up in the big, open country that we thought the US was, where people of different colors and backgrounds from all parts of the world lived and worked together harmoniously. Then we read in the papers about a new US law allowing investment immigration for people with sufficient capital."

"How much money did you have?"

"A little over a million dollars from the sale of our house and other interests."

"What did you do with the money?"

"We bought the Star Market and a house here."

"How many employees do you have?"

"Ten including me and my husband."

"What are your hours?"

"Seven A.M. to eleven P.M. seven days a week, but we arrive at six A.M. to get things ready and seldom leave before midnight, after putting away and cleaning up."

"On August 27, 1991, did you arrive there as usual at six A.M.?"

"Earlier, because we had to stop at the produce market on San Pedro Street. We had run out of lettuce and green onions the night before."

"What time did you notice Natasha Brook enter the store?"

"I didn't notice, because I was serving other customers and didn't look at the door."

"When did you first notice her?"

"I was reaching for cigarettes for a customer when I saw her walking out the door with a gallon bottle of orange juice in one hand and cheese and corn chips in the other. I didn't recall serving her and besides the merchandise was not bagged, so I called her."

"What exact words did you use to call her?"

"You mean in English?" she asked, turning to me, asking me, rather than the questioning counsel. It was impossible for the principals to zero out the existence of the translator, supposedly transparent.

"Yes, in English and in the exact tone you used," Samuels emphasized.

She looked around at the sea of American faces, cleared her throat, then said, in a somewhat hoarse unnatural voice, "Hey, you, come here!"

"Did you intend to insult her?"

"No, I had to attract her attention, let her know that I was aware of her trying to sneak out without paying."

"What did she do when you shouted to her like that?"

"She came over and stood before the counter, pushing everybody out of the way. Towering over me she yelled, 'Did you say something, Gook bitch?' I said, 'No shoplifting.' All I heard next was a scream, because she struck me with the gallon bottle of orange juice in her uplifted hand. I felt the chill of the ice cold juice over my body and a taste of it in my mouth, when a punch to my face knocked me down. I struggled to my feet, half out of my senses, and saw her right in front of me. That's when I remembered the gun, the .38 Colt we had bought for $200. My husband had shown me once how to pull the trigger but I had no intention of ever using it. I picked it up and aimed at my assailant, just to keep her away so she wouldn't hit me again, but the next moment I heard the explosion, I didn't know about its hair trigger nor the removal of the safety pin by my husband while cleaning it the other day."

But all our effort to establish an unthinking, unconscious act on her part seemed to come undone by the prosecutor's cross-examination.

"After your arrest were you taken to the hospital for treatment?" Moss asked.

"No, I was taken directly to county jail."

"Did the arresting officers carry you to the car?"

"I walked on my own two feet."

"So the terrible beating you got from the deceased, which allegedly almost knocked your senses out, did not leave any open wounds that needed treatment, did not break any bones, did not cripple any of your bodily functions."

"No, but I had a lump on my head."

"Which nobody saw."

"My hair hid it."

"Do you wear any corrective lenses?"

"No, sir."

"You can see me without any problem, can't you?"

"Yes."

"Can you see me now?" Moss asked, walking toward the witness box. Directly before her he turned around and faced the courtroom audience.

"Yes," Moonja answered.

"Do you see my back or my face?" he asked, taking a step away from her.

"Your back."

"Isn't that what you saw on August 27, the back of Natasha Brook walking away from you, not facing you to resume her alleged murderous attack?"

"But I didn't...."

"Just answer my question!" Moss bullied.

After three days of deliberation the jury reached a verdict, guilty of manslaughter, which pleased neither party. Moonja was disappointed at the American judiciary that depended so crucially on a bunch of amateurish jurors, though Bill Samuels did his best to persuade her that this was a whole lot better than the conviction of murder the prosecution had been aiming for. On the other hand, already a murmur of discontent was heard among the blacks. Manslaughter which carried a maximum of fifteen years in prison for taking a life, a young life at that? In smoldering anger they waited for the sentencing by the judge, who was given complete discretion by the jury. The sentencing was set for two weeks later but when the day came, Samuels asked for a month's postponement so he could research more and prepare appropriate responses, though it was the defendant's constitutional right to get speedy sentencing. This simple delaying tactic, he said, was to cool down the emotions involved, both in and outside the court, which generally worked in the defense's favor.

The sentence was three years, of which the defendant had served six months already by pretrial custody, the balance to be suspended. The reason: the defendant had acted under extreme pressure and was not likely to repeat the same offense, thus posing no danger to society. She was to be released immediately. She could go home, free. Her nightmare was over. If she had not been fully vindicated by the verdict, she certainly was in the penalty phase. It was a triumph for the defense, however one looked at it. If she had any reservations about the justice system of America, she had none now.

"We've done it, we've won," said Samuels, shaking my hand, eyes brimming.

He went on to be honored the trial lawyer of the year by the American Bar Association. I had my own payoff, too, with more calls from courts, lawyers, doctors, insurance companies, than I could handle. I could write my own ticket again. But our elation was short-lived. Nothing seemed settled, the DA's office having appealed the sentence. Besides, one man's gain was another's loss. The verdict and light sentence was a slap in the face of black pride. Black demonstrators surrounded the court building and demanded the immediate dismissal of the white racist female judge. The police had to take her to and from undisclosed places, hotels and friends' homes, using unmarked cars, because her apartment was unsafe. Bill Samuels had to close down his office and even I had threatening letters in the mail and had to beef up security at home with two more dogs in spite of the great distance from Los Angeles. Black gang members plundered Korean businesses openly, robbed Korean shoppers and pedestrians in broad daylight.

But the worst was yet to come during the Los Angeles Riots that erupted soon afterwards, on April 29, 1991, upon acquittal of the four white LAPD officers accused of beating Rodney King. The white policemen who had seemingly used excessive force in arresting King were all let go free by a pre-dominantly white jury in Simi Valley. This was just one ver-dict too many, demeaning black life and dignity. Angry crowds gathered at the LAPD headquarters. Held back by the phalanxes of policemen, they vented their rage by over-turning the information booth in the parking lot and smash-ing and stamping on it. Then the gas station at the corner on the same block as the LAPD building was set on fire. Next the news camera showed a building on Normandie in flames, the very building where Moonja's Star Market was located. Another fire followed on the same street. Soon fires were everywhere and engulfed the whole of Koreatown. To save themselves many building and business owners were hanging out signs, "Not Korean owned." Looting began. Mobs broke into businesses, stores, offices, and carted off everything they could lay their hands on.

We were mesmerized by the live TV coverage of anarchy and violence that swept through Los Angeles like wild fire. Whole blocks were going up in flames but no fire engine came to put out the conflagration. No police were around to stop the beatings, lootings, killings so vividly reported on TV. Suddenly we remembered Yoonhee's brother Chanho, his wife June, and five-month-old son Charles living in an apartment building in Koreatown near 9th and Vermont. We hadn't communicated with them for months since they left Orange County. Our parting hadn't been pleasant exactly. In fact, quite the opposite. The Korean restaurant he ran at our commercial property near Disneyland failed and he blamed us for his losses, demanding $20,000 in compensation. His point was that he wouldn't have left Hawaii if we hadn't painted such a rosy picture of business prospects in California. He wanted us to pay for his moving, wife's maternity, and loss of wages and profit. When we refused, he kicked over furniture, broke glasses and dishes, even threatened to shoot us.

Yoonhee dialed their home number repeatedly but nobody answered. Several frantic calls to Hawaii gave us the number of Hanyung Jo, one of his friends from Hawaii, who lived in Glendale fifteen miles from Koreatown. Hanyung said Chanho was bringing his family to his house but was probably being delayed by the roadblocks. We kept calling every other minute. Finally, at midnight June answered. Chanho was not with them. After dropping them off at Hanyung's he went back to town with a gun to guard the stereo shop where he worked.

"A gun!" Yoonhee shrieked, vaguely recalling his threat to shoot us. So he must have meant it. How close that had been! "When did he get it?"

"As soon as we came to California. He's been going to the gun club and is a pretty good shot."

"Why didn't you stop him? He's sure to get hurt."

"He says he owes it to the owner who treats him like his own son," June answered unruffled. Was it a veiled reproach to us? "You know he has a lot of loyalty."

"Loyalty to what? He should be with you and protect you, not a measly job."

"Well, I can't stop him when he makes up his mind."

"If you don't, I will," Yoonhee declared, hanging up.

She wanted to drive out to Koreatown instantly and tear him away bodily from the stereo shop, but had to abandon the plan. The news showed cars stuck for hours in the freeways accessing Los Angeles. We tried to call June again but the line was busy all night. We fell asleep, exhausted.

The phone jangled us out of bed the next morning. Choking with tears, June said Chanho was in intensive care at Cedar Sinai Hospital with a gunshot wound to his head.

He didn't regain consciousness and died a week later. After burying him and dropping June and Charles at their apartment, we drove down Olympic flanked by gaping reminders of the Riots. We had paid for his funeral expenses, only a little shy of the $20,000 he had claimed we owed him. Only if we had given him the money, so he didn't have to go to live and work in Koreatown!

As we turned south on Normandie a sickening vista of destruction came into view. Nothing remained of the many Korean-owned businesses on the block—liquor store, beauty parlor, laundry, flower shop, bakery, restaurant, indoor swap meet, and Star Market, in particular, a pile of charred rubble. Did I do her a favor, rendering her worthy of sympathy and respect? Shouldn't she have gone to prison, even to the gas chamber, condemned and undefended, for everybody's good, even her own?

Suddenly it became as clear as day: I had caused it all with my English as a second language, a little game I had played for a mercenary motive, to please my vanity. I was the arson and looter responsible for the billions of dollars in property damages, the mass murderer of Chanho and fifty-two others, who would still be alive, had it not been for my contemptible bilingual manipulation.

"What's the matter, honey?" Yoonhee asked, as I pulled over to the side.

"Nothing, just a headache."

"You sound terrible. I'll take the wheel. Maybe you have an attack of allergy from all that standing around at the cemetery."

"Maybe," I mumbled, unbuckling.

The Spells of an Ordinary Twilight

Donald Rawley

FRANCES IS FURIOUS. It is the end of a windy November after-noon in the San Fernando Valley and she has discovered, through her mechanic of almost twenty-three years, that her 1969 Mercedes is not mustard, but butterscotch. She was pregnant with her only daughter when she first bought this car. She was married, trying to be happy as her neighbors seemed to be. Frances has always maintained this automo-bile, like every other salient aspect of her life, with dedica-tion and care. And she hates the idea she is driving a candy-colored car.

Frances pulls into the garage and thinks, you go through life with a mustard-colored sedan and suddenly you find out it is butterscotch. You go through your life thinking you are an average woman and suddenly you find out the colors you live by have changed.

Perhaps they were never the right colors, she reasons. Perhaps had she worn shades of amethyst during her youth she wouldn't now be alone. Perhaps if she had worn a deep red lipstick instead of glossy peach, she would have married a different kind of man, one that wouldn't leave. And she would have had more than one child. And murder wouldn't have entered her life, an evil bringing with it a solitude so perfumed with desolation she sometimes cannot breathe.

Perhaps life would still be safe. Frances shakes her head as she walks into her kitchen. Nothing is safe anymore. Except for the end of the day, when no one calls.

Her friends used to call. After her tragedy, she talked to them on the phone and then stopped answering it. Lucille was losing a son to AIDS and would call Frances to ask her what to do. She remembers Lucille at a party with her five-year-old son, Kevin, pulling at her dress, his mouth smeared with licorice. Now Lucille is a voice, just a voice, saying what do I do, Frances, I don't recognize him anymore, he has no hair, he's only twenty-nine years old. Frances had no answers.

Another friend, Mona, would call after her husband died of liver cancer and ask Frances to come over and get drunk; Frances declined. Mona repeated herself, like a chant: you understand death, Frances, you've been there.

Frances realizes all the women she knows are now surviving someone. Like her, they wore bell-bottoms at the beginning of the seventies, smoked marijuana, had affairs, raised their children in converted churches and old apartments, then moved to the San Fernando Valley. They divorced, remarried, changed their furniture every five years. They wore more makeup in the eighties, and shoulder pads, and studied French. They were alcoholics. They tried their hand at poetry and failed. They became religious, frosted their hair, had cosmetic surgery, stopped eating, sued doctors, took up ballroom dancing. Anything for the magic again, Frances supposes. They bury their husbands and children and keep thinking, this wasn't part of the colors I chose, I wasn't meant to survive without signs and clear, impartial directions. These women are fifty years old and invisible as an old homosexual. And they are exactly like me, Frances concludes, except I know the magic.

———————

Frances looks around her living room. Her furniture is precisely arranged, clean and aging. Her cockatiel is waiting for her, and when she enters the room she hears the light rustle of transparent yellow feathers falling to the bottom of its cage. There are other sounds, a half note above silence, that she listens for—the soft bang of the house's old heater in the hall closet, the automatic sprinklers murmuring at dusk, the hardwood floors contracting in the sudden November cold.

She has taken down the photographs of her daughter and packed them in the blanket chest she bought in Marrakesh. Her husband promoted rock acts. It was 1968 and they were on their honeymoon, smoking hashish in a white-and-blue tiled house with brass oil lamps and no electricity. She would listen to the shrill morning caws of black-robed women that were indecipherable from birds and cymbals in the markets.

It was here her daughter, April, was conceived. It was the night astronauts walked on the moon, and radios all over the hot city were turned to a language no one understood, but everyone was pointing at the sky, the sleeves of their caftans waving in the sweet African wind. She was on the roof of the tiled house and her husband was on top of her. She looked past his curly blonde hair and stared at the moon as he thrust. She tried to frame it in her mind, knowing someone was there, calling to her, walking in weightless air.

Frances realizes, as the light begins to crawl away in her living room, that she hasn't traveled since. Except for now, for the last year, when she creates magic. Frances sits in her armchair after turning on the old air-conditioning unit in the den and closes her eyes. She pretends she is on a plane, tilting her head back as though it were taking off. Her air conditioner makes the exact whir of a plane's interior, and Frances is hovering over Martinique, Prague, Havana, places she will never get to. Her daughter is with her and pointing to cities clouded in dust. April wears a floral cotton dress and sandals. She presses her hands to the window, then to Frances' face.

Frances knows that when she opens her eyes, her house will be silent. This is an incantation, one of many spells of ordinary twilight, where air assumes its own color, a mauve stirred with tobacco, and light agonizes its departure. Frances never turns on the lights. She rises and goes to her bathroom mirror. It is now she is able to see her face, porcelain and devoid of age. She cannot make out her eyes and she is pleased. Only a whiteness. It is the time of day for silhouettes and thought without gravity, when she moves through a cushioned, easily numbed world, shaded by her own discretion.

This is the time for planning every luxury, then tearing its structure apart. She will have a cigarette, a scotch and soda. She will buy a mink coat, have lunch with her friends. In this winter shade Frances knows that in her life, like the history of a small town, everything and nothing will occur.

Frances murmurs a prayer for April under her breath, turns off the air conditioner, and sits back in her armchair, remembering that tonight, as she has read in the paper, there is a lunar eclipse. This evening she will converse with the moon, its face like hers in twilight, softened, devoid of pain.

Frances still cannot remember certain things about her behavior following the death of her daughter. She remembers there was no Christmas last year. She remembers screaming, having shingles and going to the hospital, then being home again and discovering that only at dusk could she move around freely.

She does remember her first day out—barely a month ago, after almost a year of having groceries sent in, of memorizing programs on television. She wore dark sunglasses and drove to Woolworth's in the white straw hat, with veil, she was married in. She bought bubble bath in a champagne bottle, and powder. Then she sat at the counter and had a grilled cheese sandwich with a grape soda in a pointed paper cup in an aluminum holder. She spoke pleasantly with the waitress who told her Woolworth's was closing. Frances replied, yes, I know, but everything is closed now.

On her way out she bought a cockatiel, cage, and food. In the car, driving home, Frances began to laugh. She said out loud, this is what older women who've lost everything do: they buy a cockatiel at Woolworth's and they drive home alone, holding a caged bird and wearing the hat they were married in.

She hasn't given the bird a name, nor intends to. She sat for almost two weeks, feeding the bird at twilight, staring at it for no other reason than the fact it was alive. And the bird stared back.

Then just a few weeks ago, during this queer and somehow satisfactory November, when a persimmon haze from the fires that ate Malibu and Topanga hung in her living room like shipyard rope, her no-name bird began to sing. It walked slowly on its plastic perch and let out clear, perfect notes, a music conceived from silence, her silence, and Frances knew her magic had begun to assemble itself. She remembers she smiled.

Now every evening, before the light is gone, the cockatiel sings. Frances has developed a ritual. She sits in her chair and travels on her plane, April at her side. She goes to the mirror and studies her face, then sits again in her chair, listening to her no-name bird. She looks out the sliding glass doors and sees how the darkness spreads like lagoon water over her rosebushes and baby palms. How it turns her grass to salt, then a true black, the only black she understands.

She considers what is now safe, what necessary drives must be made—to the market, perhaps the movies—what day of the week is safest to get the car repaired. Who to start calling again, or not. Frances no longer believes in God, but prays to the earth, the moon, the twilight.

God would never permit such a life. Frances knows it is this simple.

Then the final spell. Frances closes her eyes again and goes to April during the last minute of her daughter's life. Frances keeps her hands in her lap, and she cannot hear the no-name cockatiel's song, the monotony of her sprinklers, or the heater in the hall.

She starts by reciting the facts in a whisper. Her daughter, April, was murdered one year ago by a stranger, a schizophrenic man who hadn't been on medication. April was twenty-four years old. She had spoken on the phone to her mother about her boyfriend, who had problems with cocaine. She had hung up the phone at eight o'clock in the evening. She said she would meet Frances for lunch in the Valley the following day.

The man who killed her was from Bulgaria. It happened in Orange County, in a neighborhood similar to the one Frances had lived in most of her life. It happened in the last undecided moments of November, when leaves wilt and evening comes like an unwrapped surprise.

April was walking her dog in front of her neighbor's house. This man couldn't speak English and was deaf. How he got to Orange County, to April's cul-de-sac of ten Spanish cottages, from Miami, where he had landed, is still a point of deliberation.

He had no clothes on, and was standing in back of a pepper tree. He could run on grass and not make a sound.

There was fair wind from the Pacific. As April walked her dog, she could hear the sound of television programs from the houses around her. They were built on tiny lots. April had told her mother she wanted to move; she was tired of watching her neighbors undress. She said she wanted an apartment on the beach, with a view of the ocean and nothing else.

This is the moment that Frances walks in the dark. She pictures the man. She sees black hair, a cold, shrunken penis, arms with birthmarks positioned like constellations, eyes possessing no color except the red fright of a wild animal caught by a flashlight. He comes from behind the tree. His black hair is covered with leaves.

Frances cannot breathe. She goes back to the facts. She clears her throat and begins to whisper again, casting a spell over the hysteria that cuts its way in with scissors and spit. April was found strangled under a hydrangea bush, in front of her neighbor's house. She had not been touched except for her neck. But the dog had been cooked and eaten in a vacant lot a quarter mile away.

Frances sees a night wind rippling like chiffon used in early silent films to suggest a sea under a cardboard ship. She sees April lose her balance, her hand touch a pair of buttocks, then slide down to the grass. A crescent moon passes slowly through an ocean of stars. A cough, then a hack like an unfinished heave. Then a dog barking, running. She sees April's hair caught in leaves and flowers on the lawn. Then a man's bare feet running through wet grass. Then the sudden glassine of April's eyes catching the glitter of a night sky.

Frances opens her eyes. It is later than she thought. Her no-name cockatiel has stopped singing and is pecking at seed. She realizes she has been crying, and that is part of the spell. She rubs the tears into her eyelids and upper cheeks, like a balm. This, Frances knows, is the exorcism. The plea and penance, the eating of shadows and darkness.

She has held April's hand for one year. She has stroked April's hair and kissed her forehead, murmuring nowhere is safe, sweetheart, we're targets and we don't seem to know why. I made mistakes, April. I should have moved us to New England or Montana, where they say it is safe, but I thought California was warm and exciting and rich. He didn't know you, April, and he was sick and hungry and naked and wild.

I have seen others like him, April. They are everywhere, and I don't understand where they come from.

Frances opens her sliding glass door and walks into her backyard. The moon is out. She cranes her neck, feeling a warm vacancy in her chest and loins, the same feeling she had after delivering April. She almost smiles. This moon is not unlike her face caught in a dusk-draped mirror, her eyes two marble balls. In her twilights there are no lines on her face. Acts of defiance and magic are stretched like old velvet, creating their own brief dust.

This is the safety of ritual. Frances concludes, with a sudden satisfaction, that there are other women like her tonight, counting their dead and looking up to a lunar eclipse. They stand singular and ill-tempered in their backyards, on their balconies, at their bedroom windows.

Some, like Frances, have stored their violet resolutions of twilights and are beginning to come out, walking with the same rhythm of their forced-air heaters, knocking regular and gentle in the hall like an unexpected guest.

Some are standing, shielding their eyes in the night, thinking they will harm their vision, but this is not the sun. This could never be the sun. Some are lurching towards this absence of light like a spider missing a leg. They conjure their dead in half-lit rooms with locked doors and open windows. They are at bus stops leaving their groceries on the sidewalk, coming out of movie theaters with gloved hands and purses full of barbiturates. They are all staring at a darkened moon, wanting to float skyward, leave their keys and houses behind, if only to retrieve what they woke up and lost.

Day 'n Nite

Rachel Resnick

KATE MET TOMMY AT THE Day 'n Nite parking lot on the corner of Santa Monica and Highland. Tommy was leaning against the plate glass storefront with one leg propped up behind him, squinting at her, when she got out of the Range Rover. Bare chested, he had a banana-yellow Lacoste shirt tied around his waist, overly tight designer jeans, and filthy white Pumas a few sizes too big. A street person, his skin was burned a reddish brown by the sun, his teeth were attractively crooked, his hair greasy with natural oils from not bathing. He smelled of sweat and cheap suntan lotion. There was a white scar in the shape of a parenthesis on the side of his left eye. Kate looked at him, appraising. He whistled as she walked by.

Sexy mama, he said. He couldn't have been more than twenty-five. Kate's age exactly.

She came back out with a pack of Marlboros and hesitated. A punchy orangeish frame of light radiated around Tommy—was it the glare from polluted sun on car metal bouncing into her shades? The smog? Standing close, Kate felt an energy around him, something bobbing and weaving with her own tingling nerves.

Cig? he said. Kate slowly peeled the gold thread tab, shucked the cellophane onto the ground where it lay glittering

266

in the light, folded back the triangular flaps of silver foil and tapped the pack smartly on her palm. The cigarettes glided out the top. Staggered columns of ivory, fit for a makeshift temple. She handed one cigarette to Tommy and took one for herself. Before she could get her lighter he lit them with a silver Zippo, then bowed. The gesture touched her. They stood in the sun, the thick haze, smoked, talked, and sucked the burning fire into their bodies. Tommy didn't have a place to live so she took him home to Venice.

Kate was a successful screenwriter. She wrote about troubled girls from broken homes, drunkards, dope fiends, night lifers, psychics, child abuse prosecutors, and Marines. Even though none of her films had made it to the screen yet, they had all been bought for good prices and she was always working. With the money she made she rented a large bungalow on the canal, had two Siberian huskies, and bought expensive clothes she stored in boxes under her bed, in the closet, in drawers and never wore.

Kate was always bored, bored, bored. On top of that she was shy. Ask her on a date and she would mutter incoherently, or agree then not answer the phone until the person gave up. Industry men she considered no more men than pipe cleaners. Once she answered personal ads, but the men who said they were attractive invariably were missing an arm or a leg or were deformed in some other way when she met them for coffee at Denny's. She gave up. Concentrated on her writing. Until Tommy.

When they were driving, Tommy would point at men crossing the street and say, I did him. This didn't bother Kate because she was in love. He needed help and she could give it. She knew he was a street hustler, so what? It was a job.

Also she'd never had such good sex as she did with Tommy. It was his unpredictability that kept her hot.

Sometimes Tommy would only say the words I love you Kate the whole entire day, even when she asked him questions or when friends called him. Those times he often needed to fuck her seven or so times in a row. Other times he would sit in the den with the shades drawn and drink Maker's Mark rum.

You're the devil, he'd say. It's your fault the sun is always on, Cunt. Witch. Admit you control the weather. HAH!

He would throw her against a wall, laugh hysterically, then retreat back into the den whimpering with another bottle she kept in supply. Or he would fuck her in the ass, grind out his cigarette in her hair as it lay fanned out on the rug— the smell would tease her for days. Over the rug holes she glued patches of fabric in matching color. Kate let him do whatever he needed to, anything to calm him down. Then there were the times Tommy would go for coffee and not come back for a week, two weeks. But he would always come back, his chapped hands gripping birds-of-paradise snapped from neighbors' yards, or pockets full of rubber bones and pretzels and spiny plastic balls with bells inside for the dogs.

You don't get it, she said to her father when he ordered Kate to get rid of Tommy.

Once a friend of his stopped by when Tommy and Kate were out. The friend was impatient so he busted the living room window, made off with Kate's jewelry and let the dogs escape. Tommy apologized. Said his friend just got out of prison, he was frustrated, he'd just kicked a bad heroin habit, y'know. Kate did. She rounded up the dogs, gave them rubdowns and cooked them real calf's liver, got the window fixed, and replaced some of the jewelry which she put in the boxes under her bed. Then she took Tommy out for sushi and afterwards they made love on the beach at Zuma. The sand made them both raw.

Kate was at a script meeting at Paramount Studios. She was late and Tommy couldn't wait. Tommy opened the boxes under the bed. Silky trousers, velour jackets, gauzy flowered dresses and cotton jersey shifts. He tied the clothes in knots to each other and coiled them around the house. Looked like a magician's trick scarf—first one, then another, then another and another and another. Tommy used rum to soak the clothes, then gasoline from the garage. The silver Zippo was gone, probably the cops snatched it, the cocksuckers. He used a matchbook, lit the whole thing, sizzle, and dropped it on the clothes. Orange fingers leaped up, groped along the clothes, circled the bungalow. Ducks squawked in the canal, beat their wings against the brackish water. Tommy flicked his tongue in and out as the flames licked the sides of the bungalow. Jungle heat. It was Tommy who controlled the weather now. The dogs howled inside, but he had chained them to the pipes under the sink, a big yellow bowl of water nearby and all their toys in a pile. Tommy rubbed slowly, the flames swelled, a window bulged out then burst in a miracle of jagged hard rain.

Waiting for him to get out of jail, Kate sent photos. Racy ones. Her staring soulfully into the camera, buck naked, ash smeared over her nipples and cunt and around her eyes in black, hollow circles. She had coffee with a friend and showed the photos. Wanted to make sure she looked sexy enough. Most of them she was lounging on a red felt pool table—survived the fire because it was covered with a tarp in the garage. That's where she slept now, on the pool table in the garage. Sat Indian style and wrote her scripts on a laptop there too. The burnt smell was everywhere.

Author Biographies

KAREN E. BENDER grew up in Los Angeles, where she graduated from UCLA, and currently lives in New York. Her short stories have been published in *The New Yorker, Story,* and elsewhere. "Eternal Love," which became a segment of her first novel *Like Normal People* (2000), first appeared in *Granta* in 1996 and was later chosen for *The Best American Short Stories 1997.*

LOUIS BERNEY is the author of *The Road to Bobby Joe and Other Stories* (1991). His fiction has appeared in such magazines as *The New Yorker* and *Ploughshares.* "Stupid Girl" was published in *Story* and selected for a Pushcart Prize in 1999. He lives with his wife in the San Francisco Bay Area, where he teaches at St. Mary's College in Moraga.

KATE BRAVERMAN has been publishing poetry and fiction since 1972. Raised in LA and educated at UC Berkeley, she weaves her California experiences throughout her work. She has written three novels and two collections of short stories, *Squandering the Blue* (1989), in which "Temporary Light" appears, and *Small Craft Warnings* (1998). She lives in northern New York.

ETHAN CANIN, a physician, is also on the faculty of the Iowa Writers' Workshop. "Where We Are Now" was taken from his first collection of short stories, *Emperor of the Air* (1988). He is also the author of *Blue River* (1991), *The Palace Thief* (1994), and *For Kings and Planets* (1998). He divides his time between California and Iowa.

MICHELLE T. CLINTON has written that LA is "the place of my gruesome childhood and the root of my literary voice(s)." She was an artist-in-residence at Beyond Baroque in Venice and co-editor of *Invocation L.A.: Urban Multicultural Poetry* (1989). She now lives in the San Franciso Bay Area where she is pursuing a master's degree in theology. Her most recent book of poetry is *Good Sense and the Faithless* (1994). "Free Your Mind and Your Ass Will Follow" originally appeared in *ZYZZYVA*.

BERNARD COOPER grew up in Los Angeles where he continues to live and work—he is on the faculty of the MFA in Creative Writing Program at Antioch University of Southern California. A winner of the PEN/Hemingway Award and Guggenheim Fellowship, his books include *Maps to Anywhere* (1990), a collection of essays; the novel *A Year of Rhymes* (1993); the memoir *Truth Serum* (1996); and *Guess Again* (2000), a short story collection. "Night Sky" first appeared in *Story*.

WILLIAM HARRISON has written novels and short stories that have been filmed for movies and TV, as well as screenplays, essays, and travel pieces. His most recent novels are *Burton and Speke* (1982) and *Three Hunters* (1989). *The Buddha in Malibu* (1998), in which "The Rocky Hills of Trancas" appears, is a collection of new as well as earlier stories.

KAREN KARBO is the author of three novels, *Trespassers Welcome Here* (1989), *The Diamond Lane* (1991)—each of which were named a *New York Times* Notable Book of the Year—and *Motherhood Made a Man Out of Me* (2000). "The Palace of Marriage," a section from her first novel, originally appeared in *The Village Voice*. She grew up in Whittier and has a degree in film from USC. She lives in Portland, Oregon.

SANDRA TSING LOH is a writer, monologist, and creator of "The Loh Life" a weekly radio series on KCRW that documents that ever-twisting thing called life in LA. She has written a novel, *If You Lived Here You'd Be Home by Now* (1997), and a collection of pieces about "lesser Los Angeles," *Depth Takes a Holiday* (1996). "My Father's Chinese Wives" was adapted into one of the monologues that make up her one-woman show, *Aliens in America*, published in book form in 1997.

Lou Mathews is a fourth-generation Angeleno. His novel, *LA Breakdown*, about the city's outlaw street-racing scene during the late sixties, was cited by the *Los Angeles Times* as one of the best books of 1999. He lives in Beachwood Canyon, works as a journalist and editor, and teaches short-story writing for the UCLA Extension Writers' Program. "Crazy Life," which first appeared in *Crazyhorse*, is a Pushcart Prize winner and part of a collection of linked stories, *Shaky Town*, which will be completed this year.

Tom McNeal grew up in Orange County and received a B.A. from UC Berkeley. He later won a Wallace Stegner Fellowship to Stanford University. His short stories have appeared in numerous magazines and anthologies. "Winter in Los Angeles" became part of his novel *Goodnight, Nebraska* (1998). The selection first appeared in *The Gettysburg Review* in 1997, and won a Pushcart Prize later that year. He co-authored with his wife Laura the young adult novel *Crooked* (1999). He lives with his family in Fallbrook, California.

Rubén Mendoza was born and grew up near San Jose. In 1990 he left the Bay Area to study jazz guitar and American literature at USC. He now makes his home in Los Angeles. "Traffic" appears in *Lotería and Other Stories*, his first collection of short stories, which was published in 1998.

Walter Mosley, who grew up in Watts, is the best-selling author of critically acclaimed mysteries set there featuring Easy Rawlins, as well as two collections of short stories, *Always Outnumbered, Always Outgunned* (1997), in which "The Thief" appears, and *Walkin' the Dog* (1999). He resides in New York City.

Yxta Maya Murray lives in Los Angeles where she teaches law. She has written two novels, *Locas* (1998), about a group of female gangbangers living in Echo Park, and *What It Takes to Get to Vegas* (1999). "Girl on Fire" first appeared in ZYZZYVA. In 1999 she received the Whiting Writers' Award.

Ann Nietzke won a PEN/West Award for Best First Fiction for her novel *Windowlight* (1981). Her short stories have appeared in *Shenandoah* and *Massachusetts Review*. Her portrait of a Los Angeles bag lady, *Natalie in the Street* (1994), was a finalist for PEN West's

Nonfiction Award. A resident of Los Angeles, her most recent work is *Solo Spinout: Stories and a Novella* (1996), from which "Los Angeles Here and Now" was taken. She has been a Los Angeles resident since 1971.

TY PAK sets many of his stories in the Korean American community. He has written *Guilt Payment* (1983) and *Cry, Korea, Cry* (1999), both novels, and *Moonbay* (1999), a collection of short stories, in which "The Court Interpreter" appears. He taught in the English Department, University of Hawaii, from 1970 to 1987, when he took early retirement to devote himself to writing. In 1991 he was Visiting Professor of Creative Writing at Occidental College. He now lives in New York City.

DONALD RAWLEY is the author of the novel, *The Night Bird Cantata* (1999), and several collections of short stories and poems. His works were published in *The New Yorker* and *Harper's*. His nonfiction pieces are gathered in *The View from Babylon: The Notes of a Hollywood Voyeur* (1999). A life-long LA inhabitant, he was an editor of *Buzz Magazine*. He died in 1998. "The Spells of an Ordinary Twilight" can be found in his final collection, *Tina in the Back Seat*, which came out the following year.

RACHEL RESNICK is a writer as well as a teacher of writing at UCLA. "Day 'n Nite" was orginally published in *The Crescent Review* and won a Pushcart Prize Special Mention. Her first novel, *Go West Young F*cked-up Chick*, came out in 1999. She lives in Topanga Canyon, where she is at work on a detective novel.

Permissions

About the Editor

STEVEN GILBAR IS THE EDITOR of numerous anthologies about California, including *California Shorts* (Heyday Books). Other collections include *Natural State: A Literary Anthology of California Nature Writing* (University of California Press), *Santa Barbara Stories* (John Daniel and Company), *Tales of Santa Barbara* (John Daniel and Company), and *Reading in Bed: Personal Essays on the Glories of Reading* (David R. Godine). He currently lives in Santa Barbara with his wife, Inge Gatz, a social work consultant.